GINGERBREAD MANSION

GINGERBREAD MANSION

Lizbie Brown

This first world edition published 2009
in Great Britain and in the USA by
SEVERN HOUSE PUBLISHERS LTD of
9–15 High Street, Sutton, Surrey, England, SM1 1DF.
Trade paperback edition published
in Great Britain and the USA 2009 by
SEVERN HOUSE PUBLISHERS LTD

British Library Cataloguing in Publication Data

Brown, Lizbie
  Gingerbread Mansion
  1. National Trust (Great Britain) - Fiction 2. Aristocracy
  (Social class) - England - Fiction 3. Aristocracy (Social
  class) - Dwellings - England - Fiction 4. Historic
  buildings - Conservation and restoration - England -
  Fiction 5. Great Britain - Social conditions - 1945-
  Fiction
  I. Title
  823.9'14[F]

ISBN-13: 978-0-7278-6775-9   (cased)
ISBN-13: 978-1-84751-137-9   (trade paper)

X laid his gingerbread mansion at my feet last Monday, and incapable as ever of giving a plain answer to a plain question, I said I couldn't hear of it anyhow until my book is finished . . . But it is awful how easily one could be entrapped into matrimony with someone like that because it would *be nice to be rich.*

Excerpt from a letter from Nancy Mitford to Harold Acton, 22nd January, 1932

One

Charlie didn't set out to gatecrash the ceremony. Weddings were most definitely not his thing. But finding himself desperate – the village deserted, no children helling around, the one shop closed and shuttered – there seemed nothing for it but to prop his push-bike against the lychgate and chase after the straggling little procession making its way down the church path.

It was the second Saturday in January – one of those days when the sky seemed to have switched on its own lighting, rinsing the church and the fields behind it with a chill, blue light. Where the path turned, he skidded on a patch of frozen snow. The bride, a big girl in a blue, home-made number, turned her head to look at him, but after one distracted glance, ambled on into church. Her companions – a young man with a buttonhole of winter jasmine and a bridesmaid in a startling shade of canary yellow – disappeared after her.

Charlie said, 'Damn and blast!'

He was, to put it mildly, a bit cheesed. First, the crowds at Paddington had been so great he'd had to fight his way on to the platform. Then, after the slow, wobbling ride westwards, the train had broken down outside Exeter St David's. Also he'd eaten nothing since a gruesome sandwich and a bun thing at Okehampton. And now he was lost and would have to barge into a ruddy wedding for directions.

The church porch smelled of damp and incense. A slate knight reclined upright to one side of the studded door. The churchwarden (a stout, ruddy-faced man, crammed into a dark suit) was guarding the other.

'Now then, young man,' he said. 'Bride or groom?'

Charlie said, 'Er – neither.' He had to raise his voice to be heard above the 'Wedding March'. 'I just wanted to ask—'

'Best do that later, sir. Service is about to begin.'

'But all I need—'

'Just follow me, sir. We'll squeeze you in somewhere.'

Charlie realized that he should have resisted, but by this time the chap had his arm in a steely grip and was towing him through the door and down the aisle in the wake of the bride.

He who hesitates . . .

'Here we are, sir,' the churchwarden said in his ear. They had stopped at a pew midway down the nave. Two old trouts in grey coats topped off with fox furs shifted sideways to make more room for him.

He thought, should I shout over the organ? *Look – this is all a ridiculous mistake?*

But the music had come to its final swell. There seemed nothing for it but to take the proffered hymnal and shuffle into the corner seat.

The nearest trout gave him a sudden, alarming once-over through steel-rimmed spectacles. He must have passed the test, because she took his prayer book from him and handed him her own, open at page 307. *The Form of Solemnization of Matrimony.*

For one moment, he was taken right back to saying his prayers with his paternal grandmother in the family pew. A bored little boy with pins and needles in his bum. *Don't fidget, Charles. Sit up straight.*

The organ gave one last trill, then turned wheezy. The rector beamed at the congregation. 'My friends. We are here today to wish Samuel and Cicely a long and joyful life together.'

Not me. I don't even know Samuel and Cicely. How did I land myself in this fix?

The groom let out a rackety cough. He was painfully thin – skeletal. Sunken cheeks. Wrists enormous lumps. Charlie thought, he looks like a horror photograph. Looks like he could do with a good apple dumpling inside him.

'We will sing hymn number 33. "Love Divine".' The organ thrummed out. The clergyman started them off in his soaring tenor. Charlie cleared his throat and mumbled along with the rest of the congregation:

> Fix in us Thy humble dwelling,
> All Thy faithful mercies crown.

The bridesmaid, short of a hymnal, stood patting her hair (improbably tinted a rich conker red) and adjusting her rope of pearls, glam but bored, like a mannequin in a shop window. The bride's sister? Impossible, Charlie thought. The groom's sister? He decided not. She didn't give a damn about his cough. Didn't give a damn about anything, by the look of her.

The hymn over, the congregation sank back down, hats bobbing, feet shuffling, throats coughing. One cough above all other, that of the groom. The bride, all buxom and round and dimpled (like an apple dumpling herself) threw him a worried glance.

'Dearly Beloved, we are gathered here today in the face of this congregation to join Samuel and Cicely . . .'

The smaller of the trouts – extremely tiny, perched on the edge of the pew – fetched a hanky from her neat little glove. As the vicar rattled into the first miracle in Cana of Galilee and the causes for which matrimony was ordained, she sat mopping her eyes.

'Wilt thou have this woman' – cough – 'to thy wedded wife' – cough, cough – 'to live together after God's holy ordinance in the holy estate of matrimony?'

'I will.'

Charlie glanced down at his watch, the one he 'd inherited from his father. Ten past two. He thought, I should be the by now. What's that smell? Old hassocks. Funny thing how smells took you back. Dust and plaster to bomb sites. Wet blankets to air-raids.

Wonderful bench end, that. Sixteenth century oak. And the screen's early . . .

The prayer ended. The vicar read a psalm about letting the nations rejoice and be glad, then rambled on about the path of true love not always being flowery.

It was when they got to the blessing that the dog began to bark. A wire terrier (with a perky scarlet ribbon attached to its collar) sitting to attention by the front pew. When the bride and groom disappeared into the vestry to sign the register, the little dog trotted along after them. Charlie remembered it afterwards in a kind of snapshot. The bride, her hat adorned with pansies. The groom, his demob suit all but enveloping him. And the little dog all dressed up for a wedding.

'I don't know you . . .' The trout addressed him outside on the church path. A peal of bells came from the tower. Guests (one or two of them holding on to adventurous hats) stretched their legs and stamped frozen feet.

Here was Charlie's chance. 'Er – no. I wonder if you could direct me to Lizzah?'

'Lizzah?' Her gaze was unnervingly direct.

'It's rather urgent,' he told her. 'I was supposed to be there an hour ago.'

'In that case,' she said, 'what were you doing in church?'

Charlie glanced away, his attention caught by the yellow bridesmaid, tottering by in four-inch cork-soled heels. Finally, he said, 'It would take too long to explain. I just need directions. Mrs Jago will be wondering where I've got to.'

'Mrs Jago?' She spoke sharply. 'Not the major?'

'I have an appointment at Lizzah.' Meaning, *What's it to do with you? Nosey bloody parker.*

'Do you have a motor?'

'I'm afraid not. Just a bicycle.'

'Then you'd better leave your bicycle here and ride with Daphne.'

Well, hold on, Charlie thought. Who's Daphne? A slap of cold air hit him. The little dog leapt as the bride kissed the groom.

'Cissie's a gem,' the smaller trout confided, 'taking him on in that state. But Samuel was all she ever wanted. He was in one of those Japanese prisoner of war camps. You wouldn't believe what they did to him. But a very nice Scottish boy looked after him all the way back to Dover . . . Derek Somebody . . . brought up on the Isle of Arran . . . and Peg – that's Samuel's mother – fetched him from the hospital.' Baby-blue eyes looked pained, then cheered up again. 'They've got hold of a black market ham for the wedding supper and there's a bottle of champagne that Jack brought from France . . .'

'Splendid!' Charlie checked his watch.

'And after that, they're off to Exeter on honeymoon.' She beamed up at him. Charlie wondered if he was in one of those dreams where you run and run, but never get anywhere.

In a minute, I'll wake up and still be on the train.

'I wish them luck,' he said.

'So do I.' When she nodded, the lavender hat, skewered on, bobbed up and down like nobody's business.

'Daphne! Yoo-hoo! Over here!' the older trout called from behind him.

Charlie turned to see her waving at a shiny-faced girl in a green suit and a white piqué blouse.

'This young man has an appointment with your mother,' the trout was saying.

'With Mother?' Joining them, the girl smiled at him short-sightedly. Nice smile, Charlie thought, but otherwise not much in the looks department. Freckled face, auburn hair, enormous cheekbones.

'Exactly my reaction. I said, you must mean the major.'

'She's probably given up on me by now. I got lost—' Charlie stopped, realizing there was no way to explain getting caught up in a strange wedding without making himself seem ridiculous.

'And you are?'

'Charles Garland. I work for—' He abandoned this sentence as well, thinking that the Jagos might not want their private affairs spread round the parish. 'It's . . . um . . . legal business.'

'You're from Kendall and Brigstock?' At that, she relaxed. 'You'd better come with me. Do you have luggage?'

'Only my overnight bag.'

'You're staying?'

'Just the one night.'

'There's a bicycle,' said the trout called Mabel. 'We'll take it. He can collect it on his way back.'

'You came by bicycle? All the way from London?' Daphne Jago's face was a picture.

'No. I put it in the guard's van at Paddington. Pedalled out from Bude. Are you sure that's convenient?' Charlie asked the trout.

'It'll have to be. Mabel Petherick and Edie Medland. We live at Apple Orchard.'

'Right. Thanks. I'll wheel it round to you.'

'No need. Edie can do that.'

Just so long as she doesn't try to ride it, Charlie thought. It rattles like an old tin can and the brakes are useless. But there wasn't time to say so; Miss Jago was already halfway to the lychgate. Lifting his hat to the trouts, he took off in her wake, helped along by the vicious wind that was funnelling through the churchyard.

Motoring to Lizzah, he sat in the passenger seat of her green Rover saloon. They crawled down narrow lanes bounded by enormous, fern-topped hedges. Small farm roads criss-crossed a land of stunted oaks and narrow fields. Signposts pointed to Marhamchurch, Week St Mary, St Gennys.

'Last time,' Miss Jago said, 'they sent old Mr Kendall. He couldn't hear a word anyone said. I expect you've taken his place?'

'Actually, I've got a confession to make. I'm not from Kendall and Whatjamacallit.'

She turned her freckled face to glance at him. 'Not a lawyer?'

'Sorry. I wasn't sure you'd want your business spread abroad. The old dears were listening. The nosy one, anyway.'

'Mabel Petherick. She runs the village school.' Miss Jago drove sitting bolt upright. 'I thought you looked a trifle—'

'Untidy?'

'Unlawyerish.'

He laughed. 'That's a bonus.'

'So why *are* you here?'

Charlie reached into his overcoat pocket for his cigarettes. Knocked one from the pack and offered it to her.

'Thanks, but not now.' She steered the car expertly round a pothole in the lane. 'You're from the bank. Is that it?'

'Actually,' he said, 'I work for The National Trust.'

'Which is?'

Two short, brisk interrogatory syllables. She didn't know. And if that was the case, he would have to explain. And if he had to explain, it meant that her mother hadn't let her in on the matter. Tricky, Charlie decided.

'Well – we . . . that is, The Trust – we exist to protect . . . to save the country houses of England.'

'From what?' she asked.

Good question. There were plenty of answers. 'From rising taxation. Death duties, rates, high costs of maintenance. We take over houses that the owners can no longer cope with.'

'But they can't afford to give you a car?' Her tone was dry.

'Well . . . the thing is . . . there are four of us in the office and we have to share a second-hand Ford and I tossed for it and lost. The Trust doesn't have money to waste. It prides itself on its charitable status.'

'So . . .' She shoved the motor into second gear. 'What has any of this to do with Lizzah?'

Apart from those big, grey eyes, Charlie thought, she's totally frowsty. The kind of girl who wears riding breeches and washes the dog and makes a bed with the neatest of hospital corners and puts on a clean frock every day for lunch.

'This is difficult. From what I gather, your father's estate may be . . .' Charlie searched for the most tactful way of saying it, '. . . in a spot of bother.'

'You mean stony?'

'I was trying not to put it like that. But . . . yes.'

She pulled on the brake.

Stopped the car in the middle of the lane.

'Tell me again,' she said. 'Your appointment. My mother arranged it?'

'That's right. She telephoned a couple of weeks ago. Said a friend had told her about The Trust and she wondered if we might be able to help. And I said I'd have to see the house before I could say for sure.'

'Golly!' she said. Then, 'Does Pa know?'

Rooks, wind, the distant cry of some wild thing up there in the woods. 'I'm not sure. I assumed . . . I mean, we thought . . . One would expect—'

'She won't have told him.' She had taken off the glasses she wore for driving. 'She knows there'd be hell to pay.'

Golly, Charlie thought.

He took his time lighting the cigarette. Watched a rabbit hop across the lane in front of them. 'I didn't ask. I took it for granted that Mrs Jago was acting on your father's instructions.'

'Pa never instructs anyone. He's not the type. He's got this box he shoves bills into. If he finds things disagreeable, he simply puts them off. If my mother wants him to do something he's not keen on, she'll try and steamroller him into it. He's an old slowcoach, you see. Terribly cautious. Stubborn as a mule. You have no idea what you're walking into.'

Soon find out, though. What fun this is going to be.

'If I were you,' she said, 'I'd turn round and head back to London.'

'Not possible, I'm afraid. Old Fossett sent me down here to do a job. If I funk it, he'll fire me.'

'Well, don't say I didn't warn you.'

Charlie wondered why he'd bothered to get up that morning. The day had been a disaster from the very beginning. In the distance, a hawk swooped.

'I don't suppose,' he said, 'you'd . . . nip in ahead and prepare the ground, so to speak?'

'Tell Pa you've come to take his home away from him?' She shook her head. 'Oh, no.'

'There's no need to put it quite like that. You could say I'm here to help. Tell him the Trust really cares about these fine old houses.'

Daphne Jago sat gazing out through the windscreen at a landscape that hadn't changed for centuries. High, scudding clouds, dead bracken covering the hillside, waves of fern moving and heaving as the wind passed over it. Her gloved hands gripped the steering wheel.

Charlie said, 'The thing is, we may just be able to help him survive.'

She turned her head to look across at him. Some trick of the light made her eyes change from grey to green. 'Well, he could certainly do with some advice on that subject.' A pause. Then, 'Did anyone tell you my brother was killed in action a week before the war ended?'

There was a swift silence, during which Charlie wanted to dig a deep hole and climb into it. Finally he stammered, 'No. No, they didn't. I'm sorry.'

'Kit was supposed to inherit Lizzah. He'd been groomed for it since he was a small boy. That's all they ever talked about . . . my parents. Loving Kit was probably the only thing they ever really shared.'

She restarted the engine and put the car into gear, making it leap a little as they started off up the hill. 'So,' she said crisply, 'I just thought I'd put you in the picture.'

Charlie threw his cigarette out of the window. He thought, I know what I'd do with your picture. Tear it into tiny pieces and ram it down your plummy throat. But it wouldn't do to make things worse than they already were, so, plastering a smile on his face, he said, 'Thanks.'

She rammed the car into third. 'Don't mention it.' After a bit, she said, 'Anyway, you won't like the house. It's in a state. We had troops billeted on us. Only two or three rooms are habitable.'

Charlie said that was par for the course these days. 'There are houses mouldering to death all over the country.'

'Then wouldn't it be simpler,' she asked, 'to hold the last rites and have a jolly big funeral?'

'Not if I've got anything to do with it.'

She said, as if winding the conversation up, 'Well, I'm telling you now, my father will never ever hand the house over to your National-whatever-it-is. He'll shoot you first. And if he doesn't, Granny will!'

'Right,' said Charlie. The car shot off down the hill. Hell's bells, he thought.

Most of the old lady's days were spent trying to keep warm. She was a born shiverer. Always had been, even during that hot summer of 1911, when records had been broken and the English had shed their morals for a while and you were happy if you could just do nothing in some cool, lazy place. Even then, Evalina Jago had needed her silk shawl. But now her once-straight back was pain-crippled, and her neck, her fingers, her wrists as stiff as could be. Dear God, being so old made one ill-tempered and irritable. She had played merry hell about having to move back into the Big House with Myles and Virginia because of the dearth of servants. She behaved badly every time Tilley switched the wireless on and listened to Music Hall in the kitchen. But what made her maddest of all was everything being in such a damned muddle. The house, the country, the entire world.

Going to the dogs, all of it.

'Nothing's what it used to be,' she told Tilley, who was puffing away at the fire with the bellows. It didn't help much, because the logs were soaked.

'No, m'm.' Tilley puffed again. Wet old sticks hissed and smoked in the grate.

'Gels in the village with black babies. Bread rationed. At this rate, we shall be down to whale blubber.'

'Apple pancakes for supper, m'm,' Tilley said in her cheerful, slipshod voice.

'Dinner, girl!'

Tilley kept forgetting. But if a person had gone from parlour-maid to cook-housekeeper in one go, on account of the rest of them shooting off to work in the factories when war was declared, well . . . they couldn't expect you to remember everything.

'And rabbit pie,' she added, by way of a softener.

The old lady visibly shuddered. 'I'm not hungry.'

'You might be later, m'm.'

'I doubt it.' Evalina Jago stared gloomily out at the leaden sky. 'At least Winston's out of it,' she said. 'Getting some sea and sunshine. I wish I were.'

Me too, Tilley thought. Fat chance! She held a newspaper in front of the log until it began to crackle but there was no life in the fire and, as soon as the paper came down, it went back to its dull hissing.

'Outrageous to have turned him out after all he's done for the country! We wouldn't have won the war with anyone else in charge. And how do they repay him? By showing him the door.' The old lady fished her needlework out of the bag that sat beside her on the floor. She was pointing a cover for the piano stool. 'I still can't fathom how this Labour crowd got elected. Winston should have walked in on his coat tails. His election tour was one long triumph. They cheered him to the echo. I simply cannot understand,' she said for the hundredth time, 'why they gave him a rocket.'

Because he looked like a waxwork, Tilley thought. That's why. She had glimpsed him once from the pavement in Launceston, his open car speeding past, his face a mask of orange make-up.

'The country's turning into a zoo. It's the collapse of civilization.'

Tilley raked a smutty hand through her fine, sandy hair. Next the old grouch would be moaning about how many wars she'd seen.

'Have you any idea how many wars I've lived through? Three. Three! It has become a way of life.'

A period piece, Tilley wanted to say, that's what you are. A cantankerous old so-and-so as thinks she's a bally empress. But no hint of what was going through her mind ever appeared on her good-natured face.

'Well, there won't be any more for a while, m'm. Not after that Hiroshimy.' The gale sent a cloud of smoke back down the chimney, threatening to choke them both.

'Oh, Lord! Open the door, girl.' Covering her nose with a handkerchief, Evalina searched her carpet bag for a skein of pink wool. Untwisting it with knobbly fingers, she thought, *If I had my way, I'd drop an atom bomb on a few in this country.* Serve them right for making life so damned uncomfortable! There was a brief scurry during which Tilley banged the door open, disappeared, coughing, into the nether regions of the house and reappeared minutes later with her pinny filled with fir cones, which she proceeded to toss on to the fire. In a moment or two, as the scales opened to eject the seeds, they began to emit a homely crackling sound. Thin tongues of flame licked up.

'There!' Tilley said with some satisfaction. 'Now it's going.'

They watched, mesmerized, as flames licked up round the logs. Then the old lady looked at her watch and said, 'Where's my son?'

'Gone for his constitutional, m'm.'

'Well, tell him I want to see him the minute he comes in.'

Myles Jago liked walking the dog. It was one of his escape routes. A way of disconnecting when things weren't going right and they certainly weren't too damn pleasant at the moment. The day had started with an uneasy interview with Boscombe from the bank – a nondescript little fella overstuffed with a sense of his own importance. On two earlier occasions the major had invented excuses at the last moment, but this morning, though there was a feeling of sickness somewhere deep in the pit of his stomach, he knew there was nothing for it but to trot along and face the music. And so he'd driven himself all the way to Exeter with his army briefcase on the passenger seat beside him and marched into the lion's den telling himself there was no earthly need to kowtow to some half-baked twerp of a bank manager.

Boscombe hadn't joined up. That type never did. Too self-serving. But there he had sat, so plump that the chair underneath him was invisible, asking all sorts of damned impertinent questions: how did the major think he was going to pay off his rather substantial overdraft, and had he any thoughts about how Lizzah was to be made financially viable, and while they were about it, could he suggest how they were to settle the bills from the Borough, the Inland Revenue and various other creditors? Myles (baldish, egg-shaped head, back as straight as a flagpole) had felt a vicious urge to land a right hook on one of the so-and-so's three chins, but circumspection demanded that he placate the blighter. So, summoning up his most bracing army voice, he had invented some story about a fond old aunt who could be called on in dire emergency, a sweet old thing with a vast fortune and no offspring to pass it down to. He'd managed to fob Boscombe off, but it had been a near thing and Myles had never been too comfortable with the workings of deceit, so by the time he got outside again, he could feel his head throbbing. He'd planned to stay on in town and lunch at Partridge's – a jolly good bust to make the day feel right again – but while his heart was hot within him, he couldn't face eating and so he had set off home again earlier than intended.

It was late afternoon now, but the headache was still with him. The dog – a large, handsome pointer with a satiny loose-fitting coat – stopped to sniff at a pothole in the drive. This bit of the park resembled a battle-field. The grass was long and unmown with things dumped all over the shop – bits of rubber tubing, spent gun cartridges, an old jeep piled high with mattresses, all left from the years when the house had been occu-pied by the army. Diseased elms lay rotting where they had blown down. A sea of ghastly Nissen huts and wire fencing obliterated the view down to Apple Orchard and the village.

Blasted war! the major thought, looking jowly and mournful. If I hadn't been away for six years—

But you couldn't blame the war entirely. The steady decline had begun with the late Victorian agricultural depression and had been accelerated by death duties. 'Punch! Here, boy!' The dog was chewing some damn thing he'd dug out of the hole. He'd devour anything he could get hold of. Shoes, hats, corks . . . once, years ago, a prawning net Kit had left in the back kitchen.

'Punch! Leave it alone!' The dog looked at him for a moment, then looked away and sighed. Myles knew how he felt. All those years, he had consoled himself with the knowledge that, no matter what happened, Lizzah would be waiting; an old-fashioned sort of place cut off from England by the Tamar to the north and the great shoulder of Dartmoor to the east. The world might have gone mad, but the house would still be there, standing in a blowy Cornish landscape, always the same, only the weather changing. When you get back, he'd promised himself, your life will be your own again. You can do all sorts of things, walk the coastal path, sort out the silver cups Father won for rowing, add to your first editions . . .

But the peace he had hoped for was not to be found. He'd almost begun to wish he was back in the army again, where there was someone else to make all the decisions for you. Ridiculous, but the plain truth. Myles was as English as a cup of tea, but a growing antipathy to post-war England was building up inside him.

He rummaged in the pockets of his baggy tweed jacket for cigarettes, failed to find any, swore quietly and made himself walk on. At the turn of the drive, he stopped to gaze at the belt of horse chestnuts coiled round with barbed wire and the yew tunnel so overgrown that it was almost blocked in. The dark bulk of the house stood behind it, a brick NAAFI blocking the view of the entrance. Just as well, perhaps.

'Complete shambles,' he said. Holes in the roof and the first-floor windows; one panel of the main door splintered like matchwood.

Until now, he had never regarded Lizzah as a millstone around his neck. He loved the place – always had and always would – but what was the point of taking arms against a sea of troubles when there were only daughters to pass the old place on to? When Kit—

Myles struck out with his stick at a tangle of brambles on the path in front of him. It hurt to think about the boy, so he tried not to. Mostly succeeded. It was just that there were times when you couldn't help it. When things came back to you. Strong, painful things that cut you to the quick.

Tilley's voice, echoing down the drive, brought him out of his reverie. 'She's looking for you, sir. Wants to see you.'

No need to ask who, but he couldn't face Ma at the moment. 'Tell her I've gone down to the village,' he called gruffly. 'Tell her anything you like – but you can't find me.'

He'd take himself off to the lavatory. Take yesterday's *Times* with him. 'Safe haven,' he thought. 'Thank God for the privy.'

When the bell on the front door jangled, Tilley slipped the pie into the oven and shot up two flights of stairs to answer it. She heaved the door open and saw, under the portico, Miss Daphne standing next to a young man with a flop of dark hair and a nervous but fetching smile.

'This is Mr Charles Garland, Tilley. My mother's expecting him.' Pushing past them both, Miss Daphne took herself off upstairs at a fair old lick.

Where's the fire? Tilley thought, cursing the fact that the elastic had just gone in the knee of her pink flannelette knickers. She banged the door against the chill and, for good measure, kicked the rug hard against it. 'Can I take your coat, sir?' she asked in her upstairs voice.

The young man said he'd keep it on. Tilley didn't blame him. It was almost as cold inside the house as out.

'This way, sir.' She led him into the room to the right of the front door, flattening with one hand, as she did so, the strip of wallpaper that had been loosened by some lout of a soldier kicking a ball at it. They'd also had fun taking pot shots at the glass in the windows and breaking open the doors into the state rooms and pocketing any little bit of a thing they fancied.

Bless 'em all. I don't think! Being the soul of integrity, Tilley couldn't approve of vandalism and once or twice, she had flared right up and told the blighters so. Mostly they'd laughed, but one or two had been decent enough to feel ashamed of the tearaways among them.

Tilley bent to switch on the electric fire with a red-knuckled hand. The single filament glowed red for a moment, then died again. The electricity on the estate came from a decrepit Lister machine that was always failing without warning. It was the same with everything else in the blessed place. Furniture eaten away to nothing by the woodworm; knobs and spindles dropping off every time you flicked a duster at them; carpets wriggling with silver fish.

And only me to boggle away at it. Flog that horse that will *work.*

Eight servants and a daily, they had kept, before the war . . . But on the whole, she thought, it wasn't such a bad job, if you could face being on your pegs all day and if you turned a deaf ear to a certain sour old so-and-so who needed her behind kicking.

Tilley had never been tempted to run off and work in the munitions like her sister, Queenie. She sometimes wished she could afford a nice Plymouth-made suit for church on Sunday, instead of having to take pot luck from the second-hand boxes that the rector brought round. And she wouldn't have minded a good old blow-out now and again at one of the fancy restaurants in Bristol that Queenie kept on about. But at least she was in employment.

That was a lot these days.

She gave up fiddling with the fire and creaked to her feet. 'I'll tell madam you're here,' she said poshly.

'Thank you.' The young man crammed his hands deeper into the pockets of his coat and threw her a valiant smile. For one brief moment, Tilley almost remembered what it felt like to be warm.

Two

Charles Garland was much younger than Virginia had expected. Not that you could have any idea how old a person was simply by talking to him on the telephone, but from his voice (hesitant, but cultured – the real thing, not bogus) and the stream of facts that had poured effortlessly out of him, she would have put him down as early forties. Only here he was, a young man in his late twenties, perhaps. A very Bloomsbury young man, wearing dark town clothes and looking as handsome as a god (a god with a large, official briefcase) and for one moment, she wondered if there hadn't been some kind of mistake.

'Welcome to Lizzah,' she said in her brisk, not-unpleasant voice. 'You must excuse my shocking old sweaters. Tea gowns have gone out of the window, I'm afraid, in these arctic conditions. Mother doesn't approve, but, quite frankly, there's not much she does approve of these days. That's my husband's mother, by the way. Mine's dead and gone. Would you like tea now or after you freshen up?'

'Now, I think.'

'Then I hope you won't mind if we head for the kitchen. Mother doesn't approve of that either, but it's the only room we can afford to keep warm. How was your journey? Hellish, I expect. My husband had to dash up to town last week on army business and they shunted him into a siding and left him there in the dark for hours. I should warn you, by the way, that he'll be against this venture.'

The young man seemed embarrassed. 'I – um – I gather you haven't actually told him. That I'm coming? I mean, you may have done by now, but—' He was extremely jumpy, looking at her as though he would like to turn tail and bolt.

'No. I haven't told him. If I had, he'd have upped sticks and taken himself off.' Elegantly, she frowned at her watch. 'I'm hoping that by springing you on him, he can be made to see sense. Left alone, he'll let the place moulder until the bailiffs turn up on the doorstep.'

The writing had been on the wall for a long time, Virginia thought, but Myles didn't care to read it. He had been home since Christmas, but was more than usually silent, remote and gruff. When he was in one of his black-dog moods, there was no getting to him. It was like talking to a piece of buff paper. An army form. Once or twice, Gin had put out feelers to test the atmosphere, but it was impossible even to guess what was going on inside that rather distinguished head of his. Apart from the obvious, of course. Apart from the unutterably painful business – like sitting in a dark cupboard and knowing you will never, ever come out – of knowing that Kit was dead and gone.

Staring out at the nettlebed underneath the window, she told herself, *Don't think about it. Don't . . . think. It gives you the jimjams.*

These last few weeks, living together again at home in one big dollop, attempting to talk to each other as in the old pre-war days – both of them too utterly tired, too worn, to bother – well, it was a strain.

'Your husband's just back from overseas?' He had raised his voice, as if to bring her back to the present.

'Yes. And he's in no fit state to keep this place shored up. It will kill him. You have no idea of the costs involved. And then there's the responsibility we have for our tenants. If the bank forecloses on us, the whole village will go down the chute. Somehow . . . and I can't imagine for the life of me how . . . it has to be made financially viable.'

Leading the way back into the cold hall and down a passageway into the mustier regions of the house, she thought, *This weather doesn't help.* All these dull, grey days, one after the other, freezing your bones, your very being.

Cold hurts. It makes your hands numb and clumsy and perhaps your heart, too. Virginia thought, I can stand close to Myles, we can concoct a perfectly rational conversation, but we can no more touch each other than fly.

Pushing open a stout oak door, she led the way past rows of pantries and down a flight of stone steps. 'You'll have to take us as you find us. We're in the middle of tidying-up operations. How many other houses have you on your books?'

'Not many as yet. A score or so?' The young man followed her, his boots clattering on blue flagstones. 'But since the war ended, we've had a stream of offers.'

'And what position exactly do you hold within this Trust?'

'I'm the Country Houses Secretary.'

'And how much experience have you had?'

'I trained as a land agent. Began working for the Trust in '36.'

'And during the war?'

'I was in France and Italy. Intelligence Corps. Invalided out in '43.' He had a question of his own. 'The estate . . . you said six thousand acres?'

'Two thousand of which is woodland.'

'And, um—' He stopped for a moment, clutching the handle of his briefcase, while he aimed himself at the words he was searching for. 'I was wondering . . . Look – I heard you lost your son and I don't quite know how to approach this question, but it will have to be asked sooner or later.' He cleared his throat. 'Who will the house—?'

'Be settled on now that Kit is gone?' She made herself say it. 'There's a distant cousin. A young man we hardly ever see. Can the entail be undone, do you think?'

'Most certainly, with the aid of a good lawyer.'

'And there's the question of death duties,' she said, feeling much more than she could show.

'The National Trust Act of 1937 takes care of that.'

That was a relief, at any rate. 'Well, you seem to know your stuff. Let's just hope you can talk my husband into doing the sensible thing.' She went to open another door at the end of the lime-washed passage.

But something was still bothering Charles. He stood rooted by the jumble of old hats and coats on the pegs, a look of extreme caution on his face.

'There's just one more thing.'

'Yes?'

'Well, from what I've seen, Lizzah is a wonderful old place. But as I told you on the telephone, I can't promise anything until I've taken a good hard look at it.'

She waited with her hand on the doorknob. 'How long before you're able to give us your verdict?'

'I'll let you know before I leave.'

'Very well,' she said. 'I suppose that will have to do.'

The kitchen was wonderfully warm after the upstairs regions; the great, roaring range, built into its own smoke-blackened cave in the end wall, sent out a ceaseless heat tinged with the welcome odour of wood ash and meat stew. A massive table, bleached with years of scrubbing, filled the centre of the room. The Queen Anne dresser filling the far wall stood cluttered with brawn moulds, china dogs, brass candlesticks, blue Spode vegetable dishes and fruit-painted meat plates, with biscuit boxes and pickle jars, mustard pots and junket bowls and pie dishes whose rims were cracked and browned from having baked too long in the oven.

The scrawny maid – attired now in black, with a cap rammed down over her eyes – was toasting muffins armed with a long Victorian fork;

lining the slices up along the top shelf of the oven and wedging them between two bricks wrapped in sacking. An old woman and a girl of about eleven were already seated at the table; the girl an odd little thing with the nosepiece of her spectacles patched up with sticky tape, the old lady straight-backed and imperious with an Alexandra fringe and white, wire-like hair puffed out round her head. Her long skirt and net blouse with a whalebone collar hailed from the Edwardian era. By the side of her chair stood an enormous carpetbag.

Charlie wondered what she kept in it. A brace of pheasants? A bundle of knitting? A very small French maid?

'We have a guest for the night, Mother.' Virginia Jago raised her voice several notches above the norm. 'Mr Garland, I'd like you to meet my mother-in-law, Evalina Jago.'

The old girl eyed him up and down, decided that he wasn't worth the effort and went back to fastening her fur tippet more tightly around her neck.

'Mr Garland has come to see Myles.'

'About what, may one ask?'

'I can't tell you just now. You'll find out later.' Virginia Jago's voice came back down to a more reasonable pitch. 'Have a seat, Mr Garland. This is Penelope, my younger daughter. My husband will be along in one moment. You did call him, Tilley?'

'Yes, m'm.' The maid hitched at the side of her skirt and rushed to scatter cups and saucers and plates on the table.

Charlie selected a chair as far away as possible from the old witch and smiled at the child with the pigtails. All he got in return was a long, disconcerting stare. He wondered if that crosspatch expression ran in the family.

The maid came scurrying over a second time with a fistful of rather beautiful tea knives. Georgian, Charlie thought as she slammed one down in front of him. Circa 1810. He heard his stomach give a long rumble.

There was a pause. Then the old girl said, 'It never works, you know . . . trying to pull the wool over my eyes. You may think I'm a period piece. A foolish old woman, half-blind, half-deaf, fit only for the scrap heap, but I won't be sidelined. Is that clear, Virginia?'

'Perfectly, Mother.'

'And I won't be spoken to as if I were a child.'

'Would I dare?' Mrs Jago raised an eyebrow. In spite of the silver in her hair, she was still stunning to look at. Cheekbones like ski slopes.

'You most certainly would! Something's going on and I want to know what it is.'

'Later, Mother. I'll hurry Myles up.' Virginia Jago made for the door.

'Before you go, m'm—' The maid dumped the teapot on the table. 'I'd better tell 'ee – the seed cake had a mind of his own and come out brick-shaped.'

'Don't worry, Tilley.'

'He's a bit on the heavy side. I'm very sorry, m'm.'

'Well, we'll just have to do our best with it.'

The old girl rolled her eyes. Once her daughter-in-law had left the room, she shifted her attention to Charles. 'So . . . what is it, exactly, that you've come for?'

Charlie mumbled something vague about conveyances and land agents.

'Speak up, young man. Can't hear a word.'

Charlie glanced briefly at the child. She obviously couldn't help, so he went careering off again, this time into a frenzied account of the wedding he'd barged into.

'A wedding? You came down for a wedding? Whose wedding?'

'Nipper Trewarden, m'm.' The maid dropped a dish of muffins on the table along with a very small dab of butter. 'The one they yellow devils got hold of.'

'Nipper? What kind of name is that?'

'It's a nickname, m'm,' said the maid, rattling cups and saucers. 'He was christened Samuel, but he was the youngest, so they called him the Nipper.'

'And who did you say he married?'

'Cissie Bluett, m'm. Her father works up at the Barton.'

'So,' the old girl fixed him with rheumy blue eyes, 'You were a guest at Cissie Bluett's wedding?'

Charlie wished somebody would pour the tea and then he would have something to do with his hands.

'He's from this Trust thing.' Daphne struggled to recall the name. 'Some National Trust.'

'Never heard of it.' Her father's cheekbones hadn't yet gone purple, but they had that plummy tinge that meant they were about to. They were sitting in the semi-dark in his den; Daph on one side of the chimneypiece, her father on the other. He was wearing a battered tweed jacket and under it, a loose, camel-coloured V-necked pullover and a khaki shirt. There was a thinness to the silence. On the walls, regimental groups stood stiffly listening.

'Apparently they do up old houses that are going to the dogs and open them to the paying public.'

'Ridiculous!' He clapped his hands to his pockets, needing his pipe. 'Did he look like a crackpot?'

'He's very young and just a tiny bit pompous.'

'There you are, then,' said the major. 'Ruddy chancer. Left the army, no job to go to, travelling round trying to extort a pound or two from anyone who's simple enough to give it to him.'

Daph said, 'Oh, I don't think he's that sort. He seems respectable. Educated.'

'They always do. Well, he won't get anything out of me. Empty pockets. Empty coffers.' The major had had a thought. 'The National Trust, you said?'

'That's right.'

'There was some talk in the newspapers of nationalizing the coal industry. Wouldn't put it past Attlee to send his spies out to grab property while he's about it. I hope you were careful about what you said. An Englishman's home is still his castle. That's what I shall tell the young puppy.'

Daph gazed at him across the rug with a faint smile on her face. Really she was wondering what she'd missed most about him during the four long years he had been away. His oval, bespectacled head? The very blue eyes in their deep, bony sockets? The long, finely shaped fingers? It was all of these and more, for she adored her father. Her relationship with her mother was more remote. She could never remember sitting on Mother's knee, couldn't recall Ma ever kissing her or showing any clear sign of affection. (Nagging, on the other hand, she was good at. 'You'll never be pretty, darling, but you could at least try to look less clumsy.')

Daph had long since concluded that she was a disappointment to her mother. Not pretty. Not interested in clothes or baubles. Unable to make her laugh, like Kit did. But at least she wasn't frightened of her any more. Working for the CAB in London, at a relief centre for the bombed-out, had given her confidence. She had learned to stand up for herself without going trembly.

If there were things – people – you were frightened of, well, you just put your head down and charged at them.

'Does Granny know?' the major asked. 'About the crackpot?'

'Shouldn't think so,' Daph told him, 'or the balloon would have gone up.' She tucked her freezing hands into her armpits for warmth. Outside, the short, cold day was ending. The park had changed colour. Dark green in the distance, with slate-grey – no, purple-grey outcrops.

Behind them the door opened and her mother's voice said, 'There you are!' It was clear from her face that she had expected to find her husband alone. 'You two look cosy.'

'Nowhere in this house is cosy,' Daph said.

'The kitchen is. Tea's waiting. Didn't Tilley tell you?'

Ignoring the question, Daph said, 'I've just been telling Pa you're scheming to sell the house over his head.'

'I never scheme.'

'That's what I'd call it.'

'Then you'd be wrong.' Her mother disengaged one wrist from the sleeves of her cardigans (one in thick, sugarstick ribbing, the other a fine zig-zag herringbone) and glanced at her watch. 'I just thought – well, it would be easier this way.'

'For you or for Pa?' Daph said. 'I like things in the open and above board.'

'Of course you do, darling. And so would the rest of us, in a shiny, happy world. There's a button missing from your cuff. Did you know?'

Daph looked down at her hopelessly shabby (and creased) suit. That was what Mother did when you had a dig back at her. She found your weak point and stuck the knife in. She had become even spikier since Kit's death.

The major had no interest in the finer points of fashion. He said, 'So how long have you been plotting behind my back?'

'Look – Myles – pretending everything is fine won't work any more. Do you really want to be declared bankrupt?'

The major hitched at the knee of his corduroy trousers. 'It won't come to that.'

'No?'

'No.'

'Then I'm sorry to say you're more stupid than I took you for. It's a bit of a beast, I know, but this young man may be able to help us. You might even like him. His name is Charles Garland. He's very keen to acquire more properties for the Trust. He can't wait to see the house.'

He threw her a pained, sideways glance, as though her words had given him a sudden toothache. 'Well, you show him. I won't.'

Daph walked over to the window. Standing there listening to her mother's voice, every word chopped into its component syllables – properties – she was overwhelmed by a great surge of pent-up resentment.

Why can't she leave him alone? It's such an uneven contest.

Her mother said, 'Of course I'll show him round. But I'd like you to meet him first. Half an hour. Over tea. Just to be civil? Just to hear what he has to say.'

'Why the devil should I be civil to someone who wants to turn me out of my own house?'

'But that's just it! We don't have to leave. They would give us part of the house in our lifetime for our private quarters.'

'Big of them!' The major glanced down at his polished brogues.

The wind buffeted the panes, a piercing east wind with all the birds riding on it.

'I won't sell.' The major reached under the sofa for the dog leash. 'They can offer all the money in the world. It won't make any difference.'

'So how do you suggest we pay the bills?'

Daph said, 'You might give him time to get over what he's been through, before you start nagging him to death.'

Her mother sighed. 'Oh, I'd have laid bets on whose side *you* would take. You're going to help maintain this great barn of a place, are you?'

'I would if I could.' Daph turned her head stubbornly to the darkening window.

'If you could! Exactly so. But you haven't even taken yourself off to the Labour Exchange to get employment.'

'I can't help it,' Daph said, 'if I don't know what to do with the rest of my life.' Peace was wonderful because no one got killed any more, but it still didn't feel natural or comfortable. After fixing one's mind for so many years on defeating the Nazis, everything else was a bit of an anticlimax. *What next? What am I going to do today?* There was a yawning gap that it was best not to think about.

'I don't want to be here. I don't want to be a burden on you. I'd rather have stayed in Whitechapel where I was useful. But they can't pay me enough to live on.'

'Then you're dependent on us. Which is fine, darling, as long as you keep your nose out of any little arguments Daddy and I might be having. And as long as you stop walking round with that sulky look on your face.'

'Steady on, Virginia,' the major said.

'I think I'm keeping very steady under the circumstances. Now – is anyone coming down to tea or do I have to sink all Tilley's confounded cake on my own?'

Daph turned her back on her stylish, exasperating mother. The dog looked at the leash and went to stand hopefully next to the major, who said, 'If I don't, I suppose you'll let fly?'

'Darling, it's for your own good.'

He'll give in to her, Daph thought with a flash of resignation. He always does. He'll give in to her because it's easier and he likes a quiet life. Also because of her beauty and all that grace, even muffled up as it is now in an old tweed skirt, two cardigans and a pair of sturdy boots.

You could wrap her up in an old curtain and she'd still look chic.

Unlike yours truly, Daph thought, catching sight of her reflection in the window pane. Too tall, too ungainly, awful hair. Outside, the light from the window was winning over the blue dusk. The park, the elm avenue and the lodge gates lay in winter silence.

The green-eyed god threw up another thought. *You wouldn't be so keen to sell if Kit were here. You would have done anything to save Lizzah for my good-looking, charming, slightly spoiled brother. Oh, God, I didn't mean that.* She felt a jolt of compunction.

You loved Kit. You know you did, so why let her get to you?

Her mother said, 'Has anyone seen Fishleigh today?'

'Bad knee. In his room.' The major lobbed the leash back where it lived under the chair. The dog looked disappointed and dropped his rump.

'And I suppose Tilley's running up and down to him?'

'She doesn't mind.'

'Well, I would.'

Daph was about to tell her mother she didn't mind Tilley clomping up two flights of stairs every morning at eight with her tea. Instead, leaning forward to peer out of the window, she said, 'That's odd. There's a light.'

'A light? Where?'

'In the Lodge.'

'What kind of light?'

'Not sure.' Daph screwed her eyes up to peer more clearly. 'Firelight? Candles?'

'I'll hop over there and check,' the major said in a flash. 'There was a break-in at Jacobstow last week.'

'It's all right. I'll go.' Daph was even keener to take the escape route. 'I'll take Punch.' The dog heard his name and flung himself at her in a frenzy of joy.

It was almost dark in the elm avenue with the winter evening coming down. The trees were shrouded, but above her head, branches surged like a great sea.

Daph was glad she had a torch. Not that she was frightened of the dark. She knew every inch of the park, could have walked it with her eyes shut, but the whole place was an obstacle course now, with army debris and rotten tree trunks lying where the gales had thrown them.

She felt a snowflake on her cheek. Then another. But after the unfresh fug of London, it was exhilarating to have cold country air whistling around her ears. She could almost taste green moss and sheep droppings.

All you could smell in Whitechapel was brick dust.

For four years, holed up in London, she had longed for Lizzah . . . For the views from the windows, the unspoilt land stretching as far as the eye could see, the sense of space, the walk (twenty minutes) down through the woods to the sea. But – this was odd – now she was home again, she missed the people she had worked with in the city, where no matter how grim the news, there was always someone to laugh it off with.

Oh, she was glad the war was over, but there was this feeling of loss. The buzz of leaping for an omnibus with her gas mask slung over her shoulder, of racing at speed from one assignment to the next, of driving through the city bumping over fire hoses. Because, quite extraordinarily, there were times when you could enjoy living on a razor's edge.

Living with a capital L . . .

And no one out there in the big, wild world had ever thought of her as stupid. 'Splendid in an emergency,' her boss had once said of her. It had made Daph's day.

Virginia Jago had objected to her daughter working in the East End. She would have preferred her to join the WAAF where there was less chance of catching some dreadful disease and where she might at least meet the odd eligible officer. Instead Daph had inexplicably chosen to spend her days scrubbing down slum children in infected LCC housing blocks and ferrying them (along with their nits and their wet drawers and their colourful language) from one end of the country to the other.

'As if,' Mother had said, 'you couldn't find anything more suitable.' For suitable read ladylike.

Virginia wouldn't have been seen dead in Whitechapel, but Daphne, over-protected and under-educated before the war came along, had found the sudden swerve on to a different road exhilarating. She thought now, What I miss most is the freedom to be myself. It all seemed to be closing in on her again. But in time, she supposed, she would settle back into the slow crawl that was life in the country.

Cross your fingers and spit. That's what they used to say at school. On the whole, Daph was of a hopeful disposition.

The Lodge stood behind the fine Elizabethan gatehouse with the Jago coat of arms over the gate. Standing on the weed-filled drive, she could see a butter-coloured light in the window. Outside the gates, an old bus was parked. Its destination board read 'Crownhill' and the windows had blinds fixed round with tapes.

As a gust of wind roared down the elm walk, Daph saw the light in the window flicker. Candles, she thought, calling Punch to heel and heading for the porch. *We have visitors.* Well, it wouldn't be the first time the empty Lodge had been broken into.

At first, when she hammered on the door, it seemed no one would come. The wind blew viciously, sending whirls of dead leaves into her face. Again she rattled the knocker.

Presently the door inched open. A man peered out at her. Dark, youngish, thin-faced.

Daph said, 'What are you doing here? This is private property.'

His eyes reminded her of a watchful ferret. He wore a brown pullover and a worn jacket. 'Sorry, miss. But the kid's got a fever and Granny thought we should get her under a roof.'

'Then you should have come up to the house and asked for help. You can't just break into other people's property.'

He glanced at her, then away again. 'We was desperate, like.'

There was a pause. Then Daph said, 'Where is the child? I may be able to help.'

He hesitated for a moment, then stepped back to let her in. They passed through the cold hallway into the bare sitting room. A match-wood fire was burning in the grate. Two women, one skinny and sparrowlike in her baggy slacks and stack-heeled shoes, the other older with a face swollen with a cold, sat huddled on orange boxes. The older woman held a baby swaddled in a blanket. On an unmade mattress in the other corner sat three more children of varying ages. Beside them were two saucepans, a spirit stove with bacon frying and a green teapot shaped like a racing car.

Daph bent to feel the child. He was burning up. She said, 'What were you thinking of, travelling with him in this state?'

'He wasn't so bad when we started out.'

'Will he feed?' she asked.

The young mother shook her head. She looked dark around the eyes. 'He's too poorly. Won't take anything.'

'So where are you heading?'

'For Camelford. Or Bude.'

'We took a wrong turning,' the husband said. 'We're looking for lodgings.'

There had been a trickle of them lately. Refugees who had lost their homes when Plymouth was bombed and had never been rehoused. 'If you've come from Plymouth,' Daph said, 'then you're Plymouth's concern.'

'Oh, yes?' The man almost laughed. 'Tell that to the authorities!'

Daph's attention went back to the floppy child. 'He ought to see a doctor.'

'Can't afford it.'

'Then it'll have to be the nurse from the village.'

'And what do we pay her with? Buttons?' He probably couldn't help sounding truculent. He was at the end of his tether.

'Oh, never mind that now. This child needs medical attention.'

Sooner rather than later. It was drifting off, between sleep and coma. Poor mite.

'Lizzah is not for sale.' Myles Jago fixed Charlie with piercing blue eyes.

'The very idea is an impertinence!' his mother said. 'An intrusion on the rights of the English aristocracy.'

'I'm not sure the English aristocracy can afford rights,' Virginia said.

'What nonsense! If Myles sells up, his father and grandfather will turn in their graves. Why, in time, when the country has got itself on its feet again—'

'I'm afraid,' said Virginia Jago, 'the creditors are waiting now.'

Behind them, the maid dropped a cup. She had just passed round another plate of muffins – cut in half and touched lightly in the middle with a smear of butter. 'Delicious,' Charlie had told her, though he wasn't sure he liked the look of the burnt edges. He decided at the last minute to take two. Might as well stuff his face. If he got chucked out, it was a long walk to the village pub. Mrs Jago was pouring tea into five Mason's Ironstone cups. The old crone sat twitching at her skirt with blue-veined hands.

'We can manage the rest ourselves now, Tilley,' Virginia Jago said. 'This might be a good time for you to see to Mr Garland's room.'

'Yes, m'm. Sorry, m'm.' Head down, the girl was rattling broken china into her apron.

'Off you go, then.'

Tilley emptied her pinny into the nearest drawer and scuttled out.

Virginia Jago said, 'Have a muffin, Mother.'

'I'm not hungry. I wouldn't be here at all if my room was decently warm.'

'You have to eat.'

'When you put something decent on the table, I will. That girl is slapdash. She burns everything.'

The major said, 'She's got a good heart.'

'Better she had a brain.'

'She keeps us fed, Mother. We do better than most.'

'Living on rabbits and woodcock? They tell me the fight for civilization has been won, but I find that hard to believe, Myles, when one is reduced to eating in the kitchen with the servants. I suppose one could look on it as preparation for the time when Attlee packs us all into concrete cages and throws away the key, but in the meantime, standards are standards and, whether it's convenient to you or not, some of us will go on trying to maintain them.'

The major said, 'Things are different these days.'

'Oh, things are different, all right! We can't get staff, can't get warm and your wife is telling you to pass over your birthright to some . . . some knock-kneed little socialist scarcely out of the cradle.'

Charlie thought, I'd be safer sitting in a wasps' nest.

'I mean, are you telling me this young Bolshevik can afford to buy Lizzah? Does he look as if he had two halfpennies to rub together?'

Perhaps not, but at least I've a civil tongue in my head.

'Tell me, young man, where would you find the money?'

'How they raise the money isn't my business,' Charlie told her. 'I'm . . . well, more on the aesthetic side. The Trust employs me to say whether a house is worth saving.'

'Worth saving?' She was about to blow a gasket.

'A-architecturally speaking. Some houses we're offered are totally unacceptable.'

Her nose was turning a deeper blue. Charlie was saved by the door to the passage opening. Daphne Jago walked into the room. She looked like one of those Russians you saw in newsreels, in her belted overcoat, thick, serge skirt and lace-up boots stuffed out with two pairs of knitted socks.

'A family has broken into the Lodge,' she told the major. 'There's a sick baby, so I telephoned Nurse Gotch.'

'I hope,' the old woman said, 'it's nothing catching.'

'Nurse Gotch will tell us if it is.'

'And in the meantime, you'll have caught some dreadful fever. Is there anything in the Lodge for them to steal?'

'They're too worried about the baby to think of stealing.'

'If you believe that, Daphne, you'll believe anything.'

A new gust attacked the house, hurling itself against the windows. Not the soft violence of the west wind, but a great howling thing descending on them from the north. Even in this cosier, knock-about part of the building, it made you nervous. Something crashed out in the courtyard. The fireplace let out a great puther of smoke.

And then, without any warning, the lights went out.

Three

The bathroom (about two hundred yards from Charlie's bedroom) was large and cold and almost the size of his London flat. The red line was still in the bathtub, and there was an extraordinarily elaborate clothes cupboard and a WC pan constructed of patterned blue china. Were you supposed to turn and admire it after you'd flushed? he wondered as, hugging himself against the cold, he attempted to turn on the tap. The water, when it eventually spluttered out, was lukewarm. You had to be hardy to strip to the waist, especially when the radiator didn't work and the window was stuck open a couple of inches and had let in the snow. But at least the morning air was sharp and fresh and the view from the window – curved gables, one tumbledown chimney, an expanse of icy roof – was giving him that familiar sense of expectancy, the feeling that something important might be about to enter his life and fill it with wild excitement.

It was like setting eyes on a girl for the first time. Well, almost. The tension, the intoxication, that hit you when you found a house like Lizzah . . . A house of enormous character, half Elizabethan, half Queen Anne and wholly Cornish, with the spirit of Squire Western still hovering, in spite of its grand front rooms.

Charlie adored his job. You couldn't exactly call it a career. He was paid next to nothing and he always seemed to be on the road, but he had a generous measure of independence. He liked the fact that there were no rules laid down, because, quite simply, you never knew what you were going to find until you got there. So you more or less ad-libbed your way through each day, whirring away, all wound up. He thought of himself as a cross between a travelling salesman and an apprentice diplomat.

Before the war, he had been based in a cramped office facing a shunting yard in Victoria. The Trust had now moved to a pair of dusty old houses in Queen Anne's Gate. From there he would criss-cross the country inspecting a handful of glorious or gruesome old piles every week along with their glorious or gruesome owners; for the aristocrats going down with colours flying were often mad and sometimes barking. 'The public can't possibly be admitted to the house because they smell,' one old colonel had told him. He'd gone shouty crackers when Charlie had informed him that his crystal chandeliers were fakes, made up from snippets of old glass less than fifty years ago.

The name of Charlie's boss was Lambert Fossett. Old Fossett was a waffling bumblebee of a man with an unnatural hairline. Miss Waterhouse, who worked downstairs, was fond of him, but Charlie thought it was time the old fuddy-duddy (fond of quoting the articles of the Trust's foundation in 1895 or the National Trust Bill of 1937 in a parroty voice at breakneck speed) was shipped off into retirement.

As he scrambled to get his shirt back on, he decided he must come back with his battered Kodak and take a shot of that gable end. He did his share of crawling around under roofs, photographing venerable spiders while looking for deathwatch beetle, but there was something about these early glimpses that thrilled him no end. Fossett always told him to stick to close-up shots of the stonework or the underpinning in the foundations. 'The building is either a suitable case for the Trust or not, Garland, and no amount of airy-fairy photographs will make it so when it isn't.'

He had a quick shave and sprinted back to his room to finish dressing. He took a notebook and pencil out of his briefcase, searched for his cigarette case, then made his way along a creaking corridor and down the oak staircase (very fine, Charles II) to breakfast. Didn't want to offend anyone (well, more than he had done already) by being late. What would be on the table? Tea and toast, grilled herring and marmalade would be good, he thought. Wouldn't bet on it, though. Rationing had put paid to all that.

Minutes later, the major came mooching down the same staircase. He was fifty-four, but he looked older. This morning there was an expression of morose cynicism on his face. Strange light, he thought, staring out through old panes at the window mullions (in a bad way), the stonework (crumbling like cake), the gun-grey sky and the park sweeping up to Ham Wood. Snow, he thought. Makes everything look grubby. Well, it *is* grubby. He remembered how the house was in his grandmother's time. Blazing fires, bright damask, maids in starched aprons. The stair treads and barley sugar banisters polished until they glowed like conkers. When I was ten years old, he thought. Before the world went stark-staring mad.

This morning he felt as old as Methuselah. That was because he hadn't slept. Too many things going round in his head. It was that young fella . . . Garland . . . skulking around the place. Foppish type. Looked as if he'd be a riot with the girls. Should have sent him packing, the major told himself. Don't know why I didn't. Because Gin would have let rip, that's why. Lately, since the business with the boy, she'd been, well . . . driven. Couldn't talk about it, of course. Couldn't bring it out into the open. Grief was always there and always heavy, but in this house, they mourned in silence.

The house . . . What was to be done about it? Even in this state, it was the loveliest house in the world. And she was asking him to give it away. Well, he was damned if he would let five hundred years of family history go down the spout. It doesn't matter to Gin, he thought, clapping his hands to his pockets for his pipe. She wasn't born to it. He went on down – past the smashed balusters – to stand at the foot of the stairs, one of his favourite places. He tapped the barometer, as he did every morning. The major was a man of order. Set in his ways.

He tried to pin his mind on other things: collecting the rents; the homeless people in the Lodge; what he was going to do about Fishleigh. But it didn't work. He had hoped that the boy would bring money in by making a good marriage. And now that Kit was . . . out of the picture . . . well, you couldn't depend on the girls. Pen was too young and Daphne wasn't the sort to attract a rich suitor. Splendid girl, but not much in the looks department. Not like her mother. Odd, that. But a sensible sort of girl in a crisis. Reliable, Myles thought. Makes very little fuss. Don't know, quite, what I'd do without her.

'Myles? There you are!' Ma's voice. She spoke as she played the piano . . . mainly fortissimo.

'Here I am,' the major said.

'I wanted to catch you before breakfast.'

Myles wished he had the dog at his heels.

His mother said, 'Did Fishleigh fix the generator?'

'Fishleigh can't get out of his bed. I did it myself.'

'Servants didn't malinger in my day. I don't know why you put up with him. And I don't know what Virginia was thinking of, bringing that young man down without so much as a by-your-leave. It's one of her nerve storms, I suppose. Or her age.'

'It's been hard for her lately,' the major said.

'Hard?' His mother's hooting mezzo went even higher. 'She needs to pull herself together! I lost my father in South Africa and my husband in the Great War. It's a good thing I'm not easily felled.'

Ma was never one to spare you the cold shower.

'Three wars I've lived through. But never again, thank God! I'll be dead before the next one.'

'There's the gong,' the major said in a relieved voice.

She wasn't in the least bit interested. 'You have to bear these things. And as for the January bills, does Virginia imagine it was any different in your father's time? You won't remember this, but I could guarantee that as soon as Christmas was over, the minute the tree went out and the maids were on their knees scraping the candle grease from the carpet, down he would go with the winter glooms.'

Once Ma had you pinned down, she held her ground. She wore her morning rig-out of shawls and drapes and had piled an astonishing amount of white hair on top of her head. In one hand she held her stick and in the other a pair of spectacles (with extremely thick lenses) and her needle-work bag. Myles tried to edge past her, but she blocked his path.

'We always muddled through somehow. As you will. The idea of selling up . . . it's preposterous!' she went on. 'Of course, we know who's at the bottom of it all. The blessed Communists trying to tear the country's throat out. This Garton is one of them, mark my words!'

He wanted to tell her she was talking through her hat. The young man was more silly ass than Stalinist. But as usual, he forced himself to hold his tongue. Odd how she made him feel a grown-up boy.

Breakfast was not the most comfortable meal Charlie had ever taken. It was served, once more, in the warmth of the kitchen, albeit the table this morning was laid with good silver and a starched white cloth. The major was the only one to be served with a boiled egg. The rest of them had to make do with tea and leathery toast. The kitchen cat prowled around looking for scraps and the maid bashed away at the fire while the old woman bashed away at the major's ears. Evidently he was used to it. Now and then he dropped a crust to the dog who lay under the table.

At last, she turned her attention to Charlie. 'I thought you were leaving. Sitting there eating us out of house and home—'

Charlie felt like the butcher's boy or the man who delivered telegrams.

'He can't leave,' Virginia Jago said, 'until one of us has shown him around the house. I thought, perhaps . . . Myles?'

The major was already on his feet, clicking his fingers at the dog.

His wife said, 'Darling – don't disappear on us. I suppose you'd prefer to show Mr Garland round the park.'

'No point,' the major said.

'The point is that there are problems to face.'

Daphne Jago said, 'You should try living in Whitechapel. You don't know what problems are.'

Mrs Jago raised one perfectly formed eyebrow, then turned her attention back to the major. 'Look – Mr Garland's visit commits you to nothing. For my sake, say you'll do the park.'

He looked up and said, 'I suppose I'll damn well have to.'

'Good.'

'Myles, you're not giving in to this nonsense?' His mother glared at him. Then, with the help of her stick, she heaved herself to her feet. 'If you do, I shall consult my solicitor.'

Her daughter-in-law, dropping her napkin on the plate, murmured, 'I'm sure he'll be delighted about that.'

'Madam says to tell you she'll be with you in five minutes, sir,' the maid announced.

'Righty-ho.'

'Between me and you, sir, she's slipped off for a smoke. Don't tell the major, as he don't think it should be for the ladies.'

She hovered around Charlie like a protective shadow. Her cheerful, open face beamed at him, revealing a fine set of new porcelain teeth.

They were in the arctic space of the drawing room. Piles of dust lay under the chairs from worm borings. The smell of mould almost over-powered you, but the huge Elizabethan windows were awfully fine. As was the eighteenth century wallpaper and the superb line of Chippendale chairs.

'Don't step there, sir. You'll come a cropper. The floorboard's bust. Madam was going to call in Frank Hobbs, but the major says they can't afford it. I suppose you'll be dolling the place up, sir, if you should buy it?'

Charlie said, 'Er . . . possibly.'

'I was wondering if you'd be taking on the same staff?'

Charlie stepped round the hole under the delicately patterned Chinese silk carpet. There was old, there was in disrepair, but Lizzah was most definitely on the skids.

'Only I've never worked anywhere else. When I was housemaid, I was known as Bess, but now the others have scarpered, Madam calls me Tilley.'

She gave him a proud, porcelain grin. Charlie's eyes took in a suit of armour, rusty and brittle, and window seats criss-crossed with the trails of slugs and snails.

'Madam's all right really. Well, up to a point. She don't like you to talk back. Not that I'm that sort. I've learned to keep mum, sir. Say nothing. That's my motto.'

Charlie said, 'Really?' He tried to edge away, but she was like a limpet, refusing to be dislodged.

'I leave all that to our Queenie.'

Plymouth porcelain in that cabinet, Charlie was thinking. New Hall on the piano.

'Queenie's my sister. She's a bit of a tartar, between you and me and the gatepost. Our mother didn't mind much when Queenie took herself off to Bristol to work in the munitions.'

'That's a very fine old chimneypiece,' Charlie said.

'It was until the army blackened it. They would keep banking up the fire and it smoked like billy-oh. Queenie said *I* should get away too. Find work up country. I said, "What would I want to do that for?" and she said, "Because it's a damned sight livelier than this blinking dump." "And who would do the work up at the Hall?" I said, and she said, "Let the b . . .'s fend for themselves like the rest of us has to." As I said, sir, our Queenie's a bit of a one. Last time she come home, she brought a tin of spam from Marks and Spencers. Mother wouldn't touch it. Do you know what she said it reminded her of?'

Charlie opened his mouth to say he couldn't imagine, but he was interrupted by the door opening. Virginia Jago came sweeping in, bringing with her a whiff of perfume.

'Sorry to keep you waiting,' she said. 'And I'm sorry you had to spend the evening by candlelight because of that damned generator. I don't know how we shall get the place straight. But I remember my mother-in-law saying the same thing in '21. That was when they were pulling the house back together from its hospital days during the First War. Myles and I had just got married. It was a hot summer. All the windows and doors stood open. I remember warm winds smelling of hay.

'My mother-in-law was still in her widow's weeds . . .' She threw him a bazaar-opening smile. There was a studied graciousness about her that was effortlessly patronizing. 'Swathed in black lace. Myles's father died in a car accident during an intelligence job in the First War. She brought her son up on her own. She's a tough old bird. Had to be, I suppose.'

Charlie pulled out his notebook and Kodak and trailed after her into the dining room with its three long windows, its dark mahogany and heavy drapes. 'You won't mind if I take a few snapshots?'

'Not at all.'

'And if I come back for a second visit, I shall have to make a detailed inventory.'

'Of the whole house?'

'I'm afraid so.'

'Good God – it'll take months.'

'I hope not.' *Possible Tudor fireplace behind*, he scribbled. Then *First class pewter – tarnished*. 'Your floors are in a bad way.'

'It's all in a bad way,' she told him. 'Including the occupants.'

'But those old hangings are good.'

'The tapestries?'

'Quite wonderful.' He peered up at them. Some trick of the light made them seem to shimmer through the greenish gloom.

'Samson and Delilah,' he said. 'And Daniel in the Lions' Den.'

'They've been here since the house was built.'

You could tell. They were torn and filthy, but extremely lively.

She said, 'They're full of plaster dust. Part of the ceiling collapsed when Myles was a boy. They were too heavy to remove for cleaning.'

All the while scribbling, Charlie followed her through a well-endowed library with fat armchairs and stags' antlers and up a staircase lined with acres of family portraits (one of them an indifferent Gainsborough). The first floor guest rooms that were not a cemetery of old chairs and dormitory beds resembled junk shops piled high with ottomans and curios from the East Indies, with hip baths and hat boxes and gas mask snouts that smelled rankly of rubber. While Virginia Jago drifted along in front of him, Charlie jotted away in the notebook that was rapidly filling up. *Chairs covered with cloth-of-gold. Priests' vestments? James I bed worm-riddled. Gallery very little changed since Henry VIII.*

The house carried a cargo of rare and beautiful objects, but all of them ramshackle, neglected and thick with cobwebs.

'So – what's the verdict?' Mrs Jago asked after another mile or two of passages and staircases. They had fetched up in the nursery wing, where Charlie had to stop because he had cramp in his pencil-holding finger.

'I need to see the exterior before I can make a judgement.' He knew enough not to commit himself at this stage. 'Any ghosts?' He always asked that question. It deflected attention, gave him time to think.

'My husband got spooked by one when he was a child. He won't tell you about it, but he certainly believes in them.'

Charlie shoved his pencil behind one ear. 'Do you have any help with your accounting? Who looked after that side of it while your husband was away?'

'I'm afraid all that got neglected once the army took possession. Before the war, Nethercotts from Exeter did the annual tot-up. The rest of the time, Myles muddled along with the aid of his little helper.'

'Your daughter?'

'Good Lord, no. Mabel Petherick comes in to help part-time when the correspondence becomes too much for him.'

'The scary lady?'

'You met her?' She gave him a comic look. 'Years ago when she was young, the blessed Mabel was sweet on my husband.'

His face must have registered his shock.

'You don't believe me. It's true. They used to play together as children.'

Charlie couldn't imagine the trout as a child.

'In Mabel's eyes, my husband can do no wrong. She's not so keen on me. But I've got used to being the intruder around here. My mother-in-law isn't speaking to me this morning, by the way. Actually, I think I prefer it that way. Would you like a coffee? I think I can probably rustle one up.'

'That would be a life-saver,' Charlie said.

The baby was no longer floppy, thank God. It still wouldn't feed, but its colour was normal. It sat staring at Daph with approving friendliness.

Nurse Gotch said, 'His temperature's down. It's a good thing you called me.'

Daph wasn't sure her father would agree when the bill landed on the mat.

'They tell me they're on the way to Bude. I'd be happier if they stayed a day or two until this little one's breathing has settled. I'm sure the major won't turn them out. It's fearfully cold for travelling. Which reminds me, this place ought to be kept warmer. Can we organize something.'

'I suppose so.' Daph wasn't sure how.

Nurse Gotch shook her thermometer down. 'Good girl. How's your grandmother?'

'As cantankerous as ever.'

'That's what keeps some people going. Ill temper.'

There was a bang behind them that meant the front door had swung open. 'Hello?' Daph heard a voice call out. 'Anyone there?'

'In here,' she said.

It was Noel Boswell, who ran the estate on the other side of Ham Wood. Bos was a ponderous, good-natured young man twelve years Daph's senior. They had written to each other, spasmodically, all through the war. Daph had let off steam about under-nourished children and damp tenements. Bos had sent her closely written, methodical letters from all over the Mediterranean and the Adriatic.

When he saw her, his face brightened. 'I was coming to see you,' he said. One of the Plymouth children stood behind him, picking his nose. 'I wanted to ask your advice.' He ran a hand over his prematurely receding hairline and said abstractedly. 'I didn't know you were letting the Lodge.'

'It was news to me, too. Long story,' she said. 'Tell you later.'

Nurse Gotch shoved her thermometer case back into her bag. 'Know anyone who could shell out a bag of coal?' she asked.

'Coal?' Bos gave her a slow, puzzled smile.

'These children are cold.'

'The deuce they are,' he said. 'I'll send some over. As soon as I get back.'

'That's the ticket,' she said. 'A few groceries wouldn't go amiss either. Right. I'll be on my way.' She patted the baby's head, hoisted up her bag and took herself off. The baby rubbed a fist over its snotty nose.

Daph said, 'Thanks for coming.'

She thanked Bos, too, when the nurse had slammed the door behind her.

'Glad to help,' he said. 'Poor little beggars . . .'

Like many good-hearted Englishmen, he was bashful and awkward when it came to showing his feelings. Though he had written a note of condolence at the news of Kit's death, it had taken him weeks to bring the matter up in conversation.

'So,' he said. 'How are things at Lizzah?'

'Where do you want me to start?'

'Problems?'

'I'll say! You won't believe what my mother's been up to.'

'Believe me,' Charlie said, 'there are a great many owners in the same boat.'

'That's as may be,' the major barked.

It had turned into a fine, clear morning. The light behind the winter trees was shrimp pink. The major forged ahead in his pork-pie hat, stabbing the ground with his stick as they walked. Charlie stopped for a moment to admire the dignity of the lovely, shabby old mansion.

'The thing is,' Charlie said, 'If the Country Houses Committee agrees to accept your property, it will guarantee to let the place – or at least part of it – back to your family.'

'Damned cheek!' There was a pained look on the major's face.

He called the dog to heel, but it broke away from him and ran off into the snow. He lost his temper and bellowed at it, but the dog took no notice. The church tower was now a distant landmark behind the trees.

'You'd have unlimited access to the staterooms and you could use them whenever you wanted, but normally you would inhabit private quarters at the back. Don't you see, you could have your cake and eat it?'

'So what's the damn catch?' The major stood wrapping the dog's lead around purple knuckles. He looked worn out.

'Well, if we chose to take it on, we would need some kind of endowment in either land or cash.'

'I thought you'd have your fingers in the till! I keep telling you, there isn't any cash. Hasn't been any since about 1800.'

Seeing his chance, Charlie seized it. 'That's fortunate in a way. The old place wasn't tampered with. It's a remarkably fine example of Elizabethan architecture.'

'Hhmph.' He couldn't argue with that one.

'There are two farms, I understand?'

'Tregeare and The Barton. They can't go,' he said sharply. 'There are my tenants to consider. Responsibility and birthright still matter in this neck of the woods. Look, young man, my wife means well. I daresay she thought she had the right notion, bringing you down here, but you have no idea how many people here depend on us for a living.'

'Your tenants would be protected.'

'You say that, but how do I know you'll keep your word? Then there's the income tax to consider. If I sell, I'll be clobbered.'

'Actually, no. Under the National Trust Act of 1937, devised endowment land, provided it's classifiable as being of natural beauty and declared by the Trust inalienable, will be exempt from taxes.' Charlie could no longer feel his feet. One of his shoes was definitely leaking. 'Our solicitors would get their heads together and sort it out.'

'That'll cost. Those johnnies make a fortune.' The major's face was all screwed up with suspicion. He looked blimpish and exasperated and exhausted. 'So if I turned the show over to you . . . how would it work? Who would be in charge?'

'I would, for a while. Of course, I couldn't be here all the time. I've got a good many other houses on my hands. The general management now falls to regional agents, representatives and committees.'

'Committees?' The major evidently didn't think much of that idea.

Charlie said, 'But I'd come as often as I could to oversee the repairs. The contents of the house – the furniture and family portraits – would stay intact. After some weeding out, of course. They would be preserved by the Trust on behalf of the nation. It's hard to say exactly, but we would hope to have the house open to the public in, say, a year . . . or eighteen months?'

'Have people tramping round the place and staring at us?' The major looked appalled.

'It wouldn't be every day.'

'How many then?'

'Oh, say one hundred and fifty days a year.'

Pop-eyed with fury, the major turned and marched off. 'I won't have it. Do you hear? You can jolly well clear off. And that's an end to it.'

'Don't worry about my husband,' Virginia Jago told Charlie. 'I can handle him. If you're sure you want to take us on.'

She was sitting next to the hyacinth on the table in the small break-fast room that was now used as a parlour. Charlie said, 'The house is quite special. I've never been surer of anything in my life.'

'Good.' She threw him a coldly bright smile. 'So what happens next?'

'Well, our area agent will write a report based on my notes. And I'll need to make a second, more thorough examination to list the contents which ought to be on loan to the Trust. And to take stock of their condition.'

Mrs Jago smoothed her faultlessly cut skirt.

'But I must stress that I shall need your husband's signature on the papers before that happens.'

She got up and walked quickly over to the window. She stood staring out. 'I told you, I can handle Myles.'

'After all, you've been doing it all your life,' said a new voice from behind them. It belonged to the sour-faced dowager with a smell under her nose.

'Something had to be done, Mother.'

'It'll break his heart. You know that?'

'It'll take a weight of problems off his shoulders.'

'And take away every bit of his pride and dignity.'

'Better that than the removal men at the door.'

'I'll fight you over this with every breath in my body,' the old lady declared. 'I'll make my battle plans . . . you see if I don't—'

Charlie wondered if he could slip past her before the tirade aimed itself at him.

'And what's more, I shall put some spunk into my son.'

'Thank you, Mother,' Virginia Jago said. 'We get your drift.'

'I'll be on my way, then.' Charlie eased himself backwards towards the door.

'If you wait until after luncheon, Daphne will run you to the village in the dog cart.'

'I'll enjoy the walk. Really.'

'Then Tilley will put something together for your journey.'

'No need,' Charlie said. He had sampled Tilley's cooking.

'But I insist. She'll be in the kitchen. Tell her I sent you.'

Tilley said, 'If you could just give me a minute, sir . . .' He had walked in on her as she was emptying the crop of a pigeon over the sink top, tearing open its guts and squeezing out undigested acorns and berries. *May as well finish the job,* she told herself, *while her hands were all of a mess.* They were meaty little birds, but old and tough, so they would go into a suet-crust pie with the scraps from a ham bone. Then, later, she would pound the livers with the left-overs, some mace and seasoning to make potted meat. The pansy young gentleman looked away as her hands (red from always being in cold water) went on ripping and pulling at floppy unmentionables and flicking them into the square, stone sink. 'I'll make you a pack of sandwiches.'

'No. Really. I can s – see how busy you are.'

There was a wet, squelching sound as she disposed of the gizzards. Tilley wiped her hands down her flowered overall. 'Will bloater paste do you? 'Tis a touch salty, but I'll spread it thin.'

The young man gave a sudden grimace and vanished. Can't be hungry, Tilley thought with an inward shrug. Then she fiddled with the knobs on the radio until she found *Kitchen Front* on the radio.

Four

'I still miss the Navy Comforts Ladies. The chat, the little gatherings.' Edie Medland's hands held the skein of wool stiffly in front of her as her sister wound the end into a fat ball. 'It was topping.'

'Topping? What kind of a word is that?'

'I don't see what's wrong—'

'It's nasty, modern slang. That's what's wrong.' Mabel Petherick pursed her lips and adjusted her spectacles. You heard it everywhere these days. Films were flicks. Sweethearts were cuties. You didn't dance, you jitter-bugged.

'Anyway, I miss Wednesday afternoons knitting scarves for our boys.' Edie's hands went on dipping and weaving.

'What you really miss is the gossip.'

'I suppose you're right.'

'There's no suppose about it.' Miss Petherick tucked the end of the strand into the wedge and pushed back her chair. 'Is that the time? Good Lord!'

Well, sometimes He's good, she thought, and at others He's an absolute . . . I won't say what. An admirable spinster, pillar of the church and maiden lady of fifty-three years, Mabel was not quite embittered, though she could certainly pick a bone or two with life.

She dropped the wool into her knitting bag, mulling over the various things she would hold against the Almighty, were He to materialize suddenly on the beeswaxed linoleum in the kitchen of her well-appointed cottage. What would come first on the list, apart from the blaringly obvious – losing her fiancé in France in 1917? Having to stand on the bus all the way down to Bude this morning? Having to prop herself up in the longest fish queue she could ever remember, while being sneezed over by all the poor devils going down with the latest bout of influenza? And one really ought to have been able to get hold of a pot of white paint for the scullery and a new sheet for Edie's bed – that wouldn't be much to ask – but with all the men coming home at once, you couldn't get paint or sheets or a stick of furniture for love nor money.

Miss Petherick adjusted the neat waistband of her tweed skirt (grey herringbone, pre-war – all the best things were pre-war, in her opinion) and remembered one more thing that had spoiled her morning. The woman in the feathered hat who had pushed in front of her in the tea shop in The Strand. Too many ill-mannered people like that these days . . . A certain amount of nastiness was creeping back into everyday life.

The best thing, she thought, about the war had been seeing people come together. It was strange how at certain turning points in life, through fear or defiance or a sort of communal bloody-mindedness, people could change, almost overnight. It was as if the whole population had woken up one morning in, say, the summer of 1940, and had written in capital letters in their diaries: YOU MAY NOT BE HERE TOMORROW, SO BE AS NICE AS YOU CAN TODAY.

She stood looking at the church tower out of the window. Edie wouldn't have needed to write it down, she thought. Edie had been kind and gentle – on occasion annoyingly so – since the day she was born. But for those mere mortals who didn't find it so easy to locate their Christian kindness, war was a very pleasant corrective to normal patterns of behaviour. People started doing things for each other. They gave lifts into town. They opened their houses and took people in. Helped the old dig their gardens. During those six long years, Mabel decided, we were absolutely at our best. Now greed was returning and selfishness and the creed of all-pull-together-while-we're-in-trouble was on the way out.

'I forgot to tell you . . .' Edie said. 'Agnes saw Lil Trewarden with Another Man outside The Carriers. Agnes says she was wearing chenille fishnet stockings and her skirt was halfway up her thighs. Everything out for all to see.'

Edie's friend, Agnes Bolitho, passed on all the gossip with rococo embellishments. Edie was very well-up in chenille fishnet tales. In tales of all kinds if it came to that.

'I can't say I'm surprised. Lily Trewarden's no better than she should be.'

'I didn't like that yellow thing she wore as a bridesmaid. It wasn't suitable.'

'Lily Trewarden doesn't do suitable. You should know that.'

'It's Jack I feel sorry for.' Edie put the kettle on the boiling plate of the stove. 'And that sweet little boy.'

Small boys, in Mabel Petherick's very considerable experience, were very rarely sweet. But it was true that one should feel sorry for Jack Trewarden, who, like thousands of other young men, hadn't had much of an innings with the girls before rushing into a giddy marriage two days after war was announced.

'I thought,' said Edie, in one of her swift changes of subject, 'we could build a jolly log fire this afternoon and toast ourselves.'

Mabel said, 'I expect you've forgotten that the log basket's empty and we'd have to spend an hour chopping the jolly old logs? Anyway, I've got parish magazines to deliver.' Sometimes she was glad to have an excuse to get away from Edie who twittered away most days, non-stop, like a canary.

'Then I'll dust the front room. It needs a going over.' Edie was a naturally cheerful soul who had learned not to argue when Mabel's plans put paid to her own.

Miss Petherick gazed across the kitchen table at her dear, idiotic little sister. Edie spent her life dusting ornaments and running in and out of rooms. It wasn't a bit of good trying to stop her.

She was . . . not simple-minded exactly . . . but simple.

There was, one would hope, a difference.

When she had done the top end of the village, she cut through the churchyard, heading for The Acland. Rooks were settling round the tops of the Rectory trees. She flattened herself against the wall as one of Dan Jewell's carts came rumbling down the street. Jewell's younger girl – Daisy – was perched on the back of it, wrapped in a hard army overcoat.

Nice girl, Daisy. Shy at school. Try and get a word out of her and she would stand rolling the hem of her skirt up over her hands until you could see the legs of her knickers.

We can't all be gabby, Mabel thought. On the whole, she preferred people to think before they opened their mouths. It showed they had a brain.

The nurse's car was parked outside one of the slummier cottages in Church Row. Nurse Gotch, starched skirts crackling, would be seeing to Annie Rowe's leg. Jewell's cart disappeared round the bend by the pub. Miss Petherick crossed the road and marched her black lace-ups round to the side door of The Acland. It was a long, thatched building that had only just been connected to the electricity. The drangway couldn't decide whether it belonged to the pub or the cottage that skulked behind it. Mabel had to thread her way through beer kegs and wellington boots and drying washing.

'Hello-o-o!' she called. There was a smell of stale ale and frying. Through the door on the left was the stuffy little bar with its dartboard and the picture of King George in his naval uniform. The pub closed after lunch, but she could hear voices.

'Anyone at home?' Miss Petherick opened the door on her right and crossed a vestibule crammed with hunting prints and leather chairs. But Pru Hockin wasn't there or in the parlour, its walls swathed to the ceiling in full-blown Victorian roses, so she was forced to brave the pub proper. Flinging open the door to the bar, she saw, in the tobacco-filled gloom, a small group of the Acland's stalwarts – Wallace Truscott, Turnip Toms and Bill Ricketts – sitting round the scrubbed table against the window.

'Miss Petherick!' Pru said from behind the bar. 'What a pleasant surprise.' But she had turned a guilty pink. 'We were just having a bit of a jaw.'

'So I see.' Miss Petherick put on her grimmest face to show that she did not approve of after-hours drinking.

'About them new council houses as are going up.' Wallace Truscott's wall-eye veered vaguely in her direction. 'The missus have heard the old well's being capped off and they'll have posh bathrooms with running water.'

Mabel said, 'I brought the church magazine, Mrs Hockin.' She flapped the thing down on the bar top.

Turnip Toms took a sip from his tankard. 'They'll give you anything these days. All these young chaps turning up back home in posh demob suits. Five this week.' He looked and sounded like a thoughtful sheep. Old, snow-white and painfully thin. 'Nobody gived me a new suit when I come back from the Crimea.'

Bill Ricketts said, 'Aah, well, they found out during this last lot that the servicemen be as good as the officers.'

'That's why Attlee got in.'

Pru Hockin smiled across at Miss Petherick, who maintained her steely stare. Mrs Hockin picked up the magazine and pretended to read it. 'I'm glad they painted the name back on the church notice board,' she said. 'Funny to see it again after all this time.'

'The major arranged it,' Miss Petherick said tersely. *St Petroc's, Trewenna* had been blacked out during the war against invaders.

'He didn't fork out to pay for it, though.' Bill Ricketts knocked his pipe out on the table. 'That'll come off my rates.'

Pru said, 'Bill!' in a hiss of whispered warning.

'It's the truth. When was the last time Squire Fricking Jago saw to my leaking roof?'

Miss Petherick said, 'I won't have you speaking of the major like that, Bill Ricketts.'

'That's as may be. And I know you be in with the upper set, like. And

I know the major's a pleasant enough chap. But he don't do nowhere near enough for his tenants.'

'The major,' Miss Petherick said, 'has a good many financial commitments.'

'Aah. Folks like they always cry poor.'

Pru Hockin made a flustered palaver of extracting cash from the till to pay for the magazine.

'The regime of the landlords,' Wallace Truscott opined, 'is coming to an end. Now we've finished off the bliddy Germans, 'tis the time of the working man.'

'If I rang the constabulary,' Miss Petherick snapped, 'I could have you up before the magistrates for breaking the licensing laws.'

Pru Hockin pressed an apologetic sixpence into her hand. 'Time, gentlemen, please.'

Turnip said, 'The first shall be last . . . and the last first.'

The sound of a large vehicle passed across the windows. 'That's the sewage lorry,' Pru said, 'come to empty the lavatories.' Thank God, she thought. The smell will clear them out.

You couldn't call them rogues or even troublemakers. On the whole, Mabel Petherick thought, as she made her way back through the cluster of cottages round the church, Bill Ricketts and his little gang were stolid, decent types. All that wild talk . . . It was just the drink loosening their tongues.

Or else they'd come under the influence of a louder and less pious generation newly returned from far-flung places. Such changing times . . . Was it any wonder there was all this emotional and political disturbance?

No one has emerged from this war unscathed. Well, what did you expect? A New Jerusalem, when the country's virtually bankrupt?

Oh Lord, Miss Petherick thought, let them all stop their griping and moaning. Though, of course, one had to admit that the Lizzah cottages were in a terrible state. Myles would put that right now that he was back in charge. Dear, kind Myles. Not everyone understood that in spite of his apparent wealth, he rarely had a bent halfpenny to call his own.

'Afternoon, Miss Petherick.'

Mabel's thoughts were rudely interrupted by someone crossing the street to greet her.

'Jack Trewarden?' She was sure it was him, but the statement still framed itself as a question. The young man who stood in front of her was lean, but muscular. His hair was thick and tawny, in spite of the army short-back-and-sides, but his face had honed down. 'Welcome home! How are you?'

'All right, thanks.'

When he said, 'All right,' she wasn't sure he was speaking the truth. 'I saw you at your brother's wedding, but couldn't get over to speak. I have to say Samuel looked quite dreadful.'

'He's better than he was.'

'Then God only knows what he was like before.' Miss Petherick never minced her words. Her green eyes stared at him over a white-powdered nose. Such a good-looking boy, in his grey flannel shirt and thick jersey. A decent boy . . . She found it hard to think of her former pupils as men. 'Have you found work?'

He shook his head. 'I went for my old job down to Bude, but there were twenty others after it.'

From what she'd heard, several of the demobbed men were in the same fix. 'Six years is a long time, Jack.'

'Don't I know it?'

There was a quiet edge to him that hadn't been there before. I remember the time, Miss Petherick thought, when you fell into a patch of stinging nettles on a nature walk. You were seven years old. You had picked wood sorrel and blackthorn blossom and you refused to cry and I had to hunt in the ditch for dock leaves for your stings . . . And now you're married to a flighty piece with a gash of carmine lipstick and dyed hair.

'You'll find something,' she said with more briskness than she felt. 'You're good with your hands. And Samuel? Will he be fit for work?'

'He's going into business for himself.'

'Doing what?' Miss Petherick asked.

'He won't say. You know what Nipper's like. Goes his own way. Always did.'

Miss Petherick did her best to imagine Samuel Trewarden running a business, but it couldn't be done. Not that he was a stupid boy. He had always had a kind of native nous. But he couldn't add up for toffee.

'I suppose it's a good thing your wife is working? They tell me she runs a hair salon.'

Jack said, 'I want her to give it up.'

'Oh . . . really?' was the best Miss Petherick could do in reply. She chose not to say he might lose that particular battle. According to Agnes, Lil Trewarden had told her husband she would go crackers with boredom hanging about the house all day. 'Well, I can't say I approve of it, but a good many married women work these days.'

'My wife won't,' Jack said flatly. 'Not once I've found something. There'll be no need.'

'Have you tried The Barton? Dan Jewell needs a farmhand. The Stephens boy was killed in France.'

'I'm not a farmhand.'

She knew that. Jack had clever, useful fingers.

'Lizzah, then?'

'What would I do up at the Manor?'

'Gardening? The place is in a dreadful state.'

'Not my thing,' Jack said. 'Anyway, the Jagos are going down the plug-hole as well, from what I gather. Some chap from London wants to buy them out.'

There was silence, except for the creaking of the pub sign. Down the street came a Ford van driven by a man in blue dungarees. 'Don't be ridiculous!' Mabel snapped, squashing the magazines against her thudding heart.

Miss Petherick was a good old sausage, Jack thought, as he headed for home. One of the sort he'd missed (who'd have thought it?) all the time he was abroad. One of those tweed-wearing, sterling, bossy women who, in her sensible shoes and unfashionable felt hat, would have sorted the Germans – no contest – had they ever managed to invade.

Mouldy Mabel. That's what we used to call her. He wondered whether she still rode that terrifying old sit-up-and-beg bicycle.

He lifted a hand to Wally Truscott, who was shambling out of The Acland and turned into Forge Lane as the deep note of the church clock sounded four.

Mouldy Mabel . . . Must ask the boy if they still call her that. Not that he'd get much of an answer. Jack ducked his head against the biting wind and dug his hands into his trouser pockets.

He could understand that a kid would be wary of a father he had never met. But after two whole months, surely some of the shyness should have worn off? Why won't he talk to me, Jack wondered, when I spend half my life bending over backwards to be nice to him? OK, so I came down a bit hard when he left his clutter all over the landing. And it gets on my nerves when he glowers at me over the table. But I've done my damnedest to get him to like me.

'When's that funny man going away again?' the boy had said to his mother in the kitchen yesterday. The words still burned in Jack's brain.

He crossed the empty road and turned into Under Lane. The thing was, it took two to forge a relationship and if one of you didn't want to make friends, then you were on a hiding to nothing. *When's that funny man going away again?* Well, there were times when he wouldn't have minded clearing off because, if truth were told, his homecoming had been one hell of an anti-climax. Some mornings he woke feeling disoriented. It was like coming out of a coalmine into daylight. Everything too bright, a bit too intense. It made you blink and wonder where you were. *Who* you were. Jack was coming to the conclusion that in many ways, service life had been easier.

He passed Jessie Ching's house with its shined-up windows and trim porch. Then the Pearse's place with its wrought-iron fanlight. His own cottage, by contrast, looked less cosy. No lights to welcome you, no plants in the window. For one brief, wishful moment, Jack entertained the notion of turning tail and heading back the way he had come, to his mother's house at the top end of the village, where there was always a blazing fire, not to mention a hot cuppa and a home-made pasty on the table. Under Lane didn't yet feel like home. There were times when he wondered if it ever would.

He felt let down. Cheated.

When he banged the front door shut behind him and walked into the kitchen, he found Lil turfing clothes out of a box on to the kitchen table. 'Bloody rubbish,' she said. 'I suppose she thinks we don't know the difference.'

'She?'

'The parson's toffee-nosed daughter. "Daddy asked me to drop these in to you," she said. You wouldn't catch *her* wearing second-hand clothes.'

'You were carrying on last night because the boy hasn't got a decent jacket.'

She shoved the clothes back in the box so viciously, it was more like ramming. 'Cliffy! He's got a name.'

'Cliffy,' Jack said.

'Well, there's nothing that fits him. Anyway, I don't want their bleeding charity.'

'Beggars can't be choosers,' he told her. 'The coupons don't go far.'

'How would you know? *I'm* the one who's had to manage all these years and I'll go on managing without the blasted gentry.' Then, 'I'm going to the bug hole tonight,' she suddenly announced. 'That all right with you?'

'The bug hole?'

'The pictures.'

'On your own?'

'No. With Con.' Her vivid raspberry top clashed with her auburn hair.

'We've been twice a week all through the war, so I'm damned if I'm going to stop now.'

'Money's short,' he said.

'It's only a few pence. Anyway, I earned it,' she told him.

'What about the boy?'

'Cliffy!'

'What about . . . Cliff?'

'You can look after him.' She dumped the box in the corner by the mangle. 'So . . . is that all right?'

'Have to be, I suppose.' There was a set look on his face.

'Well, thanks for being so nice about it!' She flounced out of the kitchen, leaving behind her a trail of cheap perfume. All we ever do is argue, Jack thought. He tried to remember when they last had a quiet talk. A rather cynical voice in his ear said, You didn't ask her out for her powers of conversation. It was her legs. And the buzz that came from walking down the street with a glamour babe on your arm. And the flirting and all the pleasurable fumblings and, yes, all that other stuff that went on in bed while her father was out of the house.

Would he have married her if the war hadn't come along to accelerate everything?

Probably not. They would just have had a fling and left it at that.

Mabel Petherick drew the curtains against the wind and then poured herself a glass of sherry. Her legs were still trembling from the shock. But you knew something was going on, she told herself, as the clock in the hall struck five and the burning liquid trickled its way down to the bits of her that needed fortifying. That young man and his appointment with Virginia . . . All that nonsense about him being a solicitor. Who ever saw a solicitor with hair that long?

Myles would never sell under his own volition.

She's forcing him into it. He should never have married her. She wasn't right for him.

Mabel downed the rest of the sherry in one go and poured herself another. She never drank at this time of the afternoon. Rarely drank at all, in fact. But today she needed it. The idea that Lizzah might go to strangers . . . It was inconceivable!

She removed her favourite hat, the one with the tuft of game bird feathers. All through the war, she had kept an eye on the Manor for Myles because, well, it seemed that no one else would. As soon as the house was requisitioned, Virginia had left it to the army's tender mercies and swanned off to some south coast watering-place, taking the youngest girl with her. Myles's mother had been sent, much against her wishes because they didn't get on, to her sister in Torquay. And Daphne had decamped, as the young do, to London. So who else had been left to complain when one heard that the blighters were amusing themselves by using the stone goddesses on the balustrades for target practice and crashing their great army lorries into the park gates?

I was glad to do it, Mabel thought, launching into the second glass. Delighted to march up the Manor drive and into the commanding officer's quarters to tell him his men were a bunch of barbarians. She put a hand to the mottled red of her cheeks. Not that it did much good in the long run. Made me feel better, I suppose. Made me feel I had some recourse.

'I'd like to have seen you raising Cain,' Myles had said at Christmas when he dropped in to wish them the compliments of the season. 'Often wondered how you were. And what you were doing with yourself back home in Apple Orchard. Thanks for trying to hold things together.' Mabel didn't need thanks. She was proud that she'd been able to do something, no matter how small, to pay him back for all his kindness. Proud to call herself his friend.

She dropped the hat on the table, unbuttoned her coat and dropped into Father's old armchair rather harder than she'd intended. She remembered how, after Stephen had been killed, Myles (at home on leave) had come to offer his condolences, bringing peaches from the Lizzah hothouses. He hadn't said much. Had simply squeezed her hand and said, 'I'm so very sorry. But don't worry. We'll take care of you.'

I sat there in my dark frock, Mabel thought, feeling simply awful. Then he put his arm around me and laid his cheek against mine and we sat there so long, it seemed as if time had stopped.

Her heart swelled as it came back to her. Sometimes she felt she was still waiting for her life to begin.

When he came back from the trenches, Myles had made it his business to take her out on little expeditions. Once they had taken a picnic basket up the coast path, walking further than they meant, and he'd told her about his favourite Jago – mad old Hubert, born in 1753. Hugo had created the park from his own design, but afterwards had gone as mad as a hatter, keeping his pet sheep in the house and feeding it from a Delft bowl. He made me laugh again, Mabel thought. I loved those walks, swinging along hand in hand, talking nineteen to the dozen. Once he even kissed me. I'd caught my foot in a pothole. He put out a hand to save me and . . .

When he let me go, I was breathless.

She sat silently thinking about it. In her heart, she had always been a little bit in love with him. Myles was cultured and honourable, the best of England.

But we could never have married, Mabel thought. I was too old. Twenty-six. And too plain, although I was rather vain about my fine, dark eyebrows and my waist-length hair. And of course he had to marry someone from his own world.

But we always liked each other.

There was a spark.

As for the Manor . . . It had belonged to the Jagos for four hundred years. Living on the edge of its park all her life, Mabel cherished its every tradition. How many generations of children had she taken up there for an on-the-spot history lesson? Nicholas Jago and Elizabeth I. Or Cromwell and Lizzah.

It couldn't possibly be sold to a stranger.

'Mabel?' Edie's voice brought her back to the present. She was standing in the doorway, all pop-eyed at the sight of the sherry glass. 'Are you poorly?'

'Poorly? Of course not.' Mabel had scarcely had a day in bed in her life. How could I, she thought, with Mother and Father to look after? 'Just cold,' she said.

'Cold?' Edie said, coming further into the room. She had been cutting wafer-thin bread and butter and still held the loaf pinned to her bosom.

'That's what I said.' Mabel's voice was harsh and dry. She heaved herself out of the chair. 'I shan't be able to help with the jumble sale tomorrow. I'm going out.'

'Going out?'

'I do wish,' Mabel said, 'you wouldn't repeat everything I say the minute the words are out of my mouth. I'm going up to Lizzah to see the major.' She stalked off to the kitchen before her sister could ask why.

Edie sighed. I'm not afraid of her, she thought, but if I say the least word, she'll go off like a rocket.

In the low-ceilinged bedroom, Jack Trewarden found his wife painting her toenails scarlet. Next to her, in a dish on the bedside table, a cigarette lay smouldering.

He stood watching her with a frown on his face.

She said, 'Something wrong?'

'Your hair. What was wrong with the old colour?'

'Mouse brown? Boring!'

'I liked it. I wish you'd change it back.'

'I like being a redhead. You'll get used to it.' She flicked the ash from the cigarette and took a languorous puff. In the dimness of the room, her glass necklace sparkled. 'Jack – don't be mad at me. Not when it's been so long.'

'I'm not mad at you.'

'Don't be crusty, then.'

She went on looking at him. He had forgotten the power of Lil's cat-like gaze.

He said, 'I just don't like . . . what you've done to yourself.'

The cigarette went back in the pin tray. She sat with her legs out, wiggling her feet while the varnish dried. Toes and lips vividly matched, he couldn't help noticing. And she had solved what his mother called the terrible stocking problem with make-up.

'Don't take this the wrong way,' he said, 'but wouldn't it be better to look a bit more like the other mothers?'

'Fat and going to seed? Not likely!'

Jack said, 'It's just that people talk.'

'Let them.' Before he could say anything else, Lil took hold of one of his wrists and drew him towards her, still with her legs stretched, so that he felt a sudden flicker of desire. Sensing this, she took hold of his other wrist and placed his hands on her shoulders. Leaving them there, she reached up and began to unbutton his shirt. She smelled of something enticing . . . Jasmine? Cloves? He could feel the blood jerking through his veins.

'What about the boy?' he said hoarsely.

'He's down at Royston Lott's. Won't be back for ages.'

She flopped backwards on to the bed, pulling him with her. Jack wanted not to give in to the speed of it all. He wanted to hold back, knowing that his head didn't wholly approve of what his body was doing. But those legs, shapely and strong, were winding themselves around him. He'd never been able to resist them. When she touched his bare back with her fingers, he stopped fighting his instincts and let himself be tempted.

Five

At nine thirty the following morning, as the Reverend Hugh Matheson cast his eye over the obituaries in the *Western Morning News* and his wife rubbed furiously at a fork with her napkin, their daughter, Romily, nibbled on a piece of dry toast and wondered how she would survive the day with such a god-awful hangover.

'Jacob Furse died.'

'He's been threatening to for years.'

'I shall miss him. He was a bit of a character.'

'He was a tiresome old man who liked to make trouble.' Pearl Matheson laid the fork by her plate and moved her knife a fraction to the left. 'I don't know how his wife put up with him.'

'It doesn't do to speak ill of the dead, dearest.'

'I'm only telling the truth. Do you remember when he pushed that nurse out of the ambulance and broke her arm?'

All her life, Pearl Matheson had been a trouble-watcher. Wherever she went, she made it her business to sniff out accidents, doctor's visits, deaths (the gorier the better). This was not so that she might offer pastoral comfort or rescue the perishing, but because, quite simply, she fed off other people's disasters.

'The poor woman couldn't work for months.' There was a pause during which her attention shifted to the pink linen trousers her daughter was wearing. 'Darling, I hope you're not going out dressed like that. A nice pair in buff-coloured flannel would be just about presentable, but . . . Where on earth does one find such things?'

'They're French,' Romily said. 'The girl I shared with didn't want them.'

'Yes, well, I can see why.'

'I like them. They cheer me up.' Romy reminded herself for the hundredth time that coming home to live with her parents was purely a temporary measure. She had had enough of family prayers, Dad's fossils, endless lectures from her mother. Another month, she thought. Long enough to save a bit of money and let them see something of her and then she'd be off back to the anonymity of London. She'd find herself a job and a nice flat where she could live her own life in her own way.

So was it nerves or natural concern about her parents' feelings that was stopping her from telling them?

After the fun and freedom (well, if you didn't count the uniform and the kit inspections) of three years in the WAAF, life in an obscure country rectory was hard to take. I'm tired, she thought, of this camping-out feeling. Also my head hurts.

'So what are you up to today?' her father asked.

'I'm meeting Daphne for lunch.'

'Well, that settles it,' her mother said. 'You certainly can't go to Lizzah looking like that!'

'Daffy won't care what I'm wearing. Anyway, we're nipping into town for lunch.'

'You'll still have to put on something more suitable. Unless you want to make Daddy a laughing stock.'

'I hardly think it will come to that,' Hugh Matheson said, pushing his chair back. He was a peacemaker, consistently kind, even to his wife, which took some doing. An able man, coming from generations of country parsons, he was profoundly vertical. Six foot four with a narrow frame and a long, kindly face; he was not in the least bit aloof, in spite of his great height.

'*You* may not hear what they say about us, Hugh, but I can assure you that every word of it gets back to me. And not all of it is complimentary. Do you remember the Jewish boy you sent to work at Tregeare? The one who got kicked by the carthorse? Well, you had him living here on crutches and lent him your shortwave radio and all you got for your trouble was mutterings in the village about enemy aliens. And there was the time you tried to reorganize the choir—'

'Mother!'

'Yes.'

'What has any of this to do with my trousers?'

'Well, it's perfectly clear.'

'Not to me. I just wish—'

'What do you wish?'

'Oh, nothing.' Romy Matheson drained her coffee cup and decided to take her headache back upstairs with her. Before I throttle her, she thought.

To get to Lizzah, you took the lane that wound through the woods (the one that dipped into Devon and back again), then the footpath over the moorland past Tregeare. There was ice in the woods still. Clouds scuttled across a cold, grey sky. If you stopped to listen, you heard nothing but the wind or the odd curlew. Romy walked fast, head down, hands deep in the pockets of her old coat, her pale, shining hair stuffed into a knitted cap.

She was thankful to have escaped. Mummy had followed her upstairs after breakfast and had gone rattling on for a whole hour about how PC Eliot had informed her personally that car thefts and burglaries had gone up tenfold since the end of the war, but what could one expect when one was being invaded by the kind of homeless riff-raff who had broken into the Lodge at Lizzah? And had Romy heard that the major had offered this particular family of vagrants the cottage old Sam Vickery had inhabited before he died of his stomach complaint? Of course, such people were never grateful. The husband had had the temerity to complain about the damp and the vermin. Also they had parked their disreputable bus on the verge, where it obstructed your view as you came round Christney Corner and as a result of this, the milk lorry had clipped the wing of Fred Headon's taxi as it was taking Mrs Hicks to see her mother-in-law who was confined to bed with phlebitis. Oh, and Dorothy Hambly had sprained her ankle jumping off the bus to the circulating library in town and cook would most certainly get a flea in her ear if she went on serving them watery mince . . .

Romy had tried to lock herself in the bathroom to wash her hair with Amami, but her mother still wouldn't leave her in peace. 'I'm going to have Daisy Jewell put an edging on the sitting room curtains,' she had bawled through the locked door. 'I'd like to replace them, but you simply can't get the fabric . . .'

Romy, burying her ears in hot, soapy water, had tried to drown her mother out. But the torrent had gone on and on, even though you could only catch every other clause. 'Fraying where Essie draws them . . . that old chintz . . . cushions as well.'

You're driving me insane, she thought, and I've only been here a month. Really Daddy deserves a medal for courage in the face of extreme provocation. I don't know how he stands it. Christian duty, I suppose. Along with the ability to turn a very deaf ear.

She leapt over the little stream that was splashing its way down to the ford at the bottom of the valley. Then scrambled, steadying herself here and there on a branch or tree trunk, down the south-facing slope to the lower path. Please, God, don't let my life turn out like that. One long aggravation. An endurance test.

But it wouldn't.

She knew that for a fact.

She was half a mile from Lizzah, coming down on to the road that would lead to the gates of the Lodge, when she saw, in front of her, a figure that she recognized. Mabel Petherick. Mouldy Mabel . . . everything about her buttoned up and tight fastened. It was too late to duck back into the copse. Miss Petherick had seen her. Oh, God, Romy thought, I'll have to grin and bear her.

'Miss Petherick! How nice . . . Haven't seen you since . . . let me see . . . since I went off to Wimbledon.'

'To work as a ledger clerk,' Mabel said. 'And it didn't last. Well, I told your father it wouldn't. And what did they make of you in the WAAF?'

'They didn't chuck me out. Throw me out.' Romy corrected herself before Miss Petherick did it for her. She had spent five years kicking against Mouldy Mabel's grammar rules – along with a lot of other stupid restrictions – before her father had sent her off, at eleven, to a school for the daughters of poor clergy. 'I got fourteen days' jankers for nipping off one weekend when there was nothing to do at camp. But apart from that, I worked for the Met Office and I met people from all over the world. I loved it.'

Her companion appeared not to approve. I forgot, Romy thought, we aren't supposed to admit we actually enjoyed the war.

'So . . . how are you, Miss Petherick?'

Mouldy Mabel looked as if she regarded the question an impertinence and said that she was quite well, thank you.

'And your sister?'

A long pause. Miss Petherick took her eyes off the pink trousers and gazed instead at Romy's rainbow-coloured cap. 'We keep going. Are you on your way to Lizzah?'

'That's right. I'm meeting Daph. Daphne. She offered to pick me up, but I said I'd walk over.'

'I should think so! Walking is good for one.'

Romy, old habits dying hard, found herself saying, 'Yes, Miss Petherick.' Then she thought, I'm twenty-four, I was an air-raid warden in London during the Blitz, I have learned how to draw isobars on very big maps and I've travelled all over the country doing work of national importance. But as soon as I get home, they treat me like a child. And the worst thing is, I let them get away with it.

Mabel said, 'I suppose I shouldn't be surprised at anything Romily Matheson is wearing. She was always a rebel. Oh, she looks like a Botticelli angel. Positively ethereal. She looks as if she spent her life in a rose garden.

But if there was any mischief, little Miss Matheson was always at the back of it. You look tired. I came up to see how you are. And to ask if you need some help with the filing.'

She was standing with Myles in his office to the rear of the house. Coming in by the back way it was unlikely that she would bump into Virginia. Myles stood warming his rear end in front of the electric fire, as always. Gruffly kind, grumpily amiable, he had been pleased to see her, but there were black bags under his eyes and, though it was too early in the day for a whisky and soda, he looked as if he needed one. He wore the pork-pie hat that he seldom took off and a thick topcoat. Mabel shifted a pile of papers from the fat armchair so that she could sit down, then decided she would be better standing up.

'I don't know about filing,' she said, gazing at the paperwork strewn all over the desk. 'It seems to me a bonfire would be in order.'

'That would be one solution, I suppose. Burn the lot.' He threw her a glance, then wandered over to the window. The dog followed him, wondering if there was a walk in the offing. Myles gave him a distracted pat.

'Look here,' she said, frowning hard, not wanting what she was feeling to show on her face. 'I may as well come straight out with it. There's a rumour going round the village that you're selling up. I mean, it can't possibly be true . . . people pick things up and embroider them . . . but I had to come up and find out.'

A long silence. It was his averted gaze that struck a chill in her bones.

'Myles – you wouldn't leave Lizzah? Sell to strangers?'

He gave a shrug. 'What else can I do? Gin says—'

Hang Gin, Mabel thought. 'Look – you've carried the weight of it all for donkey's years. I know that. And losing Kit . . . well, it must seem as if there's no future. But you mustn't give up. Things will get better,' she said gruffly. 'They have to.'

'You think so?'

'Of course I do. You've hit a bad patch.'

'A damned big one, then!' He turned, now, to face her, the expression on his face gloomy, deflated, savage. 'Can't see any way out of it, Mabs. I'm getting threatening letters from the bank and there are five hundred pounds worth of bills in that drawer and nothing to pay them with. I can't even fall back on my stocks and shares. The market's fluctuating like a fever chart.'

'My dear soul,' was the best Mabel could do in reply.

'I'm not a money man, you see. I've made a mess of it all. It's a bit of a facer at my time of life.'

'It's not just you. Everybody's in the same pickle.'

'That's supposed to make me feel better?'

'It's supposed to stop you blaming yourself for something that's not your fault. The young man who had an appointment with Virginia . . . the one I met at Samuel's wedding. Is he your prospective buyer?'

Myles told her the full story, in bits and pieces, as best he could. Mabel listened, stopping him now and again to ask a question, forbidding herself to say much until he had got it all out of his system. It helped that neither of them was given to tears or hysterics; that, having known each other since childhood, they were familiar with each other in a very English sort of fashion.

'So . . .' she said when he'd come to the end, 'have I got this right? If these Trust people buy Lizzah, they will allow you to go on living here?'

'Damn it, how could I go on living here with strangers tramping through the place?' He spoke impatiently. The dog cocked an enquiring eye.

Mabel cleared the pile of unopened letters from the chair and sat down. She needed to. All the strength had gone from her legs, not so much from shock as from relief. He wasn't necessarily going to leave. She took a deep, controlling breath. The silence was that heavy kind where every word dropped into it takes on a significance.

'It might hurt your pride for a while, but does that matter, so long as you can stay where you belong?'

'You sound like my wife.'

I very much hope not!

'So if you stayed,' she said, stepping as lightly as she could on the thinnest of ice, 'you would be a sort of tenant-for-life? Is that it?'

'I suppose so,' he grumped. 'But there's no question of my staying. I shall sell up and go.'

She deemed it best to ignore this last statement. 'There are things I still don't understand. This Trust, you tell me, has no money of its own?'

'It takes round the begging bowl. Cadges funds from the government and rich patrons. Should have thought of that myself.' There was an edge to his voice.

'And the house . . .' she persisted. 'Lizzah . . . It would belong to the nation?'

'So they say.'

The ticking of the clock seemed to go on forever. 'And the village? Apple Tree? Your other properties?'

'They'd buy the lot. Do the cottages up. Keep things very much as they are.'

'So none of us would be made homeless?'

'Not if I can help it.'

'But if you leave us in the lurch, you wouldn't be here to see that they keep their word. So in point of fact, you wouldn't be able to help it.'

'Damn it, I'd have it put in writing! A legal contract.'

'That speculator who bought Nete Hall signed a contract. It didn't stop him knocking the old place down and building bungalows in the grounds.'

Myles bent to smooth the dog's head. He looked like a nice, rough old dog himself, stubbornly trying to ignore her. Our conversation, Mabel thought, has always been full of little tussles, but few of them as important as this one. Oh, God, suppose I can't make him see sense?

'But it's not just the future of the village . . .' She sat there bolt upright. 'It's you I'm worried about. Do you remember when Stephen was killed and you came to tell me how sorry you were? And you said I must never give up?'

He was gazing away from her at some spot on the wall. She couldn't read his expression, but his jaw was set and his hand, on the dog's collar, was as still as could be.

'And you weren't just spouting empty platitudes. You meant it. I know you did. So . . . if you run off and leave us to fend for ourselves and it turns bad for us . . . Well, I know you, Myles. You would never forgive yourself. Whereas if you stay and face it out, no matter how much you hate it all . . . Well, in time, one can get used to anything. Believe me.'

The sound of approaching footsteps broke into her well-meant, if fierce homily. The dog, who was wondering if he was ever going to get his walk, saw the door open and grabbed his chance. Virginia Jago dipped sideways as he shot past her. She looked terribly pukka in her green corduroy jacket and a silk scarf with horse's heads and crops.

'There you are!' she said to Myles. 'That dog smells.' When she glanced sideways and spotted Mabel, her face assumed a stiff smile. Mabel was used to this reaction and had schooled herself to respond to it with a quick nod and an offhand smile of her own. Virginia liked to intimidate. *Well, you don't scare me*, Mabel thought. I've damned well known him longer than you have and I'll come up for a chat without your permission, thank you very much.

Virginia Jago said, 'Miss Petherick! How nice to see you.'

'I thought Myles might need a little help with the office work.'

'What Myles needs is for someone to take this room by the scruff of the neck and shake it into order. I'm not criticizing, but my dear husband has the same attitude to keeping things tidy as Pen has to having her hair combed. She can't see the point.'

She was criticizing, of course. With infinite graciousness in that light and airy voice of hers. And he stood there and let her.

'If I see another rabbit . . .' Daph sat reading the menu. There was Baked Rabbit, Rabbit Pie and Rabbit Ragout. In brackets, at the bottom, it said: Beware of small bones.

Romy said, 'There's Toad in the Hole.'

'There won't be any toad.'

A big sigh. Then Daph said, 'Do you remember chocolate?'

'Not really. Bacon?'

'Fish and chips.'

They sat at a corner table in the Ceylon Café; Daph in her sporty tweed jacket, her curls pinned back with kirbigrips, Romy in the offending pink trousers and chocolate brown shirt, her hair a blonde tangle. But the tangle suited her, of course.

'I'll have the nut and carrot rissoles,' Daph told the waitress, who was waiting with her pencil poised.

'And I'll risk the macaroni cheese. So . . .' Romy said, handing back the menu, 'how's your love life?'

'Non-existent. And yours?' She didn't really need to ask. Chaps hung around Romy like wasps circling a jam jar.

'I asked first.' Romy refilled her glass from the water jug. 'Tell me what you got up to in the East End.'

'We rescued children from bombed-out houses. Found them clothes and food—'

'Not that, stupid. All the lovely men you slept with.'

Daph stared out of the window at the pavement and the river and the ducks sitting on the riverbank in the chilly wind.

'And don't say there weren't any, because I shan't believe you.'

'There was one. For a while.' Daph felt herself colouring. She hated being forced to talk about her emotions. Or sex. She had been flabbergasted when (shortly after her thirteenth birthday) Romy had insisted on telling her the facts of life. 'Don't be silly,' she had said, not believing a word of it.

'How long is "a while"?'

'Three or four months.'

'So were you in love with him or was it a passing fancy?'

'I . . . don't want to talk about it. It didn't mean anything.'

'Of course it did, or else you wouldn't have got involved.'

'All right . . . if you must know, it meant something to me, but not to him.'

The waitress was back, setting the table with knives and forks and a glass cruet.

'You mean, you were madly in love with him, but all he wanted was sex?'

The waitress stood there, all ears.

Daph's were scarlet.

'Happens all the time,' Romy said. 'Officers were the worst. I went out with one who offered to book us into a room at the Ritz and buy me some tarty underwear if I would let him do something quite unmentionable.'

The waitress was feverishly brushing crumbs, so Romy said in her girly-sexy voice, 'Could you tell cook to get a move on, please? We're starving.'

The waitress flumped off to the kitchen. Romy reached over to touch her hand. 'These things happen. Don't worry about it.'

'I wasn't.'

'Fibber.'

'No, I mean it . . . I did mind, but that was a long time ago. Anyway, he went abroad with a refugee association.'

'Good riddance to bad rubbish.'

'I'm not sure that's what his wife and children thought.'

'Sorry?'

'He was married. I didn't know until his wife walked into the office one morning.'

'Blimey! That must have given you a shock.'

'We'd had a bad raid and he'd used it as an excuse to spend the night with me. She raised the roof. Actually, I think she made more noise than the bombs.'

Daph pulled at a strand of hair that had escaped from the kirbigrip. 'It wasn't very nice. In fact, it was horrible. I didn't want to believe someone I had been keen on could be that duplicitous. Like I didn't believe, until it happened, that German bombers would ever fly over London. Anyway, I got my fingers burned. That's all there is to say.'

Except that she had been a posh, over-protected, naïve little fool. But there was no sense in brooding about it.

Romy took a sip of water. 'Well, that decides it. What you need is a cheering-up night out. I've been invited to a birthday bash on Saturday. You can come too.'

'No, I can't. I told Bos I'd go over for dinner.'

'To Trebartha?'

'Yes. What's wrong?'

Romy waited until the waitress had dumped the macaroni cheese in front of her and had served Daph with rissoles in Yeastrel gravy, then she said, 'You must admit he hasn't got an enormous amount of sex appeal.'

'Well, if that's all you can think about—'

'It's not. But *I* wouldn't go out with him.'

'I'm not going out with him. It's just dinner with a friend.'

A pause.

'Will his mother be there?'

'I imagine so.'

An ironic lift of Romy's fine-arched brows. 'Honestly, Daffy, I give up on you.'

Daph peered down at her rissoles. She said calmly, 'Good. How's your mother?'

'Dreadful. Sometimes I think I got posted to the wrong address.'

'Me too,' Daph said with a sigh.

'She treats me like a two-year-old. It's ridiculous. I mean, until Christmas I was doing a responsible job for the Met Office and staying out all night if I felt like it and now, suddenly, I'm supposed to tell them where I'm going and who with and what time I'll be back: I can't be myself and nothing interesting ever happens.'

Daph stuck a fork into a rissole and watched it fall apart. This was her chance to tell Romy about the shenanigans at Lizzah, but it seemed a shame to spoil a good lunch (well, a sociable lunch) with another sob story. Am I getting like Pa? she wondered. Putting unpalatable things off? Pretending they don't exist? She poked her fork into the rissole and took a tiny taste, as though it might very possibly bite her. 'This isn't bad,' she said.

'This morning, when she was going on and on about my trousers, I thought, Daddy's a saint.' Romy still hadn't touched her macaroni.

'Vicars are meant to be patient and long-suffering.'

'I know.' Romy sat frowning at her plate. The hair framing her face was of a startling fairness. She said, 'That's why I'm going to tell him first.'

'Tell him what?'

'The thing is, I know he won't go off the deep end. He'll let me have my say before he has his.'

'I don't know what you're talking about,' Daph said. The waitress was serving coffee over in the corner, placing the cups on the table with exaggerated care. 'What have you done this time?'

'Nothing much,' Romy said. 'Nothing that would frighten the horses in any other household. All I've done,' she added swiftly, 'is get myself engaged. To a Polish officer.'

Daph nearly choked on her rissole. 'You didn't mention *him* in your letters.'

'Didn't have time.'

Daph went on watching the waitress, but the café with its pink curtains and striped tablecloths seemed all at once more stagey and dramatic. 'You're not—'

'No, I'm not pregnant. Actually, that might be an easier subject to broach.'

'Than what?'

'Oh, Daph! You *are* slow. Easier than telling them I'm going to marry a Roman Catholic.'

The major felt the loss of his son more keenly than anyone would ever know, but he couldn't bring himself to talk about it. Instead, he had taken to acting as if the world was innately absurd, as if he couldn't be bothered to concern himself with any of it, which drove his wife wild. They sat by the round table in her sitting room waiting for Mr Garland to turn up for the contents inventory. A mild west wind was roaring in the chimney. Gin had discarded her woollen layers for a green-striped blouse and green slacks. Myles wore his tweeds. And Daphne was in grey jodhpurs with the sleeves of her jumper rolled up.

'Darling, you look a sight,' Gin said. 'You might have changed.'

'What for?'

'Because we have visitors coming.'

'A visitor.' Daphne said, 'Mr Garland won't mind.'

'He might not, but I do.'

Gin, flipping through a pile of old *Tatlers*, felt like an overstretched piece of elastic. There was a needling pain above her eyebrow. She put up a finger to rub it away. But her heart hurt too. Pain, pain, pain, like a bloody toothache nagging away at you. It made her walk fast, talk fast, snap at people, want to tear their heads off.

'You care too much about appearances,' Daphne told her.

'And you don't care enough! Look at you! Have you brushed your hair today? Washed your hands? They're filthy. What have you been doing?'

'Digging the weeds out of the front terrace.'

'There will be other people to do that.'

'Such as?'

'Mr Garland will bring someone in.'

'I don't want him to. I like gardening.'

'Yes, you would. Because you know your father and I don't approve.'

'Don't bring me into this,' Myles said.

Why did he always have to sit on the damned fence? It got on Gin's nerves. We're seeing more of each other than we have for years, she told herself, but do we want to? That's the thing.

She said, 'Do you actually want your daughter out there working like a navvy?'

Myles said, 'Nothing wrong with a spot of gardening. Lots of people do it themselves these days.'

'In a place this size? For heaven's sake, Myles.'

'You could help,' Daphne told her. 'It would do you good. Get rid of some of that ill temper.'

'Don't talk to me like that!'

They sat glaring at each other. Daphne felt an itch on her neck and started to scratch.

'And that's another thing,' Gin said. 'Why are you always itching?'

'Because I caught head lice,' Daphne told her, almost enjoying the horror on her mother's face. 'I caught them from the Plymouth family. I've dabbed myself from head to toe with chloroform and cotton wool. It kills them. Eventually.'

Gin said, 'I don't think I can stand any more of this.'

Daphne said, 'Don't worry. You won't have to. I'm going out.'

She would drive over to see Bos. He, at any rate, would be pleased to see her.

I've been a disappointment to her all my life, Daph fumed, as she drove the dogcart over to Trebartha. Why should I have to match up to her stupid standards? I can't be myself. She won't let me. I wish I could go back to London. But that would be deserting Daddy. Who would stand up to her if I ducked out?

She took the horse out of the village and down the hill on the other side at speed. It's like being back at school, she thought, only worse. If they criticized you at St Joseph's, it was at least with a certain amount of tact: 'You have beautiful hair, Daphne, but may one suggest you let it see the comb now and again?' Mother wouldn't recognize tact if it were served up to her on toast.

Home should be a place where you could relax and enjoy yourself, not a hellhole packed with family tensions. She was tired of struggling with them, weary of being a very inadequate substitute for Kit. His presence was like a ghost hanging around the place; so all-pervading that it sucked away your confidence.

The dogcart swung past Tollhouse Cottage and sailed on to the new road. Kit had always been at the centre of the picture. Now that he was gone, the perspective was all wrong.

If I only knew how to put it right again. But I don't.

And Lizzah wasn't even going to be a proper home any more. How could it be, with gawking people tramping all over it? The thought turned her anger into depression, so that by the time she had reached Trebartha and hitched the horse and taken herself up the steps and in through the side door that led to the lower kitchen, she felt so tense that she was close to tears.

It was five past three on a breezy March day. The kitchen door was open and she saw all the dear old, familiar things that she had known as a child. The settle and the green plush armchair and the vast maple-framed picture of a stag on a misty mountain. The group of honeysuckle-over-the-porch water colours done by Bos's mother as a young woman. The bureau that held games of draughts and chess and L-Attaque and farm accounts and bundles of writing paper and manilla envelopes and a box filled with old copies of the *Bude and Stratton Post*.

Everything unchanged and unchanging. Not half so grand as Lizzah, Daph thought, lingering for a moment in the doorway, but infinitely more comfortable than that cold (in every sense of the word), half-wrecked mausoleum.

Bos was sitting at the table, tapping away at his old typewriter. He jumped up when he saw her. 'Daph! I didn't expect you.'

It was the look of extraordinary pleasure on his face that got her – the sheer warmth of his reaction, so agreeable and comforting. 'I . . . had to get away,' she said, then immediately disgraced herself by bursting into a flood of tears.

Bos said, 'Good God! What's wrong?'

'I'm sorry. I'm so sorry. It's just – I can't . . . It's all too much . . . Everything's such a mess.' Then suddenly the tears got worse. She couldn't even talk any more, but covered her face with her hands and sobbed her heart out.

Bos said, 'Oh, come on now.' He looked alarmed, as if he'd never seen a woman cry before. He steered her to the settle and made her sit down, though he wasn't sure what to do next. 'Is it Lizzah? Can't you bear it?'

'I'm sorry.' Daph found a handkerchief in her sleeve and blew hard.

'Buck up,' he said. 'It's not like you.'

There was a pause during which the clock went on ticking.

'I'm sick of it all.'

'The business at home? You'll get used to it.'

'Will I?'

'I'd bet my shirt on it. I remember how brave you were at Kit's funeral. Keeping everyone else going. Arranging the music. Doing all the practical stuff.'

'Oh, yes,' Daph said bitterly, 'I'm the practical one.'

'That's good, isn't it?'

'Not at all. It's what they say about you when you're no good at anything else. When they don't appreciate you. When you're not their favourite and you never will be and they can have no conception of how deeply you care about everything because they never listen to a thing you say. Well, Mother doesn't—' She twisted the handkerchief round and round her fingers. 'She thinks I'm dumber than dumb. It's got worse since Kit died. She thought the sun shone out of his pocket and now that he's gone, she doesn't even have to pretend to care about me any more.'

'You take things too much to heart,' he said awkwardly. 'All mothers love their children.'

'All children need mothering, but not all of them get it. Some of the kiddies I dealt with in London . . . well, it made you feel sick when you undressed them and saw the bruises on their backs.'

He looked grave. He unbuttoned his jacket, then buttoned it up again.

'We've all seen too much,' he said.

'You're right there.'

'But the war is over.'

'And good times are coming?'

'Yes, of course they are. Given time.' He went on watching her.

Daph said, 'For other people, perhaps. Oh, you'll say I should be grateful for what I've got. And I am. There are thousands of people worse off and millions dead and I'm trying desperately hard to count my blessings. But there's still this sickening space between what I want my life to be and what it is.'

He dropped one arm over the back of the settle, still looking at her, though his thoughts seemed elsewhere.

'When I got home,' she went on, 'I thought there would be breathing space. Time to talk about what's happened to us. Time to register the fact that we've lost Kit and there's a gaping hole right in the middle of the family. We ought to be doing some decent mourning, but this Trust business has put paid to that. Pa's being forced to discuss surplus revenues and purchase values and the Court of Chancery and he's being very noble about it, but you can see that he's almost too tired to stand up. Yet all he says is that things aren't top-notch. And Ma's so driven that she's no use to him. No use to anybody, emotionally speaking. You can't laugh with her or cry with her. Well, I can't. She freezes me out.'

Bos still had that abstracted look on his face. He lifted a hand and pushed back a strand of her red-gold hair.

'I'm boring you,' she said.

'No.'

'So . . .' she rushed on, 'as you may have noticed, I'm in a state. We're all in a state and I've got this childish urge to cut and run. Except that there's nowhere to go. Well, nowhere I could afford.'

'You could come here,' Bos said.

'That's very kind of you, but I couldn't possibly. Your mother would have a fit—'

'Not if you married me.'

'and so would—' Daph stopped. She had a very shockable face. 'What did you say?'

'I . . . asked if you would marry me.'

'Oh,' Daph said.

It was at least thirty seconds before she added indignantly, 'You don't have to feel *that* sorry for me!'

Six

Romily said, 'You didn't!'

'Well, yes, actually.'

'I don't believe you.'

'It's simple,' Daph said. 'He asked me to marry him and I said yes.'

'You don't marry someone because you're fed up at home.'

'It's not just anybody,' Daph said. 'It's Bos.'

'That's what I mean. Old Bos. Dull but worthy.'

They were in the organ loft, waiting for choir practice to begin. The choir had recently re-formed and a concert was coming up – their first post-war event – so Miss Petherick, the self-appointed Head of Ceremonial for the village, was twitching somewhat; fussing around down in the chancel, bossing everyone into their places. The church, lit by gas and oil lamps, stank to high heaven.

'He's not dull. He's good-hearted and kind. And safe,' Daph added. 'He won't ever let me down or run out on me. That's worth a lot these days.' She gave the laces of her organ shoes a hefty tug. 'I've been on my own for six years and I'm sick of it. I'm not willowy and beautiful and I'm never going to be a charmer. Anyway, who else will I meet in this backwater?'

'You haven't given them a chance. You're making a huge mistake.'

'Oh, shut up! It's done now. I just want to share my life with a nice man who'll take care of me. And I want to be mistress of my own home.'

'Haven't you forgotten something?'

'Like what?'

'His mother?'

'She'll move out,' Daph said. 'To the cottage.'

'You're dafter than I thought you were.'

Miss Petherick's voice said, 'If you've quite finished your little chat, Miss Matheson . . .'

Mouldy Mabel took no prisoners. They were soon banging away at 'All in the April Evening'. Romy wondered if she should have another go at Daph when they got out. But it wouldn't be any use. Daph was stubborn. Once she had made up her mind to something—

'Rallentando!' Miss Petherick said, signalling to Daph to stop the accompaniment. 'Do we all know what that means? Miss Matheson?'

Lizbie Brown

'Slow down, Miss Petherick,' said Romy.

'Then why are we charging along like the Trojan army?' Mouldy Mabel's voice would have cut cheese. 'The piece is pastoral. Right. Once again. "The sheep with their little lambs" . . .'

As soon as the rehearsal was over, Romy took herself back up to the organ loft. She said, 'So have you told them at home?'

'Not yet.' Daph found the page for the first hymn on Sunday and fastened it down.

'Why not?'

'Because . . . there hasn't been a moment.'

'You're in a flap about it.'

'I am not!'

'Look – Daffy. There's still time. Tell him you made a mistake. Break it off before anyone else has heard about it.'

'I don't want to break it off. It's hardly started.' The boy who pumped the organ clattered away down the stairs. 'Anyway, he's coming over tomorrow. We'll tell them together.' Daph went on packing sheet music into her bag, along with her specs and her headscarf. She decided it was time to fight fire with fire. 'How did it go down at home about your Pole?'

There was a silence. Then Romy said, 'I haven't told them. I'm working up to it.'

'Very slowly,' Daph said with Cheltenham Ladies' crispness.

'Oh, shut up! Actually, I'd decided to do it tonight. Are you really going to marry Bos? All he does is chug along.'

'What's wrong with chugging along? If you ask me, excitement is over-rated. Bos and I like each other's company. Stop making that face. And stop treating it as some kind of joke, because it jolly well isn't!'

As they passed through the nave on the way out, Miss Petherick threw them a steely look. The kind that said they had no business hanging around chatting when she was keen to get home for her cocoa and biscuits.

'I'll need to talk to the rector about the concert arrangements,' she told Romy.

'Righty-ho,' Romy said. Mouldy Mabel's face turned even more grim, so she changed this to, 'Yes, of course, Miss Petherick. I'll tell him. Goodnight.'

'Goodnight.' Miss Petherick dragged her inverted pudding basin of a hat over her severely rolled hair. 'How is your father, Miss Jago?'

'He's . . . bearing up, thank you.'

'I'm very pleased to hear it. I never thought Lizzah would change hands in my lifetime. It's a bit of a facer, at his age. He must keep his chin up. That's the thing.'

Mabel let the girls out, then locked the great door behind her. The tall, grey tower presided over the village. She heard a whistle from the distant station.

The Matheson girl (round red hat and gypsy earrings) had disappeared through the lychgate. Mabel hoped she would remember to deliver the message. Tightening the belt on her mackintosh, her boxy tweed coat being only for Sundays, Mabel headed for home and the nine o'clock news. Not that it was the event it had been during wartime . . . news stories that knocked your spectacles askew and kept you awake at night. Now, there was only Attlee's thin, frail voice speaking of serious wheat shortages and famine in Europe.

A charming and intelligent man, they said, but as a public speaker you couldn't begin to compare him to Winston. It was like putting a village fiddler on the same platform as Paganini. All rather sad, Mabel thought. *We seem to have become smaller. I suppose the best we can hope is for things to get back to normal. Whatever normal might be.*

Romy stood in front of her dressing table mirror looking quite unlike herself in an evening blouse and a navy blue skirt. That should do it, she thought, lighting a cigarette and running a hand through her hair. Neat and tidy. Put Mother in a good mood. If that's possible.

She had practised what she was going to say. *I've got something to tell you. This may come as a shock, but I've got myself engaged to a Polish officer. I didn't say anything before, because I wanted to come home and think about it. I needed to be sure I was doing the right thing. And I am. So now I'm telling you.*

It would have been better, of course, if Jan had been here to hold her hand and charm them both with his deep-brown eyes. Sex-mad eyes, but with a bit of luck, Mother wouldn't notice. She imagined introducing him. *Mother . . . Father . . . I would like you to meet Captain Janusz Krawczynski.*

Romy remembered the night she had met him at the party in the sergeants' mess hall. Balloons and streamers. A ropy old band playing 'In the Mood'. He had asked her to dance. Swirling round the floor with him (with surprising equilibrium considering the amount of gin she'd put away) she had thought, he looks like an illustration from *Woman's Own*.

Out of all the boys she had been out with, she had known he was the one. He knew how to give a girl a good time. And he did a really snaky rumba.

Nostalgia, deep and strong, welled up inside her for all the hours she had spent with him through that long, hot summer. Lazily chatting on the grass outside the hostel. Getting beautifully merry in the King's Arms after the sun had gone down. Sitting together at weekends in dusty tearooms off the Tottenham Court Road.

How she missed the excitement of it all. Romy liked to be where the action was. She couldn't bear hanging around at home playing tiddlywinks.

After she had done the necessary, she would read his letters again. Not as many letters as she had longed for, but they were unbelievably ardent. When he had seen her off at Paddington, he had stressed that finding bread-and-butter work in London would take up a lot of his time.

Removing her earrings, she ran down to the drawing-room, where she found her father and mother sitting in easy chairs on either side of the fireplace. The rector had his head in a book. Pearl Matheson was nibbling at a biscuit and telling him how the canon's wife had had to order a new bed because the old one had collapsed under her when she sat on it to put her stockings on and how the furniture people – Farrington's of Exeter – had been most offhand.

'There you are!' The rector took his head out of his book. 'Come and sit down. How was the rehearsal?'

'Fine. Miss Petherick wants to see you about the arrangements.'

'I'll call round.'

Heavy curtains were drawn against the dark outside. A fire glowed in the grate. It's now, Romy thought, or never.

'I've got something to tell you,' she began.

'You look remarkably . . . civilized,' Pearl said.

'You noticed.'

'Of course I did. I never thought I'd see you looking nice again.'

'She always looks nice,' said the rector valiantly. 'In her own way. Interesting, I always think.'

'Yes . . . you would. So to what,' Pearl asked Romy, 'do we owe the pleasure? Are you going out? It's rather late.'

'I've got something to tell you,' Romy said. 'This may come as a shock—'

'No greater shock than seeing you with a skirt on, darling.'

'I've got myself—'

'You could do with a little brooch at the neck. Something to brighten it up. That cameo we gave you for Christmas. Did I tell you Minnie Smeeth lost her jewellery box on her way to visit her son in Ottery St Mary? It was in her bag when she left and it was there when they stopped for the usual offices in Crediton, but it had vanished by the time they reached their destination.'

The war was good, Romy thought, because it helped us run away from home. 'Mummy – I'm trying to tell you something.'

The rector closed his book, looking infinitely approachable. The state of his slippers suggested that he was as poor as a church mouse. In fact, the church mice were probably richer. 'Are you going back to London?' he asked in an attempt to help her.

'In a day or two, probably. But it's not that.'

'In a day or two?' Pearl said, 'You can't. There's the concert.'

'Mother – I can't sing. I mime along and try not to throw the others out. So I won't be missed.'

'And anyway, your brother is coming home.'

'I'm sorry, but it can't be helped.' Romy's voice was growing desperate. 'Look – I've . . . I've got myself engaged to a Polish officer. I didn't say anything before, because—'

'Peter will expect to see you. You haven't set eyes on each other for—' Pearl stopped. 'What did you say?'

'I said I'm engaged to a Polish officer. I didn't tell you before, because I wanted to come home and think about it. I needed to be sure I was doing the right thing. And I am. So now I'm telling you.'

Pearl looked frantically at her husband. 'A Polish officer?'

'He's very nice. Really he is.'

'Hugh. Don't just sit there. Tell her she can't possibly!'

'I know it's a big thing to throw at you,' Romy gabbled. 'You'd rather I married an English gentleman, preferably from the clergy. But I love him. And he loves me. And I'm going to do it and even if you disapprove, you can't stop me.'

'Love?' Pearl said. 'My foot!'

The rector opened his mouth.

'You're not old enough to know what the word means. You're just a silly girl—'

'And you are *such* a bossy-pants!'

'Romily! Language!'

'I'm sorry, but you drive me to it. I think I'd like to talk to Daddy on his own.'

'No doubt you would, because you know how to wind him round your little finger. But I'm not budging, And don't you dare give in to her, Hugh Matheson, or I shall make your life very difficult.'

'So what's new?' Romy asked.

Daphne's announcement, the following morning, went more smoothly. Bos turned up, as promised, at eleven on the dot, as solid as his gold fob watch and as good a timekeeper. At once Daph lost the apprehensions that had kept her awake for half the night. Because when she saw him standing there in the hall, touchingly kind and concerned for her welfare, with all his usual good humour, the kind of man you respected enormously, the kind you could take to tea with your old aunt (or, more importantly, your grandmother), suddenly she felt able to relax and enjoy this once-in-a-lifetime occasion.

Her father was in the library, as usual at that hour of the morning, lighting a candle to seal a letter with red wax. For the rest of her life, the smell of melting wax was to remind her of that day. At first, when Bos explained his mission, the major was so surprised that he couldn't bring himself to reply. The dog seemed surprised, too, fixing its gaze first on one face, then another. But then, after a string of ums and ers, Pa had said, 'Right. I'm with you.' And, 'Bless my soul! When did this happen?' He had congratulated them both warmly and brought out a bottle of very good old Graves, seemingly glad to drop all thoughts of the impending arrival of the Trust's architect and the daily tussles over all sorts of tricky questions with young Garland to concentrate instead on toasting the happy couple.

Mother, very much the Lady of the Manor in her green linen suit with pearls in her ears had been on her way out to lunch with a friend, but when the car wouldn't start and Fishleigh had been unable to fix it, she had been forced to change her plans. When Pa called her into the library, she had at first looked irritable. Then, like Pa, she had gone through a stunned phase. But Bos's bluff good humour and lovely manners had forced her to dredge up a smile and, after that, it was more or less plain sailing.

'Good to have something positive happening for once,' Pa had said over and over. And, 'Shan't lose you, that's the thing. You'll be just over the way.' Then, when at last they had had a moment to themselves, Bos had drawn out of his breast pocket the diamond ring that had belonged to his grandmother. Thinking back, she couldn't quite remember what he had said when he eased it on her finger, except that they could get it altered if it was a little tight. He would take it to Brownings in Plymouth. It would be no trouble.

'It fits perfectly,' Daph told him.

'Suits you no end,' said Bos.

And then she had let him kiss her. It felt a little awkward, but that was because she was half afraid someone might be watching – Tilley or Mr Garland, who was wandering all over the place with his notebook and camera.

There was one thing Bos had said that she clearly remembered. 'As long as you're happy. That's the thing.' Remembering the words upstairs in her bedroom later, with the window sashes rattling and a south-west wind sloughing the treetops, she had wanted to cry.

When the rector called on Mabel Petherick the following morning, he sat making conversation with the pleasant dexterity of a dedicated clergyman, but Mabel could see that he was distracted. Once the concert arrangements had been dealt with (church hall, hand-drawn posters, Mrs Badcock to organize the refreshments) she drained the coffee pot to refill his cup and set herself to the task of finding out what was bothering him. 'And how is Mrs Matheson?' she asked.

'Pretty well, as far as I can make out,' he added jokingly. 'Some days, what with one thing and another, I scarcely see her.'

Which wouldn't be a bad thing, Mabel thought. Pearl Matheson was always making problems for her husband. She had a flair for upsetting people, for telling them what they didn't want to know and saying the thing that would upset them most. On purpose? Possibly.

'And Romily? It must be good to have her safely home again.'

'Um. Yes.' Stretching his long, thin neck, he busied himself with his coffee.

So that was it. You would have made things easier for yourself, Mabel thought, if you hadn't neglected your daughter's education in favour of your son's. That cheap boarding school you sent her off to did her no favours. The girl has a brain, but it has been allowed to run riot.

And we all know what that leads to.

'Mabel! There's someone at the back door.'

Mabel looked round and there was Edie gesturing with some kind of dumb-show from the doorway.

Mabel frowned. 'Can't it wait?'

Edie was still pulling faces. 'I just think you ought to— Well, it's difficult.'

'For heaven's sake—' Apologizing to the rector, Mabel marched out to the kitchen.

Samuel Trewarden stood in the back porch, talking tenderly to his little dog. He stopped when he saw Mabel and smiled with a hint of his old impishness. It reminded her of the time he had filled the inkwell on his school desk with glue. Her heart softened.

'Samuel! How are you?' she asked.

'Oh, you know. Fraping along, Miss Petherick.'

Her gimlet gaze took him all in. 'You've put on weight.' He had moved on from skeletal to scrawny. He was wearing a drab demob raincoat that all but enveloped him, topped off with an orange knitted scarf. 'So what can I do for you?'

'I was wondering if you could do with any butter.'

'Butter?'

'Under the counter, like.' The expression on his thin face said that if she had been anybody else, he would have winked at her.

For one moment, Mabel couldn't think what to say. But, when she had got her wits back together, she said, 'And where has it come from, may one ask?'

'Never you mind about that, Miss Petherick.'

Mabel hesitated. She didn't approve of the black market, but rations had been tight for years and would go on being tight. In the end, she ditched her principles and said, 'I'll have a pound. But I don't want my business spread around the village.'

'Good enough, Miss Petherick.' He tugged the scarf more tightly round his neck. 'Don't suppose you want any nylons?'

'What would I do with nylons?' Mabel said, with a glance down at her sensible, lisle-clad legs.

Samuel got the picture. 'I'll be back when it's more convenient, like.'

When it got dark, he meant. Mabel wondered if it was the ghost of the young Samuel or the daft-eyed little dog that had made her succumb to temptation.

She went back to the rector. 'Just a hawker,' she said crisply. 'I hear we're going to discuss street lighting at the next parish meeting. Street lighting! Whoever heard of such a thing?'

Most of the floors and ceilings would have to be taken out because of the dry rot that went right through that part of the east wing. The panelling, too. Charlie had taken photographs of the worst affected areas; every room, every bit of crumbled plaster, every stain and crack. Now he stood studying the ceiling in the king's bedroom with the architect, Tom Fermoy, who had brought the plasterer along with him. 'Should, by rights, be pulled down,' he said to the architect.

Fermoy made a rueful face.

'But it's so very fine.'

'Exceptional,' Fermoy said.

'Can we keep it, do you think?'

Tom looked at the plasterer, who made a desperate face. 'Should just about be possible,' he said.

He had arrived just before lunch, having spent the night at an inn near Okehampton. He had apologized for being so late. He had lost his Ordnance Survey and had got foxed by the impenetrable lanes and wandered all round the compass. Cornwall seemed to have a lot of gorse bushes, he had joked, leaving his open sports car by the NAAFI block in front of the magnificently grand front windows.

Charlie liked Fermoy. He and the young architect had worked on a couple of National Trust projects together. When taking in a room, Tom would lean against the wall, gazing and thinking, as motionless as a statue. You had to keep mum until this process had come to a natural end. Then he would suddenly be galvanized into action, scribbling notes and thumb-nail sketches all over his sketchpad. After that, it would be safe to chat, which was when the fun started. Tom had a wry, dry sense of humour that was at odds with his somewhat terse exterior. He was in his late thirties, of medium height, with curly hair and clear eyes that didn't believe in hiding things. But the most important thing about him was his impeccable flair for knowing what to do with old houses.

Charlie said, 'I suppose we'd better tackle the roof next. Deathwatch beetle?'

Tom looked underwhelmed at the thought of spending half a day crawling on hands and knees under the roof. He strolled over to the window, rubbed a hole in the dust with his sleeve, and stood looking out. 'When the house opens,' he said, 'the landscape will be one of the stars of the show.'

Charlie joined him and rubbed a porthole of his own. When you stood close against it, you saw pale grey trees and the park tossing with wild daffodils.

'What's the family like?' Tom asked.

'You'll see for yourself later.'

'That bad?'

'I've known worse. Don't go near the major's mother. She'll have you for breakfast.'

'Not keen on the Trust?'

'Let's just say she might be in favour of liberty and fraternity, but she definitely doesn't trust egality.'

Fermoy laughed. 'So you're back to London tomorrow?'

'First thing in the morning. Catching the early train. You all right without me?'

'Have to be,' Tom said. Then, 'Yes, I'll be fine. Don't worry. I thought I saw your car outside.'

'It is. But James is picking it up to drive down to Truro.'

Fermoy turned from the window. Took a deep sniff. 'Somebody should bottle it,' he said.

'Bottle what?'

'That authentic country house smell. Dry rot and mackintoshes and mouse pee.'

It was four o'clock by the time they finished the roof inspection. Tilley was in the kitchen kneading bread. When she saw the state they were in, she said, 'Good God Almighty, sir, I thought you was the sweep!'

'Rolls of dust up there, I'm afraid.' Charlie's eyes grinned at her through his blackened face. 'We came to ask if there would be any hot water. Can't go back to The Acland like this.'

'I'll put the kettle on,' she said. 'Miss Daphne took what I had. She's washing the dog in the scullery. Let somebody else wash the bally thing, I said. Specially with that blinking great diamond ring on your finger. You heard she got herself engaged, sir?'

'I did.'

'I thought there was something going on when Bos – Mr Boswell – turned up with his jacket all buttoned.'

A stifled yelping was coming from the direction of the scullery.

'They been having a regular old fight. He got in the cesspit, see, and come in shaking himself over the covers. Miss Daphne had to take a stiff brush to him.'

'Perhaps she should take the brush to us,' Charlie said.

'Well, at least you don't 'um,' Tilley told him, forgetting her aitches.

There was a crash. Then the scullery door banged open and a very wet, very handsome pointer came tearing through the passage and into the kitchen.

'Oh, hang!' Tilley said.

The pointer proceeded to shake himself violently all over them. Charlie ducked. Tom Fermoy laughed, then, shoulders hunched, attempted to catch the animal. The dog raced round in circles, then leapt on top of the table. Down went Tilley's bread and the bowl and the tin that was waiting for it and a pile of plates.

'Punch!' That was Daphne in the doorway.

'Here, boy!'

'Grab his collar!'

'Hasn't got one.'

The dog went round the kitchen like a blast of wind. But this time, Charlie and Fermoy cornered him. Tom held on to him. Punch struggled ferociously. When he sagged to the floor, Tom slid on top of him.

'I couldn't hold him,' Daphne said. 'He pulled his collar off.'

Tom reattached the thing. Daphne, shiny-faced, soaking wet, gave a relieved sigh. Charlie picked up the broken bowl and said, 'Miss Jago, I'd like you to meet our architect, Tom Fermoy.'

Daphne blushed a fiery scarlet. She put a hand up to her dripping hair, then, realizing it would do no good, brought it down again. 'How do you do,' she said, with as much dignity as she could muster. 'I'm most frightfully sorry!'

'Don't worry,' said Fermoy. 'It's all in a day's work.'

Tilley couldn't wait for her afternoon off, so that she could tell Mother. She gazed at the three of them and shook her head. Very clever people, but half dotty, she shouldn't wonder.

Charlie had arranged, for this second visit, to stay at The Acland, the idea being that it would be warmer than the Big House and the company a tad more welcoming. Besides, when he was about to put an estate to rights, he liked to get his ear into village voices.

He parked the Ford in the street and grabbed his bag from the dicky at the back. A squally wind tried to shove him across the road. Having failed to do so, it picked up a pile of dead beech leaves, the colour of rust, and tossed them at the pub windows. There was fitful March sunshine, but the black sky behind the church was faintly menacing. That faint roar was the sea, three miles away over the headland.

Until the war this had been an isolated settlement in a remote parish that few strangers ever penetrated, a backwater where nothing happened except the cycle of the year. Charlie stood gazing across the empty street at the dark and insanitary-looking row of cottages that stood behind the baker's van. There was something so dank about them, so bleak and condemned-looking, that he felt a sense of relief that the Trust was taking them over. Really, the tenants would be better off. He wondered how much of a shock it would be to them that the Jagos were on their uppers?

Charlie's thoughts, as he stepped off the kerb, were interrupted by a frantic squealing of brakes and a 'Look out!' Stopping in his tracks, he saw a flash of scarlet. A girl on a bicycle, swerving to avoid him, skidded sideways and sailed into the forsythia bush by the bakery wall. Her bicycle clattered into the flower bed of the cottage next door.

'I'm terribly sorry!' Charlie said, rushing over to help her up. 'I was miles away. Didn't hear you coming.'

'That's obvious.' Swearing hard, the girl was brushing the mud from her scarlet trousers. Pointedly, she ignored the hand he held out to lift her to her feet.

The stroppy type, Charlie thought. Just my luck. 'Are you all right?' he asked. 'No bones broken? You've cut your hand.'

'Lucky it wasn't my skull.' She wore a corduroy coat topped with a knitted scarf that was wrapped twice around her neck. 'Damn!' she said. 'There's a hole in my stocking.'

'I'm so sorry. I'll replace them.'

'And how are you going to do that, when you can't get stockings for love or money?'

There was no answer to that. Charlie fished her beret down from the top branch of the forsythia and handed it to her, then crossed the road to retrieve her bicycle. The chain was off, so he upended the machine and began the tricky process of fixing it back on.

'You won't manage it,' the girl said. 'Ted at the garage says it's a bugger.'

'I'm used to bikes,' he told her. 'Fix mine all the time.'

'Yours is probably quite normal.'

'Actually, it's ancient.' He slipped the last cog into place. But then . . . flop. Down the thing came again. The thing was, she was unnerving him. He was very aware, if only out of the corner of his eye, of her nippy little waist and all that carelessly flung-back, shining hair.

'Look – I'll walk it home.'

'No need,' he said, cursing the thing for slipping and sliding. His fingers were coated in bicycle oil. He had one last stab at looping the chain back up.

She said, 'I'd better tell you. You've got oil on your chin.'

Gritting his teeth, he forced the chain back on. Immediately, it flew off again.

'I'll take it round to Ted,' she said. Was that laughter in her voice? Charlie counted to ten before righting the bicycle and wiping his hands on the handkerchief he had fished from his overcoat pocket. 'You'll send me the bill, of course? Charles Garland. I'm staying at The Acland.'

'Rather you than me,' she said.

He took his eyes off her hair. 'You wouldn't recommend it?'

'Only if you're desperate,' she told him. Then she took the bicycle and pushed it down the hill in the direction of the garage.

Pru Hockin, who had been keeping a weather eye on the proceedings from the tap room window, opened the side door to the young gentleman (a very pleasant, if greased-up, young gentleman) and carried on for some time about the state he was in before leading him up to the best bedroom – the front one with the mahogany bed, a scriptural text above the washstand, and Granfer Hockin's horsehair sofa. As was her habit, Pru lingered to chat for a minute or ten about the Ministry of Agriculture and Food cutting fats and animal fodder, and about all the uprooted people drifting in and out of the village, and about the cheap ukelele her son had brought back from overseas. She was assured that she need not apologize for the fact that they weren't yet wired up to electricity.

Thank the Lord, Pru thought, Mr Garland wasn't one of those snooty types, the sort that grumbled about prescribed menus and the apple and custard she served up for afters. No, this young man had perfect manners. You could tell that by the way he'd struggled to mend the blasted bike. With that silly maid standing there lording it over him.

The parson's daughter met with the brawny force of Pru's disapproval. Girls these days, she thought, were too full of themselves. They had kept the country going, in the factories and such, while the men were away, but it had brought them on too much. They didn't deserve polite, dependable young men. But there, she thought, I don't suppose they'd want them either.

Seven

Evalina Jago's voice was dauntingly brisk. 'I have an appointment with Mr Boscawen Senior.'

'I'm sorry, madam, but Mr Neville's in court today.'

Evalina gazed at the girl behind the desk. A pretty gel, but all made up. 'In York?'

The receptionist raised her voice. 'He's at the police court.'

'No need to shout.' Evalina stood there in her toque, her hair all coiled round at the back. As a girl, she had learned how to stand properly by walking with a book on her head. 'When will he be back?'

'I'm afraid he won't,' the receptionist said.

'You're new. What happened to the other girl? Moira.'

'Laura. She's expecting a baby.'

'Are you sure? She was getting on a bit. And I can't say I ever noticed a wedding ring.'

A throat was cleared in the doorway behind them and a stolid young man with a charming smile stepped forward to take charge. 'Mrs Jago!' Nicholas Boscawen wore a tweedy suit and a country solicitor's shirt with a starched collar. 'You were hoping to see my father.'

At this particular moment, Evalina didn't care to be smiled upon. She drew her fur wrap more closely round her shoulders. 'Not hoping, young man. Expecting. I think you'll find my name in his book for ten thirty.'

'Well, yes, but he's been called away, I'm afraid.'

'Called away?'

Nicholas Boscawen's smile did not waver. 'He sends his most sincere apologies. Asked me to deal with whatever it is you wanted to see him about.'

'Young man,' said Evalina, 'I do not discuss my affairs with junior partners.'

Nicholas said, 'Coffee, Sybil, right away, please.'

'And I never drink coffee. It plays havoc with my innards.'

'Tea, then.' He took her arm. Evalina shot him an icy look. 'And shortbread biscuits.'

'*I* was always taught that if one has difficulty in keeping an engagement, one should have the grace and manners to write and say so.'

'You're right, of course.' Nicholas steered the old lady in the direction of his office. 'But in this case, there was no time. So . . . how are we keeping? Well, I hope?'

'No. Not at all well.'

'I'm sorry to hear that.'

'Old-fangled and useless. That's how one feels when one's whole life is being dismantled around one.' Evalina gave up the frosty act. She needed to let some of her frustration out. 'You'll have heard what's going on up at Lizzah?'

'Um. Not exactly,' Nicholas manoeuvred her through the open door. 'Not officially, so to speak.'

'Yes . . . well . . . that's because the young Bolshevik is insisting that everything is handled by his own lawyers. What do you think of that?'

'Depends who his lawyers are.'

'Exactly so!'

'McKewan and Swann, I hear. Tabard's Inn.'

'How the devil did you know that?'

'Have a seat. No, not that one, it's too low for you.'

Evalina stalked across to the upright wing chair by the window. She said in her hooting mezzo, 'Well, *I've* never heard of such a firm. Are they sound?'

'As a bell. Pretty swish, between you and me and the table leg.'

'I'm relieved to hear it. But my son is still making the biggest mistake of his life.'

'You think so?'

'I know so. I can't eat, can't sleep. I thought about getting right out of it and taking myself off to live with my sister in Torquay, but then I said to myself, no, I'll ask Neville Boscawen if there's any way I can put a spanner in the works and stop the whole ridiculous affair.'

Nicholas closed the door. 'To tell the truth,' he said, 'I'm not so sure there is.'

'Nonsense! You're a lawyer. It's your job to sort out other people's messes.'

'That's one way of looking at it.' Nicholas sat down behind his desk. 'Trouble is, the owner of the mess has to dump it on my desk himself, so to speak.'

'You're telling me I'm interfering in my son's affairs?'

'Wouldn't dream of it. Ah . . . tea.' Nicholas leapt up again as the door opened. He took the tray from the girl, who looked flustered, and found space for it on the desk. 'Thank you, Sybil.'

'It's just that he hasn't the strength to stand up for himself. It's my daughter-in-law who is forcing him into it. I don't know if anyone ever told you, but she's the domineering type.'

'Really?'

'Yes, really. And, of course, losing the boy unhinged them both.'

'That was sad. Black or white?'

'Black. Do you have children, Mr Boscawen?'

'Um. No. Not at the moment.'

'Well, don't bother. That's my advice. They'll break your heart. Myles hasn't said a word to me in two whole weeks. I know I rattle on. Try to stiffen him up. But that's a mother's job, surely?' Her eyes, a washed-out blue, seemed distressed. She watched him lift the teapot and begin to pour. 'All he does is take himself off for walks with the dog. How does he think that will help?'

'Man's best friend. Comforting.'

'He used to disappear with the dog after his father died. Not the dog we have now. A cocker spaniel called Jack. Funny the boy took it so hard, because Alexander was never much of a father. Never spent time with the children. Hated the country. Preferred to be in town where he could blue money and charm the ladies and . . . well . . . live for the day.' She became aware that she was rambling on and turned her mind back to the subject in hand. 'We've been under a strain, all of us. We've survived the Germans and the Allies. What I can't see is how we're going to survive the peace.'

Nicholas came round the desk to hand her a steaming teacup. 'If anyone survives, you will.'

'Not for much longer. I'm an old crock.'

'A spry old crock.'

Evalina told herself that the boy was becoming far too familiar. She said, 'I shall consult your father on this matter just as soon as he has a free moment. In the meantime, you can draft me a letter to a very old friend of mine, Field Marshall Fairfax Boughton. The field marshall was at school with my husband.'

Nicholas said, 'And the . . . um . . . thrust of the letter?'

'The field marshall was a military adviser to the PM during the Great War.'

'I'm sorry. I don't see—'

'What don't you see? You seem a little slow, if you don't mind my saying so. The field marshall always ran a good campaign. I intend to ask what he would do if he were in my shoes.'

Nicholas said, 'You could write to him yourself.'

'I don't seem to be able to get my brain together for letter-writing.' Evalina set the cup down on the windowsill. 'Anyway, it's complicated. Needs legal jargon. And paragraphs. I'll give you the gist of what I want to say and you can cobble it into some sort of order.'

Nicholas Boscawen had been careful not to say so, but the truth was that his father had purposely made Mrs Jago's appointment on a day when he was certain to be absent from the premises. 'You deal with her, m' boy. Got to start sometime. Daft old bat. Gives me a headache.'

'Is she always like that?' Sybil asked when the old lady had taken herself off.

'Independent?' Nicholas grinned.

'Cantankerous! I tried to help her down the steps, but she batted me away with her stick.'

Nicholas eyed the jumbled notes on the sheet of paper in front of him and wondered how he was going to turn them into a coherent whole. He poured himself another cup of tea – half cold, but Sybil *did* make good tea – while he pondered Mrs Jago and her correspondence. Mostly, Boscawen and Boscawen (wily old Neville and nicer young Nicholas) were on the receiving end. For forty years or more, she had aimed missives at them with astonishing regularity, always in the same fine copperplate, like a letter from one's aunt, always in the same dark blue ink and always with the same mixture of patronage and complete disregard for anyone else's point of view. The cupboard behind Nicholas's desk had a corner that was stuffed with neat packs of them. '*I want your advice on a family dispute . . . I should be grateful if you would give me your opinion on a point of law . . . I believe you must have the envelope containing carbon copies of my mother-in-law's will. It was lodged with you. I distinctly remember.*'

As for Mrs Jago's six-monthly visits to the office to change her own last will and testament ('Not that there's actually anything to leave,' her daughter-in-law had been heard to mutter), well, they had become an office joke.

Nicholas shuffled the notes into some sort of order and dropped them into the baize-lined box that served as an in-tray. A wet wind kept smacking away at the window and when he went to tighten the catch, he caught the cool, sweet scent of the daffodils that Sybil had arranged in a jug that morning.

In the street outside, branches were thrashing like the tail-end of a heaving sea. A country solicitor, thought young Nicholas, is a therapist, putting on a performance, complete with refreshments, for his dottier clients. It was one way to build a successful business, he supposed.

It was one of Charlie's habits to try to deal with the more boring practical matters by correspondence whenever possible, so that on returning to a property after the initial visit, he could devote every precious bit of time to the house.

Accordingly, in the dozens of brusque and sometimes bristling letters that had passed between the major and Charlie over the last couple of months, they had established that the major, if given a two-hundred-year lease, would hand over, along with the house and the park, two thousand pounds in three percent war stock to build up a reserve fund for capital repairs. In return, the Trust would provide one thousand pounds for expenditure on practical improvements such as the heating system, re-wiring, new boilers and repairs to the structure. That was more or less the gist of it. Not that anything had been signed and sealed.

'We would hope to open in, say, fourteen months,' Charlie said over a good malt in the major's study. 'That would take us to . . . let's see now . . . June next year.'

'A bit soon, wouldn't you say?'

'It's pushing it, but spring is a good time for house openings. People are restless for an outing. Hopefully they'll turn out in droves.'

'You'll have to prohibit access to the park. That's where the pheasants gather. I won't have anyone walking there in the late summer or early autumn.'

'We might have to do some negotiating on that. I thought,' Charlie said, deftly changing the subject, 'you might like to help with the guide book. We could make it a joint effort. Illustrate it with a print or two from your library.'

'Have to think about that,' said the major, sending his gaze back to the run of Wisden – daffodil yellow – on the shelf by the fireplace. 'I suppose the old place will be unrecognizable by the time you've finished with it?'

'I hope not. The last thing I want is to see it dolled up like some vulgar hotel. We just want to . . . well . . . rescue it, don't you see?'

'Hrmmph!' The major brushed back his thinning hair. There was an expression of morose cynicism on his face.

'The only place we let rip on is the tea rooms. Jolly colours, printed tablecloths—'

'Tea rooms?' The major was shocked to the core.

Charlie shot him a glance, then kicked himself for letting the subject slip in before it was strictly necessary. 'Don't worry. We'll hide them in the stables or somewhere well out of the way. You'll hardly know . . . They won't be visible—'

'Of course they'll be damned well visible! Otherwise how will people find them? Well, I won't have it, d'you hear? Won't have you running a blasted tea shop on my estate. A fine figure of fun I'll look! Quite apart from the fact that it'll be unmanageable. What'll happen, for instance, when they've had their nice pot of tea and they start rummaging around the place looking for the privy? Thought of that?'

'Well, of course, we would accommodate extra . . . facilities . . . behind the—'

'Facilities? What facilities?'

'Well, all the usual . . . amenities.'

'You mean public lavatories?'

'Well, yes.'

'Be damned, you will!'

Oh, hell, thought Charlie. Talk about putting your foot in it. And I wanted to talk to him about the entail . . .

Jack Trewarden no longer expected peace and quiet at home. Lil's idea of marriage was a running fight. As soon as she got home from work, the bickering started. It was mostly about the state of the house. Jack liked things spick and span. Lil would have been at home living in a pigsty. One Saturday, when he found a pan of mouldy mashed potato under a mound of ironing, he said, 'I can't stand this. Why can't you keep the place clean and tidy?'

'Because I'm out at work all day. That's why.'

Jack said, 'I put the place straight after you've gone. Then you come home and mess it up again.'

'You and your army spit and polish!' she flung back at him. 'You weren't like it before you went away.'

'It's not spit and polish. I like the place to look decent if anyone comes in.'

'Meaning your mother, I suppose? Well, if she's got anything to say about the state of my house, tell her I can't be at home all day polishing and baking like some I could mention, because her precious son hasn't yet landed himself a job. For God's sake, Cliffy, get those things out of here.'

The boy said, 'But—'

'No buts. I won't have vermin on the bloody table.' Cliffy was feeding bits of grass to the lizards that he kept in an old Cow and Gate tin with holes in the lid. He slammed the lid on and stuffed the grass into his pocket. He reminded Jack of himself as a child. Wrists out, collar crooked, nothing ever seemed to fit him. 'I used to catch lizards with Uncle Nip,' he told the boy. 'Sometimes their tails came off.'

'They grow again,' said Cliffy flatly. He picked up the tin and took himself off. Jack felt the distance between them stretch even further.

Lil fished a packet of Weights from her pocket. 'Kids! I ask you!'

It wasn't that she didn't care for the boy. It was just that she felt no need to show it. She was a rough, loving mother, like a bitch with a puppy. Jack wanted to ask if the boy had learned to act cold and careless because it was what he had taken in with his mother's milk. Instead, he took his jacket from the peg by the door and shrugged himself into it.

'I'm off up to The Barton. Heard there's work going.' He flattened his hair with the palm of his hand and headed out before she could make him feel even more irritable.

On the way, he called at his mother's. Peg was removing the brains from a calf's head ready for the stew pan. She wore a flowered overall over her frock and her reddish hair was tied up in a scarf. She was a lanky, loose-limbed woman, warm but abrasive, and she put things straight in your head when you talked to her. 'I didn't expect you today,' she said. 'What's up?'

'Nothing.'

'Her been at you with her tongue again?'

'Lil?'

'Who else? Anything less like a lily you never saw. Unless it's one of they exotic foreign things that smell to high heaven.' She put the brains in the stew pan with a little salt and water and stuck it on the range.

Jack said, 'I fancied a bit of your saffron cake.'

'What you should do,' his mother said, 'is tell her you've been fighting for six years and you didn't expect to have to carry on with it when you got back home. Any work yet?'

'I'm just off up to Dan Jewell's. Heard they wanted a cowhand.'

'You're no cowhand. You're better than that.'

'It would only be until I could find something permanent.'

Peg said, 'I suppose they have good food on farms.' She filled the kettle and set it down next to the brains, which were hissing on the hob. 'Nip was in last night. Brought me a box of chocolates and some novels. God knows where he laid hands on them. He calls it doing a little business on the side. He's bought a car and he's teaching Denny Aunger to drive.'

'But he hasn't got a licence.'

'Denny has. He knows somebody who forges them. I'm worried the bobbies will catch up with him, Jack. Worried about him, full-stop.'

'It takes time to adjust,' Jack told her. He still felt strange . . . uncomfortable . . . in grey flannels and an open-necked shirt.

'It's more than that. I can't get through to him. And he seems . . . I don't know . . . reckless.'

Jack told himself he would go for a stoke-up at The Acland with Nipper. A pint or two in the spit and sawdust of Pru Hockin's establishment might make it easier to ask what it had been like in the prison camp, what exactly the bastards had done to him. Jack had been trying to approach the subject for weeks, but hadn't been able to work himself up to it.

He was fond of his little brother, but it wasn't the kind of closeness that easily put itself into words.

So familiar was every twist and turn of the lane up to The Barton that he could have walked it in the dark. He knew every stick and stone, every field gate. Nothing had changed – the scent from acres of farmland, the blowing woods, the flights of wood pigeons with their wings clapping.

The Barton was a small yeoman farm with walls of cob and the inevitable clutter of machinery rusting among the nettles. The dog came out barking, then stopped and sniffed him amiably. Soft pigeon cooings came from the roost above the barn. Jack studied the cluster of lichened roofs, the ancient pump, the flurry of chicks around the baler and still felt he was in a dream, one of those where everything seems familiar yet unfamiliar. There was no one about, but the stable door was open, so he crossed the yard and stood on the threshold for a moment, breathing in the smell of hay and saddle soap and leather and horse manure.

Here, the war might never have happened. Sparrows flew in and out of the arches, motes of dust floated peacefully in the bar of sunlight that stretched from the gable window to the tackle on the wall in the end stall.

Then something rattled above him and a warm and friendly female voice said, 'Can I help you?' Glancing up, Jack saw a girl in a green pullover and Peter Pan blouse leaning over the edge of the hayloft. An old-fashioned kind of a girl with a wide, lovely mouth.

'I'm looking for Dan Jewell,' he said.

'He's gone to market.'

'It's Wednesday. Damn. I didn't think.'

'It's Jack, isn't it?'

'That's right,' he said, still gazing upwards. The girl had turned herself round and was climbing down the wooden ladder. Jack couldn't place her, but he took in her sandals, hand-knitted stripey socks, dungarees, and a mass of brown hair fastened by a slide.

'Jack Trewarden,' she said. 'You don't remember me. I'm Daisy.'

Jack stood frowning at her.

'Daisy Jewell,' she said. 'Dan's daughter.'

'You can't be.'

'Why not?'

'Daisy was a skinny little thing with tight pigtails.'

'That was six years ago. I'm eighteen now.'

'Good God!'

'You've changed too. I wasn't exactly sure it was you.' Her face was flushed, her eyes shining.

Jack gazed at the soft lines of her jaw, her rounded chin. It was a long time since he had seen a girl so . . . dewy.

'Father won't be back for hours,' the girl said. 'But I could take a message.'

'I heard there was work going,' Jack said.

'I'm sorry,' Daisy said. 'He took on someone last night. One of the Facey boys from South Tamerton.'

Her gentleness eased the disappointment that ran through him. He said, 'Never mind. It can't be helped.'

'We'll need extra help for the hay.'

'I know. It's just that I need work now. If you hear of anything, would you let me know?'

'Of course.'

'Thanks,' he said, smiling down at her. 'I was sorry to hear you lost your mother.'

'Yes . . . well.' Her face had lost its tranquillity. 'It's five years next month.'

'Peritonitis, Mother said.'

'That's right.'

Jack wished he hadn't brought the subject up. His eyes were still on her face. She wore no make-up. Didn't need it. For a moment, she made him remember what it was like to be young again.

It was as well that he couldn't see into Daisy Jewell's mind. She was thinking, sadly, how much older he looked than when she had last seen him at the pageant her mother had done the costumes for in the summer of '39. Jack had played young King Henry in a mulberry silk tabard. His hair had been almost flaxen, his eyes full of fun. But we're none of us the same, she thought, and life's not perfect like it used to be. She held on, for a moment, to the picture of Mother with her needle in her hand, mending a tear in the mulberry tabard. Then let go of it. Looking backwards got you nowhere. Especially when there was butter to be churned and a flasket of clothes in the kitchen that needed ironing.

On the way back, Jack stopped to lean on a five-barred gate. It was an extraordinary delight to gaze at the view down over Pen Head. But he still missed the camaraderie of service life.

Only yesterday he'd found a curly-edged photo of himself in the camp rugby team and he'd felt a stab of . . . what? Nostalgia? Ridiculous, when he remembered the army for what it was: the officers thinking of themselves as a superior race; the class divide between them and the ranks.

When he was a sergeant-major serving in Cairo, a large number of the clubs and hotels had been out of bounds to the ranks. Them and us, he thought, remembering the night in the barracks when the results of the General Election had come through. The men had gathered eagerly around the radios, while a group of officers, sullen or poker-faced, had withdrawn to the far end of the room, distancing themselves from the would-be rebels. There had been comments about 'mob rule'. You could imagine them thinking the tumbrils were going to come out. For three days, no officer was saluted. They had had to introduce saluting patrols to get it back.

A patch of sunlight broke through down in the valley. The tradition of deference was over and done with, Jack told himself. I won't be like Father, going to an early grave after a lifetime of punishing labour. I won't be touching my forelock to the gentry either.

Winston was a grand old man; he had brought them through the war and his country would always be grateful to him for it. But he was tired and spent and outmoded, like his high-crowned bowler. Take that speech he'd made telling people that if Labour introduced Socialism, they would need some sort of Gestapo to silence the criticisms. Extraordinary! What a blunder, to accuse the men he'd worked with for six years – Attlee, Bevin, Morrison – of being no better than the Nazis! It had been an unwarranted smear, but now the Tories had been savaged and the Liberals annihilated and the old warrior had got his comeuppance.

'Serves him right,' Jack said.

Hitting a bunch of dock leaves with his stick, he strode on down the hill. He spotted a rabbit in the field on his left. It was nibbling hard, oblivious to the fact that it had company. There were rabbits everywhere. *If I could get hold of a gun . . .* He stuck a stalk of timothy grass between his teeth and cut down across the copse to the pack bridge.

The young beeches were touched with green. A delicious scent of bracken shoots, gorse and heather was coming off the moor. He had crossed the bridge and was rounding the bend on the hill on the other side, when he came across the Bentley, stuck in the middle of the lane.

In the back was a female passenger wearing a formidable toque. The driver, a man in a golfing cape and pork-pie hat, stood peering rather hopelessly under the bonnet. The major. He looked short-tempered and on the verge of blowing up.

Jack said, 'Won't she go?'

'Died on me halfway up and won't start again.'

'Want me to have a look?'

'Do you know anything about engines?'

'Should do. I spent six years driving an armoured car.'

'This isn't an armoured car,' called the passenger. 'You are not to let him touch it.'

'It's something to do with the ignition,' the major said.

'I'll see what I can do.'

'You will not!' the passenger insisted.

'Carry on,' ordered the major.

'It'll be the setting of the ignition and choke.'

'If you say so. Haven't driven her for years. Useless with anything mechanical, that's the thing.'

'You've got to get the right position when you swing. And just a gentle touch on the advance lever.'

'Not my cup of tea . . . engines.'

Jack bent to have a look at the ignition. He liked tinkering with cars.

'Myles – did you hear what I said? Send him to Davey at the garage with a message.'

Jack looked up to see a sour-faced, dissatisfied-looking old woman climb stiffly from the car. The tartar. The old battle-axe. From the look of all those furs, she had half an animal around her.

He adjusted something, fetched the starting handle and went round to the front of the Bentley.

'We've got stables with no horses,' the tartar said, 'a greenhouse with no heat and a motor that refuses to function.'

'Better than a grave in France,' Jack said. Then wanted to kick himself when he remembered the major's son. He gave the handle a quick swing. Nothing. Then another. And another. At last the engine roared into life.

'Good show!' the major said. 'Get in, Mother. Quickly.'

'I can't do anything quickly, Myles. You should know that.'

'Just get in. I'm very grateful, young man. Care to hop in? We'll take you down to the village.'

'Thanks, but no,' Jack replied with a considered disrespect.

'Oh, get in. It's a fair step. Least we can do.'

The door was open and the hill ahead *was* steep, so in the end, Jack ditched his principles and climbed in, ignoring the old woman's glare.

'I'm most grateful,' the major said as they started off up the hill. 'Can't thank you enough.'

'Every engine's different. You have to get the feel of them.'

'Daresay you're right. Fishleigh used to see to it, but he's crocked up.'

'Should be pensioned off,' said the voice from the back.

The major ignored it. 'I know your face,' he said to Jack. 'Can't put a name to it.'

'Jack Trewarden.' He refrained from adding the word, 'Sir.'

'One of Margaret's boys?'

'That's it.'

'Nice woman, Margaret. Sense of humour. Good thing in a woman. Anyway, good to see you back in one piece.'

'Thanks. I was . . . er . . . sorry to hear about your son.'

'Yes, well, you know.' The major kept his eyes on the road ahead. 'These things happen. The hedges are coming out. Catkins. Daresay we shall see daffodils soon.'

Eight

'Did you have a chat with Nip?' Peg whispered.

'Not yet,' Jack said. 'I will, though.'

It was a Saturday night – the fifteenth of April – and in the church hall, the Roof Fund concert was under way. Lights slung over the rafters illuminated the tiny stage. Mabel Petherick's swooping contralto and her sister's wavering soprano were making a meal of 'Love's Old Sweet Song'. Mabel was wearing her best beige frock, which only came out on special occasions, and her hair was set in rolls. Edie, her shoes fastened with pearl buttons, sang as she did to the gramophone at home, sweetly, unselfconsciously, without a care in the world.

'Thank God that's done with,' Peg said as they took their bow. 'Can't be doing with bad salads.'

'I've got something to tell you,' Jack said. 'I had a note from the major. I think he might be offering me a job. A month's trial as his chauffeur.'

'Good God! I thought you didn't want to work for the nobs.'

'I don't,' said Jack. 'But beggars can't be choosers.'

'So what's he offering?'

'Seven pounds a week.'

Peg gave a whistle. 'I thought they were skint.'

'There's skint and skint,' Jack said.

At the piano, Miss Jago flipped pages of sheet music. She turned her face towards the audience as if to say, 'Quiet, please.'

'You've been at the Cherry Blossom,' Peg said, taking in the gleam on her son's shoes. She glanced down at her programme to see who was next. 'Dear Lord,' she said, 'it's Ron House.'

Ron House with his comic monologues. He stood, centre stage, hands clasped, waiting for Miss Jago to get through the pianoforte introduction. Then he beamed at the assembled company, screwed his face up and began:

I took to the army like a cat does to water . . .

'Whose idea was this?' Peg asked, sotto voce.

'Yours. You bought the tickets.'

'Had them forced on me. So what does Lil think of the job?'

'Not a lot.' She had said surprisingly little until he had told her she could give up work now and stay at home to look after the boy. Then the trouble had started. 'Who the hell do you think you are, telling me what to do? I'm not turning into some kitchen skivvy! I like going to work.'

'So who's going to look after Cliff?' Jack had asked.

'He can look after himself. He's used to it. Annie next door keeps an eye on him.' Jack hadn't thought much of that idea. Kids needed a mother around, he'd told her, and if she didn't like staying at home, she could lump it. That was when she had really blown her top.

Now you know what Mother always says. Don't do anything you hadn't oughter.

Ron House kicked up his heels and broke into a dance routine. When he had finished his turn, he gave a smart salute and exited left.

Peg said, 'Thank God that's over.'

George Facey sang a bass solo entitled 'They Who Do Lie Under the Dark Rushing Sea'. Victor Rowse performed conjuring tricks. Then, as the spotlight turned rose-coloured and Miss Jago drifted into an arpeggio, a girl stepped on stage.

You'd be so nice to come home to
You'd be so nice by the fire . . .

A hush fell over the audience. Her voice – not strong, but clear and sweet – held them effortlessly.

Where the breeze on high sings a lullaby
You'd be all that I could desire.

'Daisy Jewell,' Peg murmured. 'Nice little maid. No side to her.'

'Sssh!'

Daisy threw a smile around the audience. Innocent, Jack thought. Countrified.

Under stars chilled by the winter
Under an August moon burning above . . .

The audience sat spellbound. Even Peg stopped her rattling. She was smiling dreamily, taken back to long-ago times in a guiltless world.

You'd be so nice, you'd be paradise
To come home to and love.

There was no artifice, no attempt to flirt the song up. Every word was heartfelt. The honesty in Daisy's voice sent a tingle up Jack's spine.

'*To come home to . . . and love.*'

'Now that's what I call a lovely song,' Peg said, clapping herself silly as Daisy took three curtain calls.

That's what I call a lovely girl, Jack thought, waiting for the rush of adrenalin to subside. Daisy rented a room in his head all that week.

* * *

'Who *are* all these people descending on us?' Evalina Jago asked Charlie.

'Museum experts,' Charlie told her, trying to make it all sound like one big lark. 'They give us advice on all sorts of things. Let me see now, Elizabeth Wootton – the one with the hideous feather in her hat – runs The Royal School of Needlework. Edwin Rowse knows everything there is to know on Goanese work – that's Portuguese bed-hangings. Then there's our art expert, Bernard Nagel. Impossibly posh voice. Spends half his life rushing up and down ladders like a squirrel with a torch. I have to butter him up like nobody's business, because we can't afford to pay him.'

Evalina twitched the throw over her pain-crippled legs. 'Nagel?' she huffed. 'What sort of name is that? This country is being taken over by foreigners. We are swarming with them.'

'I hadn't noticed.'

'I wouldn't expect you to. The young never notice anything. So what did your Mr Nagel think of the Jago portraits?'

'Well . . . they're of historical and social importance, but as to value . . . I'm afraid there was nothing of any note.'

'Nothing of any note?' She was outraged, but Charlie knew better than to pursue the matter, so he said, 'There's a possible Grenville portrait going up to the Portrait Gallery for identification.'

'I knew old age wasn't going to be any fun,' Evalina told her sister when she came visiting two days later, 'but I never imagined it would be this damned, long, drawn-out purgatory.'

They were in Evalina's room taking a sherry together. Hesther islanded on a chintz armchair and her older sister hogging the circular table with its heavy embroidered cloth. There was something about Hesther's serene expression that irritated Evalina beyond measure. Or possibly it was the informality of her get-up. The greyish cardigan, the floppy trousers that might have been discarded by some man or other, not to mention the silver blue of her loosely waving hair. Evalina thought it was high time she learned to dress her age.

Hesther said, 'It's good news about Daphne's engagement.' She beamed at Evalina, who glared back at her balefully.

'Is it?'

'Well, of course,' Hesther said in her calm, matter-of-fact voice. 'Have they arranged a date for the wedding?'

Evalina said, 'How can one arrange anything with strangers roaming around the place? I wish it could be a wedding in the old way. The long grass scythed. Wasp-waisted gowns and flower-garden hats.'

'Weddings are a joy anyway. What does it matter what anyone wears?'

'Of course it matters! When I remember my own wedding . . . Ribbons and hats and lace. Spats and canes . . .'

The old lady got up and creaked with difficulty to the bureau. She fished out a pile of snapshots from the well-ordered drawer. She tapped the top one with her finger. 'Look at this. A striped marquee on the lawn. Buckets of Pimms. Pa in his tailcoat and his off-to-the-wars moustache. All those housemaids,' she said. 'Sometimes I think I can hear them, running up and down the stairs, chattering like magpies. Do you remember how hot it was that summer? The men bathed naked in the river. Alex loved the heat. Revelled in it.'

'That wasn't all he revelled in.'

Evalina sat down with the photographs in her lap. She could play deaf when it suited her.

Hesther said, 'What I remember most was that immense wedding feast. Ten different jellies.'

'Yes, well, you always were a gluttonous child. Here's our wedding photograph taken in the library. I had to lean over Alex's shoulder and pretend to read the book he was holding. An enormously heavy old tome that the photographer picked off the shelf at random. It was probably the only book he ever read in his life.'

'Myles and Virginia . . .' Hesther asked. 'How are they . . . well, you know . . . coping?'

'I wish I could answer that question,' Evalina said, 'but I really haven't the faintest idea. *She* stalks around like a caged animal. Myles hides . . . like he did when his father was killed.'

Her webbed old eyes – chalk blue, like the butterflies – gazed through the window as if the answer to all her problems might be found somewhere between the wet lawns and the wind-tossed elms. 'Everything's falling apart. I wrote to Field Marshall Boughton, but no one answers letters these days. Ink isn't the same, either. Have you noticed? It's impossible to find one that doesn't fade.'

'Have you had your eyes checked?' Hesther asked.

'What have my eyes got to do with it? They miss nothing, I can assure you, Essie.' She glanced down at her watch. 'Thank goodness. It's time.'

'Time for what?'

'To get some blessed warmth into our bones. Sunday is the one day we are allowed a fire in the drawing room. There's wood on the estate, but no one to cut and gather it. Who would ever have thought a roaring fire would be a sinful luxury?'

*   *   *

Jack had spent the week ferrying experts to and from the station. Three of them had arrived this morning on the eleven fifteen from Exeter: a jolly hockey sticks woman, very posh and very loud; a cocky bloke in brown suede shoes; and a bald chap with a stiff leg. After he'd dropped them off at Lizzah, he'd had to deliver three great files of papers to the agent in Bude and now he was on his way down the lane by the new council houses, hoping that Bess Tilley would have something even halfway edible for him to tuck into when he got back.

A little puff of May air came through the open window. He was beginning to feel easier about driving for the major. He still couldn't bear The Tartar and he certainly wasn't willing to kowtow to any of them, but working at Lizzah no longer seemed odd. He saw the Jagos as penniless people who spoke nicely, a sad lot, when you thought about it, slipping from the top of the greasy pole with all the dignity they could muster. The major – affable yet distant with his khaki socks and his army brusqueness – mooched around the estate talking to his dog as if it understood him. 'What do you think, old girl?' he had asked Punch the other day. 'Shall I live to regret being a blasted guinea-pig?' Yet there was a directness about him that Jack found he could live with.

The road bent itself round and followed the wood. Driving the car down Bracken Hill, he wondered if the major felt as fidgety as everyone else who had made it back home after having been on the move for six years. *We've come down to earth with a bump that's knocked us endways.*

The trees overhead were still and quiet. In the lavender distance, he caught a glimpse of the sea. Must take the boy to the beach, he thought. Back when Father was alive, they had walked to Pen Head on many a Sunday. Mother carrying pasties wrapped in greaseproof paper in her shopping bag. Father rattling along behind with the kettle and the stove. *And us kids charging through the woods playing Tip-and-Run.* Mother had always worried about what the rector would say, but Father, never a religious man, had said it was safer to see things straight from the very start, then you wouldn't have a shock when you found out there wasn't a heaven. On the other hand, Jack thought, Father was the most principled man you could wish to meet, a man who knew right from wrong and cared too much what happened to other people.

'One of nature's gentlemen,' Jack said, feeling memory tighten inside him.

A sharp turn at the ford took him back up again, past the river, past the old mill and towards the manor. A girl was hurrying up the hill – a girl in a cream suit with her hair tucked into a summery hat. She was light on her feet, but the steepness of the slope and the bundle squashed under her arm was slowing her down. Jack stopped the car and leaned over to open the passenger door.

'Want a lift?' he asked.

Daisy Jewell's face lit up at the sight of him. She said, 'Oh, would you? Father dropped me off in the village and I said I'd walk the rest. But Agnes Bolitho caught me outside the shop and wouldn't stop talking and I'm late.'

'Late for what?'

'I'm supposed to be at Lizzah at twelve with some skirts I let down for Miss Penelope.'

He smiled at her and said, 'I enjoyed your song the other night.'

'I was scared stiff.'

'You hid it well. Lovely voice.'

Her cheeks flushed at the compliment. They drove on through patches of sunlight, past a clearing where he used to play Robin Hood with Nip.

Daisy said, 'I heard you were working for the major. I was so pleased. Does it suit you?'

'It'll do until something better comes along.'

'I don't suppose you've heard anything about the tenants? Father's afraid he'll lose the farm.'

'No use worrying before it happens.'

'That's what I said. The major's always been straight with us. He won't throw people out when they've been here for generations. Do you ever miss the war?'

The sudden question took Jack by surprise. He said, 'Now and again.'

'It sounds funny, but I miss the sound of planes droning overhead on their way back to Germany. Jerry running home, Dad called it. It's so silent at night now.'

He glanced across at her blowing hair, at the lovely line of her – supple, graceful – from hip to knee. 'Silence is good,' he said.

'You're right. I'm not grumbling. Honestly.'

Jack looked at her. He said, 'It can't be *that* quiet, with all the young men hammering on your door.'

Daisy went pink again. 'There aren't any. Not at the moment,' she told him. 'I went out with someone for a while, but it didn't come to anything.'

'I was only teasing,' Jack said.

'Oh.' Daisy gazed out at the passing woods.

He said, 'What I miss most about the war is playing rugby union. And my mates. One particular mate. His name was Ted. Ted Reresby. We went through the desert campaign together. Then he copped it.'

'I'm sorry.'

'It was like losing a brother.' Why had that come blurting out, when he had never even told Lil?

Because Lil wouldn't be in the least bit interested, that's why.

Daisy was interested. You could tell by the way her grey eyes watched and listened. Daisy was soft, she made him feel like a boy again . . . a seventeen-year-old, half mad with excitement.

When they reached the Lodge gates, she said, 'I'll walk from here. They wouldn't like it if you took me any further.'

'Who cares?' Jack said.

'I care. I wouldn't like to get you into trouble. Not when you've just started.' Then when Jack hopped out to open the door for her, she stood in a patch of shade and said, 'It was so good of you to stop. Thank you.'

A pause. A long one. 'It was no trouble,' Jack said.

It occurred to him that this was what he had been fighting for. Girls like Daisy. And Mother, of course. And the boy.

It was only when he restarted the motor that he told himself that by rights, Lil should have been in there somewhere.

In the railway carriage at Bude, Charlie sat waiting for the early morning train to get steam up. It was raining a little – a light spring shower – but the air was soft and the bank opposite studded with primroses. He watched a porter trundle a luggage cart past the window, and hoped the couple having an altercation by the news stand weren't going to finish up in his compartment. Two other people had just come through the archway. A tall clergyman and a fair girl in a grey beret and plaid trousers.

The girl whose bicycle he had walked into.

She was saying goodbye to the clergyman, stretching on tiptoe to kiss him on the cheek. Then she picked up her bag and started to walk towards the train. She's heading in my direction, Charlie thought. Dammit, he had promised himself a good six hours' work on the guide book. There was no corridor on the train, so no way of slipping off into another compartment.

Her bag appeared in the doorway, followed swiftly by the plaid trousers. 'Oh, hello. It's you. Strange how you keep bumping into people . . .'

She had the kind of voice that quickly filled with laughter. It made you feel, somehow, like a stooge who had been outwitted on stage. 'I know who you are now. Daph told me. Actually, the whole village knows. There are all sorts of wild rumours flying around over breakfast tables.'

She slung her bag into the rack above their heads and sank into the corner seat opposite. There was something very vital about her – the vivid lipstick, the blue eyes, all that carelessly flung-back fair hair.

'My mother heard from an impeccable source that you are going to throw the whole village on to the street. She can't go shopping in town without meeting someone who had their house rifled. The thing she loves most in the world is a drama. So she's married to the right man, I suppose. The rectory pew's like the front stalls at the theatre.'

Charlie said, 'You're the rector's daughter?'

'For my sins. Romily Matheson.'

'Charles Garland.' Briefly, they shook hands.

'How far are you going?' she asked.

'London.'

'Me too.'

There was a slamming of doors. The train lurched. She leaned forwards and waved frantically to the clergyman, who was disappearing in a rush of steam.

'I don't like leaving him,' she said. 'He's cross with me, but won't say so. You think I'm going to rattle on all the way to London. I can tell by your face. Don't worry. I've got a novel with me. Picked it up at the jumble sale last week. The dust jacket's a bit lurid, but it's actually quite interesting. It's about a black sheep son who gets shipped off to relatives in Africa and has a fling with a beautiful heiress. Oh, all right. Put like that, it's rubbish. I shoved it into the bottom of my bag so that Daddy couldn't see it. So . . . how are you getting on up at Lizzah?'

'Oh, let's see now . . . we've got to tear half the house apart, put it back together again, install a new heating system, new drainage, re-wire the place and put in new boilers. Apart from that, it's a doddle,' Charlie told her.

'I wish somebody would put a new heating system into the rectory.'

Charlie smiled. 'How's the bicycle?'

'Fine, except for a dent in the front wheel. There's a room at Lizzah called the king's room. Did you know? Charles the Second stayed there when he was Prince of Wales and on the run from Cromwell. Miss Petherick used to walk us up there and tell us about Charles the Martyr.' She did a very passable imitation of Mabel Petherick's steely voice. '"Regicide, children! Do we know what the word means?" We hated her at the time, but she was a good teacher. One afternoon, she marched us round all the Jago portraits. My favourite was Richard Jago, the black-bearded buccaneer. Is this a good thing, your Trust taking over? I suppose it must be, but Daph's horribly upset by it.'

'It's the best solution under the circumstances.'

'The circumstances being that they haven't got a penny left to bless themselves with?'

'I wouldn't have quite put it like that, but . . . yes.'

'You get the feeling that a whole social system is breaking down. It's sad. Daph's my oldest friend. When you ask her about it, she says, "Don't worry, really, it will all be fine, I'm sure I'll like it once I get used to it." But really she hopes one morning she'll wake up and find it was a bad dream.'

Charlie didn't have any answer for that. He gazed out at wet leaves, wet trees, wet everything.

For the biggest part of an hour, the train creaked its way towards Okehampton, while Charlie scribbled away at his notes and his companion read her novel. When they changed for Exeter, they grabbed a coffee at the buffet and Miss Matheson, lean and lithe and energetic, followed him across the bridge to the opposite platform, talking nineteen to the dozen and seemingly taking it for granted that they were stuck with each other for the rest of the journey.

Sampford Courtenay, Crediton, Newton St Cyres, Exeter St David's.

'I wish you could just shut your eyes and be there,' Romily Matheson said as they caught the Paddington connection with just four minutes to spare.

On and on, past the Exeter suburbs to Honiton, where the train buried itself deep in a stretch of damp, cloudy woods, then steamed purposefully through one country town after another. By twelve thirty, Charlie was ready to break into the packets of sandwiches Tilley had stuffed into his overcoat pockets and it seemed only civil to offer to share them. Though, as he told Romily, he couldn't guarantee what would be in them or whether they would be fit to eat.

She laughed. 'Don't worry, I've got some of my own.'

He opened the first packet and took a tentative bite.

'Well?' she asked.

'Seems to be some kind of cheese.' That was a relief.

'Where do you live in London?' she asked.

'I've got a flat in Bayswater. It's pretty small, but there's a piece of roof you can climb out on. Nice in summer.'

'Girlfriend?'

'Sort of.'

'Sort of?'

'Now and then.'

'That's an odd sort of arrangement.'

'It's an odd sort of a world at the moment,' he told her.

Bridget Holway – Biddy to her friends and Red Biddy to those she worked with, on account of the colour of her hair and her political persuasions – worked in Charlie's office. He couldn't pretend he was absolutely in love with her, but in a casual way, things occasionally got a bit torrid.

'I'm engaged to a Polish officer,' Romily told him, picking a piece of crust off her apple tart.

His eyes went to her left hand.

'He gave me a little ring,' she said, 'but I haven't been wearing it because I knew there'd be trouble at home. Mother hit the roof when I told her.'

'And your father?'

'Daddy wants to meet him. Well, he doesn't really, he's just saying that, but he's always scrupulously fair, so I'm going back to tell Jan and to fix a visit. Jan's a poet.'

'Really?' Charlie pulled a fleck of cheesecloth out of his sandwich.

'You don't have to look like that.'

'Like what?'

'As if you don't believe poets exist.'

'I'm sure they do.'

'But you don't get married to them?'

'Not if you want to eat,' Charlie said, then at once regretted it. He was getting a look. From those dazzling eyes.

It's immaterial to me what you think, the look said. You're too ancient to know anything about poetry or romance. So why don't you take yourself back to your stupid little flat and chuck yourself off your bit of flat roof?

Nine

Virginia opened the door to the dusky room. A boy's room still, with its caps and silver cups and racquets and odds and ends of sports tackle. In the corner, on Kit's old botany table, were the presents they'd given him for his eleventh birthday – the yellow kite, the camera and a small tent. He'd rushed around the house hugging people to death. Then they'd driven up to Bursy Tor to fly the kite.

In her head, Kit's voice said, *Never thought you'd be so sentimental, Ma. You know what I told you that day about mooning around? If anything happens to me, just get on with your life.*

Easier said than done. There was a pain like a cramp around her heart. She closed the door and reached into her pocket for a cigarette. Myles didn't care for it, but up here, she could do as she liked. Tilley would clear away the incriminating evidence. She had orders to clean the room once a week, then lock it up again.

Secrets, Ma. Don't worry. I won't tell. Hey, do you remember that walking holiday we took in the Black Forest, just you and me, before all this madness started? You went up to your room to fetch cigarettes and that cow-like woman tried to pick me up? Listen to the row the wind's making in the chimney. I used to think it was ghosts. I suppose I'm one now. That's a bit rum, don't you think?

Rum and a lot of other things, Gin thought. She bit her lip and walked over to the bed. So is this what they call depression? Hearing voices that aren't really there? Walking around in a fog, as if your brain isn't anywhere inside your body?

'I must keep busy,' she said, putting out a hand to touch the pillow-case that was stuffed with Kit's letters and photographs. 'Soldier on. Keep on top of this damned campaign.'

That reminds me. What the hell is going on around here? People taking furniture away . . . crawling around under tables to see if they're fakes. All a bit hideous, don't you think? Like the dirges they sang at my funeral. You don't mind me saying that, do you? Only I always preferred something you could whistle along to. Surprised you didn't remember that. Didn't have your mind on the job, I dare say. That grass out there has grown daisies, all in a day. And take a look at the chestnuts in the churchyard next time you're passing. Sticky buds . . .

Kit had loved the great outdoors. He'd spent most of his boyhood fishing, exploring, looking for birds' nests in the hedges around the hall.

You look a bit blue, Ma.

No, not blue. Dark grey.

Can't you snap out of it?

Well, no.

Oh, she would walk downstairs in a moment and act a part. She would fidget around, snap at people, be argumentative and Virginia Bloody Jago with the hump, but that didn't erase this sense that she was feeling her way round in the dark. Funny how none of them seemed to notice she was saying one thing and feeling another.

Straight-backed and beautiful, Gin straightened the books on the shelf. She supposed there were times when an ill wind brought benefits. Impossible to imagine how silent the house would be without this flurry of lawyers and experts and Ministry of Works people and insurance agents passing through it. Maybe that was why she could talk so calmly to Myles about handing the place over to strangers. Because as long as there was Trust business going on, they wouldn't have to address the more painful personal matters that dwarfed the other into insignificance.

A bit deep, Ma, for the likes of you and me.

I know. We don't do deep. When you were around, all the horrors turned into jokes. There was a laugh to be had out of the gloomiest situation.

She was caught by a sudden piercing memory of standing out on the drive saying goodbye to him at the end of his last leave. He had said something silly to force a smile out of her. She had managed to hold it while the car disappeared down the elm drive. If only, she thought, I'd gone up to London to see him off properly.

Kit . . . with his blue eyes and his easy smile and hair the colour of spun treacle. The best friend she ever had in the whole world. If only she had caught it instead of him. Her eyes gazed through the window at a park that was flooded with daffodils. The if-only thing was a pointless exercise.

Stop punishing yourself.

That's what survivors do, Ma.

Is it?

But I punish, Myles, too, she thought. What's that about?

The comforting smell of wood smoke slowly invaded the room. Myles threw on another log of apple wood and the fire crashed. A shower of

sparks flew up the chimney. He sank back into the most comfortable
armchair by the mahogany bookcase, settled a copy of *The Field* on his
lap and wondered how long it would be before one of them came in to
disturb the peace. The room had three long windows that looked out on
to the terrace. Damned if he didn't think it the pleasantest in the house,
with all those old panes, the deep window seats, the tapestry curtains,
the patch of panelling broken by Cromwell's soldiers and never quite put
back together again. His eyes took in the Queen Anne chairs with their
original coverings, the gently faded prints in their frames – one of them
a minor Gainsborough – the Lowestoft teapots collected by his great-
grandmother and the small wind-up gramophone with an album containing
Mendelssohn's Violin Concerto.

The door opened and his mother came into the room. Sometimes she
reminded him of the large-faced clock in the corner. Always some sonorous
note or other booming out of her.

'It's still cold in here, Myles.'

'It will warm up.' Reluctantly, he offered her his chair by the fire, but
she refused it, saying that she had to have something higher that she could
heave herself out of.

'Anno Domini,' she said with a heavy sigh.

Aunt Hesther almost laughed, but got her face back under control and
said pleasantly, 'Well, this is nice. Eva tells me you have a cold, Myles.'

'A whopper.'

'It's the stress and strain,' she told him. 'You're dog tired. We all are.'

'Dare say you're right.' By the way he kept his head in *The Field*, she
knew he didn't want to discuss the matter.

The fire was burning brightly now, the crackling of the flames making
the afternoon suddenly seem more cheerful. Hesther said, 'You must be
pleased with Daphne's news.'

'Certainly,' the major said. 'She's a good girl.' And Bos was a good
sort of fellow. An honest fellow. The sort you'd want to have as your
son-in-law. Daphne would be all right with him. He sat staring at a
picture of a dead hare and trying to chart how many minutes it would
be before he could switch on the radio for the weather forecast. One
of the proofs of peace was that the forecasts had been restored and
Myles wouldn't dream of missing one. There was something comforting
about breaking one's day up into predetermined sections. The eight
o'clock, the twelve o'clock, the three o'clock. Did everyone feel that
way? That you could detach yourself? Detach from yourself? Push the
nervy stuff away while you listened to the clear, reassuring tones of

the BBC chant about Dogger, Fisher, Bight . . . Humber and Heligoland. This morning, for instance, bright intervals had been promised. Hadn't materialized yet, but the mere promise of them made one feel more hopeful.

The door opened again and Charlie Garland walked in. Gin's Bloomsbury young man, her blue-eyed all-provider. He had his notebook in his hand. The major sighed. That spelled trouble.

Garland threw a charming smile at the three of them. 'I . . . um . . . wondered if I might have a word.'

Evalina said, 'Certainly not. It's the Sabbath.'

'It will only take a moment.' He sounded intelligent, respectful, but quite unshiftable. 'It's just that we ought to discuss the question of finding staff.'

'Staff?' Evalina's fingers stopped ferreting around in her bag. Her eyes went from Garland to Myles, shrewdly.

'If we're to open next year, we shall need to recruit an experienced housekeeper and people to scrub and clean.'

'Servants,' Evalina said, 'are a distant memory, young man.'

'There are always village ladies . . .'

'No one these days wants to do an honest day's work.'

'Don't suppose it would be possible to take on a chauffeur?' Myles asked. 'Only I bumped into a young fellow who seemed the right sort. As a matter of fact, I jumped the gun and engaged him for a trial period. He's very capable.'

'I don't care for his attitude,' Evalina said. 'I preferred Fishleigh.'

'Well, Fishleigh's on sick leave with his sister and young Trewarden would be a sight more use. Gets it from his mother . . . Margaret. Now there's a woman I wouldn't mind employing.'

Garland looked thoughtful. 'A chauffeur wouldn't be my immediate concern.'

'But if he doubled up as handyman and steward?'

Garland said, 'I'll put their names on my list of possibles.'

'Possibles?' Gin had slipped into the room unnoticed. She was wearing a flowered frock Myles hadn't seen before and her amber beads. Her eyes, though smiling, looked like blue stones.

Garland filled her in.

'Staff?' she said. 'Where on earth are they going to come from?'

'We generally manage to find them locally.'

'Yes, very good, any more silly stories while you're at it?' Her expression was entirely disbelieving.

'We may be able to pull a rabbit or two out of the hat,' Garland said. He was standing there in his beautiful suit, admiring the Lowestoft.

'You mean pull strings?'

'Let's just say we have . . . contacts.'

'And who would pay these people, supposing you were lucky enough to find them?' Evalina demanded.

'The Trust, of course.'

'I thought you hadn't a bean to your name.'

'We have money for the essentials. It would be impossible to get the place straight with only Tilley at our disposal.'

Virginia said, 'I hear you unearthed more tapestries from the attics.'

'Three,' Garland told her. 'All quite rare but quite filthy. Tomorrow, if you don't mind, we have to start shifting and sorting furniture. I was hoping you'd be on hand to make sure we don't eliminate anything particularly dear to you.'

'Eliminate?' Evalina jerked her head like an old war horse.

'Our craftsmen will rescue what they can, of course, and we shall do our level best to keep the house's original character, but I'm afraid there will have to be a clear-out of surplus effects.'

Silence, in which the ticking of the clock seemed to go on forever.

'What do you mean? Clear-out?' Evalina asked.

'Well, quite often we have a sale . . .'

More silence.

Myles said, 'Here? In the house?' One finger rubbed away at his right temple.

'We sometimes hold them in the grounds. Best place, really. Then we can spread the stuff around the lawns and people can . . . well, you know . . . browse.'

'I shall be an anchorite,' Evalina said. 'I shall simply shut myself away until my time comes.'

Myles stood up. The warmth from the fire no longer made up for all the hoo-ha. He said, 'Must catch the forecast. Anyone mind? Call me when tea arrives.'

Never think further than the next meal, that was his secret. He sometimes felt he had dealt with six years at war by concentrating on one thing, one hour, one day at a time. Keep your head down, and perhaps everything would be tickety-boo again.

'Damn tea,' Gin said. 'What I need is a stiff drink.'

Minutes later, she found him in the library. He was tuning the dial on the radio, frowning at the thing with heavy concentration.

'Thought I'd see if you were all right,' she said in a moment of kindness.

'Oh, you know . . . pegging along.' He turned the dial a fraction to the left, then asked abruptly, 'Isn't there any way we can reverse this situation?'

'No, I don't think there is.' Sad for a moment, knowing how much pain he, too, was going through, she said, 'It's the only way, believe me.'

'I thought something might come along to stop it.'

'Such as?'

'God knows. A miracle?'

'Not too many of those around these days.'

'Right. Nothing for it, then. Stiff upper lip and get on with it.'

'I'm sorry, Myles.'

The phone rang. Draping her Afghan cardigan around her shoulders, Gin went to the desk to answer it.

'Trewenna One Seven One.'

'Virginia. Freda Boswell here. I meant to have spoken to you before, but you know how it is. I just wanted to say how delighted I am about Daphne and Noel.'

I very much doubt it, but we'll go along with the fiction.

Gin said, 'Yes. They seem very happy. We're delighted, too.'

'Have you any idea when the wedding will be? Noel says they haven't made any decision as yet.'

'Haven't a clue, I'm afraid, but I don't suppose they'll hang about.'

A silence at the other end. Gin imagined Freda's eyes, wide with horror. Oh, dear, she thought, now you've upset her. Isn't that just too bad.

'Look, I've got to go,' she said. 'Someone here. I'll call you if I hear anything. Goodbye.'

Myles was listening to the forecast, making a solitude for himself where no one could get at him. Squally showers, the announcer was saying with enormous solemnity. Clear later.

I hope so, Gin told herself. Oh, God, I hope so.

Lizzah, dead for the last year, now buzzed with activity. Charlie and Virginia spent days weeding out surplus furniture from the state rooms to make space for the public to pass through. After that, they tackled the rooms upstairs that were over-brimming with stuff that was never likely to be used. Half of the set of twenty-four chairs in the salon were found to be reproductions. Bundles of Civil War tracts found in trunks under the upper seaward windows were so hopelessly mouldy and riddled with silverfish that Tilley had to make a bonfire of them in the kitchen garden. Innumerable bedsteads of wood, iron and brass were unearthed in innumerable bedrooms. Suits of armour, ebony cabinets, flowered washstands, Regency chests were noted down on the sheaf of paper they lugged around with them, and painstakingly labelled. They developed a system: pink labels for the stuff to be moved to the stables for storage until sale day; white for the items to go on loan to other more sparsely furnished Trust houses.

'Don't worry,' Charlie told Gin towards the end of the operation when they stopped for a makeshift picnic lunch in one of the still rooms in the extensive servants' quarters. 'We won't lose sight of them. They'll be listed as having come from Lizzah.'

Gin said, 'Some of the chairs in the drawing room are a sight.'

'The needlework sofa that your dog keeps nibbling? We tend not to recover them unless they're irretrievably threadbare. But, as I said, we'll need a needlewoman to help re-back the curtains and hangings. Had any thoughts on that?'

'There's a girl called Daisy Jewell. Her mother was a needlewoman and Daisy's quite skilled. It seems to me she's exactly what you asked for.'

Charlie helped himself to one of Tilley's pasties. 'Splendid. We'll have her over for a chat. I've arranged for a chap to come and sort through the books, by the way. There's one he'll find very exciting. An Erasmus. Can't swear to it, but it's possibly illustrated by Holbein.'

He leaned his back against the oak-grained door.

'I wondered if you could broach a tricky subject with the major for me. Might come better from you. The Trust takes a risk in committing itself to guardianship of valuable items of furniture that are still, after all, your property. As tenant-for-life, your husband can't exactly give these things to us, so all we can do is suggest he might persuade his new heir to give an informal undertaking to do so. Would that be feasible, do you think?'

'No point in dealing with the new heir,' Virginia said. 'The person you'll have to win over will be his wife.'

Agnes Bolitho fell on the news of impending job interviews up at the manor like a starving dog on a bone. Agnes had heard there would be hundreds of positions on offer. She knew for a fact that they were looking for a French cook, and that a wing commander with royal connections would be vetting every single applicant, even the dailies for the rough work.

'Agnes has heard that the wing commander is very well-thought-of at the Air Ministry,' Edie Medland told her sister. 'Apparently he has the use of an apartment at Buckingham Palace.'

'Agnes's mouth,' Mabel said, 'is a damned sight bigger than her brain.'

'Mabel!'

'I'd muzzle her,' Mabel said grimly.

They were spring cleaning – taking down the cardboard from the grate in the front bedroom, removing the old bag stuffed with rags that someone had pushed up it to keep the draught out and boarding it all up with three-ply wood that Samuel Trewarden had procured for them from an unnamed source.

'I don't know what you've got against Agnes,' Edie said with dignity. 'She speaks very well of you.'

'To my face,' Mabel said. 'Hand me that hammer. And put the kettle on before I get into an even worse temper.'

Edie took herself off down the stairs, like a nun scuttling away from pirates.

Nipper Trewarden was perhaps the only person in Trewenna not to care tuppence whether there were openings up at the manor or not. That was because Nipper had made a vow never to bow his head to authority again. He would never go hungry again, either. During the three years, six months and two days that he'd been beaten and half starved by the Japs, he had sworn to himself that if he ever got out, he would bloody well run his world according to his own rules.

So to hell with the Labour Exchange, Nipper thought, as he turned the car with the brand-new set of L-plates into Chapel Lane. And to hell with the bobbies and the risks involved in what his mother called profiteering. He'd been all but dead when they found him in the camp. It seemed a miracle, even now, that he could get his legs out of bed and make them walk. But he had come through it. And they bloody owe me, he told himself, swinging the wheel so that he could pull in by the village pump.

It was a quiet day with a smell of spring in the air. He turned the engine off and sat waiting for Denny Aunger to turn up. On this April morning, the indignities he had suffered in the camp seemed all but inconceivable. He remembered the time those monsters had bound him like a chicken and left him in the sun for hours and hours. The mouthfuls of excrement they had forced him to eat. The three-tailed whip. The tree with the harness . . .

Every night in the small hours, the feeling of absolute helplessness came back to him. He wanted to tell somebody. Anybody. But he hadn't been able to breathe a word to a soul. Not even Cis. Least of all his gentle Cis. It would make her weep. Hurt her too much.

Gazing at the pink valerian coming into flower on the granite wall, Nipper told himself he had to concentrate instead on bringing enough money in to keep the baby that Cis was now expecting. Then perhaps, given time, the hellish stuff would fade.

Nipper closed his eyes. A baby. A kiddie growing up in this quiet spot where rooks circled and seagulls wheeled. A child that you wouldn't be able to prevent yourself from getting attached to or from worrying about. He asked himself how he felt about that.

No answer.

The dog gave a yip from the back seat. He had spotted Denny's lanky figure coming up the road.

'All right, boy?' Denny came round to the driver's door and waited for Nipper to slide across to the passenger seat. Then he climbed in and slammed the door behind him.

'Right, squire,' Denny said. 'Where we off to?'

Nipper glanced at his watch. 'Tell you when we get there.'

There were times when he let his old mate into his confidence on black market matters, but as the dog had more chance of understanding what was going on than Denny, it seemed easier to fudge the issue.

Denny pulled on the starter and got the engine humming. He let the handbrake off, they jumped downhill a yard or so and skidded to a halt.

'Try again.' Nipper said. Only the twitch at the corner of his jaw showed that he had turned a hair. It was going to be a long morning.

On the second Friday in May, the major's nephew and new heir, Arthur Jago, called with his wife, Julia. It was a fine morning, all bright light and high skies and gorse and blackthorn in blossom, but in the morning-room, there was a chill in the air.

'I don't see why,' Julia said, 'Arthur should have to sign the contents over.'

Evalina, sitting in a patch of yellow sunshine, was in a quandary. Half of her wanted to agree with Julia, but she disliked the woman intensely – her pushiness, her sharp and thin and querulous speaking voice, the bony, high ridge on her nose – and so she glared back at her and said, 'Well, strictly speaking, of course, he can't. He doesn't yet own anything in this house, thank God.'

'Neither does Uncle Myles,' Julia said, 'from what one hears.'

Arthur's attention seemed to have been caught by the pear blossom outside the window. Julia often embarrassed him, but he felt far too inadequate to crack her over the knuckles for it.

'Of course,' said Julia, raising her eyebrows, 'all we know is what we've been told by outsiders. We would have appreciated it if someone had put us in the picture earlier.'

'None of your business,' Evalina said.

'Of course it's our business. The estate is settled on Arthur—'

'Well, he won't inherit. The estate will now be vested in The National Trust.' Evalina, cutting off her nose to spite her face, shot a glance at Myles. He was tapping his fingers on the arm of the chair, as if listening to some tune inside his head.

'We'll see about that,' Julia said. 'You can't bypass the rightful heir.'

Arthur transferred his gaze to the dog.

Pointedly, Virginia said, 'The rightful heir is not your husband.'

Julia rose to her feet. 'We'll see about that. Arthur – we're leaving.' He cleared his throat. She said, 'Don't waste your time being polite. It will be wasted on them.' Arthur hesitated, then eased himself out of the chair. 'You will be hearing, in due time, from our solicitors,' Julia said, viciously doing up the buttons of her jacket. The dog ambled over and sniffed at her. She said, 'Get away from me. You smell.'

Julia swept out, leaving her husband to follow her. When the door closed behind them, there was the clink of a spoon against a teacup. 'If Arthur were not married to that shrew,' Evalina said, 'I would be quite prepared to believe he was one of those nancy boys.'

Julia had stopped on her way out to make a foray into the drawing-room. With the eyes of a cat, she was prowling. Her hand snapped out. She tucked something into her pocket. Something bright and silver.

'Julia!' In the doorway, behind her, Arthur was shocked.

Her hand went out again. This time it was a snuffbox that went into her pocket along with a Staffordshire figure.

'I don't care,' she said. 'These Trust people will skim off the best stuff and we shall have nothing.'

'But—'

'But nothing,' Julia said grimly.

When the major got the go-ahead to take Jack on permanently, he suggested a move to the old head gardener's cottage on the edge of the park. 'On the spot, so to speak. More convenient.'

Lil didn't find it more convenient. She grumbled like mad. The rooms weren't big enough, the furniture wouldn't fit, the poky, diamond-paned windows were hell to clean (not that she ever did) and, worst of all, there wasn't a single neighbour to talk to.

A week after they had moved in, Jack heard her heels clacking down the stairs. (She didn't like *them* either. Too narrow, too steep, a bloody death trap.) She negotiated the last bend while powdering her nose from a gold compact. Her legs were a deep golden bronze from sunbathing on the salon roof in her brassiere and shorts in the lunch hour, her hair was up in a bang, Rita Heyworth style, and her décolletage was fearless.

Jack said, 'You're late this morning.'

'I told Dora I'd be in by eleven.' She was fiddling with her hair. The red dye had mostly washed out. She was now brightening it for the summer with Hiltone. 'I'm the boss. I can go in whenever it suits me.'

He sat in the sun-filled room watching her reach to the top cupboard and hitch out a bottle of Camp coffee. He told himself, it beats me how she got that business up and running. She's hopeless with money. But then, he thought, she lights up in company. She can make a cat laugh provided she's in the right mood.

'Fancy a coffee?' she asked.

'I don't want that muck.'

She said, 'Ooooh. Fussy!' — but in a perky, expansive sort of way. This hot weather improved her temper. He watched as she filled the kettle and stuck it on the primus stove. Through the open door, the garden was a shimmer of faintly buzzing stillness. An American comic with lurid cartoons lay on the table beside a half-full can of milk.

He flicked it open. **PAGAN LEE – GANGSTER'S MOLL,** it said. **A GOOD GAL GONE BAD**. 'Where does he get this rubbish?'

Lil was spooning treacly liquid coffee into her cup. 'God knows. Probably swapped it for film star postcards at school.'

'Miss Petherick would tan their hides if she caught them.'

'Miss Petherick's eyes are nowhere near as sharp as they used to be.' Fag in hand, Lil waited for the kettle to start singing. 'Actually, I like a gangster film.'

'So I noticed.' He told her the major was to have a new housekeeper.

'I thought they were supposed to be on their uppers.' Lil poured boiling water into her cup. 'Con feels sorry for them because they lost their boy. I told her, they've got more than most by way of consolation. Con's too soft. That's how she finished up with two kids from two different fathers and the little one as black as your hat.'

She poured milk into the coffee and stirred it round with an apostle spoon that Jack's mother had brought back from a Sunday school outing.

'The oldest one's Fred's. She fell pregnant when he was home on his last leave.'

Fred Pearce – they had been at school with him – had copped it at Dunkirk.

'She had to give up her job in the typing pool at the munitions factory.'

'Poor old Con.'

Jack couldn't imagine the shy, skinny Con he had known at school struggling to bring up two kiddies on her own. 'And the second kid?'

'His father's a Yank. From Mississippi. She met him on the train on her way back from Okehampton. He was sitting next to her and he fell asleep and his head dropped on her shoulder. Con says she couldn't help it. Honest to God, Jack, I don't know what world she lives in, but it isn't the same as you and me.'

'Never was,' he said, remembering Con's daydreamer's gaze.

'She says he was ever such a nice boy.' Lil rolled her eyes. 'Not nice enough, I said, to write and ask if you've got enough money to feed his kid. I told her she should be getting half his pay as an unmarried wife. But will she get the authorities to track him down? Will she hell.'

She brought her coffee to the table and sat down next to him. 'Remember when you bet Fred he couldn't climb that lamp post and the copper stopped to ask what he was up to?'

'And he said he was trying to find out where the pub had gone.' Jack wanted to smile at the memory, but found he couldn't.

'Don't look so sad.' She rubbed her cheek against his shoulder.

Outside, a blackbird was whistling. Hay lay in swathes, the smell of it mildly flirtatious.

He said, 'It's a long time since anything felt right.'

'You worry too much,' she said, and then, as she cradled her cup in both her hands, 'So . . . what were you doing giving Daisy Jewell a lift?'

'Daisy?' He blinked.

'You didn't see me. I was on my bike. I thought, If the major finds out, there'll be hell to pay.'

'I came across her in the lane. She was late for an appointment with Mrs Jago.'

'You'll get yourself in trouble, picking up the local talent.'

Jack's hackles rose. 'Daisy's a nice girl. Natural.'

'In a minute, you're going to tell me she hasn't been around.'

'I don't think she has, actually.'

'If you believe that,' Lil said spitefully, 'you'll believe anything.'

'They're not all as tough as you,' he said. Then he said, 'They didn't all spend their war glamming themselves up to work in a salon.'

Lil drained her cup and slammed it on the table. She said, 'I'd rather work in a salon than heave dung for a living. You went up to The Barton looking for work. How many times have you been back there since?'

'I haven't.'

'Expect me to believe that?'

'It's the truth. I don't care if you believe it or not.'

She got up and rammed her chair under the table.

'All I said was that Daisy's a nice girl.'

'It wasn't *what* you said. It was the look in your eye when you said it.'

'Oh, for God's sake.'

'Don't look at me like that.'

'Like what?'

'Like I'm boring you to death. Like I'm someone you never met before—'

'If only—'

He shouldn't have said it. Too late. She picked up the cup and smashed it against the wall.

'Hello?' called a voice out in the porch. A sharp rap on the knocker. 'Hello? Anyone there?'

Jack walked out of the room and went to the door. Mabel Petherick stood in the porch. She wanted to enlist his help for the summer fête. The skittles, perhaps? Or the bowling alley? She hoped she hadn't come at an inconvenient moment.

'Why, Miss Petherick,' said Lil's voice, sweet as pie, from behind him. 'We were just talking about you.'

'Really?' Miss Petherick's eyes were still sharp enough to notice the scarlet patches on Lil's cheeks.

'I said to Jack, I'd love to coax you into the salon. We could fluff you up a bit. Do you a fancy new cut?'

Fixing her with a gull's eye, Miss Petherick declined the offer.

Ten

Jack Trewarden guided the Bentley down through May woods. High earthen hedges were splashed with bluebells. The lane curled and zigzagged, dropping ever deeper into the coombe.

Daphne said, 'You'll see the house in a moment, over the tops of the trees.'

She sat in the rear seat next to the elderly insurance expert. The old buffer had tired eyes in a pale face. He wore small wire spectacles, grey spats, patent leather shoes and kid gloves. His left hand gripped a stout, unfurled umbrella and a folded mackintosh lay in a neat square on his lap. He's too tall, Daph thought. His legs are all folded up like a deckchair.

'There. Now. See the purple roof?'

'I'm afraid I'm somewhat shortsighted.'

'You have to know where to look.'

'Quite.'

'There! Now. Slow down, Trewarden, would you?'

'No, really,' the insurance man said, 'there's no need.'

Passing over the hump-backed bridge at the very bottom, the Bentley gave a hiccup. Having been laid up since 1940, it was a trifle out of sorts.

Daphne shifted unobtrusively in her seat. Her blouse was stuck to her skin and her linen suit crushed and crumpled. It was too hot for the time of the year. One of those days when the weather caught you out. She couldn't wait to get home and change into something cooler. Rolling down her window, letting the smell of damp moss come flooding in, she asked herself if the trip up to Exeter had been worth the effort.

All that time spent in exclusive drapery shops fingering crêpe-de-chine and triple ninon and silk organza, dithering over underslips and satin shoes and Honiton lace and fending off fearfully affected saleswomen, she was coming home, at the end of it all, with the grand total of one good silk shirt.

What a waste of a glorious day!

And what was the point? That was what she had been asking herself all the way back. She didn't feel impatient with the idea of getting married; it wasn't that. The problem was all the fuss it entailed. I am not a pomp and ceremony person, Daph thought. What I'd really like is an unsmart wedding. A simple frock and a hat. The church, the rector, a burst of music and confetti and then off we would go, leaving them all behind to eat wedding cake and exchange gossip with the maiden aunts and curious cousins.

Trewarden steered the Bentley through the lodge gates. The back of his head was rather handsome, sunburned and rusty-haired under Fishleigh's peaked cap. It was his stiff and abrupt manner that she didn't care for. The offhandedness lurking at the back of his eyes when he opened the door for you. Fishleigh had been such a dear old thing. Not quick, not even terribly efficient if truth were told. But he had taught her how to bicycle on the gravelled forecourt, pretending not to notice her hurt dignity every time she landed up in the flower bed. '*Never you mind, Miss Daphne. You'll get the hang of it sooner or later.*'

Well, he was gone now to live with his sister in a cottage near Barnstaple and there was no point in feeling nostalgic. When Bos opened the Bentley door for her two minutes later and bent to kiss her on the cheek, she told herself that there were things to be said for the here-and-now.

'You're late.' His stolid, well-fed face radiated affection.

'Got stuck at Okehampton waiting for the other train to come through.'

'Never mind. You're here now.'

He was always dropping by to bring her flowers from his mother's garden or a few eggs from the farm or a book he wanted to share with her. At weekends, he had got into the habit of turning up to take her for a jaunt in his ten-horsepower little motor, all neat and shiny with its picnic basket on the back. First he would get the map out and uncrease it, then point out all the possible routes. Daph was always given the choice of two outings because, Bos said, these things had to be arranged for the enjoyment of all concerned. 'Boscastle would be topping, though,' he would say if she showed the slightest hesitation. 'We could tackle Beeny.' Once, sitting with him on the rug halfway up Rocky Valley, he had caught her hand and kissed it.

'You're all the world to me,' he had said in a low voice.

That was it. No more, thank God. He would never say anything to make you blush or feel embarrassed. He was that rare thing, a man who felt much, but behaved decently.

Now, she said, 'This is Mr Freeman. He's an insurance expert.'

'Jolly good,' said Bos. He stood with his wrists poking out of the sleeves of his Norfolk jacket while the insurance expert unfolded himself from the car. 'Wizard weather.'

Mr Freeman gave a dry smile and smoothed his hair, much of which, like his personality, had sadly departed.

These days, it seemed to Charlie that he was always humping around some terrible old piece of furniture that had been eaten away to nothing and had to be removed and treated before it disintegrated altogether. This afternoon, breathing hard and manhandling a Jacobean chest down one of the many staircases, he had almost been flattened when Trewarden's end had slipped and hit the wall with a fearful crash.

'Is everything all right?' Virginia Jago's voice asked from the landing.

'Well, my neck aches, my back is breaking and I may have fractured my little finger – but apart from that, everything's hunky-dory.'

From the top of the staircase came a sound that was almost a laugh. Mrs Jago stood dusting down her blue siren suit, which was covered with a fine layer of worm dust.

'The leg's dropped off,' she said. 'Leave it there. I'll collect it.' She waited until they had manoeuvred the chest round the turn of the stairs, then said, 'So this will go off to some old chap who will douse it in something absolutely foul to kill off the worm, and when it comes back it will smell to high heaven.'

'I'm afraid the whole house will smell to high heaven. We've got to douse the rest of the furniture with Benzine-Bentol as well.'

'We?' Virginia's blue eyes looked, Charlie thought, horror struck.

'Don't panic. There's another old chap I know – a retired craftsman from the V and A – who will come down and see to it.'

'Thank God.' Virginia had had visions of herself crawling around the place with a succession of smelly rags. She felt filthy enough at the moment and thought, suddenly and longingly, of a deep, hot bath; but that wasn't going to happen because the boiler was playing up again.

Also, Daisy Jewell was waiting downstairs . . .

After Charlie had inspected and been impressed by the work he'd asked Daisy to bring, he asked how much time she could spare if she were taken on.

'As much as is needed, I suppose.' She could fit her farm duties in between.

'Good. You seem very able. But I should warn you, it's not a job for the faint-hearted. You will have to learn a great deal in a very short time. Someone from the Royal School of Needlework will be in and out to set you off and keep an eye on everything.'

Daisy said nothing, but her eyes shone with anticipation.

'The most precious items will go to London to be restored.'

Thank God, Daisy thought.

'But the rest of it will keep you very busy. There are Jacobean bed hangings that will need renovating. Chairs and sofas to re-cover. Also the worst of the curtains will have to be replaced.'

Virginia Jago was gazing slantwise at her. 'Somehow,' she said, 'I expected you to look daunted.'

'Mother always said that if you're doing something you love, it doesn't feel like work. I love sewing. The more you throw at me, the better I'll like it.'

Mrs Jago said, 'You may regret that you said that.' She fiddled with one of her earrings. Then she said, 'I have no idea what the Trust will be able to pay you. Mr Garland sees to all that.'

I'd do it for the fun of it, Daisy thought, admiring the cut of her prospective employer's pleated grey crêpe-de-chine trousers. Although she had to admit that the money would come in handy. She wanted to ask what was going to happen about The Barton, but there were dark shadows under the older woman's eyes and her mouth was set hard, so maybe it wasn't the time.

I'll tackle her, Daisy told herself, when she's in a better frame of mind.

Charlie and Trewarden heaved the chest down two more staircases and out into the courtyard where it seemed to stand blinking in the sudden sunlight. Charlie stood blinking, too. He said, 'Another wonderful day!' The air was sweet with a shifting mixture of scents: plum and pear and apple blossom, lilac and wallflowers. He wondered why he wasn't skiving off to sit under a tree with a picnic and a bottle of bubbly and a pretty girl to share it with. Biddy? Not sure. Biddy, with her thick black stockings, cropped hair and weirdo make-up, was fun, but she didn't do pastoral. Oh, she was always going on about the oppressed peasants and how something had to be done to improve their lot, but she wouldn't be seen dead actually talking to one on his humble doorstep. No, Biddy was more at home in town delivering leaflets about Keir Hardie and the more-cake-and-jam future you would get under the Communist Party

Not Biddy, then.

So . . . who?

His mind went instinctively to the rector's daughter. He imagined her sitting in a sea of cow parsley. 'Oh, come on!' he told himself. 'She's another rattling smartyboots. *Yes, but intriguing.* A smartyboots with a face to die for.

She hadn't been so lively when he had left her on the platform at Paddington. She'd been tired and dispirited because her Pole hadn't turned up to meet her as promised.

'He'll be stuck in the tube,' Charlie had said. 'Or in a traffic jam.'

'I know. It's just that I've been longing to see him. He's never on time. Doesn't even own a watch. But I thought today—'

Heart-shaped leaves shook themselves on the lilac tree over the court-yard wall. She had been upset, remembered Charlie, though she tried to stay aloof and nonchalant. There had been desperation at the back of her eyes.

The sun burned warm on Daphne's back. She had been working for almost two hours, but bracken and weeds still flourished all around her. She straightened up and wedged a hand on to her aching back. She quite liked pulling up weeds but you could have too much of a good thing. The handle had snapped off her hand fork and she had just torn her thumb on a bramble that had wrapped itself round the roots of the untended fig tree.

Oh, rats! she thought, fishing a handkerchief from the pocket of her gardening dungarees to wipe the blood away. It would stop her playing the Toccata in D Minor in church on Sunday. Her thoughts skipped from Bach to the Beethoven discs she had bought in a second-hand shop in the Cathedral Close. Shouldn't have done it, she told herself. At least, not with the money Pa had donated for wedding finery – even if that nice old man *did* let her have them at a special price. The temptation had been too much. She would pretend, if anyone asked, that she had borrowed them from the rectory.

No, that would never do. Can't tell fibs about a gentleman of the cloth.

A voice said, 'There you are!'

Daph came out of her thoughts and saw her mother on the terrace. She thought, Oh, God, here comes the Inquisition.

For the moment, however, Mother's face wore an expression of studied affability. 'I forgot to ask what you bought yesterday. I suppose it's no wonder with all this going on around us. Look at me! I had a wash, dusted myself with bath powder, put on a clean frock and the workmen chose that moment to start hammering on the roof. So now my hair is full of dust again.'

Daph shoved a hand through her own thick, bright curls. 'I hope the ceilings stand up to it.'

'Quite. So what did you buy in Exeter?'

'Oh . . . this and that.'

'This and what exactly?'

Daph gazed at a clump of tulips under the fig tree. Pale, pointed petals flopped open to the sun.

'A shirt.'

'A shirt?'

'Yes. Rather a good one. White silk. Useful for all occasions.'

'Is that all?'

'There wasn't much else,' Daph said defensively. 'Nothing I liked. I did try. It's just that I don't know where I am with finery.'

'I should have gone with you.' There was exasperation in her mother's voice.

'Actually, I don't much like weddings,' Daph said. 'I like to watch them. I like playing the organ at them. But I never really imagined myself taking part.'

'What are we going to do with you?' Virginia spoke despairingly. 'Look – you'd better get on with it. Time slips by and finding what you want is a nightmare, what with the coupons and the shortages.'

'I'll go up to London. Marina's good at clothes.'

'Marina?'

'Marina Nicolson. The Marina I was at school with. She came to stay once. We went swimming at Bude and she nearly drowned.'

'The girl who jumped in the deep end when she couldn't swim?'

Which just about sums Marina up, Daph thought. The breeze brought a sour whiff of currant bushes.

'Romily might like to help.'

'Romy's tied up with her Pole. The officer she got herself engaged to. He's staying at the rectory. She brought him down to meet her parents.'

'Come and play Ping-Pong,' Penny said.

'Can't,' Daph told her. 'I'm busy.'

'Gardening's stupid.' Penny wore her usual skimpy plaid skirt topped off with a hand-knitted sleeveless sweater. She poked at the pile of weeds with the toe of her shoe. 'They'll only grow again.'

'Not immediately. You could stir yourself and help.'

'Not likely.'

'Fresh air and hard work are good for you.'

'Who said?' Penny's wire-rimmed spectacles were perched crookedly on her nose.

'The cat.' Daph's arms were coming out in freckles. She hated them. 'When are you going back to school?'

'Next week. It's much more interesting here. I love it when things are happening. That insurance expert hit his head on the beam in the rocking horse attic. It was very funny. He wanted to yell at me.'

He's not the only one, Daph thought.

'Why don't tulips smell,' Penny asked, 'like daffodils and bluebells?'

'No idea.' Daph tugged at a dandelion clump, but it snapped off with the milky root still in the ground.

'Am I annoying you? I'll leave you alone if you give me just one game of Ping-Pong.'

Daph stuck what remained of her fork into the dandelion root and said, 'Clear off before I lose my rag, there's a good girl.'

By the steps, there was a sage bush covered in long, mouse-pink buds. It would have to come out. Not grand enough for the front terrace, Mother would say.

I could leave it in, of course, and argue the point . . .

She turned and saw the architect, Tom Fermoy, crossing the grass towards her. He was in his shirt sleeves, his hair all wavy and a bit wild.

Daph said, 'Hello. We weren't expecting you until next week.'

'The sun was shining. Thought I'd get out of London. You've taken on something here.'

'Don't I know it.'

He said, 'By the time you get all round, you'll have to start again.' When he smiled, his eyes creased at the corners. 'Be sure and yank out that guelder rose. The big-branched thing at the top of the steps. The leaves and berries are poisonous.'

'Really?'

'The birds must have brought it in from the woods.'

Pen said, 'How poisonous? Would I die if I touched it?'

'Not sure, but I wouldn't try if I were you.'

Pen thought it over, frowning hard.

'Want to hear a garden joke?' he asked.

'Go on.'

'What did the Egyptian find at the bottom of his garden?'

'I don't know,' Pen said.

'Pharaohs.'

'I don't get it.'

'There are pharaohs at the bottom of my garden . . .'

'That's rubbish!'

'Pen!' Daph glared at her.

'Well, it is.'

Tom Fermoy said, 'There's some grapefruit squash in my car if you'd like some.'

'Grapefruit squash?' Pen's eyes lit up.

'You'll have to fetch it, though. Oh, and we'll need a jug of water and some glasses.'

Pen bounded off.

'You're a marvel,' Daph said. 'She was driving me up the wall.'

'I've got younger sisters of my own.'

How many?'

'Three.'

'Good gracious!' Her eyes were very round and large and green. 'Where did you learn about guelder roses?'

'My mother loves her garden. She wears this old straw hat,' he said, 'with a collapsible brim and a pair of canvas shoes you wouldn't be seen dead in.' He stood looking at her with that slaty grey concentration. 'This is the most wonderful old place. We're so lucky to have found it.'

'Not sure my pa would agree.'

'He'll come round when he sees it back together.'

'I hope so.'

Standing on the edge of the terrace, they gazed out at may blossom and pink hawthorn blowing and growing, at dog daisies and charlock and, beyond the park, the gold of gorse.

Daph said, 'I'm afraid the army left rather a mess.'

'We'll get that straight. The NAAFI hut's coming down next week.'

'Where does your mother live?' she asked.

'Sussex.'

'Do you see her much? I missed Pa so much during the war. Couldn't wait to have him home again, but . . .'

He didn't say anything. He just waited.

'He's not himself at the moment. He's taken himself off somewhere. In his head, I mean.' She shoved her hands in her trouser pockets and watched the clouds blowing in a summery wind.

Fermoy said, 'A defence mechanism. He'll come out of it.'

He smiled down at her. Sincere, Daph thought, and intelligent. She liked his friendly mouth and direct gaze.

'I suppose so.'

'Funny things, parents,' he said. 'For a while, you think they know everything and then it suddenly changes. You're looking after them instead of them looking after you.'

'You wouldn't dare look after my mother,' Daph said.

'No?'

'No.'

But Pa was another matter altogether. If only there were some way to get through to him. Daph looked at her hands, all grimy with soil. The diamond in her ring caught the sun; there was a fleck of dirt in it. Next time she would be sensible and take it off.

After lunch, she sat in her bedroom and asked herself what, if anything, she should do with her afternoon. There seemed to be three alternatives. She could stretch out in a hammock and bury herself in *Woman's Own*. She could do something more useful, like visiting the Lodge family to see if they had everything they needed for the children. Or she could do what she really wanted, which was to call at the rectory to inspect Romy's Pole.

Lazing in the hammock was not a serious option. There were too many workmen hammering on the roof and anyway, she wasn't in the mood for reading.

It had better be the Lodge family.

But the thought of doing nothing but Good Works on such a summery afternoon made her feel restless. 'What if,' she said, 'you drop in on the Lodge family on your way to the Rectory?

Yes, that would do.

She glanced at her wristwatch. If she wanted to kill two birds with one stone, she would have to get a move on. She got her mirror and powder compact out of her bag. Not that it mattered what she looked like – a dab of powder would do.

Peering at herself in the dressing table mirror, she caught a reflected movement from the garden below her window. Charlie Garland was loading a couple of paintings and a small footstool into the dicky of his car. Just about anything could disappear, she thought idly. Who would know? Not that she didn't trust Charlie. He reminded her of those boy-next-door movie stars from the wartime years, with that charming face of his that could do comic as well as the deeper stuff.

The little table with the squash jug was still out there by the fig tree. But Tom Fermoy's green Riley had gone. She pulled a linen frock over her head and tweaked it so as to slide it over her hips. She smoothed the skirt and wondered what he must have thought of her in those terrible old dungarees.

Not that it mattered. Well, only a tiny bit.

She fastened the four big mother-of-pearl buttons on the bodice and stood staring down at her silk-stockinged toes. The house seemed dark after the brightness of the garden. The tree at the window looked unnaturally green, like painted scenery, and the sky wildly blue.

She wondered if Tom was gone for good. Again, not that it mattered. Only she had enjoyed his company. He made me laugh, she thought, but it wasn't only that. It was his enthusiasm. He was one of those people who would never be bored. Or boring. She shoved her toes into her favourite two-tone shoes. He went to concerts. Had heard Pablo Casals play *La Sardana*.

'Absolutely stunning. I can't tell you,' he had said.

But he had gone ahead and described it anyway. They had sat on the bank while Pen made a pig of herself with the grapefruit squash and, stretched out with his head propped on one elbow, he had told her about the hushed wartime audience, the ensemble of cellos and the baker's van the great man had loaded his instrument into afterwards.

'That was in France. The unoccupied zone,' he had told her. 'I was so lucky to have been in the right place at the right time.'

She had liked him immediately. His warmth and enthusiasm. She remembered his crisp, white shirt. The smile he had thrown her at the end when he was walking away, with Pen tagging along behind him in the hope that he would offer her a lift down to the village. A summer moment, she thought, can fix itself in your mind's eye.

But anyway. She must clear away the grapefruit jug and the glasses. And slip off out before Pen wanted to come too . . .

She walked the two miles to the village. Four bread and jammy children greeted her in the doorway of Smart's Cottage, which Pa had thought more suitable than the Lodge. They looked healthier and more energetic than when she had last visited. I'd like children, she thought, handing the tallest child the bag of rhubarb she had brought with her. Four or five at least.

Bos would approve. She imagined him teaching them all to ride and telling them stories about what he did as a boy. Only last week he had told her how, setting off for his first term at Blundell's, he had clutched in his pocket, for comfort, his favourite book: *Aesop's Fables*. In her memory, she heard his voice say, 'I liked the miller and his son carrying the donkey over the bridge. Made me laugh. And none of the stories went on too long.' She smiled for a moment, imagining him reading bedtime stories.

Though the picture she was framing in her head stayed the tiniest bit misty. She supposed it wouldn't get sharp and real until she was married to him and living at Trebartha.

The children's mother and granny were sitting together on the stairs, where they appeared to be sharing a cigarette.

'Good afternoon,' Daph said. 'I brought you some freshly picked rhubarb.'

This didn't make much of an impression.

'It'll make a nice pudding for the children,' Daph said brightly.

The children had had a bite already. The oldest boy was spitting it out. 'Sour!' he said.

'It will need sweetening. With honey. The Miss Pethericks at Apple Tree would sell you some. Has your husband found work?'

'On the buses.' The young woman on the stairs took a moody puff.

'Jolly good.' Daph smiled encouragingly. The baby she had been so worried about beamed at her from his pram and blew a bubble shaped like a barrage balloon, which burst suddenly, turning into a dribble on either side of his pointed chin.

Romy's Pole turned out to be a terrifyingly handsome young man in a black overcoat with dark hair and a piercing gaze. Good-looking men made Daph uneasy. 'Hello,' she said, holding out her hand to him and drawing it back again when he ignored it.

'Jan wants to be an artist,' Romy said.

'*Is* an artist,' the Pole insisted.

'Sorry, darling. He *is* an artist. We met at a party over sausages and cheese straws,' Romy went on. 'One minute we were all droning on about margarine coupons and shortages and postings and it was as dull as ditch-water and I was thinking I'd go home early, and the next, Jan was asking me to dance and the room was buzzing. He's a party animal.'

'Really?' Daph said. If anything, the young man seemed cool and distant. He had barely glanced at her before taking his attention back to the view from the drawing-room window.

'He did a wonderful portrait of me. It's called "Woman Talking". It's all spikes and dashes and there's actually three of me. Terribly clever. Like a Picasso. I wanted to keep it, but he's going to sell it for a lot of money. It's in his flat in London. He has agents coming round all the time. And dealers. Hasn't sold any yet. But he will, I'm sure.'

'Is hot in here,' Jan said, flipping his hair back and stalking dramatic-ally out.

'Poor dear. He feels it all so much. Having no money, nothing but his enormous talent. I'm sorry I haven't been around to see you, but Jan . . . well, to tell the truth, he can be difficult. It doesn't help that Mummy glares at him as if he's about to rob the poor-box.'

'Oh, dear.' Daph could easily imagine that spikes and dashes wouldn't be Pearl Matheson's line.

'She wants to know what we're going to live on. And I said it hardly matters. Then she said, why couldn't I take a leaf out of Daphne's book and marry someone rich and reliable, and I said I couldn't bear to, and she said if I married Jan, Daddy would cut me off without a bean, which, considering he hasn't got a bean anyway is pretty ridiculous. You've got a funny look on your face. You don't like him either.'

'We've only just met.'

'He's not usually so abrupt. Honestly. He doesn't know what to do with himself out in the sticks.'

'He could paint,' Daph murmured.

'No. He couldn't. Skies and trees and cottages are not his thing.'

'Ah.'

'He says they're tedious. And then I have to stop him from trying to creep into my room in the middle of the night. When I told him we couldn't . . . not here . . . it would upset Daddy, he went all . . .'

Romy looked at Daph as if she didn't know whether to finish the sentence or not. As if, for one moment, she was at the end of her tether.

But that couldn't be right, because Romy had always been utterly confident of her power over men. She could wrap them round her little finger. All men. Ever since she had learned to flutter her improbably long eyelashes.

Daph wandered over to the window seat. The Pole was sitting in the garden with his back against the mowing machine. She took in his surly expression, the sullen pose, the clever fingers flicking matchsticks at the sundial and she thought, *I wouldn't live with you if you paid me.* Damn the good looks, give me Bos any day. Plain but comfortable, like a good country overcoat.

But she kept her mouth shut and let Romy ramble on. 'We went to a beer garden in Holsworthy last night.'

'A beer garden? In Holsworthy?'

'Yes, I know, it doesn't seem likely, but they've done it up with tables and music. Actually, it wasn't such a bad evening. I got as whizzed as a newt on Pernod.'

Daph said, 'When are you going back to London? Only I thought we might go wedding shopping—'

'Daphne! How lovely! We haven't seen you in ages.' Pearl Matheson had appeared, looking very Pearlish in a blue frock that matched the waterlily tiles in the fireplace. Selecting a chair, she dropped into it and sat drumming her fingers on her lap. 'Wedding shopping. How delightful. But you mustn't attempt it in this heat. My mother-in-law once fainted on the top deck of an omnibus. That was in August, of course, but the summers are getting hotter. She had her little dog with her – a poodle – and he ran off. He was found two weeks later in the wilds of Hammersmith.'

Daph said, 'That was lucky.'

'She went by bus because she hated travelling underground and I don't blame her. It's the escalators. I hate the point where you have to stagger off. And the wind that comes round the corners and blows your hat off.'

'I rather like that bit,' Daph said. 'The warm wind.'

'The last time I travelled on the tube, it was packed with servicemen. And their rifles and gas masks and tin hats and haversacks entirely blocked the stairways. My dear, I swore I would never attempt such a thing again! I suppose you've met our friend from the east?'

'Mother – I'm warning you!'

'There's no need to use that tone on me, Romily.'

'I'm just off,' someone said.

The rector, tall and vague in his black cassock, was hovering in the doorway. In his steady, friendly voice, he added, 'Diocesan meeting. Might be late back. Apologies, Daphne. Stay for dinner. Romily will like that.'

He didn't say why, or stay to keep the peace between his wife and daughter. He went off at a lope, through the hall, past the big gong and out into the sunlight.

Eleven

The rector took the short-cut through the churchyard, past headstones lapped in long grass. He had escaped before there was another blow-up between his wife and his daughter, though if truth were told, when Romily left home to join the WAAF, he had almost missed the rows, along with her bohemian disorder and offbeat view of the world. 'Church vestments aren't rationed,' she had said to him one day on the telephone. 'If you were to order an extra surplice, I could cut it up to make a dance frock.'

The thought of losing her completely – watching her leave the rectory for good with a new husband – filled him with the most enormous sadness. But perhaps it wouldn't happen for a while. Perhaps she would grow out of the idea. Romily liked a jaunt, there had always been a streak of adventurousness in her nature, but she didn't always stick with things. That was the hope that he was clinging to, anyway.

Dear God, he had prayed last night, let me not feel so utterly weary when I look at this young man she has brought home with her . . . this Jan Whatever-his-name-is. Let me not be prejudiced against him because he has no manners and because his egotism makes me want to boot him out of the front door. Every man has in him something of God, but in my day young men showed some respect to their elders. If I have to force myself to listen one more time to his diatribes about Cubism and Futurism and multiple viewpoints and the analytic phase . . . I'm sorry, Lord, this is wrong of me, but he is nowhere near good enough for my beautiful daughter.

The rector loped on through the churchyard and out through the wicket gate at the back. All down Fiddle Lane lacy branches were coming into leaf. Clarrie Badcock had tied up her sweet peas with binder twine. He took a right turn and went on at a fast clip up Church Street to call on Miss Petherick.

She ushered him into the front room, where the grandfather clock was wheezing in preparation for its half-hourly chime. 'I must apologize for the state of the windows,' she said, waving him into a chintzy chair under a framed picture of a sour-looking Queen Victoria. 'The old curtains were threadbare and, as we didn't have enough coupons for new, we eked them out with panels of cheap cotton, which turned out not to match.'

She was wearing a brown stockinette frock that adorned her bosom with pin-tucks. The room smelled of methylated spirits and furniture polish.

'But it's very nice to be able to draw them back as far as they can go,' Mabel said. 'I was sick and tired of the blackouts. So . . . what can I do for you, rector?'

'The summer fête,' he said. 'Difficult, this, but I was wondering about the possibility of holding it up at Lizzah, as we used to do before the war.'

'Have you asked the major?'

'Didn't like to. To tell the truth, I wasn't sure if he would be able to give his permission.'

'Why in heaven's name not?' Mabel's voice was sharp and snappy.

'Well . . .'

'Who's been telling you the major's no longer in charge? He may be moving to private quarters in the west wing, but he's not leaving. There's no reason why we should go to anyone else for permission.'

Miss Petherick picked up a copy of *The Ladies' Knitting Journal* and slapped it down again.

'I thought the Trust—'

'The Trust!' said Mabel. 'Fiddle, faddle!'

The rector thought, I've ruffled her feathers. 'Well, perhaps you could contact the major and have a discreet word.' Then he took refuge in the traditional English pastime of discussing the weather. 'I do hope we get a fine day. People spend more if the sun's shining and there are some big bills coming in for the repairs to the vestry roof. I wondered if I might ask the archdeacon to come along to open the proceedings?'

'Can't we find someone with a bit more oomph? The archdeacon is about as exciting as the Shorter Oxford Dictionary.'

The door behind them opened. Edie gave a little cough and came in with an envelope in one hand and a tangle of parsley in the other. 'A letter for you from the major, dear. I thought I'd bring it in at once.' As she handed it over, she said, 'I'll put the kettle on, Rector.'

'No – thank you. I'm in rather a hurry.' He smiled at her vaguely.

Edie smiled back. 'What a shame. It's not often we get a four o'clock guest. I made a seed cake. I'd like to have made a lemon curd tart, but you can't get the lemons. But it's a pleasure to have time to bake again after the turmoil of spring cleaning.'

Mabel had prised open the envelope and taken out a single sheet of thick, expensive notepaper.

Edie said, 'And how is dear Romily? I saw her the day before yesterday in town with her young man. I was puzzled to see that his coat collar was turned up. Is he suffering from a stiff neck? Or neuralgia? Vapex is good for that kind of trouble. Not that Mabel will let us take anything. Best to let your body heal itself, she always says. Mrs Toms had a stiff neck when I saw her in the fish queue. She put it down to that new bus driver throwing her sideways when she was about to get off. Did you know that Mr Hutchings will provide his own wrapping paper again for the fish?'

'No, I didn't,' the rector said.

Mabel was studying the letter with a frown on her face.

'It was such a nuisance having to take your own,' Edie said, yattering on. 'And not only for the fish. You had to take your own newspaper to the greengrocer's and—'

'I remember it well.' The rector stood up, awkwardly. 'I must be going.'

Mabel didn't seem to have heard him. When he was halfway to the door, he said, 'I'll see myself out.'

Edie said flutteringly, 'You can't do that. Can he, Mabel?'

Mabel Petherick, looking up, seemed to stare right through him. Then she said, as if from the distance of another room, 'Can't do what?'

Widemouth Bay came into view at the end of the lane. Jack dropped his speed down from thirty to twenty, to take a long lazy look at it. The Atlantic, dotted here and there with a tiny boat, stretched from horizon to horizon. A gentle surf broke on the beach below. Further out, turquoise shadows were blowing towards the shore, though the sky was still perfectly clear. It was Sunday afternoon. He was to drop the old lady at Efford Court, where she would take tea with the canon before attending evensong at St Michael's. So he would have a couple of hours to waste before picking her up again and driving her back to Lizzah.

'Don't dawdle, Trewarden. The time is getting on.'

When doesn't it? Jack thought. She had been talking at the back of his head all the way down from Lizzah, droning on about the new influx of builders laying drains and paths, the electricians tearing up the floor-boards and the chaps from Gilbert's foundry who had come to take one of the great wrought-iron gates for renovation. And about her brother, Jocelyn, who had, at the age of seventy-nine, decided to grow tobacco plants to augment his pipe ration.

Once, briefly, about a mile back, she had paused to throw a question at him to check that he was listening, but she hadn't expected him to supply an answer.

Looming large in a walnut silk ensemble in the seat behind, Mrs Jago continued her peppery monologue. 'I lost my other brother in the summer of 1917. Arthur. He was ten years younger than me . . . the baby of the family. When he was very small, I used to sit him on a chair while I polished his hair with a silk handkerchief.'

Like most old people, she was more at home in the past than the present. Granny Trewarden was the same, Jack thought, except that her monologues ran more along the lines of Mother's seed cake and Father's prize-winning runner beans and the fox that had once crept acro⁓ ⁓he churchyard to kill every single one of his ducks. She would be seve⁓ ⁓nine at Michaelmas and could be every bit as obstinate as the old girl in the back.

'Arthur was a beautiful child and he grew into a perfectly splendid young man. We were hoping, as time went on, that he would survive the war, but he got a leg wound that turned gangrenous in the mud and the wet. We were still in mourning for him when peace was declared. We went up to London for the celebrations. The streets were lined with flags and Princess Mary waved to us but all I wanted to do was howl because Arthur wasn't coming back.'

The past, for these tough, no-nonsense old women, was thick with stories that were their old friends.

'But as I said to Dr Owens only last week, howling never brought anyone back. Now there's a particularly useless young man. Can't cure my arthritis. Or the neuritis in my back or my rheumatic elbow. I told him, doctors in my day came dressed properly in a square wing collar and a frock-coat. And while we're on the subject of clothes . . . I was sitting at the window the other day taking in the view across the park and I said to Tilley, "Who *is* that extraordinary young woman on the bicycle?" And Tilley informed me that this person – who was wearing what I believe is now termed a sunbathing rig-out – was your wife, Trewarden. I should tell you that though such get-ups might feature in the worst of the Sunday sheets, one does not wish to set eyes on them in the park at Lizzah.'

Jack resisted the urge to stop the car and clock her one. He changed gear and drove on along the coast road, eyes front, shoulders squared, sweeping them round a series of bends down into Bude.

'You may leave the Bentley in the canon's stable yard. I would like you back there at seven thirty, then we shall be home at a reasonable hour. After nine o'clock, I drop off my perch.'

If only, Jack thought. He stuck out the indicator and drew the Bentley to a careful halt in the canon's driveway.

'Seven thirty,' Mrs Jago said again as he helped her out of the car. 'And don't, on any account, be late.'

It would be good – very, very good – to get away from the sound of that foghorn voice.

Jack left his jacket and tie and his chauffeur's cap in the car and strolled aimlessly in the direction of the beach. The day was perfect. He walked over the swing bridge and past the warehouses on the wharf and tamarisks in sandy gardens. He sat on a bench outside the Lifeboat House and let the salty sun and the haze from the sea soak into him. He wondered if the canon's ears were aching yet. Did the old lady ever think of letting anyone else get a word in? She was preposterous. A dreadful dowager of the sort – and class – that he had always hated. And yet, Jack thought with a certainty that leapt from behind to surprise him, there was something about her that he could not altogether dislike. A verve. That was it. She was unquenchable . . . . . . unsinkable.

Go on, admit it. You like her spirit. Funny, he thought, getting up and wandering down the steps to the beach, how last night in the pub he had found himself defending the Jagos against mutterings in the village about how much was being spent up at the hall. 'What does it matter,' he had told Bill Ricketts, 'as long as your leaky roof gets mended while they're at it?'

Skirting the remains of the wire entanglement and the concrete tank barrier, he climbed to the top of the dunes. He sat there letting a handful of sand run through his fingers. Hot blue sky. Pure seaside light. I don't mind the major either, he thought. Oh, he wasn't the sort of chap you could easily exchange confidences with. Hours would sometimes pass without him uttering anything except wrathful harumphings. But Jack had got used to chaps like that in the army. The good officers . . . as English as leather saddles, cricket balls and *The Book of Common Prayer*.

He watched a wave break in the distance. Another thought came to him. I've been recruited into the major's new army, the one that Charlie Garland is mustering from the village to get Lizzah back on its feet. Did he mind? Not really. Not any more.

'Hello.'

Jolted out of his reverie, he was startled to see Daisy Jewell, in a sprigged cotton frock and white canvas sand shoes, clambering up the dune to greet him.

'Hello!' Jack made a desperate attempt to sound normal. 'Didn't expect to see you here.'

'I come most Sundays.' Sea-lit, her face was so lovely that he felt a thud of his heart. 'Father drops me off. He's gone to see Aunt Jem. All on your own?' she asked.

''Fraid so. I'm working.'

'Oh, really?' She thought that was funny.

'It's true.'

'I believe you. Thousands wouldn't.'

He told her about Mrs Jago and the canon, making it as theatrical as he could. 'She's a semi-deranged old bat,' he said, 'but if you don't mind that, she can be quite entertaining.'

'Mother used to say she was well-bred, but not all there.' Daisy dropped down beside him and, tucking her skirts around her knees, chatted happily about Aunt Jem, about the old jumper she was unravelling for her aunt to knit it up again in a different pattern, and about the airmail letter her father had received from a GI from Ohio he'd palled up with, and about the new young schoolmaster who had moved into Badman's Cottage and who may or may not have been a pilot, but he looked the part and kept an officer's hat on the bust of Mozart in his sitting-room window.

'All sorts of odd bods are moving in,' Jack said.

'Agnes Bolitho says we're in the middle of a crime wave.'

'Agnes Bolitho said Hitler was going to be tried at the Old Bailey.'

'Daft old bats aren't confined to the gentry.' Daisy peeled off her white cotton gloves.

Jack couldn't stop looking at her slim arms (as brown as a nut) and her hair (fairer than he remembered). But mostly, it was her face that held him, that wide, expressive mouth, the slender tanned neck.

'So . . .' he said, feeling as if he was driving into the curve. 'Still no young man?'

'None that I really like.'

'You're choosy. That's good.'

'Is it?' she said. 'Father wouldn't let me go out with the Yanks.'

'Not even the one he was friendly with?'

'Bud? He looked like Groucho Marx! Anyway, I hate little black moustaches.'

'Don't we all?' Then he said, '*I'd* be knocking on your door if I was young and single.' As soon as the words were out of his mouth, he regretted it.

'Joking apart,' he added quickly, 'your father was right to keep you locked up. Too many innocent things have been spoiled by this war.'

'That sounds heartfelt.'

'It is.'

She glanced at him and then away. 'My brother says coming back home was odd.'

'Flattish,' Jack said. 'Funny that, because it was all you ever thought about.'

'If you look forward to things too much, they're always a disappointment.'

You're not. He sat staring at the summer heat. 'What I said just now . . . about knocking at your door. I'm sorry. I embarrassed you.'

'No.'

'I wouldn't like you to think I made some cheap pass.'

Daisy's hand came out to touch his arm. 'I don't.'

'Honestly?'

'Honestly.'

'That's all right then.'

Only it isn't, he thought, because the calm certainty with which she said it tells me I'm the last man in the world she would ever think of being attracted to. And what's so surprising about that? I'm twenty-nine years old. Practically an old man.

He felt like someone who had built a perfect sand castle with all sorts of turrets and pinnacles, only to see it washed away by the tide.

Daisy said suddenly, 'There's Father.'

'Where?'

'On the wharf. He'll be wanting his tea.' She jumped up. 'Well, goodbye.' She tucked a strand of hair behind her ear.

''Bye. See you another Sunday perhaps.'

'Not sure about that. I'd hate to stop you working.'

She was already running down across the sand to the river, laughter floating behind her on the breeze. Jack felt giddy at the very sight of her.

On Wednesday, after he had written the note to Mabel, Myles had spent the rest of the day turning out huge wooden chests in his grandfather's den, the contents of which included glass plates going back to the time of his great-great-grandfather, tin box after tin box of celluloid negatives, and album after album from the pages of which stared out the faces of long-dead uncles, aunts and cousins. Grandpa had been a founder member of the Bude Photographic Society.

Once, when Myles was a boy, not more than nine or ten, Grandfather had made him sit for what seemed like hours on a plinth on the terrace while he fumbled interminably with lenses and the camera hood. Myles had tried not to wriggle, but in the end his numb bottom had got the better of him. He had slipped and gone crashing on to the slabs. Not that there had been any sympathy. 'What's the matter with you, boy? St Vitus' dance? Now I'll have to start all over again.'

Suddenly, remembering this, he saw Grandpa watching him from the red chair in the corner. '*Myles,*' the old man said, '*there are strangers in and out. What are these extraordinary people doing in my house?*' And he found himself trying to explain to the old man what was happening. *You see, Grandpa, the country is winding itself down like an old grandfather clock. And we're going down with it.* He wanted so badly for the old man to understand. For them all to understand, all the ghostly faces that stared up at him from the sepia-tinted photographs. Aunt Let in her 1920's suit with a shortish pleated skirt and two-tone organ shoes. Her brother, Henry, killed on the last day of the Great War. Her father, Great Uncle Jocelyn, who had had friends in the Pre-Raphaelite Brotherhood. And towards the further past, a long, misty line of fidgety ghosts gathering to rail at him. Until now, he thought, I was fond of them. And vice versa. But I no longer feel at peace with them. Feel like a ghost without a beat myself.

He fixed his gaze on the dog. 'The past puts out its hand and touches you,' he said, 'and it feels real. Frightens you half out of your wits.'

The dog lifted its head and licked his hand.

That night, Myles dreamt he had wedged a chair behind the door, against the things that might try and get in, but instead, they had squeezed themselves through the window. They started to open and shut doors, rap the panelling and knock the shades off the lamps. And then Kit had arrived. Dear Kit. And the other things had all shot, with a hissing sound, into the mirror. 'You can't come back,' Myles had told the boy, 'because there's nothing for you to inherit.' Kit had just smiled and put a finger to his lips. He closed the window and very gently drew the curtains. Turning back to Myles, he had said, carefully and calmly, 'Ssh! I'm not supposed to be talking to you.'

He woke next morning with a thundering headache and thought, for one moment, that the boy was still there.

'We thought we would have a fancy dress competition,' Mabel told Myles. 'And the rector's going to dig out the maypole, if he can remember where he put it back in '39. He thought it was in one of the rectory attics along with a couple of chairs that need mending, but he couldn't find it. He's wondering if Dan Jewell might have carted it up to The Barton.'

They were in the church vestry, where Mabel was attempting to shove a sprig of lilac into a cut-glass vase. It was her week for the altar flowers. But though she loved her flowers, she was hopeless at arranging them. She said, 'I thought this might be as good a place as any to talk. We won't be disturbed.' And no one, she thought, would think it odd that they had bumped into each other. Myles was a good churchman, always in and out of the place. At Kit's birth, he had given every villager a prayer book.

He took off his hat and dropped it on the vestry table. 'Grateful to you for coming. Thanks.'

He sat on the hard-backed chair tapping his fingers against each other. Sunlight filled the tracery of the windows. There was a sense of time trickling past.

Mabel said, 'So what's up? Your note sounded . . . well, urgent.'

He didn't appear to be with her. He was fiddling with a sheet of crumpled airmail paper that he had taken out of his pocket, folding it into half, then into quarters. At last he said, 'I was going to burn it and not tell a soul, but in the end, I couldn't do it.'

'Burn what?' Mabel asked. There were too many blessed leaves flopping over the blossoms. She stripped one or two off, scattering water over the lace cloth on the table. But the arrangement still looked top-heavy.

'So I hid it away in my gun case. Couldn't let Gin set eyes on it. It would break her up.'

'Myles – you're not making sense. Start at the beginning.'

He spoke agitatedly, not looking at her, but vaguely in her direction. 'It was a good thing the postman was early for once. Normally, you can time your watch by him. Seven thirty in the morning and three in the afternoon . . . bumping and threading his way round the potholes on the drive. But that day, he was early. She wasn't down. She didn't find it.'

Standing with wet lilac leaves in her hand, Mabel studied him with loving concern: the way his hair had turned silver at the temples, his bright blue eyes under their heavy lids, the strong line of his jaw . . . despite the slight sag where the broad angle of it met his chin.

'You received a letter that upset you,' she said.

'Well, yes.'

'So who was it from?'

'Didn't I say?'

'No. You didn't.'

'It was from Kit,' said Myles, as if she should have known all along.

'My dear soul!' Mabel sat down hard on the vestry chair.

Twelve

'*They march, twelve abreast and in perfect step, through the heart of bomb-pocked London,*' the BBC commentator intoned from the kitchen window. '*Sikhs in turbans, high-stepping Greeks in pompommed shoes, Arabs in fezes . . .*'

His voice, toe-curlingly top-drawer, changed direction. Edie must have given the radio a jolt to get rid of the hiss. It was a grey and damp June day. Mabel had cleared the ground of early potatoes and was planting leeks, choosing the thickest seedlings and cutting the tops back by a quarter of their length. A soothing occupation, she thought, making neat holes with the dibber and dropping the plants in at six-inch intervals. Good, sensible things, leeks; hardy, easy to grow, little maintenance required.

'*A specially warm tribute of applause is forthcoming from the crowds watching the victory parade as the troops of our Allies march by. After the American contingent come the troops from China, occupying the place in the procession originally reserved for the USSR.*'

I should think so too, Mabel thought, hitching at her gardening apron. Stalin was always a reluctant ally. He'll have his own victory parade in Moscow, now that half of Europe is under the boots of the Red Army. Damn the old devil, she thought, shifting one of her old gum boots into the next furrow. But her mind was not quite on the goings-on in London. It was dear Myles's predicament that she kept turning over in her mind. The business of the letter. When he had first produced it, she had mistaken what he was trying to tell her. 'You mean, Kit's alive?'

'Of course he's not alive. He's in the churchyard.'

'Then how——'

'The letter got held up,' Myles said. 'God knows where it's been for the last twelve months.'

Mabel said in a shocked voice, 'Lord above! And you've read it? Yes, of course you have.' She sat staring into space, wet leaves flopped between her fingers.

'Over and over. It's as if he's talking to me from the grave.'

At that point, he had handed it to her to read. She hadn't really wanted to. It wasn't right, somehow, but how, after all, could she have refused? The letter (abominably spelt, but you couldn't say so) had spoken of the war ending before too long. *I can't tell you where I am*, Kit had written, *but the rain's coming down in streams and there's a cluster of elms thrashing around above my tent. It's been frantic for the last week or so, not to mention noisy. Thanks, Ma, for the snaps. I like the one of Daph with the kids on the train. Tell her it's time she had a few of her own. I shall, when I get back, pretty smartish. Case of making up for lost time, don't you think?* There was a lot more about coming across a chap he'd once known at school and about the CO of a neighbouring unit copping it. And then came the paragraph that Mabel couldn't seem to get out of her mind. *One day, when I'm home again, I shall spend a whole day lying in the heathery sun up at Tregose. I just want it all to be still and quiet again. But I wouldn't mind hearing the wood pigeons carrying on in the park.*

Mabel straightened her back and gazed at a fowl back-kicking the dust under the gooseberry bushes. She wondered if she had misjudged the boy. To tell the truth, she had never been fond of Kit. Oh, he'd had great charm, when he chose to switch it on. Like his mother. But there had seemed little depth.

The fowl gazed inquisitively back at her. 'I suppose there might have been more to him,' she said.

She remembered Myles's stricken face in the vestry and her floundering attempts at comfort. 'You know what you told me when Stephen died. You must try not to fret,' she had said, speaking with a gentleness she reserved for him alone.

'Easy to say, Mabs.'

'I know.' In a funny way, she was glad of the chance to return his kindness. But losing a son, she thought, was far worse than losing a fiancé you'd only had for six months. Losing a son . . . well, it was your future and past gone in one fell swoop.

Had he told Virginia about the letter? It would churn her up, but she would want to see it.

Miss Petherick's thoughts were interrupted by the snick of the wicket gate. An emaciated young man with a dog at his heels was coming up the path.

'Good morning, Samuel,' Mabel said.

'Morning, Miss Petherick. Back-breaking work—'

'But rewarding. What can I do for you today?'

He tapped the left-hand pocket of his flannel trousers. 'Best seen indoors, Miss Petherick, if you know what I mean.'

'Oh. Right.' Mabel gave a little cough. 'Go on in while I get my boots off. Tell Edie to put the kettle on.'

By the time Mabel had exchanged her boots for her indoor shoes, Edie had fetched out the embroidered tablecloth and was feeding Samuel up with a wedge of saffron cake and the little dog with stale sponge fingers. In the centre of the kitchen table, disconcertingly, stood two bottles of their favourite sweet sherry.

Mabel picked them up and stowed them away in the bottom of the dresser. 'How much do I owe you?' she asked.

'I paid him.' Edie took down two more of Granny Petherick's Asiatic Pheasant plates. She said to Samuel, 'Mabel hates having to fetch it from The Acland, out of hours. She tells Pru it's to put in the trifle, but—'

'The kettle's boiling,' Mabel said.

Edie, rosy and breathless, went to see to it. A burst of military music accompanied her. '*And at the end of the parade,*' said the plummy voice, '*in a crowd-pleasing, Union-Jack-waving climax, come at least ten thousand men and women from the armed forces and civilian services of His Britannic Majesty, King George VI . . .*'

Edie said, 'You should be marching up the Mall with them, Samuel.'

'Not too keen on parades, Mrs Medland. Not my style.'

'Maybe not,' Edie said. 'But you did your share. More than your share. And how is dear Cicely? Well, I hope? Mabel is knitting a matinee set for the baby. She likes to have something on the go while we listen to the wireless. Before that, she was knitting garters. So much better than the flimsy shop variety—'

'Use the everyday teapot,' Mabel said. 'And make sure you warm it.'

'Of course, dear. India, Samuel, or China? Do you like the colour we painted the ceiling? It needed three coats. We're very pleased with ourselves. Next week, we're going to put up a buffet in the back kitchen—'

'We'll have the tea today and not tomorrow, Edie,' Mabel said. 'And use the everyday teapot.'

'Sorry. Yes. It's the right size for just the three of us,' she explained, in case Nipper interpreted Mabel's instruction as discourtesy, which he didn't.

Mabel said, 'I hear your mother's working up at Lizzah.'

'Yes, Miss Petherick.'

'Cleaning, is it?'

'Yes, Miss Petherick.'

'You could do worse than apply to the major yourself for employment.'

'Not me, Miss Petherick.'

'Your brother would put a word in for you.'

Better up at Lizzah, she thought, than falling foul of the law by illicit trading. Samuel sat on the edge of the carver as if on the point of flight. He reminded her of the White Rabbit in *Alice in Wonderland*. Alert, all of a twitch, always scuttling,

All the dammed up energy he'd possessed as a boy seemed to have turned into something slightly different. Nerves? Some kind of fierce distress? Or was she imagining things? As she pondered the question, Mabel studied the two-pronged scar above his right eyebrow. He didn't have Jack's good looks, but there was something about Samuel she had always been fond of. For one thing, he'd had the horse sense to choose himself a pleasant little wife instead of some Fancy Nancy.

Samuel asked if they'd be interested in a few tins of black gloss paint. Or some strips of pine for shelving.

Edie said, 'Pine? We could make new headboards.' But Mabel clattered the cups into their saucers and told Samuel again that he could do worse than apply to the major.

'This Trust thing will bring a certain stability to the village. Heaven knows, it is needed. The dog is full, Edie. Feed him any more and you'll be cleaning up vomit.'

'He likes sponge fingers,' Edie said. 'Mother used to smuggle them into our pockets to keep us quiet during funerals. Funeral fingers, that's what they were called when I was a girl.' She bent to tickle the dog's ear. 'Yes, you're a lovely boy! He reminds me of a dog we had that used to chew the legs of the piano stool. A little gentleman. We always had gentlemen dogs because . . . well, you didn't have the problem of puppies.'

There came a burst of cheering from the wireless in the corner. The dog gave a yip. 'You'd like to be there,' Edie said. 'Wouldn't you just?'

'For heaven's sake!' Mabel said. 'He's just a dog.'

'You're wrong there,' Nipper said, contradicting Miss Petherick for the first time ever. 'He's more than that.'

'He's your very best friend,' Edie said, taking courage from Nipper's little rebellion.

Mabel looked at her and despaired.

Nipper called at the pub on his way home to pick up what Pru owed him for the nylons and a roll of canvas from the Plymouth Blitz, after which he went home to Church Row. Cis was sitting on one of the kitchen chairs looking pale but relaxed. The smell of roast mutton was seeping from the range. On the starched blue cloth stood a warm fruit tart and a junket topped with nutmeg.

Cis smiled her slow smile. Nipper dumped something wrapped in brown paper on the table.

'Present,' he said.

'What is it?' she asked, looking wary.

'Open it and you'll find out.'

After a worried glance in his direction, she did as she was told. 'A maternity smock,' she said.

'Don't you like it?'

''Course I do.' Her plump fingers touched the hand-stitching around the seersucker collar. 'It's just – well, I wish you wouldn't. Folks might wonder where the coupons came from.'

'You worry too much what people think.'

'It's a small place, Sam. People talk.'

'Who cares?'

'I do.' Her face had flushed right up, making her look ten years old again. 'I'll wear it later on. When I'm bigger,' she said stubbornly, by which Nipper knew that she would hide it in the well-polished wardrobe upstairs and go on wearing her one, neat navy-blue maternity costume for best. He felt a spasm of irritation.

Cis laced her fingers over her growing bump. 'Jack called by. He wanted to know how you were.'

'God help us,' Nipper said, 'How many more?'

'He was only asking.'

'Well, I get sick of folks asking! *How are you today, Samuel? How's the cough, Samuel? What does the doctor say, Samuel?* I wish they'd mind their own fricking business.'

'It's because they care about you,' she said quietly.

'I might not want them caring about me. Following me with their eyes and talking about me behind my back.'

'Sam!'

He hated himself for taking it out on her. It was happening too often. But though he tried to keep the anger inside him, sooner or later it came up like a geyser.

'What's got into you? Is it the baby?' She hesitated, then said, 'We used to talk about having children. Have you changed your mind?'

For her sake, he twisted his face into a smile. ''Course not.' It was new life, after so many deaths. But there was this sense, as he stood trying to ease things back to normality, that Cis was ridiculously young and that he was older than Methusalah. Older than the world itself.

He thought, *I wish to God I could feel something. Anything.*

Cis said, 'I'll get up in a minute. I was feeling bilious.'

'Stay where you be. I'll see to supper.'

'You wouldn't know how.'

'I can follow orders,' Nipper said. He looked down at her. Then he said, 'You bide still,' and he gave her shoulder a small, clumsy pat before escaping to the pump in the yard.

By this, Charlie's third visit, Myles was more used to his presence and had even offered him a room in the east wing. It involved a nightly walk along the upstairs passage to the cavernous bathroom with the window that wouldn't shut, and Charlie rather missed Pru Hockin's excellent goose pudding (made from an elderly goose stuffed with onions, wrapped in suet pastry and boiled in a cloth), but being on the spot, so to speak, was considerably more convenient.

'I'm most grateful, sir,' Charlie said to the major. The old dragon had come down for tea and gone back to her room – but not before telling him how disgraceful it was that there were two Communist MP's in Attlee's government. Now, on an exquisite summer's evening with the sound of bells floating in through the open windows, Charlie was telling Myles that the National Art Collections fund had turned the Tudor wine cup down, but the V&A man had reported the Erasmus genuine.

'It'll fetch a pretty sum,' Charlie said. 'And the wine cup will go to Sotheby's along with a good many other items.'

'Rather like to have kept the Erasmus,' Myles said gruffly. 'Don't care about the silver, but I hate the books going. It's a damned shame.'

Charlie gave him a sympathetic smile and nodded ruminatively. He wondered if it was safe to re-introduce the tricky subject of the sale.

'But there's nothing to be done about it,' the major said. 'Empty purse, that's the thing. Might as well shoot myself and be done with it.'

Charlie made a demurring sort of a sound, so the major said to the dog, 'I'm the fag-end of an old stock. What do you think of that?'

The dog dropped his head on to his paws and gazed at him balefully.

'Yes, I know. You're depressed, too . . . poor old chap.' He turned back to Charlie. 'I've had a letter from your people. Something about an Act of Parliament. Seven or eight pages of gobbledygook. Hardly any full stops. Need you to translate it for me.'

'I'll do my best.' Charlie said.

'So is that it?'

'Not quite. The sale of effects—'

'Not on. Won't hear of it. Things that have been in the house for centuries . . . never moved an inch. Feels like shoving old friends out—'

'It will only be the minor effects. Stuff that's fit only for the local auctioneer.'

'So have him come and collect it.'

'He wouldn't know where to start. The thing is, we'd make more if the sale was held in situ.'

'You plan to have the whole village pawing over our personal possessions in my own house?'

'Not exactly. What I thought was, if the weather's good, we could set the sale up in the park. Put up a marquee. Hold it over a couple of days. In July, possibly. Those we've held before have been most successful.'

'Preposterous notion,' the major huffed. 'Won't hear of it.'

Twice a week, Wednesdays and Sundays, Bess Tilley was free in the afternoon. Twice a week, Wednesdays and Sundays, she cooked supper for her mother in her two-up and two-down in Under Lane and after supper, Wesley Colwill came courting.

He had courted Bess for five years before the war, for six (by letter from Saskatchewan) during, and now, because Wes was a cautious man and nothing had ever quite come to a head, Bess figured he would go on courting her till the cows came home.

They had met at chapel at one of the faith suppers. Wes had landed up next to her on the hard, wooden form. He hadn't said a word. Too busy eating, Bess thought now, as she wandered, arm in arm with her young man down to the ford. Four pieces of saffron cake, as she remembered, three splits with jam and cream, half a dozen fancies and that was only when she'd been counting. But a week or two later, he'd taken to hanging around outside the house. She had been fifteen, Wes a couple of years older. It had taken six whole weeks for him to ask her out, but Bess didn't mind because he was steadfast. They had an understanding.

She turned her head to gaze at him. He was togged out in his Sunday best and when he moved, his shoes creaked. 'What they need is a dab of goose grease,' Mother had said, but Wes went right on creaking and squeaking.

Elderflowers blew in a warm breeze. Bess said, 'I feel ever so sorry for the major. There's going to be a sale in the park. All the old rubbish.' Or what passes for rubbish, she thought, among the gentry. 'When I took in his tea this morning, he looked proper down. They still get their tea from London. I said to Jack when he changed the batteries in the wireless,

I said, it comes by special van. Did I tell you Peg's helping out with the cooking? With so many in and out, I didn't know if I was coming or going. She likes it better in the kitchen, out of madam's way. They've had one or two little spats.'

'Well, now,' said Wes.

'See, Peg can be peppery and madam gives as good as she gets. The old lady's giving Miss Daphne her tiara and earrings as a wedding present. I heard them talking about it. I wasn't earwigging. It's just that they was having tea on the lawn and Her Majesty kept me running in and out with garden cushions and rugs and her blinking Japanesy sunshade. Between you and me, I don't think Miss Daphne was all that interested. It was Mr Boswell as kept saying that's very good of you and thanks awfully.'

Wes slipped an arm around her shoulder.

'It'll be a June wedding. They was having a grand old time in the drawing room last night. Mr Fermoy – he's the young architect – nice chap – you can have a bit of a joke with him – well, Mr Fermoy asked if he could put the gramophone on and Mr Garland found one or two dance records and before you know it, they'd rolled the carpet back and they was taking it in turns to dance with Miss Daphne. It was good to hear a bit of fun in the place. I could hear it all the way down in the kitchen while I was putting the rennet in the junket.'

'Proper job,' Wes said, this being his notion of amorous banter.

''Course it didn't last. Her Majesty had me say they was disturbing her rest. Only thing you can disturb in this place, I almost said, is the dust. Or the dead. 'Rose of Tralee'. That's what they was dancing to.'

'I like a good tune,' said Wes, his left hand sliding from her waist to her breast.

'Here – cheeky!' Bess had lost her thread.

'Fancy a kiss?'

'No, I do not!'

But when he sneaked one anyway, all thoughts of Lizzah, tea, gramophones and rennet was put out of her mind.

Romily telephoned from the rectory, her voice light and hurried.

'Daph? It's me. Listen, Daddy heard in the village that your Mr Garland is driving back to London tomorrow. Apparently Tilley told her mother and Agnes Bolitho dropped in on Mrs Tilley . . . Anyway, if he is motoring back, is there any chance he could give us a lift? Only the wretched signals are jammed on the Okehampton branch line and we'd have to do that bit by bus and we wouldn't get into Paddington until ten. So if he could, it would be extremely kind. Could you ring back and let me know?'

'Of course.' Daph said, 'He's here somewhere. Taking down the drawing room curtains, I think. I was hoping to see you before you went back.'

'Not possible, darling. Jan got talking to this chap and his girlfriend in the pub last night and he's insisting on us going back tonight. They got him very drunk on double whiskies. I didn't like them much.'

'Then don't go.'

'If I refuse, he won't speak to me for days. And I can't stand that. I'll catch up with you next time, I promise. Oh, I bought a super pale blue silk dress at Burrows. But it cost so much, I've had to give up smoking. Again.'

Charlie was on the little terrace outside the drawing room windows. He was talking to the old lady. Or, rather, she was talking at him. Her clear, stentorian tones would have filled the Albert Hall.

'They will have to toughen up to handle the country in the state that it's in! The Communists will tear its throat out. I'd line them against the wall and shoot them.'

This last week or so, she had taken to following him around, seeking company and conversation, as old people do when they feel the world has passed them by. Also, she was keeping an eye on what he was up to.

She had parked herself on the wicker chair with her carpet bag at her feet and was rummaging into its depths, pulling out skeins of wool. Her deep-brimmed straw hat gave her a less stern air, or perhaps it was that the silvery grey silk of her dress made a welcome change from her usual black and navy. She fished out a length of pink wool and said, 'I was listening to a programme on the wireless the other night – I only listen to the Home Service and the Third Programme, you understand, not that other nonsense. They were asking whether there should be intelligence tests for MPs. And I thought, my hat, there should! That would send a few of your Labour men packing.'

Charlie said, 'It's an interesting thought.'

'Winston would pass with flying colours, of course.'

'I imagine he would.'

'He's in Amsterdam, you know, at the invitation of Queen Wilhemina.' She snipped off a length of thread. 'Fêted all over the world, but discarded at home.'

'What are you stitching?' Diplomatically, Charlie changed the subject.

'Covers for the window seat in my room.'

'You're very skilled.'

'Should be. I've been at it since I was a gel.'

'The same covers?' He risked a little joke.

She obviously thought it a rotten one, because she looked down her nose at him and said, 'You're very grubby this morning. What have you been up to?'

'Shaking the moths out of the drawing-room curtains.' He had brushed himself down, but dust and loose silk threads clung to his shirt and his hair.

'I was asking Virginia what happened to my Venetian dishes. They came back from my honeymoon with me and you certainly won't be selling those to boost Communist party funds. They were the most exquisite things. Rose and gold-spangled stripes. Caught the light of the candles. I was fond of them.'

'I'll look out for them,' Charlie said.

'They used to be in the dining-room cabinet next to the Waterford jam pot, but that was back before the Boer War.'

'The Boer War?'

'Oh, yes. I am extremely old, young man.' She sat back in the chair, admiring the honeysuckle that was scrambling over the top of the wall and romping its way down the other side.

'I was twenty-nine when it began. Myles was eight. On the day Alex was packing his bags for South Africa, one of the servants, Nelly, went down with typhoid. And Mrs Shepperson, the housekeeper, was kept running up and down the stairs to the servants' quarters all day with jugs of icy water. We had to send Myles off in a great hurry to stay with my mother in London. And he was in floods of tears and Alex lost his temper and told him not to be such a blasted baby.'

'*My* father was pretty tough on me,' Charlie said.

'I remember the white dress I wore when I went down to Southampton to see my husband off. It had a matching hat trimmed with partridge feathers. We were wildly extravagant and stayed at the Regent's Palace for the night. Only I didn't see much of Alex, because he sat up playing cards until three in the morning and then we overslept and he had to rush off before I was awake. He left a bunch of white violets on the pillow. I didn't see him again for four years.'

She had dropped her needle and thread and sat gazing into her own thoughts.

'What happened to Nelly?' Charlie asked.

'Nelly?'

'The servant with typhoid.'

'Oh, she died. People did, in those days. Quite suddenly, with the least possible warning. Pneumonia. Diptheria. Rheumatic fever. And then there was the influenza epidemic in the black winter of 1918.'

I wish I hadn't asked, Charlie thought. Inside the house, the telephone rang.

'Peace came at the beginning of a spell of bitter weather. I remember the bells going into a wild peal down at the church. And the vicar – now what was his name? Horridge? Harridge? He had sticking-out ears and looked like a schoolboy with an overgrown moustache. Anyway, he got the flag out and flew it from the tower and later he added a bit of bunting, but it was only a matter of weeks before the influenza hit us. The black-smith's wife was the first to die. The sturdiest woman you ever saw. Then Isaac Sampson, who ran The Acland in those days. The worst affected were the strong and the middle-aged, not the very old and the very young as you would have expected.'

'Odd, that.' Charlie edged sideways, skirting a circular wrought-iron table. Could I slip away through the French windows? he wondered.

'I lost a very good friend to that outbreak. Cut down, never to return. All my friends are dead now. Believe me, it's no joke when you outlive them all.'

The telephone had stopped ringing. Charlie checked his watch. He was taking an experimental step backwards when she changed tack. 'This opening of the house to the public—' Her sharp gull's eyes pierced his. 'You can't let people just wander around. Things will get damaged. Or disappear into pockets.'

Charlie said, 'We'll have guides in each room to keep an eye on things.'

'Guides? I don't follow.'

'We shall advertise locally. You'd be surprised how many sensible, intel-ligent people there are around once you look for them. Women who would be grateful for a few hours interesting—'

'You propose to bring in villagers? Surely *they* won't be involved?'

You sound, Charlie thought, like a horrid old snob. Not that I would dare say so.

Mrs Jago said, 'We had them up here for Red Cross sewing parties and such. But to have them standing around one's house as if they owned it—'

'I can only tell you, from my experience, that if we want things to absolutely run smoothly—' He didn't have time for all this. Frank Hobbs was due at any minute. And there were quarters to arrange for a visiting stonemason.

He was saved by someone coming out through the French windows. Daphne Jago, in blue trousers, holding a book in her hand.

'Did you know,' her grandmother asked, 'that we are to have guides from the hoi polloi?'

Daphne said, 'I did actually. I've come to ask a favour of you, Mr Garland. I understand you're going back to London tomorrow? Only my friend, Romily – I think you've met – needs a lift back to town. We wondered if there would be room for her and her fiancé in your car?'

'Of course,' Charlie said, feeling his irritation dropping away. 'Only too pleased.'

Evalina Jago said, 'I didn't know Romily had a fiancé. No one tells me anything.'

Daphne made a comic face. Charlie wanted to laugh, but didn't. 'I'd planned to leave quite early. Say . . . nine o'clock?'

'Thanks awfully. I'll tell her you'll be there at nine.'

Thirteen

The wheels of the Ford scrunched on the rectory gravel. Charlie parked the car in front of the house and climbed out. He stood for a moment, letting the quiet of the place soak into him. The morning mist was clearing away. Behind the house stood the vast yews that hid the church, except for the tower, looming high above.

The herbaceous borders were lovingly tended. There were clusters of creamy roses, canterbury bells and delphiniums thickening to a deep, dark blue. An old rambler lolloped over the upper windows of the house, a square granite-built, Georgian place.

Charlie walked towards the stone porch, but before he could knock on the door, it was opened by the rector.

'Mr Garland. My wife spotted you from the window. Do come in. I'm delighted to meet you.'

'How do you do, sir,' Charlie said. 'I hope I'm not too early.'

'Exactly on time. Though I'm afraid my daughter is nowhere near ready. She has many talents, but punctuality isn't one of them.'

The rector wore an alpaca jacket and grey trousers and his distinguished, enthusiastic voice reminded Charlie of the service he had gatecrashed that first day. That odd little wedding. The dog with the ribbon.

Love Divine, all loves excelling . . .

'Don't worry,' Charlie said. 'I've got sisters.'

'Then you'll know all about it. Let me offer you a cup of coffee while you wait.'

He followed the rector through the book-lined hall to a dining-room with angling trophies in glass cases, where he found a young man and a woman in a mauve frock sitting at the polished table.

'May I introduce my wife. Pearl, this is Mr Garland.'

Mrs Matheson, hastily putting down her egg fork, took command of the conversation. 'It's so very good of you to offer to take Romily back to town.'

'It's no trouble,' Charlie told her.

'The poor child would have been in a fix if she'd had to depend on the wretched trains. These days you never know where they are going to deposit you and when. I had a letter from my cousin Margaret yesterday. Now she had an unfortunate incident on the train. They were in the restaurant car and fast approaching a tunnel. She had ordered the soup, but when it came the lights failed and there was a hissing noise and . . . well, you can guess where it ended up. Have you met my daughter's . . . fiancé?' She said the word as if holding it in two fingers a good way away from her. 'Mr Carsinski.'

'Krawczynski,' corrected the young man, who was dark and lantern-jawed with lank, black hair hanging over his collar.

'I can never get it right.' She came across to shake Charlie's hand. 'I remember seeing a film once about a man whose name no one could remember. It ended with a runaway wagon scene.'

The rector said, 'The young man would like some coffee, dearest.'

'It's been made some time, I'm afraid.' She reached for the pot and dithered about over by the sideboard in a search for a clean cup. 'So . . . Mr Garland, you must tell us all about yourself. Where are your family from?'

She poured his coffee and led him to a chair at the far end of the dining table. The Pole helped himself to more toast and marmalade.

'I was born in Wales,' Charlie said. 'But my parents now live in Dorset.'

Krawczynski bit a chunk out of his toast. Not much of a conversationalist, it seemed. Not the chummy sort. Charlie took his attention back to Mrs Matheson, who had embarked on a story about some woman she had once met on holiday in Dorset.

'It was supposed to be a yachting holiday, but the house was ten miles from the coast. Quite a poky little house, too, in a steep valley where it never seemed to get properly light. There was a—'

But Charlie never heard the end of the tale. The door behind them opened and Romily Matheson came flying in. 'I'm late. I'm sorry. I've been searching for my ration book. I can't think how it got under the bed.' She looked very fresh and pretty in a lime green cotton dress with a scarf the colour of cherry blossom around her waist.

'Good morning,' Charlie said, 'I hear congratulations are in order.'

'Oh. Yes. Thanks.' She threw a bright smile in the direction of the Pole. 'We should be going.'

'I will finish this,' he told her.

Her smile faded. 'Yes. Of course.' She turned back to Charlie. 'I'm afraid I've got a few things to take back with me. I hope there's bags of room?'

The few things turned out to be a suitcase, a small radio, a tartan rug, a pot plant, a box of books, a pile of glossy weeklies tied up with string, and a very old, very battered teddy bear.

'His name is Tug,' she said when she saw the expression on Charlie's face. 'I didn't take him while the bombs were dropping. I didn't want him to be blown up by the Luftwaffe. But now that things have settled down . . .'

'He can sit next to me,' Charlie said, laughing. Krawczynski threw him a look that tried hard to intimidate. The collar of his dark jacket was up, which made him look even more like a surly undertaker. Was his English so bad that he couldn't join in a conversation? Or did he think it made more of an impression if he chose to be silent?

It was the rector who helped Charlie carry her things out and stow them in the car. 'Now I don't want to hurry you,' he said when the pot plant had been wedged on top of the pile, 'but you had better be off, if you want to get back at a reasonable time.'

'She can't go yet,' Mrs Matheson protested. 'She hasn't had breakfast.'

'Not hungry,' Romily said. 'I'll have something later.' She threw her arms around the rector and held him for a long time. 'It was lovely seeing you, Daddy. Take care of yourself.'

'And you, my darling. Telephone when you get there.'

'I will,' she said. 'Bye, Mummy.' Dropping a kiss on her mother's cheek, she slipped into the passenger seat. Krawczynski, who had finally decided to join them, slung his bag in the back and climbed in after it.

No word of thanks or farewell. The rector's gaze met Charlie's. 'Drive carefully,' he said. 'Look after her.'

'Don't worry, sir.' They shook hands.

Mrs Matheson came fluttering out in her husband's wake with her own request. 'Next time you're down, do call. Any time.' Her voice dropped to a near whisper. 'And, if you have a moment, drop in on Romily. We're worried about her.'

'Thank you for the coffee. I'll . . . do what I can.'

There was nothing else he could have said.

The roads were empty; still no signposts on the lesser ones. Charlie drove through summer lanes with corkscrew bends. They crossed the Tamar and the heathery ridges of Dartmoor appeared in the distance with the odd farmhouse anchored in the heaving ocean of the moor.

A motorcycle passed them and went roaring on ahead. 'Silly devil,' Charlie said.

He was very aware of her slim arms and fine wrist, as she sat beside him. And of the way her fingers were intertwined round one brown knee.

'I'd like one of those.' Romily opened the window even wider.

'A motorcycle?'

'Mmm. What fun.'

'If you want to break your neck.'

She made a face. 'Didn't you ever ride one?'

'Once or twice.'

'Where?'

'In France.'

'You didn't break *your* neck.'

'I went into a bad skid once.'

'Whereabouts in France?' she asked.

'Normandy. Paris. All over.'

'Do you miss it?' she asked.

'The war? Sometimes.'

'Me too. Everything you did then was automatic.'

'I shouldn't have thought you were the automatic type.'

She laughed. 'What I mean is, you didn't have to think what to do with your life. It was all controlled by the flight sergeants and the squadron leaders and the Air Ministry Board. You never had to think for yourself. Well, only about which lipstick to buy and where to go to dance and if you should go to a gramophone concert or the cinema on your weekend off. Now that they've given you your life back . . . well, some of us don't have the faintest idea what to do with it. A life is a big thing to chart, don't you think?'

Charlie said. 'Plenty buried in Europe who would like the chance.'

Out on the moor, fresh greens ran up into an opal sky.

'You're right. It's not that I'm ungrateful. It's just . . . well . . . every now and then, your spirits dip.'

Mine would, Charlie thought, if I had to deal with that sleazeball on the back seat. With one hand, he flipped open a packet of cigarettes and offered her one. She shook her head. 'I stopped. It's absolutely bloody.'

She reached into her pocket and rustled a cough drop out of its wrappings. 'Daph bet me five bob I won't last. Which is pretty pointless because neither of us has a penny to bless ourselves with.'

'For friends, you're not at all alike.'

'You don't have to be like someone to be friends with them.'

That's true, he thought.

Romily said, 'We used to get invited to the same parties when we were infants in crêpe-de-chine dresses and dancing pumps. Daph hated having to be sociable. She would find a corner and hide herself away. Once, when it was time to go home, no one could find her. She was sitting two floors up in the nursery, watching the piano tuner. Her mother used to get wild with her.'

'I can imagine.'

'Kit, on the other hand, could do no wrong. He was charming, handsome, spoiled to death. I don't mean completely awful. We had a lot of fun, the three of us. Kit made up all the games during the hols. It was just that you had to play by his rules. One time, when Daph refused, he chucked her music book on the fire.'

They drove past a thatched cottage with pinks and sage under the windows.

Romily crunched on her cough drop. 'She told everybody it was an accident. I suppose the thing is, if it's your brother, you love him no matter what. She was devastated when the news came that he'd been killed. Not that you would have known. Daph isn't one to make an outward show of her feelings.'

Charlie thought of Pru Hockin's comments.

Miss Daphne's her own person. You can't help respecting that. She'll always give you a please and a thank you when she wants something. Unlike some you could name. Her mother now . . . she's a fully paid-up member of the awkward squad.

He said, 'People seem fond of her in the village.'

'That's because Daph taught Sunday school and took the Brownies and Girl Guides, all the village activities her mother was never interested in. Which makes her sound dull, but she isn't.'

'No?'

'No.' She looked at him. 'You don't believe me.'

I believe you're a loyal friend, Charlie thought.

Romily took another cough drop out of her pocket. 'She's good fun when you get to know her. And she has the most beautiful mezzo soprano voice.'

He smiled. 'So her fiancé is a lucky man?'

'His extreme luck is about the only thing he has going for him.'

'You don't approve?'

'I like him well enough. He's kind, pleasant, upright . . .'

'But?'

She thought for a moment and then said, 'Well, marrying Bos would be like getting yourself hitched to a St Bernard dog . . .'

They drove down the steep hill into Okehampton. It was market day and the streets were thronging with stoutly built farmers. At Sticklepath, they got stuck behind a tractor and trailer, loaded with sheep. Krawczynski turned over and muttered something to himself as he did so.

Romily said, 'Poor darling, he's exhausted.'

Charlie said nothing, but changed gear. They were down to a slow crawl. She glanced across at him and said, 'I know you must think him astonishingly ill-mannered, but there's a reason for him being so silent.'

Oh, yes? It had better be a good one.

'He's angry because no Polish officers took part in the victory parade. He says they were our first allies, they fought side by side with us from the beginning and now, when it's all over, we call them bloody Polacks.'

'I suppose he might have a point.'

'And Churchill is Stalin's friend and has allowed his Communist army to take over Poland.'

'It might be just the tiniest bit more complicated than that.'

'Not to Jan. He can never go home. Think what that must feel like.'

Charlie tried, but he was still of the opinion that someone should tell their friend on the back seat that it was illegal in England to spread despondency and darkness of spirit.

Five miles from Exeter, Krawczynski stirred. The sky had clouded over. Small streaks of rain speckled the windscreen. Romily asked Charlie how many other houses he was working on.

Charlie said, 'Well, in the last week, I've written up twenty houses. A lot of stately home owners are going under.'

'You English are obsessed with property,' said Krawczynski from the back seat.

'Are we?'

'It's all you ever talk about.'

'That's not fair, darling. If old houses are Mr Garland's—'

'Charlie,' said Charlie.

'If old houses are Charlie's thing, then of course he's going to talk about them. So the Trust has sprung up since the war?'

'God, no. It was started fifty years ago by an eccentric clergyman. A bit of a tub-thumper.'

'The English are all eccentric,' said the Pole.

'Are we?' Charlie shot Romily a glance. She stared straight ahead of her. 'Anyway, this particular English eccentric had a parish in the Lake District and fought to stop a railway being built by Derwentwater. And then in 1895, he sat down with a group of like-minded souls and founded the National Trust. Its first property was bought in 1902. Bought by public subscription, actually. A female worker from Sheffield sent him two shillings and sixpence to help keep the lakes for others.'

'How wonderful,' Romily's face lit up.

'The poor handing over what little they have to buy out the landowners?' Krawczynski said. 'How very stupid.'

Her smile faded. Charlie swung the car round a hairpin bend. He was tempted to slam his foot on the brake, open the rear door and chuck the bastard out. But he couldn't because of Romily. So he drove on with his jaw set and jabbed the heel of his hand on the horn when, a mile or so on, a dog ran out in front of them.

'We'll stop for lunch when we get through Exeter,' he told her.

'Actually, I *am* hungry.'

'I am not hungry. I would prefer to keep going.'

'Sorry,' Charlie told Krawczynski, 'but you're in the minority.'

'Then I shall stay in the car.'

'Just so long as you don't mind me locking you in. Only I've got one or two priceless items for Sotheby's in the boot.'

Charlie enjoyed the black look that he caught in the rear mirror. He began to whistle, lightly, under his breath. 'The major just had some good news. The army has offered dilapidation money to repair some of the damage they did during their residency.'

'So they should,' Romily said.

'Tilley's pleased. She made a plum duff to celebrate.'

'Was it edible?'

'Almost.'

They were now on the outskirts of Exeter. The roads were beautifully empty. They crossed a bridge and drove alongside a rushing river.

'Old Mrs Jago says plums aren't as big as they were when she was a gel. And they never get properly ripe. It's all to do with the gardeners absconding. Daph caught her listening to Jimmy Dorsey last week.'

Charlie said, 'You're kidding?'

'No. She told Daph the radio had gone wrong and kept tuning itself to the wrong station.'

He started to laugh. Romily turned her head to gaze back at the Pole as if to include him in the conversation. The expression in her eyes was a fine mix of anxiety and conciliation. Cheer up, it said. Please. After a moment or two, she gave up and sat twisting the beads of her necklace.

'Jimmy's the one who plays the hot alto?'

'I think so,' she said.

'Soft. Romantic. You need the lights dimmed.'

He pointed out the cathedral spire. Krawczynski said he thought it out of proportion. 'There is something lacking,' he said. 'A sense of grandeur.'

'I think you'll find—' began Charlie. But Krawczynski was just getting into his theme.

'I find this with many English edifices. People go on about how ancient they are and how impressive and venerable, but too many people in this country make a fetish out of age and tradition. I get tired of hearing how wonderful are your so-called national treasures. To me they are just dead old piles of stone. You would not want to go back and see them twice.'

And a jolly good day to you, too, Charlie thought. Romily was avoiding his eye. He hoped she wasn't scared of the bastard. From the way her fingers were laced together, he very much suspected that she might be.

They stopped for lunch at a hotel overlooking a wooded valley. Krawczynski, choosing not to be locked in the car, stalked off through the gates. What a relief, Charlie thought. It was like turning off a radio that was giving out depressing news.

The hotel was an old-fashioned sort of a place with a formal dining room looking out on to heathy shrubbery. He chose a table by the window. 'Will this do?' he asked.

'Absolutely.' Romily flopped into the chair he held out for her. 'I'm sorry Jan's being so awful.'

'Not your fault. Why should you apologize for him?'

'Well, you're driving us back. He sounds so ungrateful.'

He couldn't argue with that. To take her mind off her ungracious friend, he started to read from the menu. 'Vegetable soup . . . Probably made from potato parings and cabbage stalks.'

'I'm tempted to have the suet pudding.'

'Won't have any suet in it.'

'You're right.'

Her hair shone brightly as she sat in the oak carver. Not tinted, not even curled, but thick and luxurious with its own halo of light. 'I'd have the chicken,' she said, 'only it might be tinned. I had some in town once and it reeked of aspic.'

'So where exactly do you live in London?' Charlie asked.

'I've got a flat in Victoria. Well, a room with cooking facilities. And I work in a little bookshop round the corner.'

A cadaverous waiter appeared with a water jug. He said, 'The weather has turned a trifle inclement, sir.'

'Dry enough in here,' Charlie said cheerfully.

'You have a point, sir. May one take your order?'

In the end, Charlie ordered soup for two, roast mutton for himself and herrings in tomato sauce with a salad for Romily. He watched the old boy shuffle back to the kitchen. 'This might take some time,' he said.

Not that he minded. It would serve Krawczynski right if he got drenched.

'So do you like your flat in town?' Romily asked.

'Absolutely. It has the most charming views. Three bombed out houses on one side, two on the other, plus a church across the way with its steeple blown off.'

'Sounds great.' There was, at last, a smile on her face. 'How long have you lived there?'

'Since the last tenant took off without paying his rent. About a year.'

'And your sort-of girlfriend comes and goes?'

'She works in the Trust office. We've known each other for years.'

'So it's not the kind of relationship where rockets are going off?'

'Not at the moment. No.'

'But they did once?'

'For a while.' He saw his chance and went for it. 'What about you and your friend out there?'

He could see her considering her reply. How much to let out and how much to keep to herself. The latter a considerable amount, judging by the set of her mouth.

'Lots of rockets,' she said at last. 'Bits of them falling back down to earth to burn you, but I don't really want to talk about it.'

'Right.'

Damn it, she had cut the conversation off just as it was getting interesting.

'Vegetable soup, sir. Madam.'

The soup was very thin and very pale. Lettuce and cress? And the mutton, when it came, was thin and as tough as old boots.

'Wish I'd had your herrings,' he told Romily.

She glanced at her watch.

'It won't hurt him to get wet. He's probably found the local pub. Holed himself up in the chimney corner with a pint.'

'That's what worries me. He might not come back.'

'Then we'll go on without him.'

Romily said, 'I know he deserves to be left.'

Charlie said, 'He'll be back. There isn't a bus or train station for miles.'

'You're probably right.' She fished a bone out of the herring.

'Does he do this often? Take himself off?'

'Now and then. He's highly strung. I suppose *we* would be gloomier if the Nazis had grabbed our homes and everything that belonged to us. His father had an estate outside Warsaw, but they had Jewish blood and had to leave it all behind. Actually, I think he's probably a bit jealous of you. Not you personally, but the way you're able to go tootling round the country in your little car. People give you meals and put you up. And you've got a job that you obviously adore and you— Well, you belong. And he doesn't. So it makes him a bit savage.'

I only asked a simple question, he thought, as he refilled her water glass, and I get all this nervous chat. One day, I'll find out exactly what is going on to make her so defensive.

They found Krawczynski hanging around in the porch as they emerged after lunch. He was thoroughly wet and even more ill-tempered if that were possible. He kept up a brooding silence for the rest of the journey. It was after six when they got back to London. The view from the car windows had gradually changed from fields and trees to chimney tops and blown-up houses. Charlie negotiated his way through several miles of bomb-site jungle and finally stopped the car outside Romily's flat in Frances Street.

Krawczynski muttered something to Romily, then strode off without a word of thanks. Standing by the car, with a radio wedged under her arm, Romily watched him go. Charlie watched him, too, but whereas her eyes were forlorn, his were angry.

The Pole might have helped carry her stuff up to her flat.

Charlie wanted to say something reassuring, but he couldn't think of anything, so he grabbed her suitcase and the tartan rug from the boot of the car and stuck to practical matters.

'Got your key? Right. Lead on, Macduff.'

'You don't have to,' she told him. 'I can manage.'

'It's no trouble. Which floor are you on?'

'The top, I'm afraid.'

She saw the expression on his face. 'You can leave it in the hall.'

'I was joking,' Charlie said, twinkling at her to prove it.

The house was a four-storey terraced, very tall and very thin. By the time he had run up and down the ninety-seven steps with the suitcase, the pot plant, the box of books, the glossy magazines and the teddy bear, he was out of puff.

'That it?' he said.

'That's it. Thank you so much.' Standing at the window by the patched-up wallpaper, she said, 'Can I make you a cup of tea?'

'Thanks, but I'm meeting someone.'

'I hope we haven't made you late?'

'Not at all.' He buttoned his jacket, unbuttoned it again, brushed a non-existent bit of dust from his sleeve, then dug a hand into the sagging pocket of his suit and pulled out a small, cream-coloured card.

'Here's my address and telephone number. If you're ever desperate for a lift home or . . . anything . . .'

'That's very sweet of you.'

No. It just makes me feel better about leaving you on your own, when you look so vulnerable.

'Well, goodbye,' Charlie said.

''Bye,' she said, and managed – just – to smile at him . . .

Romily's smile stayed in Charlie's head until he walked into his flat and heard the phone ringing. Swearing softly, he hurried into the sitting room and picked it up. 'Charles Garland.'

There was a crackle on the line. Then it cleared and he heard Virginia Jago's slow drawl. Only tonight, for some reason, it seemed to have speeded up. 'Oh, Mr Garland. I'm so glad to have caught you. I'm afraid we've had a bit of a disaster.'

'What's happened?'

'The workmen have been banging around on the roof all day. They stopped at about five thirty and I was just thinking, thank God, we shall have a bit of peace. Then there was a deep rumble and the Yellow Room ceiling collapsed.'

Bugger. Now I shall have to drive straight back again.

Fourteen

July was gloriously fine. On the south terrace, an explosion of china roses stretched from the house down to where the discarded army jeeps were buried. Gin put on her long-distance spectacles to gaze at them one morning, saw every single petal and couldn't bear it, so she took them off again.

This was the day Roland Kerslake, the auctioneer, was due to start the dreadful business of humping acres of stuff for the sale down to the coach houses, where his men would endeavour to put it into some sort of order. God knows how on earth they will do that, Gin thought.

Old Ned Kerslake had died quite suddenly one Christmas while his son was home on leave from the army and within weeks of being demobbed, young Roland had been forced to take the reins. Roland's Sunbeam was parked, now, down in the driveway. He was a sensitive-looking young man in a grey suit and a trilby that was a smidgeon too large for him. She had just seen him cross the lawn to the orangery, then, realizing that he had gone wrong somewhere, make his way worriedly back round the side of the house.

I only hope he's up to it, Gin thought. Still, if rumours were correct, he was modernizing the offices. The sign over the firm's windows had been changed to Edward Kerslake and Son and electricity had been installed so that the secretary could work that most modern of inventions, a dictating machine.

A little breeze lifted rose scents through the window. Gin glanced down at the list she had just made.

> Rector
> Myles
> Jewell's sheep
> Soapwort – Trewarden's boy

Charlie Garland had spent a whole hour showing her how to boil soapwort root before infusing the whole plant to make a gentle, clove-scented cleaner for the delicate silk of the dining-room curtains.

'You can use it as a shampoo,' he said, rubbing the leaves in warm water to show her how well they lathered up. 'But don't get it in your eyes. It's toxic.'

The Yellow Room curtains, once in dull tatters were now, if not quite as good as new, then better than they'd looked for centuries and Daisy Jewell was working her needlewoman's magic on them in the attic sewing room. Thank God, thought Gin, we took them down before the ceiling collapsed. Imagine having to wash out all that filthy plaster dust.

She'd thought it impossible to find enough of the herb to deal with the other bedroom hangings, but Charlie Garland had once again come up with an answer. 'Send Trewarden's boy to find some,' he had told her.

'Send him where?'

'Oh . . . fields, hedgerows, on the banks of streams. It likes damp soil.' He was a walking encyclopaedia. 'Tell him to take his gang with him.'

'What if he hasn't got a gang?'

Charlie grinned. 'All boys belong to a gang. Give them an old sack each and Bob's your uncle. But make sure they wash their hands afterwards.'

She found Trewarden down in the hall helping Kerslake's men move a set of chairs. He said he didn't see why the boy – Clifford – shouldn't make himself useful. 'Keep him out of mischief,' he said in a careless, disinterested way that put Gin off her stroke. She had the urge to give him a dressing down, but there was no point in trying to wither someone who wouldn't be withered.

'We need it as soon as possible,' she said brusquely. 'If you send your boy to the kitchen, Tilley will give him a piece of the plant to show him what he's looking for.'

Trewarden strode off with the chairs. Kerslake's man dipped his head and scuttled after him. If only she could clear them out of the house and bang the door on them! I'm not sure I can do this any more, she thought. The getting up, the walking around, the sorting, the clearing, the emptying . . . And yet what was the alternative? How else to survive, except by allowing herself to be swept along, with no time to look right, left or front, in the hope that if she got the house back straight, her life would go back to what it was.

But it won't, she thought. The past can't be restored. Once a time is gone, it's lost for ever.

Myles was sitting at the small mahogany table in the breakfast parlour. Gin said, 'Charlie suggests we ask Dan Jewell if we can borrow some of his sheep.'

'Sheep?' He raised his eyes from the newspaper. 'What the devil for?'

'To get the grass down in the park.'

'But last week he made us buy a motor mower.'

'For the lawns, not the park. That's decided then. I'll send a message to Dan via Daisy. She was telling me how much she enjoyed the course.'

'Course?'

Sometimes she wondered if he was with her at all.

'At the Royal School of Needlework. Three days on Jacobean work and two on gold-work with silk. She's really very skilled. Apparently, in the twenties her mother quilted for agricultural shows and WI events.'

'Winifred. Nice little woman. Always gave me milk straight from the cow. I used to go up with Father when he collected the rent. Liked the ride through the woods. Remember when we used to ride up there?'

Of course I do, Gin thought with a bittersweet mixture of love and regret. I'd had my hair bobbed and I wore flapper dresses and I was madly in love with you. I couldn't believe it when you took out your great-grandmother's diamond ring and went down on one knee and laid your gingerbread mansion at my feet.

It had felt wonderful, but terribly unreal . . . like a fairy tale that might, at any moment, all disappear. And now it had, which just goes to show that life should never be confused with fairy tales.

'Long time ago,' she said. She wanted to say, '*We had Kit just a year later*,' but the words wouldn't come out.

Myles flapped the paper until he had turned it inside out. 'Jewell tells me the beeches want cutting back. It's the right month, but there's no one to do it.'

'Too much to do here.'

'That's what I told him.'

'Must ride up there again some time.' There was a pain in her chest, as if a horse had kicked it. For one brief, ridiculous moment, she was tempted to drop to the floor at his feet and rest her head against his knees. Like in the old days, when Kit was small.

Don't be silly. He'd have a fit.

She poured herself a cup of coffee and stood there on a lemon and gold patch of carpet. Finally, she forced herself to broach the subject that had been on her mind all week.

'I'm meeting the rector later.'

'Arrangements for the fête?'

'No.' Gripping the back of the chair in front of her, she said, 'I want to talk about a memorial window in the church.'

Wait. Give him time to let it sink in.

'Something to remember him by. Kit . . . Nothing fuddy-duddy. No angels or harps or saints with halos. Something very simple but modern. Something very plain, I thought, and engraved. Kites . . . birds . . . a landscape . . .'

He said nothing. She ploughed on. 'Something, essentially, that he'd approve of. What do you think?'

'If you wish.' Bright blue eyes gazed at her for a moment, then away again. His shoulders hunched as he went back to the newspaper headline: **NEW WORLD ORDER**.

Is that all? Gin thought. Couldn't you even attempt, just this once, to help me?

'I don't know how we're going to afford it. I'll sell something, if necessary. Obviously nothing that belongs to the house . . . A piece of jewellery perhaps. It just sits in the bank. I never wear it.'

Except my engagement ring. In another moment, I shall have to cry.

The world, for Lil Trewarden, had not improved since the Yanks left town. She missed the buzz of things going on, the comings and goings, the hullabaloo, the sheer, ring-a-ding fun of it all.

She missed Glen Miller and American wolf whistles and all the boys and the dancing and the flirting. She missed the exciting sound of GIs marching down the street in soft-soled boots and Yanks lounging wherever they could find a wall. Lusty, carefree Yanks . . .

Most of all, she missed her *particular* Yank calling her his cutie and his hotsy totsy. Joey Venuti – cheeky eyes and disarming grin – had bought her chocolates and perfume and silk stockings and primrose silk scanties; comics and sherbert papers for Cliffy (she'd had to lie on her feet to Jack about that). And, once, he'd even given her a whole bottle of perfume.

Just don't ask where it came from, baby.

Joey had burst into her life at a dance at The Pavilion, taking a flying leap from the balcony on to the dance floor and twirling her away from the bloke she'd been jitterbugging with. On that never-to-be-forgotten Friday night, he had quite literally swept her off her feet and sometimes, now, she felt as if she was still spinning, only in great wobbly lurches, like a top going out of control.

Lil pedalled her bicycle along the edge of the hayfield and up over the steep bridge in the middle of the park. It wasn't that she'd thought the fling with Joey would last forever. Because she had known that sooner or later all those cliff-scaling rehearsals down the coast would have to be put to use. It was just . . . well, she hadn't expected them to vanish into thin air like that, while she slept, just before D-Day, with no warning and not even a 'See ya, honey!'

Freewheeling down the other side of the bridge and along the dusty lane, Lil asked herself if she regretted cheating on Jack while he was away fighting for king and country. Well, occasionally she felt bad about it, if she stopped to think. Let's face it, she was still fond of her husband. He could still turn her on. And now and again, she could almost pretend to herself that they were back in the early days of their marriage.

But there were the other times when he was unhappy, edgy, without an ounce of fun. So all in all, she was glad she hadn't wasted the best six years of her life waiting for him to come home, only to be bitterly disappointed.

Warm air and dog rose scents caressed Lil's face and her bare shoulders. Remembering Joey, a dreamy look came into her sharp eyes. No, no regrets.

She thought, I'll be an old hag soon enough.

The rector had a habit of writing light, almost humorous sermons on large, grim subjects. He had once been known to say, leaning genially over the pulpit, that death was a remarkably underhand fellow. A kind of thief who nipped into the house when your back was turned and stole your most precious possession without so much as a by-your-leave. Which had prompted Pru Hockin to say after the service that she wished the wily old so-and-so would come and take her mother-in-law, but if he did, he'd be getting a blessed sight more than he'd ever bargained for.

Standing now, at three in the afternoon, at the back of the church with Virginia Jago, the Reverend Matheson wondered if the loss of a son could, in loose terms, be compared with a moving picture disappearing off the cinema screen. If he might suggest that life, in all its flickering beauty, was by its very nature a transitory thing; but how wonderful to have had a moving picture at all.

But now, glancing at her face, he had second thoughts. For one thing, sitting there in the pew next to him, she looked so dreadfully pale. There were violet smudges under her eyes. The rector knew abject misery when he saw it. So, abandoning more fanciful approaches, he said simply, 'This must be an absolute agony for you.'

'Quite bloody,' she said with scant regard for the sanctity of their surroundings. And then she said, 'You can't imagine. Well, I expect you can. You have sons.'

Sons. Plural. It made Hugh feel enormously guilty that his boys had survived the war; also more blessed than he had any right to be. 'Well, quite,' he said.

'I want it – the window – to be very present-day,' Virginia said, fishing a packet of cigarettes from her bag, then, realizing where she was, shoving them back in again. 'And I'd like it to be in the Jago chapel. Possibly to replace that dim old thing on the east wall . . . Moses in the ´desert.'

Hugh knew the one she meant – pious Victorian and of absolutely no artistic value. 'I shall have to ask Bishop Paul, but I can't see there would be any objection.'

'I can't go into any detail at the moment – can't think straight because of the mess we're in at the manor.'

Another difficult area, the manor. Hugh gazed down at the font in which his boys and Kit had all been baptized.

'I shall have to find someone to design it.' She sounded weary. 'When there's a minute. When, if ever, we get back into some kind of order. Kerslake's men are in. Did you know?'

'I *had* heard,' Hugh said. 'Pearl says it's to be an . . . outdoor event.'

Virginia whisked an imaginary speck of dirt from the blue cotton frock that matched her chenille turban. She appeared to be searching for a suit-able reply. 'It's absolutely necessary to clear the decks.'

'But painful?'

'It's what you find,' she said, 'when you do the sweeping out. Things you're not prepared for. Things you'd forgotten about until you reach in and pull them out of some blasted cupboard.'

Hugh's gaze shifted to the memorial plaque for the men who had died in the First War. Three Rowes. Two Hockins and half a dozen others from the village. Some christened here, some married, but very few of them laid to rest with their ancestors.

'Like yesterday. I found Kit's electric torch. In his fishing basket.'

'Corker of the Yard. The detective game.'

'You know about it?'

'Kit would lay clues up in the attics, then flash a signal for my boys to come and sleuth. They played it at the rectory too.'

Virginia's eyes were bright with unshed tears. 'You think you're the only one who remembers these things.'

The rector laid a kindly hand on her shoulder. 'We all remember.'

'Perhaps we'd be better off not remembering.'

'I don't believe that and neither do you.'

Virginia said, 'Sometimes I do.'

'Kit most certainly wouldn't want you to forget him.'

'A weak argument, Hugh,' Virginia said. 'But as he's lying out there in the churchyard and we can't ask him, I don't see any point in arguing the matter.' She saw the look on his face. 'I'm sorry. I didn't mean to upset you. The thing is, you believe in happy endings. Vicars have to. God will wipe away all tears . . . All that hokum. I can't.'

'I never thought of it as hokum.'

'Well, you wouldn't. I don't suppose Bishop Paul would either. But at the moment, all my life seems to consist of is pushing an enormous stone up a very steep hill. So you must forgive me if I can't believe in your shiny, sunlit heaven with sounding trumpets.'

'Not quite sure I see it that way either,' the rector said. 'Celestial realms not really being my forte. Heaven, if it's to be found anywhere, will be here on earth.'

He edged a kneeler back into position in one of the pews and offered her his gentle smile. Virginia thought, The thing about really good people is that they make you feel so unutterably shallow.

After she got back from the church, she sat for a while in one of the garden chairs under the trees and then cut some roses for the parlour table and the little bureau in the breakfast room. Pieces of furniture, paintings, carpets, curtains and books had been passed out of the windows and doors and stood stacked up on the drive. Peg Trewarden, in a rollicking hurry, was rushing the vacuum cleaner up and down the first floor landing. Gin wished she would stop. The noise was making her head worse and the heavy smell of disturbed dust reminded her of the time she had been standing on the basement steps of her London solicitors' office during an air-raid and the ground had collapsed beneath her. The same smell, the choking sensation.

'What wouldn't I give to put one of these round my front-room rug,' Peg shouted over the din of the hoover, 'instead of having to brush it with tealeaves!' She had never handled such a machine before, but seemed to be making a pretty good fist of it.

Gin beat a hasty retreat from the rattle of the hoover and took herself along the passage to check on Evalina. When she got there, she found the old lady asleep in her favourite chair overlooking the park, her hair braided up into two plaits, a half-worked circlet of flowers in floss silk thread lying in her lap. Gin tiptoed away from her mother-in-law's room and headed for the kitchen to ask Tilley for a pot of tea. At the top of the back stairs, she could hear Charlie Garland's voice; he was having a yarn with Frank Hobbs. She rang the bell in the passage outside the kitchen and eventually Tilley came scurrying out. Gin asked for tea and aspirin and climbed the staircase again to her own room.

She kicked her shoes off and lay on the bed. The conversation with

Hugh Matheson was still wandering around her head. Heaven, if it's to be found anywhere, will be down here on earth. Also hell, she thought. The gods were right when they told Orpheus not to look back. To some extent, everything the rector had said was true; there was a magic to memory. Memories could act – for a while – as a shield against the horrors of cold reality. But you could get tired of switching your mind, like the dial of the wireless, from memory to memory until you found one that didn't hurt so much as the others.

So perhaps the best option was to switch off.

The sun glimmering through a haze of leaves outside the window helped her doze for a while despite the scattered commotions going on around her – Kerslake's men shoving a heavy piece of furniture through a doorway that was too small for it, Daphne playing something bright and tinkly on the little gramophone in her room, the telephone bell ringing at the end of the vast, cool hall.

Then the door banged open, waking her with a start. Tilley, her face all screwed up with concentration, came backing into the room with a loaded tray. 'Here we are, m'm. A nice pot of tea.' She made room for the tray on the bedside table. 'And I brought a couple of my biscuits as well, as you oughtn't to take pills on an empty stomach. At least, that's what our mother says.'

She clumped over to the window and drew the curtain against the sun. 'I'm sorry it took so long, only Farmer Jewell's boy turned up with a load of plums. Not that we shan't be glad of 'em. You'll never guess what I just heard on the wireless. Bread's going to be rationed. The announcer chappy said 'tis something to do with the world food shortage and us having to feed all the refugees in Germany. I said to Mrs Trewarden, us've got a big enough job feeding ourselves.'

There was a thump outside in the passage, followed by a disastrous crash. Tilley said, 'What the dickens is going on?' and went to find out.

The tea had been poured and Gin was shaking an aspirin from the bottle, when Tilley's head popped back round the door. 'They dropped the tallboy. And I forgot to say, m'm, that the major would like to see you. When you've had your tea. He's in the library.'

Myles stood in front of the fireplace with the dog. 'How's the headache?' he asked. 'Better?'

Gin crossed to the armchair and sat down in it. 'Not really.'

She could see him trying to gauge what sort of mood she was in. The air wafting in through the open window was hot and midsummery. He had the look, she thought, of someone waiting on a station platform for a train to come in. Only now that one had, he couldn't quite decide whether to board it or not.

'Wonderful show . . . the roses,' he said. 'Just been admiring them.'

She said, 'The delphiniums would win prizes, too. Myles – did you drag me all the way down here to talk about flowers?'

'No.' He fixed his eyes on the seat cushion above her head. 'Daph around?'

'Up in her room.'

He thought that over, absently rubbing the back of his neck.

'The thing is . . . well, there's something I must show you. Something that might be a bit of a shock.'

He pulled something papery and crumpled from his jacket pocket.

'A nasty shock?' she asked.

'Yes. No. The fact is . . . I've had it for a while.' He unfolded the piece of paper and thrust it at her.

She smoothed the two sheets of airmail paper out and, in the afternoon silence, stood staring at them.

'Didn't quite know what to do about it. Wanted you to see it, but then I couldn't make up my mind. Tricky, you see. Might have upset you. Bound to, under the circumstances.'

'This is Kit's writing.' She didn't know what to make of it. On her face there was a tangle of emotions: amazement, anxiety, fleeting delight, and finally complete bafflement. 'I don't understand.'

'To tell the truth, I nearly burnt it. But then I thought, no, if it's the last letter we'll ever have from the boy—'

'The last? But . . . when did it arrive?'

'Turned up a few weeks ago. Postie brought it.'

'A few weeks ago?'

'Got held up somewhere. You'll see by the date. Army mail bag went astray. I said to Mabel, it'll have been halfway around Europe. Suppose it's a miracle that—'

'You showed it to Mabel Petherick?'

The major pulled his pipe out of his pocket. He looked, if it were possible, even more uncomfortable.

'Needed advice. I can talk to Mabel. I knew she wouldn't—'

Gin felt the fury rising inside her.

'You've had this for weeks and that . . . that crab-faced old cat gets to read it before I do?'

He blinked. He had assumed that she would understand. 'Look, old girl—'

'Don't call me "old girl"! I'm not that old. Feel it sometimes. All the time, actually.'

'Look, Ginny,' he said, 'I wasn't sure if you'd cope—'

'Then you're a half-wit,' she said with a ferocious glare. 'A bumbling half-wit! Did you really think I wouldn't want to read Kit's last, precious — very precious — words to us?'

'I wasn't sure at the time.'

'Absolutely, typically ridiculous!' She had gone scarlet with indignation.

'You're right. I'm sorry. Clumsy of me. I didn't think.'

'No. You never do.'

Myles glanced at her. She sat with Kit's letter scrunched up against her breast, her elbows digging tight into her ribcage as if trying to stop her feelings from bursting out.

'Headache bad?' he asked. 'Want to see the doctor?'

'No, I don't bloody want to see the doctor!'

'Look, Ginny—'

'Don't talk to me. Don't even talk to me!' she said.

But Myles, miserably trying to put things right, said, 'The thing is, I never know how you're going to—'

'The thing is,' she told him, 'that all you ever want to do is find a pile of sand and bury your head in it. Oh, I know it's easier not to talk about Kit, about the pain of it all, but it just won't do. Because, sometime, Myles, some of it has to be faced. And how the hell are we going to do that when all we do is plod silently along in our separate, well-worn tracks? I'll tell you something now, even if you won't ever say a word — a meaningful word — back. I don't exactly know who I'm here for any more. The other day, when that ceiling fell in and I was damned near underneath it, my immediate thought was: I wish it had killed me. Then I'd be out of my sodding misery.'

Her head was thudding so hard, she had to get out of the room. She ran, with Kit's letter still tight in her hand, past the cleaners who were buffing up the marble hall, past the fox heads on the staircase, past armchairs and tottering china stacks and plasterers and builders, to the blessed gloom of her bedroom.

I wish, oh how I wish my brain would thump its way out of my skull so that I didn't have to think any more.

Fifteen

Penelope Jago no longer believed a word that grown-ups told her. This was because, during the war, they had hoaxed her into thinking that carrots were nicer than a sponge cake, that her father and brother would both be home again before long, and that she would be quite happy in the dump her school was evacuated to – a muddy village in the middle of onion fields in deepest, dullest Norfolk.

So when, on the morning of the auction sale, Daphne tried to tell her that Mother and Pa would soon be back on speaking terms, Pen said, 'I'm not stupid, you know. And I'm not a child any more.'

Daph watched Roland Kerslake unfold the stepladder that served as his improvised rostrum.

'They haven't spoken for two whole weeks. You don't think they'll get divorced?'

Daph said, 'Of course not.'

'Only I don't know anyone whose parents are divorced. Why are you wearing a frock? Are you practising for when you get married?'

'Don't be silly.'

'What's silly about it? You never wear fluttery frocks.'

'Voile. It's called voile.'

Pen wasn't interested in the finer points of fashion. 'Can I come with you to fetch Tom from the station?'

'No, you can't.'

'Ohh! Why not?'

'Because I've got other things to do first and you'd be bored and you'd be a nuisance.'

'Oh, please!' Pen poked at the gravel with the toe of her sandal, restlessly pushing it into little dykes and furrows. 'He said he'd bring me an old pair of skating boots that belonged to his sister. We're the same size. Isn't that lucky?'

'And where would you go skating,' Daph asked, 'even if it happened to be the right time of the year?'

Pen made a face.

'Just asking,' Daph said and took herself off to talk to the auctioneer's clerk. Prospective buyers were ambling around the park, picking up this and that, making notes on catalogues, and eating sandwiches that they had brought to sustain them for the long day ahead. Some were there for the bargains, others out of sheer nosiness, for the house had had a pull on the collective imagination for over three hundred years.

It was good, she supposed, that so many had come.

A voice behind her called, 'Daph. There you are!'

Bos was making his way towards her through the crowd. It was odd: he had been all the way across Italy, France, Germany and yet he didn't seem able to cross the lawn with any ease. The thing was, he would keep stopping, with old-fashioned, amiable politeness, to let people go round him. He was not a jostler, even when desperate.

At last he made it. As he bent to kiss her, he smelled of old tweed and tobacco. 'Jolly good turn-out,' he said.

'Yes.' Daph watched the auctioneer's trusted factotum, in shirt sleeves, lift a chair for a lady to inspect. 'I can't imagine where they've all come from.'

'What's it matter as long as they cough up?'

He was right, of course.

'How's your father?'

'Tired and cantankerous. He's taken himself off up to High Moor with Punch.'

'Can't say I blame him.'

'Actually, I'm worried about him. He's not sleeping. He's had this terrible row with Mother. And last night he said if the old place is to be turned into a cross between a museum and a public park, he may as well shoot himself.'

Bos tightened his tie, then loosened it again. He put one hand on her elbow, squeezed it, then, not knowing what to do next, took it away again. The auctioneer, hammer in hand, mounted his stepladder. 'He doesn't mean it.'

'I hope you're right.'

Young Roland Kerslake consulted his late father's watch, which was attached to the gold albert chain crossing his waistcoat. He was dressed with scrupulous care – grey three-piece job, panama hat and crisply striped tie. Nervously clearing his throat, he began his auctioneer's puff. 'Ladies and gentleman, we are here today to begin a four-day sale to dispose of the surplus effects of Lizzah Manor, a mansion which has its place in the history of this parish and in our nation's great history. The sale will commence in the park and proceed through the house, room by room, from the stable block via the breakfast room, the dining and staterooms to the bedchambers, the nursery, the servants' quarters and the attics.'

Daph felt the bottom drop out of her stomach.

'Lot one,' Kerslake said. 'Granite feeding trough. What'll you give me for it?'

Bidding had commenced.

A sunny morning on a damp park. Under a light, still sky, the grandest house in the parish braced itself and, ignoring the unseemly hullabaloo going on under its windows, gazed, calm as ever, out over the valley to the distant sea.

Beyond the gates, the hay was cut and lying in bundles. In the lane that ran down to the village, the breeze carried a scent of summer grasses and Mabel Petherick's sister, Edie, said, 'Oh, my!' when a twenty-eight-seater charabanc all but squashed her into the ditch as it passed her on its way up to the sale.

Emerging from the makeshift tea room in the orangery with a tray in her hand, Peg Trewarden spotted Edie chattering away to Dan Jewell, a stocky figure in his best brown jacket and farm gaiters, and young Daisy, who had set her hair so that it was nice and wavy.

'Mabel says we're to look out for a length of carpet for the box room, but what I've set my heart on,' Edie said, 'is a piece of china. Willow pattern or that other pretty one with an acorn and oak leaf border. I don't mind if it's cracked. And I don't care if it doesn't match anything on the dresser because you can, well, fling all the blues together on a shelf and they'll get on. Don't you think?'

'Morning, Peg,' Dan said.

'Lot fifty-two . . . a quantity of sand buckets, two with broken handles.'

'Did you ever see such a load of old junk in all your life?' Peg folded her arms over the empty tray. 'But it's Goering's medals to an oven door that someone will be daft enough to buy it.'

'I should turn out *my* old rubbish,' Dan said.

Peg was about to go on speaking, but she spotted Jack in the crowd and waved him over.

'Trewardens all over the shop,' said Dan.

'I think of it as helping the major out,' Peg said. 'He's a decent chap. And having a hard time of it at the moment, between you and me and the gatepost.'

'Mother's turning into a right old Tory,' said Jack with a wink when he joined them.

'That's one thing I'll never be. But you can't help feeling sorry for him. The old lady's in a foul mood and madam's rapping out her orders like nobody's business. Well, they've got a full house, Jack. Mr Garland says there's dealers here from all over. Exeter, Plymouth . . . London even. And them as aren't buying are having a good nose.'

'Nothing wrong with that.' Jack smiled at Daisy, noticing her pretty hair and the way the wind was flapping her skirt round her brown legs. He couldn't have said what she was wearing, except that it was something soft and green and summery that set her off without having to shout about it.

Daisy, later that evening, remembered his toughened, sunburnt neck above the crisp white shirt of the chauffeur's uniform. His brown eyes, his tawny hair. And the way his hand rested affectionately on his mother's shoulder.

'Also,' said Edie, who had all this time been thinking about the treasures waiting to be sold, 'I would rather like to find a nice old oil lamp. Mabel says their time has gone, but a room looks more friendly in lamplight, I always think.'

Old Ned Kerslake had seldom indulged in levity – a joke would have been an experiment that was something quite out of the ordinary. But Mr Roland, as he was called by one and all at Kerslake's, was the kind of young fellow who could get away with a touch of dry humour. 'Lot one hundred and twenty-five,' he said, taking a quick sip from the glass of water handed to him by his lady clerk, 'Three boxes of medical books. Entertaining and companionable fireside reading.'

After a tentative start, he was getting into his stride, Charlie decided. Rattling through the lots at a fair old lick. Even Biddy was impressed.

She had pulled off her knitted jersey to reveal a white blouse worn with heavy beads, Russian émigré style. You would never mistake her for a waif. The flattering word to describe her figure would be bonny, Charlie decided.

She turned to see if he was still there. 'I'm glad I came,' she said.

'Thought you'd enjoy it.'

Last night they had stayed at The Acland. Separate rooms, of course. Mustn't frighten the natives with any London carryings-on. Charlie hadn't exactly planned on bringing Biddy down to Lizzah. He'd mentioned the sale and she'd said, 'Sounds like fun,' so he'd said, 'Why don't you come down then?' half regretting it before the words were even out of his mouth.

He wasn't sleeping with her as a matter of *policy*. It was more that when she hopped into his bed, he didn't know how to tell her he was beginning to find the whole thing a tad tiresome.

Look, he wanted to say, you and me. The sex thing. Well, it's a bit like eating boiled sweets. Quite enjoyable . . . especially after a long time without any. But I've got to the stage where it seems like a childish occupation.

'*Mr Garton.*'

Charlie thought, Damn! Then turned and beamed out a smile. 'Mrs Jago!'

The old bat was wearing a grey silk frock – lace at the neck, mother-of-pearl buttons and the skirt to within six inches of the ankle. Her shady hat was trimmed with partridge feathers. She looked more than ever like an imperious, blue-nosed old empress. And she was clearly annoyed about something.

So what's new? Charlie thought.

'Would you tell me why Kerslake's catalogue includes a framed drawing of my husband, Alexander Crispin Jago?'

'Your husband?'

'Yes. Lot four hundred and two. My son certainly didn't give you permission to include it in the sale.'

'I'm most frightfully sorry—'

'Sorry is not good enough, young man! What I would like to know is, how many other of my personal possessions have been secreted into the auction without anyone either knowing or caring?'

'Um—'

'You may well hum and haw. I suppose you thought I wouldn't notice? You think I'm a stupid old woman who's easily hoodwinked—'

'An ill-tempered old woman,' Biddy said.

'I beg your pardon?'

'And ill-mannered. How do you expect Charlie to answer your questions if you never let him get a word in edgeways?'

They stood glaring at each other, Biddy holding the cup of coffee she had just fetched from the stall by the orangery, while Charlie put a mental bet on which of them would trounce the other.

'And you are?'

'Bridget Reilly.'

'Ah. Irish,' the old lady said, as if it explained everything.

'And proud to be.'

'You don't sound Irish.'

'That's because I was born in London.' Biddy squashed out the stub of her cigarette on the terrace slab. 'My mother came over here in the twenties to nurse.'

'Taking jobs from our own workers,' Mrs Jago said.

A mistake. The colour flared into Biddy's cheeks. 'Well, at least she made an honest living. She didn't exist on unearned income like some I could mention.'

There was a silence. Mrs Jago's sharp eyes considered her. 'I suppose you're one of these young bolsheviks who peddle the *Socialist Weekly*?'

'I'm on the side of the people in the class war. Yes.'

'And how,' Evalina asked acerbically, 'do the people feel about that?'

Charlie, making an attempt to defuse the situation, said, 'Um – Perhaps we should check your picture with Kerslake's secretary.'

'I'll hang on to it,' Evalina said, 'thank you very much!' Then, 'I always knew you were a Red.'

'Charlie? A Red?' Biddy started to laugh. 'He spends all his time hoisting nasty old Tories like you back on your feet. God knows why. I wouldn't.'

'I suppose you would line us up against the wall and shoot us?'

'Not really.'

'You surprise me.'

'I'd stick you in one of your damp little cottages,' Biddy said, 'so you could find out how the other half lives.'

Charlie was reminded of the competing barrage of sledgehammers wielded by workmen repairing bomb damage in the street below his flat. Why had no one ever bought Biddy a pair of kid gloves? The old lady was aggravating, yes, and autocratic, but it was rotten bad form to hit her so hard when she was . . . well . . . old enough to be your great-grandmother.

'Sorry,' Biddy said, after the old lady had stumped off. 'But she's a useless, parasitical old harpy.'

'We'll all be old and useless one day,' Charlie said. He thought, Romily would have handled the situation with far more charm and tact. He'd found himself daydreaming about her lately, remembering over and over the ironic lift of her fine-arched brows, her laughing voice (when she wasn't thinking about her surly Pole), the way she rattled artlessly on.

As a matter of fact, he had telephoned her a couple of days before. He'd come in from a meeting of the Historic Buildings Committee feeling unaccountably restless.

So he had picked up the receiver and dialled her number.

'It's me. Charlie. Er . . . Charles Garland.'

'Oh . . . hello,' she said.

Now, standing staring at himself in the hall mirror, he'd felt the beginnings of stage fright. 'It just occurred to me . . . well, I wondered . . . will you be going down to the Lizzah sale? Only if so, I could offer you a lift.'

A brief silence, then, 'That's very kind of you but—'

'You've made other arrangements?'

'No.' A silence. Then, 'I'd love to go, if only for Daph's sake, but I don't think I can make it.'

'That's a shame.'

'Yes.' A silence. 'It's just . . . well, it's difficult. Getting time off work.'

'Right. Well, it was just a thought.'

'A very kind one.'

'Not at all. So how are you?'

'Fine. I'm fine.'

'You sound tired.'

'Do I?'

Was he imagining the hint of panic in her voice?

'Perhaps I am, just a little. It's so hot. In my flat, I mean. The heat seems to collect under the roof.'

'And in the tube.'

'Yes. Well, thanks anyway. It was good of you to call.'

She didn't mean it. There was no bounce in her voice. He missed the flippant, madcap girl who had come running down to greet him at the rectory.

He wondered where that fearless and strong-willed girl had gone.

All morning, the crowds milled around Kerslake's rostrum. All morning, a powdery rose scent hung in the air. The bidding continued. 'Lot number two hundred and twenty-five. A desk with red-ink pot, black-ink pot and a quantity of first-class blotting paper. Who's going to start me off?'

An aircraft wandered high overhead.

'Lot two hundred and forty. Dog basket containing part of a dinner service. Pretty little pattern. May even be a bone or two tucked away underneath.'

Seagulls wheeled and rooks cawed over the square fruit gardens and the symmetrical coach houses and the medieval barn. Mabel Petherick bought a patch of carpet big enough to cover a dozen boxrooms, also a green jug with lavender trim. Edie acquired a whole box of assorted blue china and a big, wide armchair that no one else wanted.

'I felt sorry for it,' she told Mabel as they ate their sandwiches on a couple of striped deckchairs.

Mabel said, 'Where are we going to put it, that's what I'd like to know?'

'I'll have it in my bedroom.'

'And how do you think you'll get it up the stairs?' Mabel's face wore the same grim look as it did on the first Monday of every month, Budgeting Day, when they sat at the front-room table and totted things up. Or rather, Mabel did. Edie would sit nervously awaiting the verdict.

Edie thought it safer to change the subject. 'I hope young Mr Kerslake will last out. He's as hoarse as a crow.'

'I daresay he'll survive. He's making a packet. What did you put in this sandwich?' Mabel asked.

'Lettuce, dear.'

'Anything else?'

'A small piece of Samuel's ham.'

'A very small piece, if you ask me. And we don't want any more mention of where it came from.'

'But, Mabel, everybody knows—'

Mabel sighed. 'Yes, yes. Everybody knows but nobody talks about it.'

Edie couldn't see that it made any difference one way or the other. She wondered if Mabel would notice that one of her bodice buttons was undone. But she hadn't. Oh, dear. Now she'd have to tell her—

Too late. Virginia Jago was making her way across to them. 'Don't get up, Edie. You look well, Mabel.'

She reminded Edie of a delphinium that had somehow escaped from the flower bed. Tall and willowy, drifting across the grass in her blue linen frock and French grey slingbacks. Absolutely beautiful, though Mabel didn't seem impressed. 'You're as well as you feel,' she shot back.

'You don't feel well?' Virginia asked.

'I feel for Myles. This is a sad day. Haven't seen him. Where's he got to?'

'He's taken himself off.'

'I don't blame him.'

'No. You wouldn't,' Virginia said acidly.

Mabel bridled. 'And what, exactly, do you mean by that?'

Edie felt her heart jump as Virginia said, 'I mean, Mabel Petherick, that you don't seem to mind the streak of yellow in Myles. That is possibly because you've always had a schoolgirl crush on him, which is really rather foolish for a woman of your years.'

Mabel gave an audible gasp. 'Now look here—'

'No. You look here—'

Edie shot a glance at her sister, thinking, I really ought to say something to intervene. Like, how well your garden looks, Mrs Jago, or would
you care for a piece of my special sponge cake? Only neither of them
seemed . . . well . . . appropriate under the circumstances.

'Gardens are at their best,' she ventured, 'at this time of the year.'

But neither of them took any notice. Mrs Jago carried on where she
had left off, saying to Mabel, 'My husband tells me he showed you a letter
that came from Kit.'

'Lot two hundred and forty-nine,' Kerslake said. 'Nice little Regency
table with wormy legs.'

There were crimson circles on Mabel's cheekbones.

'You look uncomfortable,' Virginia said. 'And so you should be.'

Mabel's tongue seemed to have stopped working. For years now, the
Petherick sisters had dug for victory, knitted for seamen and endured a
thousand and one fearful moments, but Edie had never, ever, seen Mabel
look so flustered.

'Myles needed . . . advice,' Mabel said at last.

'Then he can go to the rector or his doctor or . . . or even his bloody
commanding officer, but I won't have you reading other people's private
correspondence. And I am sick of you assuming the role of his special
friend and helper. Is that clear?'

There was a pause and then Mabel said stiffly, 'I'm sorry if my seeing
the letter upset you.'

'Upset me? Of course it did! What did you damned well expect?'

'There's no need to use that kind of language.'

'I'll use any kind of language I damned well like. And I'll tell you this.
If I ever again catch you having little heart to hearts with Myles about
my son behind my back, I'll . . . I'll tear your head off.' The conversation
came to an abrupt end as Virginia stalked grandly and spikily off.

Half an hour later, Edie's knees were still shaking.

Daph hitched the horse to a post in the station yard. The train was
already in. It stood steaming next to the buddleia bushes that edged the
little platform. Watching Tom Fermoy chatting to the porter who was
manhandling his luggage, she wished that she hadn't put on the fluttery
voile frock that was so unlike her usual sort of thing, along with her
pearls and the sandals with straps. (Not to mention the dab of Coty's
Vertige from a flask on her dressing table.) Her legs looked horribly
bare and thick and white. She stood trying to straighten her raggle-
taggle hair. He hadn't seen her yet. Perhaps if she sloped out through

the booking hall, he would think they had forgotten him and take Davey's taxi.

Then, 'Hello there!' he called. 'You look summery.'

'Do I? Mother was nagging me to look like a perfect English lady.' She knew as she said it that it was not the entire truth. 'How was your journey?'

'Not bad. It's good to be out of London. The air's so sweet.'

'That's the buddleia. I've brought the dogcart. Do you mind?'

'Not at all. As long as you don't want me to drive it.'

'Impy wouldn't let you.'

'Who's Impy?'

'The pony. She's got a mind of her own.'

'That's okay. I like independent women.' His smile had warmth and a sweetness about it. Sometimes, Daph thought, the way he looks at me, I'd swear—

But, no. She was imagining things.

Tom hoisted his bag into the back seat and climbed in beside her. Impy turned right, without being told to, out of the station yard then trotting briskly on out of town. Already the station seemed far away, a mere wisp of smoke puffs back in the distance. The hedges were thick with leaf. They turned off the main road and into a small wood bordered by a stream that was all bright light and silver water. 'There's the sea,' she said as they left behind the small Cornish oaks and skimmed up over the rise. They were bowling along so fast that she had to rein Impy in.

'She hasn't been out for ages,' Daph said.

She heard herself rattling on, telling him about how mad it had been all week: about the crowds milling around at home; how the birds had been scratching around where she had been weeding, scattering earth all over the steps, so she had fetched a broom and swept it all up. She told him about Arthur Jago and his wife, Julia, turning up as they were having a hurried breakfast, along with great-aunt Sarah and cousin Hermione and various other mongrel family members. Then she asked if he had been listening to the BBC talks on the Peace Conference live from Paris.

'I caught most of them,' Tom said. 'Odd to think that Winston was at the 1919 conference.'

'Isn't it?' She turned her head to look at him, and saw the clean, bright green of new bracken and pink valerian flying by. 'Granny says he's the only one who ever had the measure of Hitler.'

'Granny might very well be right,' he said.

'She can't stand Attlee.'

'Neither can my grandmother. They're Victorians.'

'I suppose. Granny likes everything done formally. Calling cards and maids bringing this and clearing that. She can't bear this new take-us-as-you-find-us world. She told me off just now for coming out gloveless.'

'Funny you should say that. I thought, when you turned up at the station, there's something missing—'

Daph laughed. 'Sorry. I'll remember next time. How long are you here for?'

'Depends how long it takes to check on the dry-rot treatment to the staircase hall and the sagging timber floors in the top bedrooms and the external stonework repairs and—'

'Quite some time, then?' All at once, sitting on the striped cotton seat beside him, she felt enormously happy. In his light summer suit and blue shirt, there was something sinewy about him. Very clean and . . . What? Attractive? This last thought shocked her. She pushed it away.

'A few days at least.' He asked how her parents were coping with the sale.

Daph stared straight ahead. She said, in a rush, 'Pa said last night he feels he's let go of the tiller. And that the house knows it and is blaming him. He said it's like taking the one love of your life and handing her over to someone else. I tried to tell him he was saving the old place, but he wouldn't have it. We were in his den and he got the best port out and we both got tipsy and he started telling stories about when he was a boy.' She hesitated for a moment, then hurried on. 'Some of them were quite funny. When he was about ten, he decided he would sleep in a different room every night until he'd been all round the house, but Granny found out and she forbade him to sleep up in the servants' quarters, so he had to give up on the project. But after the drink kicked in, he went all maudlin. He started talking about his father's coffin resting in the drawing room until the funeral and – this is the bit that worries me – about an uncle of his who died when he was out shooting. His foot slipped and he managed to shoot himself in the head. And what I'm scared of is that he might do something silly. You don't think he would, do you? I don't even know why I'm asking you. I mean, how could you possibly be expected to know?'

'I can't. But the thought's better out in the open.'

'Yes.' The dogcart swayed as they swung round another corner.

Tom said, 'He's bound to be distressed at this stage. But if anyone can get him through this, Charlie will. He's an expert on handling distraught owners of stately piles.' A pause. 'I don't know if I'm supposed to tell you this, but he's got plans to take the major up to Montacute to see what's been done there. He thought that showing him the end product might cheer him up. Let him see there's light at the end of the tunnel.'

Daph said, 'That's a wonderful idea.'

'Isn't it? Charlie's not the type to throw his weight around and he wears his knowledge lightly, but he *always* – and I mean always – knows what he's doing. Except with women.'

'I don't believe you. He's very good-looking.'

'Ah, well, that's the problem, you see. He's such an admirable specimen that he gets chased by the wrong kind of women. And when it comes to the tipping point, he's never brave enough to tell them to buzz off and leave him alone.'

'Perhaps he doesn't want them to.'

'You haven't seen the women.'

'Pa's at a kind of tipping point,' Daph said, after a pause.

'The whole country's at a tipping point. So many things of the old ways gone. So many unknowns waiting in the offing . . .'

Daph thought, He seems flippant and light-hearted, but there's a depth to him. His smile's so warm, you could drown in it. I really have to stop thinking like this . . .

'I shall be glad,' she said, 'when the ground stops shifting under our feet.'

Tom fixed her with his disconcerting gaze. 'Actually, I quite like the ground to tip a bit. Before the war, I was working for an old-fashioned sort of architectural practice near Baker Street and I was bored to death. They offered to take me on again last September and I thought, do I really want to spend the rest of my life doing this? And then a client I'd once worked for recommended me to Charlie and he wrote to ask if I'd consider working for the Trust. And here I am racketing like a spinning top around the country, never quite knowing where I'll eat or sleep from one night to the next. And it's a dream to be working on all these wonderful old buildings. Liberating. Restorative.'

There was a hesitation, then he added, 'I was in Dresden, you see. The damage we did there . . . well, it's not easily forgotten. I know that what our air force did was necessary . . . at least, I hope it was necessary. Tens of thousands killed. Homes, churches, a wonderful old city destroyed in a firestorm. And the women and children who survived having to surrender to the Red Army. I can't do anything about their fate, and I can't go over there and help rebuild their flattened homes, but—'

They were nearing the hall. Daph could see it behind the trees.

She said, 'There are hundreds of flattened homes in the East End. Their need is greater than ours.'

'Yes.' Tom accepted that. Then he said, 'I suppose I should have known, from the missing gloves.'

'Known what?'

'That you're a raving socialist.'

Daph drove the dogcart expertly through the gates and past the lodge. *He's teasing,* she thought, *and I don't mind in the least.* She felt light-hearted and a little light-headed.

She said, 'Not raving. I'm sorry. I stopped you in full flow.'

'All I meant was, there's a lot of stuff to be put back together in this country and that, working with Charlie, one can't help but be optimistic.'

She thought this over.

Optimism I like, she wanted to say. *Also the way you're not embarrassed to be passionate about your work.* But there was something else that had to be said. 'It's hard for us to feel optimistic with Kit lying in the churchyard.'

He took the reins from her and pulled Impy into the verge.

'I'm sorry. I'm a clumsy oaf.'

'No.'

'Yes, I am. You're mad at me.'

'No.' Not mad, but hit, unexpectedly, by a wall of grief. How could you feel so good one moment and bad the next? 'It's okay.' She struggled to get herself under control. That took about five seconds. Then she had to find a new topic, so she said, 'I was wondering last night how many concerts you would have been to since you were last here.'

'Let's see now. Mozart's *Requiem*.'

'I love Mozart.'

'And *Aida*. And next month I've got tickets for Sullivan's *Golden Legend*.' Tom sat there holding the reins, and then he said, almost casually, 'You should come with me some time. If you ever come up to town.'

Daphne sat there, her red-gold hair glowing in the sun. Leaves rustled above their heads. Up by the yew hedge, people were strolling away bearing their spoils. She wanted to fold the moment up in tissue paper and keep it for ever and ever.

In the morning, Jack Trewarden went down to the kitchen to make tea and found Lil hanging over the kitchen sink being sick. So he filled an enamel jug from the old pump outside the door, poured some into a glass and handed it to her.

She took a couple of sips, then poured the rest of the water into a bowl and splashed her face with it.

'Something you ate?' he asked.

'If only,' she said.

'Something you picked up at work?'

'You don't pick up being pregnant,' she said, reaching for the tea towel to dry her face on.

Sixteen

The office Morris, doing a smacking forty miles per hour, was speeding towards Montacute. Charlie, at the wheel, reached for a cigarette and lit it. The major sat with his knuckles resting on his knees. Their overnight bags were stowed away in the boot. It had been – still was – one of those long, yellow days of August. They had set off in the late afternoon and had stopped for an early dinner just before Taunton.

The major, all the way up through Devon and Somerset, had kept up a stream of questions about Montacute. Who had owned the estate before the Trust had taken it over? What sort of state had the house been in? Who had it been entailed to and how the devil, if such a good bag of stately homes – Cotehele, Laycock, Arlington Court – was dropping at Charlie's feet, was he going to manage them all without going bankrupt himself?

After the grilling, Charlie felt like burnt toast that was crumbling at the edges. Under the major's gruff, tough exterior it was not difficult to sense a man of some kindness, but would he ever learn to loosen up? He was now rummaging distractedly through his pockets, searching for something. The rummaging was sending out a slight smell of mothballs and something else. I know, Charlie thought. That dark brown soap with the healthy smell. The one that cracks on top and grows jelly underneath when you don't use it for a while.

'Something wrong, sir?' he asked.

'My pipe. Must have left it at the hotel.'

'Too far to go back, I'm afraid.'

The hotel, a safe but boring choice with a nondescript menu, was now a good fifty miles behind them.

'There's an acid drop in the glove compartment, if you're desperate.'

'No. Thank you.'

Charlie offered him a cigarette. 'It was good to arrive at a hotel and get dinner without booking days beforehand,' he said, but the major just dug his hands in his pockets and stared out at the passing hedges.

'How far now?' the major asked abruptly.

'Ten miles.'

'Good show.'

These days, it seemed to Charlie that the Jagos were an extension of his own family and that, in spite of, or even because of their little eccentricities, he was growing as attached to them as he was to the mansion they inhabited.

'Good to flee the field, so to speak, for a day or so.' The major stuck an elbow out of the open window. 'Good to get away from all that hammering.'

'It won't be forever.'

'The visitors will be forever.'

'Yes,' said Charlie, 'but they shouldn't be too much of an inconvenience.'

'Hrrmph.'

They went on gazing out at hazy fields. For the last three weeks, high pressure had kept the countryside in a trance. 'There's another thing,' the major said. 'When you walk in, the house smells different.'

'Benzine-Bentol, plaster and sawdust,' Charlie told him. 'In a few months it'll change to paint and beeswax.'

'Preferred it as it was in the old days.'

'Ah, but which old days? Lizzah has had so many pasts. Edwardian, Georgian, Elizabethan . . . I like to think that in Shakespeare's time, the house would have smelled of cold mutton and uncleaned woollen clothes.'

For a single fleeting moment, the major looked him in the eye. 'Not my cup of tea . . . philosophizing.' Then, 'I suppose what you're saying is that it doesn't matter who owns it, so long as the house – and its whiffs – go on?'

'Something like that.'

A silence. Then the major said, 'So when did Montacute open its doors to the public?'

'A month ago. We had one hell of a job to meet the deadline, but I'm proud of how it's come together. I hope this visit will go some way towards quelling your fears about . . . well, everything really.'

'Spindly corn in that field,' the major said. 'I'd like to be on a cricket field in white flannels.'

Daisy trailed down the wooden staircase from the sewing room on the attic floor, through the barrack-like gallery and down two more flights of stairs to the back quarters of the house where she took her morning break with Mrs Trewarden and Bess Tilley. This morning, the kitchen smelled of plums. Bess was filling a row of jars with them, snapping the rubber rings carefully round the bottles and then giving them a rough wipe with the dishcloth to remove any sticky patches. Daisy sat down at the table next to the cup of tea that had been poured for her and unwrapped the twist of biscuits she had brought from home.

'I keep telling you,' Bess said, 'there's no need to bring your own.'

'She might prefer her own,' Peg Trewarden said with a wink in Daisy's direction.

'There! That's done,' Bess said, chucking the dishcloth at the sink. 'I remember the year we made fifty pounds of plum jam. That was when you could get the sugar. So how's Lil getting on at the cottage, Mrs Trewarden?'

'Same as she does anywhere else,' Mrs Trewarden said. 'Never does a stroke of work if she can help it.'

'I suppose er've got the salon to run.'

'Salon my foot!' Peg Trewarden said. 'She's the laziest madam it's been my misfortune to meet. I went round to cook Cliffy's supper once, during the war, and all the cupboard contained, except tins, was a bottle of sauce and half a loaf of bread. They eat a sight better now that Jack's home, that's for sure.'

'You mean he has to do the cooking?' Bess was astonished.

'And the cleaning. This is between you and me and the gatepost.'

The thought of Jack having to run the home, of no one looking after him or the boy, shocked the tender-hearted Daisy. She had been thinking about him upstairs as she pulled together a frayed coverlet with a line of meticulous herring-bone stitches, wondering miserably why he had crossed the road to avoid her when she had come across him in the village. He had seen her, she would swear to it, but he had turned his head away and ducked off into Rectory Lane.

What had she done to upset him? Why had he looked right through her? Was it something she had said? Was it because she had smiled at him? Had she seemed too forward?

See you another Sunday, he had said. Oh, she knew it couldn't actually happen. You shouldn't even think about meeting a married man. But in her head, ever since, she had been building up a fantasy about walking on the breakwater with him in a cotton frock copied from a sketch of a Christian Dior dress she'd seen in the new *Woman's Weekly*.

A fantasy in which Jack was holding her hand and turning his head to smile at her . . . The dress had little cap sleeves and a nipped-in waist and yards and yards of wide, sweeping skirts. And St Michael's clock was tanging and the sea was shimmering and all the little boats bobbing at their moorings . . .

Was it possible that something of all this silliness had communicated itself to him? I hope not, she thought, coming over all hot. Actually, she thought, he probably didn't even notice me. Why would he?

Mrs Trewarden took a bite of ginger cake. 'I remember the first time he brought Lil home. She was wearing a tiger-print fur jacket and I thought, "You've got the wrong one there, my son." But you have to let them make their own mistakes, same as we did. Nice moist bit of cake, Bess.'

'It come out surprisingly well,' Bess said, 'considering I left the oven door slightly open and all the heat went out of it.'

'And how are you getting on with your sewing, Daisy?' Mrs Trewarden asked. 'I hear the old battleaxe has taken to sitting with you.'

'Actually,' Daisy said, 'she's been quite a help.'

'When I took her coffee up, she had a face like stewed prunes. That's the one she wears when she's having a good day.'

Daisy laughed. 'She reminds me of Granny Jewell. They're in their eighties, they're lonely, and they don't know what to do to fill their day, so they play you up.'

'You can say that again. I expect she finds fault with every stitch.'

'She did until I asked her to show me what I was doing wrong. So she did and I let her carry on and she ended up doing half the work on the Red Room chairs.'

'Well, I never!'

'Actually, I think she likes feeling useful again.'

'You've got a better opinion of her than I have, that's all I can say. Well,' Peg drained her cup, 'this won't feed the plum cake for Miss Daphne's wedding. Mr Boswell's taking her out to lunch. He wasn't anywhere near the front of the queue when looks were handed out, but he's a nice enough chap and that's all that matters.'

Bess begged leave to say that a bit of money didn't hurt either. There was an artistic pause for dramatic effect before she added, 'And a nice old place like Trebartha.'

So far as Daisy was concerned, it didn't matter two pins if a man had money just so long as when he smiled at you, you got a warm feeling in the pit of your stomach.

In the servants' hall, on the way back upstairs, she told herself that when you were older . . . say fortyish . . . you'd be happy to settle for someone dull and kind. But in the meantime . . .

She was on the bottom stair when she heard a drawer slamming and the major's voice saying, abruptly, 'I've admitted to being in the wrong. Several times. Don't quite know what else you expect of me.'

'I don't expect anything.' That was Mrs Jago, sounding as businesslike and competent as ever. They were in his office with the door half open. 'I used to, at one time, but that was when I was young and foolish.' There came the sound of more drawers banging. Mrs Jago said, 'What on earth are you searching for?'

'My roll of Tums.'

'Are you ill?'

'No. Indigestion.' More rummaging, then he said, 'Be damned — where've they got to?'

'No need to swear,' his wife told him.

'I'll swear if I want to. Pa swore. Not much of a father, but he lived his own life.'

Daisy's heart began to thud. She stood in the stairwell, knowing that she ought to run on up, but her feet wouldn't seem to move.

'*You* live your own life.'

'Not any more I don't,' muttered the major. 'Nagging womenfolk glaring at me behind my back.'

'And how would you know if I was glaring at your back?'

'You know what I mean. Never been any good at words.'

'Oh, I don't know. You manage to talk to the blessed Mabel.'

'Mabel doesn't keep sniping. There isn't hell to pay if I express myself badly.'

My goodness, Daisy thought wildly, she goes to a London hairdresser and she's got all those wonderful clothes and she looks like the Queen of Sheba and she's jealous of old Miss Petherick!

She ran on up to the sewing room and swung herself behind the huge rack that had been rigged up to hold the coverlet while it was being repaired. The room was sunny and the mother-of-pearl shell she had picked up on the beach that Sunday sat on the window sill looking like an elegantly polished button.

She wondered whether it would be possible to make the little Dior number out of no-coupon muslin or even one of the off-ration furnishing fabrics. It would have to be something lightish. She would have a poke around Hennings' on Saturday.

The door opened and old Mrs Jago came creaking in, breathing heavily and rattling her stick on the floorboards. 'Those stairs don't get any easier,' she said. Then, 'Did Perrin deliver my note about the bed linen?'

'Yes, she did. But—'

'I wrote it at two in the morning. I don't sleep, you know. At least, I sleep for an hour then wake up with a million things in my head. Mostly morbid. I decided last night that I would ask the canon if I could be buried without any church service.'

Daisy didn't know what to say.

'At first he tried to persuade me against it, but when he saw I meant business, he said that he couldn't see any reason why not. I would have to write a formal letter to the bishop, of course, to ask permission. I've been thinking about it for a while. I don't see why I should lie there in my coffin with people spouting religious platitudes over me when I don't have beliefs any more. So . . . anyway . . . the note. What did you think?'

Daisy didn't know what to think, because the writing on the scrap of paper had been practically illegible and she had only been able to make out two words. 'Well, actually, I've been puzzling over it all morning.'

'Puzzling?' With her white, wire-like hair puffed out round her head, she looked like an impatient, hawk-like bird. 'What is there to puzzle about?'

'I . . . didn't understand the bit about the barley and the threadworm.'

'Threadworm?' said Evalina Jago blankly. There was a pause, then she said, 'Didn't they teach you to read at school? I was asking if you needed help with the drawn threadwork on the bolster case. The one with the rose and barley embroidery.'

Marina telephoned and said, 'It's me.' Daph could imagine her at the other end of the line. Terrifyingly smart. Pale, sculptured hair and varnished nails. 'I got your letter.'

Daph said, 'I hope you didn't mind me asking.'

'If you could come and stay? Darling, don't be silly.'

'And James won't mind?'

'James isn't here. Actually, I'm divorcing him.'

'Oh, my goodness.'

Daph couldn't think what else to say.

'You'll want to know why. Well, he cheated on me. And I racked my brains for an adequate reason why I should stay married to him, but there wasn't one. There's nothing to get the wind up about,' Marina said airily. 'His family were awful. And there are compensations. I'm having a full day in bed. I promised myself one when the war was over.'

'It's been over for months,' Daph said.

'I know. But I've been working at one of the ministries and they wouldn't give me time off until this week. I've just had a whacking break-fast and I'm halfway through the papers.' There was an infinitesimal pause, then she said, 'I'm sorry about your brother, by the way.'

'Yes, well . . . you just have to get on with it.'

'And I'm sorry you're losing the house.'

'We're not exactly losing it. Just moving to the east wing.'

'That's all right then. So . . . what about this engagement of yours? I nearly died of shock. What's he like? Has he got plenty of cash? Was it like a bomb going off inside you the minute you saw him?'

'Not . . . exactly,' Daph said.

'Hmm. I shall have to come down there and inspect him.' Marina, who had always dominated their friendship, proceeded to ask what Daph was doing about birth control.

'Birth control?' Daph said.

'Yes, birth control. You know. Volpar gels—'

'I'm not sure—'

'Sweetie, he must have pounced on you?'

'Did I tell you I've got tickets for a concert?' Daph's voice was defensively high.

'He hasn't. Sweetie, he's not religious? Or a cold fish? Because that would be worse than having a randy so-and-so like James.'

Daph said, 'I've been offered a ticket for a Wigmore concert.'

'He's not old and decrepit?'

'Of course not! So . . . would you mind if I took myself off one night while I'm up?'

'Just as long as you don't expect me to come with you.'

'No. As a matter of fact,' Daph said quickly, 'a friend got the tickets. So I'll have company. It's Schubert. And Debussy.'

Marina let out a yawn. 'Fantastic, darling. We'll continue this chat when you get here. When do you want to come?'

Daph let a few drops of delicious oil fall into the bathwater. The decision had been made. She was going to a concert with Tom Fermoy. He had telephoned the previous weekend. Daph had attempted rather breathlessly to refuse, telling him that the tenth of October was Pen's birthday, but that had only made him say, 'Will she really mind? It's the Nash Ensemble.' It was very wrong of her to have said, 'The Nash? Don't tempt me,' and then, on finding that it was Schubert, to have added instinctively, 'Perfect!'

She put a wet flannel on her head and lay there wondering what on earth she had done. Her friendship with Tom seemed to be progressing in little leaps, each one leaving an intense pleasure that seemed to remain in her bones. There is nothing intrinsically wrong with sitting next to a man at a concert, she told herself. We'll enjoy the Schubert and I'll thank

him for a lovely evening and we'll stand on the pavement outside for a
moment or two talking about . . . oh, I don't know . . . the *Winterreise* or
the *St Matthew Passion* or the violets on the hat of the woman who sat in
front of us. And when he asks if I want a coffee, I'll say, 'Better not.
Marina will be waiting up,' and after a moment of awkward zing, we'll
say 'Goodnight,' and that will be that.

So.

Nothing to be uncomfortable about.

Only the fact that you haven't told Bos. She swished the water around with
one toe. She had spent the day up at Trebartha and Bos had talked endlessly
about his Greyfaced Dartmoor sheep. An old friend of his from Tavistock
had put him on to them. They were good milkers, capable of rearing twins.
Deep-bodied, short-legged, they had immense strength of constitution.

'I say, I'm boring you,' he had said at one point.

'No.'

But you'll never set my heart on fire.

He hadn't an ounce of romance in his body. Daph opened her eyes
and saw sunlight on the wall. She got out of the bath, dried herself and
dusted herself down with bath powder. I shall have to own up, she thought,
about the concert. The thing was, she couldn't think how. Bos was such
a nice old stick. Why risk upsetting him just to square her conscience?

'I'll ask Tom to bring Charlie along,' she said, dropping the towel and
reaching for the comb. 'A threesome would be quite all right.'

Once the idea had occurred to her, she felt more comfortable. This
pash she had for Tom . . . the flippy-floppy flight of her heart when he
spoke to her, the wild joy that grabbed her every time he popped into
her mind . . . it was just a stupid crush that would die a death.

And if it doesn't? I'll pull it up like bindweed.

The thing was, the more you thought you had killed a bindweed root,
the more it sprang up somewhere else. Well, it won't have to, she decided,
because I'm marrying Bos in March and I can't back out at this stage,
not without hurting him dreadfully.

And how could she do that when he had been so very good to her?
She wrapped herself in a dry towel and thought of the wooden box from
India, painted delicately with charming butterflies, that he had given her;
the pots of lavender; how he planned to have the big old bedroom overlooking the dovecot done up before the wedding. The only fly in the
ointment was that she couldn't for the life of her imagine herself in bed
with him. Or him *pouncing*, as Marina put it.

Did that matter?

Possibly.

As she came to this uncomfortable sticking place, Pen came barging into the bathroom, 'You should bolt the door,' she said. 'I might have been anybody.'

'And you,' said Daph, 'should try knocking.'

Ignoring this, Pen stood gawking at her. 'You look better with your hair in a mess.'

'My hair's always a mess.'

'And better without your clothes.'

Daph raised her eyebrows. 'Is that a compliment?'

'No. I just wouldn't be seen dead in most of your outfits. They're out of the ark.'

'Well, thanks for that.'

'Don't mention it. The thing is, they make you look horribly sensible. Like Miss Gardner.'

'Who's Miss Gardner?'

Our maths teacher. All her clothes are the colour of brown sauce.' Standing there in her sand shoes and her Liberty's smock, she smiled at Daph. 'Don't worry about it. Bos won't care. Oh, God – I'm desperate. I'll have to use the outside lavatory.'

At the end of that week, Charlie let himself into his flat in Balfour Gardens. At one time, half the street had been lined with unoccupied, empty houses and flats whose owners and tenants had left London in a hurry. But now, as he dumped his bag in the tiny hallway, he could hear radios playing and footsteps thumping above his head and laughter coming from somewhere across the landing. He dropped his mountain of post on the table and his jacket on the chair and stood at the window watching great splats of rain – as big as hailstones – hitting the pavement below and drying out almost immediately. Light thunder was rolling round the streets and the green and blue of the plane trees filtering into mauve. There was a feeling of a mood changing. Well, it can do with changing, he thought. He was feeling . . . what? Restless? A bit seedy? Not jolly, at any rate. He had lunched alone at the Maison Basque in Dover Street. Had gone on to Batsford's to choose illustrations for a guide book, but on coming out, had found his battery flat, so the car had had to be pushed through the close summer streets to start it.

He pulled on a jersey, got himself a scratch meal of poached eggs on toast, and asked himself why he felt so cheesed when the week had actually gone well. The major had seemed impressed by Montacute; had been pleased to see that it wasn't too vulgar. He had admitted – praise indeed – that the Trust seemed to run a pretty good ship.

So . . . it wasn't work. It was the fact that his personal life felt . . . off the cuff, haphazard, nothing ever fully intended. There were two of him, he felt. The Charlie who went about working hard, chatting to people, enjoying himself, even; and the other self, unnervingly isolated, who stood waiting around for something significant to happen. Waiting for a change of season . . .

The evening drifted on. The rain stopped, though clouds still lay over the green sweep of the park. Charlie wrote a schoolmastery page for the guide on seventeenth-century Lizzah. He put a record on the gramophone and sat down at the typewriter again, but his thoughts kept wandering, so at half past ten he decided to turn in.

He lay awake for ages. Then, when he did sleep, he dreamt he saw his army chaplain in a summer wood. The chaplain, his voice young and edgy, was singing 'O God, our help in ages past'. Leaves rustled against a sharp, blue sky. Then a shot rang out and the chaplain was a goner, picked off by a German sniper. Then the big guns started. Bang, bang, bang, one after the other.

He woke in a sweat, only to realize that someone was thumping on his door and calling his name. At first he thought he was still dreaming, but as he listened, the sound was repeated. 'Mr Garland! Phone!'

At a quarter to midnight? Charlie pulled on his dressing-gown and went down the two flights of stairs to the hall. Mrs Kingham, his landlady, was standing by the telephone waiting to have a go at him. 'This isn't good enough, Mr Garland. Waking people in the middle of the night.'

'Yes, I know. I'm sorry. It must be some emergency.'

His father ill again? Had somebody died?

The voice at the other end was desperate. 'Mr Garland? Charlie?'

It was her . . . Romily . . . and she was sobbing. 'I'm so sorry to ring at this time of night. I didn't know who else to call. Could you come over? Right this minute? I need someone . . .'

Seventeen

Charlie parked the car halfway down Frances Street. He was struggling to remember the number of the house. Sixteen, he thought. Or was it eighteen? Then he remembered the triangular rose bed in the front garden.

He had tracked this down and was opening the squeaky gate when the front door sprang open and Romily called out to 'm. 'Thank God!' she said.

She came running down the path and threw herself at him. She was shaking all over. In the light from the doorway, he could see that she had blood on her face and there was something wrong with her eye.

'All right. It's all right. I'm here.' Charlie stood holding her, trying desperately to behave in a rational manner. 'What happened? Tell me.'

'He hit me.' She was letting out dry, hard sobs.

'Who hit you?'

'Jan.'

'Bastard.' He couldn't help it. The word just came out.

'He said I was seeing someone else. He was drunk. I told him to clear out and I was terrified that he wouldn't. Then when he did go, I was scared he'd come back.'

'No need to be scared.' Charlie could smell the evening and the damp dust from the streets. 'Look – we can't stand here. We'll wake the neighbourhood. Do you want to sit in the car?'

'No. I'm cold.' Her teeth were chattering. 'Come in. We can bolt the door.'

She did so. The house, miraculously, was still silent. Gripping his hand, she led him up the two flights of stairs to her flat.

It was only when she closed the door behind them that he could see clearly the cut on her forehead and her swollen, discolouring eye.

'Good God,' he said.

'Actually, I feel a bit peculiar.'

'Sit down.' She was as white as a ghost. 'I'll bathe it. Have you got iodine?'

Fetching water from the washstand in the corner, he took a clean handkerchief from his breast pocket and did the necessary. Then he lit the gas fire in the hearth and made her hot, sweet tea. 'Do you want to call the police?' he asked.

'No.'

'Why not?'

'Because he'll deny it and he'll come back in a foul temper and hit me again.'

'Has it happened before?'

Silence.

'Romily? Tell me.'

'Once or twice.'

'I am going to call the police.'

'No – please . . .'

Charlie's gaze was heavy with thought. At last, he said, 'Will you let me call them if he can't find you?'

'But he will.'

'Not if you're not here.'

'Where else could I go?'

'Home to the rectory?'

'Looking like this?' She shook her head. 'I couldn't.'

'All right.' He had made a decision. 'You can stay at my place.'

'I can't do that.'

'Why not?'

'Because . . . well, I hardly know you.'

'You knew me enough to ring for help.'

'Yes.' She sat looking at her hands.

'That's settled then. Pack a bag. Enough for a few days. You can have my bed and I'll sleep on the couch.'

'I can't steamroller you into taking me in.'

Charlie had never seen anyone less like a steamroller in his life. She was more like a Rolls Royce, he thought. Beautiful (in spite of the rapidly swelling eye), svelte, elegant, classy.

He would have to smuggle her in past Mrs Kingham. And in the morning? He would say she was his cousin up from the country. That she'd been in a car accident and had to rest up for a couple of days.

And after that?

He had no idea, but he'd think of something.

A week later, Pen wrote in her diary:

> A bit of a row at breakfast when Mother had the brass neck to call
> me difficult and I said it was the pot calling the kettle black. She

is such a bossy-pants! Walked up to The Barton with Pa to collect the rent. Gusty day. Larks and pheasants and buzzards. Farmer Jewell kindly let me ride one of the big horses. When we got back, Mr Garland was in the back hall on the telephone. I think he was talking to a WOMAN, because he gave me a frowny look and kept his voice down. I pretended to go on upstairs, but sat on the bend and listened. He said, 'What about having dinner at The Perroquet on Friday night?' She said (I think), that she didn't want to. He said, 'But you mustn't worry about your face.' I wish I could have heard what she said next because she went on for ages and he kept fidgeting with the cord and raking his hand through his hair (which is what heroes do in books) and he couldn't get a word in at all until at last he said, 'Of course you're not causing me a lot of trouble, I'm perfectly comfortable in Tom's spare room and he doesn't mind me staying in the least.' Then he said, 'No, I didn't call the police.' And, 'Now you've handed in your notice at the shop, that madman will never find you.' And then he asked, (and this is odd) 'Don't you think you ought to tell Daphne?' Well, that properly put the cat among the pigeons because he had to keep saying, over and over, 'All right,' and, 'Don't worry,' and, 'Of course I wouldn't tell her without asking you first.' In the end, they arranged to meet at the Charing Cross station bar and after he'd hung up, he looked all tired and battered-looking and moony and he stood staring at his feet for I don't know how long. So what's wrong with her face? If it's the girl he brought to the sale, she's plainish (and fat), but not THAT ugly. I'd go to The Perroquet with him, if he asked. Fat chance!!! I had a thought. Maybe she's had the measles. Or chicken pox. I don't know where he gets his shoes from but they're quite, quite beautiful.

Keeping in touch with Romy by telephone was the only option Charlie had during the week. It didn't stop him worrying about her, but hearing her voice gave him some relief.

'I'll have to find another job,' she said one night.

'In a week or two,' Charlie told her. 'When you feel better.' He meant, when the bruising had gone down. She hadn't wanted to leave her job at the bookshop, but Charlie had persuaded her that she was better safe than sorry.

'If he can't find you, he can't cause any more trouble. You can stay at my place as long as you like.'

'But it's not fair, turning you out of your home.'

'You didn't turn me out. I offered.'

As they chatted, he liked to imagine her in his untidy flat opposite the bomb site; solid stone fireplace, deco rug on the floor in front of it, bookcases, desk and the Duke of Wellington's bust used as a doorstopper. It was easier, somehow, talking to her down the wires. If he couldn't see her slim throat, that exquisite hair, the colour of honeysuckle, and her tormenting figure, then he couldn't be unsettled by them. The inner essence of her was enough, shimmering in the ether at the other end of the line. While she told him what she had been doing with her day – cleaning the sooty windows, re-reading *Treasure Island* and *Huckleberry Finn*, fetching herself a custard tart from the bakery on the corner – Charlie listened and wondered what she would say if he told her she was the only person in the world who could possibly look beautiful with a black eye, that he was quite, quite gone on her, and that he had found it difficult to restrain himself from rushing round to wherever the Pole lived and killing him with his bare hands. Instead he said, 'Your landlady was a bit grunty when I collected your stuff.'

'Grunty?' Romy said. It was good to hear her laugh.

'She wanted me to pay two extra months for leaving at short notice. When I only gave her one, she hit the roof.'

'I'll pay you back,' she said.

'No hurry.'

Another night he told her he'd called at the rectory to see her father.

'Why?' Her voice filled with alarm.

'Why? Because I bumped into him in the village and he asked me to.'

'You didn't mention—'

'Of course not.'

A relieved pause. Then, 'How are they?'

'Getting ready for the harvest supper. Your mother and I had a long conversation about scarlet fever.'

'Oh, God.'

'Your father has been visiting a family whose child is in the fever hospital, so she thinks she might hang sheets soaked in Jeyes on the rectory doors as a precautionary measure. What colour is your eye today?' Charlie asked.

'Pale yellow.'

'That's an improvement.' Charlie said. 'I like your father.'

This was the mere gist of what he wanted to say, which was, he supposed, that there was an appealing simplicity about the rector. When he considered you with his clear, grey eyes and smiled at you with enormous kindness, you felt captivated by . . . Well, the phrase that came to mind was *the beauty of holiness*. In any other circumstances, Hugh Matheson would have been the perfect person to confide in. In fact, at one point, Charlie had come appallingly close to doing so; but though the idea had been tempting, it was also quite barmy.

Because how could you tell a father who preached that God is love, and who thought well of everyone he came across, that his daughter had been knocked around by a plastered Pole who had been posting foul-mouthed, threatening letters to her last-known address in London?

I'd ram them down his throat if I could catch him, Charlie thought. Thank God he had collected and burned them before Romy laid eyes on them. She had sounded moody the last time he'd called. Was she still holding a candle for the bastard? Not possible. Surely?

The thing was, you never knew with women. One minute you were talking to them and they were sassy and uplifting and full of gorgeous aplomb . . . then in an instant, they were as vulnerable as hell and sobbing on your shoulder.

Charlie's face softened. He sighed.

Come on, he told himself. There's loads to do. Those damned partitions separating the gallery into an orderly room and officers' mess have to come down, and there's the stack of porcelain we found in the cellars, and another thirty rooms to clean and the major's new will (ten foolscap sheets and no punctuation whatsoever) to be looked over, and we shall have to get the tapestries out into the garden before the weather breaks to check for moths . . .

He still didn't know how he was going to get through the three days until he saw her again.

'I heard on the nine o'clock news that the Duchess of Windsor's jewels were stolen. She was at some country house party.' Evalina sat waiting for breakfast to be served. 'They won't see her, you know – the king and queen. If I were in their shoes, I wouldn't either. What do you imagine he sees in a woman with no more flesh on her than a skinned flea? Of course, the thing about falling in love is that it doesn't always bring happiness. Or ease. Or comfort.'

She peered past Daph at Bos, who smiled back at her amiably. He had come to drive Daph to catch the early train to London.

'One hears that she's a difficult woman to live with. Pigheaded. Gets on her high horse.'

It takes one to know one, Daph thought, glancing at her watch. The porridge was bubbling at a fast gallop. Tilley threw another handful in and stirred like mad. 'We should be going,' she said.

Trewarden was charging around the lawns with the motor tractor, leaving the dead grass lying. Daph tugged at the tweedy jacket handed down from her mother. It was at least a size too small and a bad match for the sage green woollen dress she had unearthed from the back of her wardrobe. She had considered running back upstairs to change it, but there wasn't time so she had rejected the idea. Her bag was the wrong colour, too, and her face felt stretched with too much nervous smiling. She wasn't used to making strategic arrangements and she was certain Bos would sense her guilt.

Serve me right if he does, she thought. What I'm about to do is like a story from a bad flick. I shouldn't even be thinking of it, but I *so* want to. Best get on with it, then, before anything happens to stop you.

She gave Bos a determinedly warm smile. He looked bronzed and shiny with health and, somehow, big and clumsy.

'If you're ready . . .' she said.

Bos said, 'Righty-ho.'

'So what exactly,' Evalina asked, 'is the purpose of this trip?'

'I need to buy off-ration white lace from Bourne and Hollingsworth. And stockings and . . .'

'And what?'

'And things for my trousseau.'

'If you mean underwear, why don't you say so?'

Pen was smirking into her porridge plate. Daph shot her a look. Then she buttoned her jacket and said to Bos, 'My bag's in the hall.'

Bos expressed the hope that Mrs Jago would enjoy her breakfast. Evalina said that, given the state of her innards and the smell of burnt oats emitting from the stove, she very much doubted it.

On Sunday morning, Myles and Virginia attended church together. The major wore a very correct collar-and-Eton-tie outfit with a crisp khaki handkerchief stuck in the breast pocket. His wife wore a tailored suit with a wisp of blue crumpled chiffon at the throat.

It was the harvest service. The nave smelled of chrysanthemums. The rector preached at length about beating swords into ploughshares, but all the talk in the church porch was about Goering swallowing a cyanide pill in his cell before they could hang him. The rector said that justice had now been done. But Mabel Petherick, in her storm-proof hat and shoes, said, 'Justice? My grandmother's foot!' Then stalked off with Edie running along behind her.

At the church gate, Charlie Garland said to the major, 'I'm thinking of asking Miss Petherick if she's interested in acting as a guide when the house opens.'

'You are joking?' Gin said.

'No. Now that the new chap's taking over at the school, she'll have time on her hands. She knows an awful lot about the history of Lizzah. And she's lively and intelligent and—'

'And she would cause more problems than you could ever imagine.'

The major fixed his eyes on the horizon, as if gazing out over the great crashed continent of Europe.

Gin said, 'Mabel Petherick runs things in this village because no one will stand up to her. She's like an air-raid warden. As soon as people hear her coming, they dive for cover.'

'So,' Charlie said, 'what do you think, major?'

The major seemed to be combing through all possible options. He settled for, 'Well . . . Mabel's a very capable woman.'

'And about as congenial as a wet winter's afternoon,' Gin snapped as she yanked open the lychgate. 'If you think I'll agree to that woman—'

The rector and his wife were coming down the path, so she was forced to stamp out the blue touch-paper.

Gin climbed into the car and sat staring at the back of Trewarden's head. He had never exactly been a gloriously endearing type, but today he seemed even more truculent than usual. One had to pretend not to notice, but it was difficult when even the back of his head sent out an aura like a highly effective people repellent.

Oh, what I'd give, she thought, to run off up to London like Daphne. Imagine leaving all these petty irritations behind. Imagine walking into the Dorchester to find a delicious luncheon waiting for you on a white starched cloth with gleaming silver and good wine in Waterford crystal and that blatant smell of prosperity.

Myles climbed into the back of the car beside her and Trewarden, poker-faced, jerked the Bentley into gear.

Imagine gorging yourself in that little restaurant in a side street in Kensington where we used to go before the war. The one with the plushy seats, where the waiters were all very old, but very dapper. Nice old tortoises, Myles had called them. But that was in the days when they still knew how to share a joke.

Eighteen

'Hell's bells,' Marina said, 'is that what you're wearing?'

'I thought so. Isn't it right?'

'Frumpish, darling. Take it off. I'll lend you something.'

'I wouldn't get into your things.'

'Nonsense. You've got more bust than me, but apart from that—'

With much flapping of blue trousers, Marina led Daph through the double doors into her bedroom, where everything was very luxurious, very elegant, in spite of the cluttered dressing table, the clothes thrown all over and yesterday's tea tray on the sofa at the bottom of the bed. Marina dived into her wardrobe and dragged out a blue silk number and a grey crêpe dress with daisies all over it.

'Here. Try these on.'

'I couldn't possibly—'

'Oh, for heaven's sake—'

Marina sat on the bed and lit a cigarette as she flicked through the pages of a glossy magazine. Daph slipped off her navy jacket and the high-necked white blouse that she had thought perfectly suitable for the concert, but her underwear didn't pass the Marina test either.

'You're not still wearing thick, white utility cups?'

'I don't have the coupons for fancy brassieres.'

'Sweetie, pretty undies are an absolute necessity. You beg, borrow or steal. Here—'

Marina dragged open a drawer and whisked out a handful of grey lace. 'I suppose you're wearing service knickers as well?'

'They're comfortable,' Daph said defensively.

'So's that old cushion, but I wouldn't dream of wearing it for a date.'

'I keep telling you. It's not a date!'

'Honestly, Daph,' Marina said, 'you must take me for a nincompoop.'

She went off laughing, to the kitchen, to make coffee. Daph swapped her utility brassiere for Marina's wisp of gossamer-fine lace and told herself that it wouldn't make any difference what she had on underneath. But it wasn't true. The crêpe daisies dropped enticingly over the frankly more startling shape. And wasn't it amazing what a few inches of lace could do to the shape of one's bum?

Was she all in? It appeared so. The grey print subtly changed the colour of her hair and gave her a slight but unmistakable air of sophistication.

She stared at her reflection in the mirror and met a gaze that was not entirely easy. 'Enjoy yourself,' Bos had said as he kissed her goodbye, slipping a couple of banknotes into her hand and telling her to treat herself to something old Eva would disapprove of.

Such a dear, Daph thought. I like him so much. I won't spend it. And I'll change back into my own things.

Marina came in with a jug of steaming coffee and hot milk. 'Much better!' she said approvingly. 'With just the right crazy little hat and a dab of lipstick—'

'I don't like make-up. It's not me.'

'But that's the whole point, darling. We don't want it to be you. What we're after is a far more exciting Daphne. So . . . who's this chap you're meeting? You've got quite a crush on him. No, listen, darling, I'm not blaming you. You're sex-starved and I see no reason at all why you shouldn't have a bit on the side before you go into wifey mould with your nice old fogey.'

The bit on the side phrase hurt. Marina made out that life was such a scream, but actually it wasn't. Well, not that kind of scream.

Marina said, 'What's wrong?'

Daph said, 'Nothing,' and wished it was the truth.

An hour later, she cut through an alley that led into Harley Street. The nippy little borrowed hat that Marina had skewered to her head had slipped a little and her carefully arranged hair, ruffled by the wind, now reminded her of an Abyssinian lion she had once seen at a zoo. She would have to hope that the concert hall was badly lit or that Tom Fermoy didn't mind being seen with such a fright.

She'd telephoned him the night before. 'Are you still on for the concert?' she had asked.

'Absolutely.' At the other end, his voice was warmly enthusiastic.

'So shall I meet you there at about sevenish? Is that too early?'

'Not at all. Make it as early as you like.'

'Um – I'll be there just before seven, then.'

'Good.'

Daph had said, 'So . . . I'll see you tomorrow?'

'I'll look forward to it.' Me, too, she had thought, but now that she was within minutes of actually meeting him, she felt as nervous as a bird.

She turned from the window, glanced at her watch and hurried on into Queen Anne Street, where she saw, in the leaf-strewn violet haze, the lemon-coloured lights of the Wigmore. The city looked better at this hour, she thought, with twilight and autumn mists blurring its scars and bomb sites. Tom stood on the pavement, waiting for her, looking as bohemian as ever in a floppy blue jacket and cream cords.

'Hello,' she said.

He turned and for a second or two looked right through her. Then his face changed and he said, 'Good Lord!'

Daph felt impelled to apologize. 'Marina said I looked frumpish. She insisted on dolling me up. I knew it was a mistake.'

He looked at her. 'Who's Marina?'

'We were at school together. I'm staying at her flat. She's very glam. I don't know how we ever got to be friends, except that she made me laugh and she used to chivvy me along and make me play dance music so that she could practise her foxtrot with Wendy Wetherall, who would dance the boy's part if you bribed her with mint humbugs.' An Octoberish draught was riffling the light hem of her frock. 'Do I look totally ridiculous? If so, I'd rather you told me.'

He was still gazing at her. There was a pause and then he said, 'You look stunning.'

Daph went pink. A queue was forming under the glass arcade. He took her arm and they joined the end of it.

He said, 'The thing is, I've never seen you in town before.' The queue shuffled forward. Guiding her through the doors into the lovely marble foyer, he said, 'You haven't seen me spruced up either. I should have worn my London suit. I dig it out for pinstriped days. Solicitor's meetings and funerals. Actually, there's not much difference between the two. You've never seen such a dreary hole as Finch and Hennings in Lincoln's Inn Fields. Makes the average funeral parlour look positively cheerful. Charlie said thanks for the invite, by the way, but he couldn't make it. He's otherwise engaged.'

They handed over their tickets and made their way to their seats in the Edwardian auditorium. The gas lights sent flickering shadows over the plum-coloured walls. Daph sat blissfully gazing at the polished Bechstein, the green curtains, the lavish cupola over the stage decorated with figures representing The Soul of Music.

'I love this building.' Tom rested his elbow on the arm of the seat between them. He unbuttoned his jacket and handed Daph a programme. 'It's both grand and intimate. A hard trick to master. So how long are you staying up?'

'Until Tuesday. Then I've got to help sort my great-grandfather's photo collection. Charlie wants to display it in the gallery. So is he seeing his girlfriend tonight? The one he brought to the sale? Pushy girl. I forget her name.'

'Biddy? Charlie dropped her when your friend moved into his flat. Well, apparently she still chases him at the office, but apart from that—'

The string quartet was tuning up. The seats around them were filling up fast. Daph thought, I don't know what you're talking about. 'My friend?'

'The girl from the rectory. Blonde.'

'Romily?'

'That's the one. Poor old Charlie's got it bad.'

'Romy's at Charlie's flat?'

'You must have heard? This chap of hers – the Pole – was knocking her around and Charlie came to the rescue. He took her round to his place and she's been using it as a hideaway.'

'She's living with Charlie?'

'No. Charlie's been sleeping on my sofa. You have no idea what a night-mare that's been. He snaffles all the cheese ration and hogs the phone and bungs up the bathroom while he's shaving. I have to practically kick him up every morning and if he manages to get himself to the breakfast table, his only conversation is about Jacobean chimneys and half-timbered wings. But as from tomorrow, the place will be my own again. He's found a new flat for . . . what's her name? . . . Romily . . . and he's spent the day helping her move her things.'

Two cellos, a violin and a viola lifted and blended, a perfect mix of sweetness and the darkest night. Daph's mind was in such a whirl that she scarcely heard a note. She sat there thinking, poor Romy. How awful for her, but then again, I could see how he bullied her, so I'm not as shocked as I might have been. She might have told me. How is one supposed to help if one doesn't know what's going on?

Strings and cellos shivered, the music soared like a bird. Worry about Romy later, she told herself. Use your ears instead of your mind. But Tom's arm, only a hair's-breadth away from her own, was another powerful distraction. The tips of his long fingers, pressed together, forming a curve like the upturned prow of a boat. His thick hair flying in all directions like a rumpled Botticelli cherub. The set of his mouth, amusing and inter-esting, but with an intensity at the corners.

He turned his gaze to meet hers. 'What do you think?' he whispered.

'Wonderful.'

'Isn't it?' His smile would have dazzled angels.

The Haydn flew by. Then the Shostakovich. The interval gave them a chance to get some air. 'Hot in there,' Daph said. 'The Shostakovich was . . . striking.'

'Too striking?'

She laughed. 'Not my cup of tea, as Pa would say.' She hesitated, then said, 'Romy rang me for a chat a couple of weeks ago. Why didn't she tell me she was in trouble?'

'Pride?'

He had hit the nail on the head. Daph said, 'She's the kind of person whose life has been a delicious mixture of men, parties, fun . . . I used to wonder what would happen if she had to come down to earth like the rest of us. I must go and see her. Could you get her address for me?'

'I'll call Charlie in the morning.'

'Thank you.'

There was a tiny beat and then he smiled at her and said, 'Don't mention it.' Daph felt as if she was floating a couple of inches above the deep, red carpet. This attraction thing was totally unnerving.

When the concert was over, Tom asked if she fancied going to a pub – he knew a good place just around the corner.

The Warwick Arms had leather chairs, oak boards and beams and the odd customer still in khaki. 'Gin and It?' he asked.

'Yes. Thank you.'

It was a comfortable old place with a framed portrait of the king and queen above the fireplace, a jug of chrysanthemums on the bar and a stuffed owl that sat watching you from the window. Daph chose a table in the corner and waited, all shy again, for him to bring her drink.

'I ordered cheese sandwiches.' He sat down next to her. 'There won't be much cheese, but the landlady makes her own crusty bread. I used to bring Fi here when she came up to stay.'

'Fi?'

'My sister. Two years younger than me. We argue a lot, but we've always been close. She's a doctor. She lives in Somerset and she's married to another doctor. He was wounded at Dunkirk and never went back to front-line fighting.'

'Do you see her often?'

'Not as much as I'd like to. She's more tied now that she has the children.' He said, 'But she came up to see me when I got back from Germany. We talked for a day and a half without stopping. How's the major?'

'He says he feels homeless.' She took a sip of her gin. 'I had to get sharp with him. We can't stay in a time warp. I hate to sound like Mother, I said, but if Charlie's working like blazes to get the house on its feet again, then you'll have to stir yourself too.'

'And how did he take it?'

'Oh, he bristled a bit and went off to worm the dog. Deal with a minor problem instead of the big one. That's his way.'

'At least you can talk to him,' Tom said.

'You can't talk to your father?'

'I suppose it's better now than it's been for ages. But he had his heart set on me taking over his practice and I couldn't do it. I tried medical school for a year, to please him, but I hated it, flunked the exams and got the biggest dressing down of my life. Did I know, he said, how many young men would like to have an established practice waiting for them to walk into? Yes, I did know, and they were welcome to take my place, I said, because I wanted to be an architect. He hit the roof. No one in his family has ever been arty-crafty and if I thought he was going to finance such a namby-pamby, frivolous occupation, then I'd damned well got another think coming.'

'But he relented?'

'Like hell he did! Granny Henning – my maternal grandmother – paid for my architectural training. She was a bit of a rebel, in her young days, and she enjoyed subverting my father. They had the most ferocious rows, but she could hold her own with him.'

'I owe her such a debt. She died in '44, before I could get to see her. I went up to Norfolk for the funeral. It was one of the saddest days of my life. I hadn't seen her for a while, but her letters followed me all over Europe. Funny, sharp little letters, telling me about her bulb bowls and cook's troubles with the range and what had been said at the Women's Institute committee meetings. She kept me sane. I never got to tell her how much they meant to me.'

An extraordinary notion came to Daph, that she might take his hand and hold it in both of her own. There was such a mixture of regret and deep affection in his voice.

She leant against the back of her chair and looked at the stuffed owl, because she didn't know where else to look. She said, 'I'm sure she knew.'

'I asked the organist to play the Mozart *Sonata in C* at the funeral service. Granny taught me to play it. We used to stay with her every August and it was the only piece I ever mastered and even then I could only do the andante. My real piano teacher – Miss Dorothy P. Browne – used to rap me over the knuckles with a ruler. Why are all piano teachers weird old spinsters?'

'Because so many of them lost their fiancés in the First War and had to make a living any way they could?'

'You're right. I'm an unfeeling idiot. And I was a terrible pupil. Deeply lazy about practising. Is your fiancé musical?' he asked, making a sudden disconcerting turn.

Daph turned madly pink.

She eventually settled on an almost-safe answer. 'He likes army bands. And a jolly good sing in church.'

He nodded. 'I was talking to him at the Lizzah sale. He'd just bought a particularly gruesome vase for his mother. Don't take this the wrong way, but I wouldn't have thought he was your sort.'

Actually, Daph felt quite defensive. 'You're going to say he's dull. Well, he isn't.'

He said consideringly, 'Not dull. Nice chap, but restricted, I suppose I mean, in his interests.'

'You can't be that restricted when you've been all over the Middle East.'

'It's not where you've been. It's where you travel in your head. Some people are more . . . vivid than others.'

'I'm not vivid.'

'You look pretty vivid from where I'm sitting.'

'Yes, but I won't in the morning.'

'Like Cinderella?'

'Exactly.'

He studied her. 'It's just that I can't see him being the highlight of your day. Tell me I'm wrong.'

The landlady said, ''Ere's your cheese. Lovely frock, miss. My daughter wore printed crêpe for her wedding. Was there anything else? A pickled onion? No? Well, I'll leave you to it.' She waddled back to the bar, shoes flapping.

'I was right about the cheese,' Tom said. He tore off a corner of new bread. 'Have some. You think I'm an arrogant so-and-so. I can tell by your face. It's just that I don't want you to make the same mistake I did. I got engaged to my childhood sweetheart the day I joined up. She was very sweet, very pretty, but on my second leave, I realized that we didn't have a thing to talk about except the war.'

There was a silence.

Daph said, 'He's not my childhood sweetheart.'

'Even so.'

'He's just a very old friend. I don't mean *he's* very old. Just a little older than me. Six years actually. He used to ride out with me when he was home from school and I was about nine and they worried because Light – my favourite pony – had a tendency to bolt. So are you still engaged to her?'

'Angela? No. She met someone else and married in a great hurry.'

'Did you mind?'

'Not after I'd got over the shock of the Dear John letter. If I'd married her, we'd have finished up murdering each other.'

Daph swallowed some gin. Looking at Tom, she thought, You keep coming at me like a curved ball. Which ought to make me feel uneasy, but I feel more and more comfortable with you. I just wish I didn't.

An unexploded bomb had closed off one end of Marina's square. They walked across the leaf-strewn park to get to the other end. It was raining slightly, a dampening drizzle. London's a sad old place at the moment, Tom thought. Sometimes it hurt to look at the gaps, the great, untidy open spaces, the streets that had been turned into silent stone quarries. The night air was still bronchial; when he came in from work, his clothes had that heavy, asthmatic smell of brick dust and stale mortar.

'You don't have to walk me home,' Daphne said. 'Your car's miles away.'

'That's no problem.'

Tom let his glance rest on her face. He wondered what it was about Daphne that stayed with him. Not just her blue, believing eyes, or that vivid hair, or the shine on the end of her faintly freckled nose. No, it was some quality that came from inside. Most girls these days he found sterile. They had been around, slept around; they dressed smartly and had glossy red lips that flashed you the kind of smiles they reserved for men, but when it came down to it, there was nothing even vaguely original or interesting about them.

Oh, he'd had the odd fling, mostly in London while on leave. There was a girl he'd been keen on down near Aix-en-Provence, where he'd spent the whole of the summer before the war. But nothing more permanent.

No one who really mattered.

Certainly not a girl who was wearing another man's diamond ring.

He honestly didn't know why he was letting himself fall so hard for a girl who was engaged to someone else. It would end in tears. Taking Daphne's arm to steer her round a hole in the path, he told himself that throwing off the bonds of both caution and common sense was pretty damned stupid. But even the most dependable man acted recklessly now

and again, and what the war had taught him was that you had to take
what pleasure you could from the moment. And anyway, he was fed up
with trying to keep his conscience all polished and shiny.

He held open the park gate for Daphne and she walked past him into
the light of the street lamp. The leaves above her head blurred into a
luminous haze.

'We're here,' she said. 'Number twenty-seven. I'd ask you in, but
Marina might have gone to bed.'

'Nice old houses. Timeless.'

'Yes. Marina's is the ground floor flat. So could I phone you for Charlie's
number?'

'Tell you what, I'll get him to give me Romily's address. Then I'll drive
you round there tomorrow.'

'Oh, no.' She looked startled. 'You mustn't—'

'Why not?'

'Because . . . well . . . I've taken up enough of your weekend.'

Tom said, 'Not at all. I'm at a loose end. Nothing else to do.'

'You're just saying that.'

'Why would I do that?'

'Because you're so nice.'

Nice? Tom gave her a comic look, there was no other way to describe it.

Charlie said, 'Well, this is fun.' He stood leaning against one corner of
the fireplace. Tom had parked himself on the other side – they looked
like a pair of bookends. Daphne and Romy sat on the over-stuffed sofa.
'Fancy us all being up in town together. We should have lunch somewhere. What do you think?'

No one seemed to think anything, so he went rattling on. 'How was
the concert? I've never been to the Wigmore. Prefer the theatre myself.
We went last week, as a matter of fact. A mad little comedy. When you
rang, I thought, Romy won't half be pleased that Daphne's in town. I've
got another idea. Perhaps you girls should have lunch together. Tom and
I can take ourselves off.'

'I might not want to,' Tom said.

'Right. All I meant was, if the girls want to have a chat, catch up with
each other, have a bit of a gossip, we could . . . we could . . . make coffee.
That's it. In the kitchen. What do you think? Should we . . . um . . . leave
them to it?'

Tom said, 'Coffee. Fine. Tell you what, let's go the whole hog. I'll nip
out and get some custard tarts.'

Charlie headed (with some relief, Daph thought) for the kitchen. Tom raised his eyebrows at her and disappeared downstairs.

She heard the front door bang. There was another silence. Romy sat staring at a copy of *Tatler* that lay in her lap; Daph gazed at the cover of the Lizzah guide that Charlie had just given her. It's like being back at school, she thought, like doing silent reading.

'Why didn't you tell me?' she said at last. 'About the trouble you were in?'

'Oh, Lord!' Romy chucked the magazine on the table. 'I didn't want you to know I'd made an utter fool of myself.'

'I might have wanted to help.'

'You weren't here,' Romy pointed out.

'I could have been, if you'd told me. I'm quite angry at you, actually.'

Romy sat tying and untying the ends of her soft belt. 'I didn't want Daddy to know.'

'Which means you don't trust me to keep my mouth shut?'

'Of course I trust you! But sometimes things slip out. And there's no prizes for guessing what everyone at home would say. They saw what he was and I didn't. What kind of a chump does that make me?'

'You made a mistake. It happens to all of us.'

'Well, I'm mortified that it happened to *me*!' Romy gazed down at her madly tapping foot, then said, 'Anyway – you keep things from me. What are you doing in town with Tom Fermoy?'

'I'm not in town with him.' It was Daph's turn to look uncomfortable. 'He just . . . happened to have some tickets for the Wigmore.'

'Happened?'

'Yes.' Daph smoothed the skirt of her dress.

'Also,' Romy said, seeing her advantage and building on it, 'you walk in here looking like a fashion plate. Where did you get that frock? Have you been to a beauty parlour? Talk about scrubbing up well! Honestly, you might have warned me!'

'And you might have told me you've been living in Charlie Garland's flat. He's very jumpy, by the way. Is there something going on between you two?'

'Going on?'

'You know what I mean.'

'No. I don't.'

When Daph gave her a tough look, she said, 'Well, nothing I can't handle. Nothing you couldn't tell your maiden aunt about.'

Daph refused to let her look soften. 'So are you still working at the shop?'

'No. I had to change jobs in case Jan came in.'

'You're scared he'll find you?'

'No. Not really.'

It was the 'not really' that spoke volumes. 'So you've broken off your engagement? Given him his ring back?'

'Charlie did, actually.'

'Charlie?'

'Yes. He went to see him to get back some things of mine.'

'Things?'

'I wish you'd stop parroting everything I say! The thing is, Charlie used to go round and pick up my post. And one day, there was a note from Jan . . .'

Daph said, 'Go on.'

'Well, the thing is, he had some letters I'd written him and he was threatening to send them to my parents unless I told him where I was living.'

'What was in the letters?'

Romy said, 'Stuff I wouldn't want Daddy to read. Steamy stuff, making it perfectly obvious that we were sleeping together. I'd made up my mind to go round there, but Charlie wouldn't let me. He went himself.'

'And?'

'And there was a big bust up. Charlie told him that if he ever came near me again or contacted my parents, he'd call the police and make sure he was charged with attempted blackmail.'

'Well, good for Charlie!' Daph said

But Romy said, 'I'm not so sure. Jan can't find me, but he knows Charlie's working down at Lizzah and I'm really worried that he'll go down there and . . .'

'And what?'

'Oh, I don't know, but if he's been drinking and he's holding a grudge—'

In the kitchen, Charlie was rattling china around. Down below, a door slammed and footsteps came thumping up the stairs. 'No custard tarts,' Tom said, 'but I brought ginger nuts from the ciggy shop. I just had a thought. Why don't we all go to the flicks? We could catch the matinee. What do you think?'

It wouldn't hurt, Daph decided. It's probably just what Romy needs. And nothing can happen, can it, so long as we stay in a foursome?

Nineteen

Jack removed a dried-up leaf that had wedged itself beneath the windscreen wiper and crushed it between his fingers. In his head, he could see Daisy skimming away from him across the bridge, up the steps and along the canal path. He hadn't spoken to her since Lil had dropped the bombshell about the baby. In one way, there was a kind of relief that he no longer had to struggle with his conscience. But going out of his way to avoid Daisy and ignoring the sweet, hesitant smile she threw him when they *did* bump into each other made him short-tempered both at work and at home.

Lil was as snappy as hell, too She didn't want any more kids, she told him, and if she'd had the spare cash, she would have done something about it. But she didn't and so she was stuck with the morning sickness, the inconvenience of it all and the fact that she was getting to be the size of a bloody house.

Jack fetched the sponge and the bucket and spent half an hour washing the Bentley down. The major appeared, briefly, to give him his orders for tomorrow. Shift the piano, take Mrs Jago to the station (she had a hair appointment) and take costumes and props to the rectory. 'For the Mother's Union theatricals,' he said.

Theatricals was the last thing Jack was interested in. He got plenty of those at home, thank you very much.

The major dragged his hand through his thinning hair. 'Did you find that photo?' he asked.

'Not yet, sir. I'm still looking.'

'Right. Good. Time you knocked off, I should think.'

The air, as Jack walked back to the cottage, was crisp and cold. Scratchy twigs against a dishcloth grey sky. He walked through the door to find the boy – thin pullover, knee-length socks, flimsy plimsolls – lying in front of the range listening to *Children's Hour*. Jack threw some more coal on and slipped him the sherbert paper that had been a week or more in his pocket.

Cliff almost grinned.

'Don't eat it before supper. If there is any supper.' He couldn't smell anything good. 'Is she back?'

The boy shoved the sherbert into his jacket pocket. 'In the kitchen.'

Lil, breasts lolloping over the top of her blouse, was making sausage meat cakes at the kitchen table. The sink was piled with unwashed dishes. Jack opened his mouth to ask why she hadn't done them after breakfast, then shut it again. Her expression was savage. She got like that when she had to cook or do necessary chores.

'Mother found my old train set,' he said. 'It was in her attic.' He was intending to clean it up to give it to Cliff for Christmas.

Lil's fingers were all stuck up with sausage meat. Slamming a lump of the stuff on to the table, she said, 'And you think that's a decent Christmas present? A load of old junk from your mother's attic.'

He said, 'It was good enough for me when I was his age. I had hours of fun with it.'

'Well, children expect a sight more these days.'

'They'll have to expect, then. There aren't toys to be had.'

'I always managed to get him a decent present. All the way through the war . . .'

'All those Yankee plane models?' He said, 'Why didn't you get him Spitfires?'

'Spitfires?'

'Yes, you know, the things our boys flew for years before the Yanks deigned to come over here and risk their dainty necks.' He was so irritated by the conversation that he almost fetched Cliff in to ask if he wouldn't prefer Spitfires. But Cliff had just taken himself off up the stairs. He didn't want to be enlisted on either side of an argument that was growing nastier by the minute.

'What time's supper?' Jack demanded. 'That looks disgusting. Why can't you make something nourishing for once?'

'Because I haven't got time, that's why. I'm a working woman.'

'Not for much longer,' he said.

'Oh, yes – you had to bring that up. I'm not leaving the salon. There's no way I'm going to stay home and wet-nurse a baby.'

'So who else will do it? Oh, I know. We'll hire a nanny in a starched uniform. Tell you what, while we're at it, we'll have a live-in housemaid to clear up this mess. And a cook so that we'll get a proper meal now and then.'

'Sarcasm,' she said, 'is the lowest form of wit.'

'That may be, but decent women don't work after they've had a baby.' Daisy wouldn't, he thought.

'Decent! I hate that word.'

'So I noticed.'

'You've changed, Jack Trewarden. I said to Con the other day, the army's made him as hard as nails.'

Jack didn't need to be reminded of the fact. When you were at war, all the rules disappeared. If in doubt, you shot first and asked questions later. Kill or be killed. Of course it hardened you.

He turned on his heel and strode upstairs. Cliff was on his bed with his legs tucked under one of the old coats that served as extra blankets. Jack walked into his own bedroom, a square, cold shape with a window under the eaves, and began to search for the curly-edged army rugby team photo he had promised to show the major. It wasn't in the mahogany box where he thought he had left it. He wondered if it had got into one of the dressing table drawers and began rummaging through them.

The bottom drawer was stuffed with jumpers, vests, flowered overalls and a leopard-print scarf reeking of cheap scent. He slammed it shut and tried the next one up, which should have held his pullovers and socks. But no. It was overflowing with lingerie, fishnet stockings, twinsets and, buried deep at the bottom, a bottle of whisky. Jack took it out and gazed at it. Well, damn me, he thought. He frowned at it for a moment then put it down on the lino next to him. When he opened the third drawer, he found his own things – grey shirts, braces, jumpers, socks – but no photograph. He almost gave it up as a bad job, but then he thought he might have shoved it into the top left drawer with his cufflinks. The cufflinks box was buried under powder, lipsticks and a tube of that brown muck that Lil smeared on her face. He rifled through them with no luck. The last drawer was crammed with more knick-knacks. Necklaces, curlers, a green snood, a couple of boxes of embroidered handkerchiefs and then— Glory be! A photograph.

Good.

He slammed the drawer shut and turned the snapshot over to look at it. His eyes, already a dark, deep brown, turned even more unfathomable.

He took it to the window to examine it in the light.

'What are you doing?' Lil's voice said.

Jack turned. She stood in the doorway wiping her hands on her overall.

Jack said, 'And who would this be, I wonder?'

'Sorry?' Lil said. But she looked flustered.

'Your GI buddy.' Jack tilted the photograph to one side. He read out the scribbled message in the left-hand corner. 'For my Honey Bunch. All my love, Joey.'

'It doesn't mean anything,' she said. 'You know Yanks. They'd chase anything that moves.'

He stopped gazing at the cocky-looking Yank and said, 'If it doesn't mean anything, why keep it?'

'I didn't keep it! Honest. I didn't even know it was there.'

'Liar.' Jack said, 'This baby – is it mine?'

'Of course it's yours!'

'Because I may be slow on the uptake, but I'm not a complete fool.'

'Look – the Yanks left months back.'

Jack said, 'I bet he had his fill before he went. You didn't keep *me* waiting long. Nor any other man. Did he sleep with you in our bed?'

'Of course not!'

Jack tore the photograph into tiny pieces.

'You've got to believe me—'

Well, I don't, Jack thought. Of course he came home with you. That was where the comic books came from and the other Yankee junk. He felt a stabbing pain in his head. 'Tell you what, let's ask the boy.'

Lil said, 'No.' She had hold of his arm. Jack shook it off.

'Cliff! Come here!'

Lil stepped back on to the landing. Jack dropped the snapshot pieces on the floor. She glanced down at them as if she would like to pick them up. The boy, scared-looking, came out of his room. Jack knew he shouldn't be doing this, but he couldn't help himself. He heard himself asking, in a quick spurt of words, 'Did your mother have any Yanks to stay while I was away? I want the truth.'

The boy looked down at his boots.

'Well?'

'They . . . didn't stay,' the boy stammered.

'They?'

'Leave him alone,' Lil said, 'you great bully.'

'Shut up,' Jack said. Then, to the boy, 'How many came home with her? I want to know.'

Head down, Cliff muttered something.

'Speak up. Can't hear you.'

Cliff grabbed the stair knob and dashed off down the stairs.

Jack said, 'Too many. Why would I even have to ask?'

'Look – Jack – for the last six years, we've had no cigarettes, no tobacco, no sweets, no chocolate—'

'You mean, if it wasn't for sex, there'd have been no pleasures left.'

'No. Yes. You're twisting my words. Making it sound worse than it was.'

Jack said, 'How could it be worse? I missed my youth, missed seeing my son grow up and all that time, you were sleeping around like a cheap little whore.'

'I missed things too, you know! Like a proper home with a man in it.'

'A proper home? Would you recognize one if you saw it?'

'That's not fair. I brought Cliffy up on my own and I made a good job of it.'

'On your own? You mean with the help of half the American army. Did they pay you for your services? Did you give good value?'

She slapped his face – a hard, stinging slap that would have stung if he'd felt sane enough to register it. He wanted to hit her back, but he couldn't. Not in her condition. The front door slammed. A breath of cold air came up the stairs. Lil swung herself awkwardly back down, her face mottled, her hair a wild bird's nest because the pins had fallen out.

As he watched her, Jack thought: *Oh, Christ . . . Oh, Christ . . . Oh, Christ!*

'I'm going to walk out to the breakwater with Val,' Daisy had told her father on Sunday afternoon. 'I'll be back at Aunt Jem's in time for tea.'

Father hadn't minded.

'As long as you're back by five,' he said. 'No later, mind.'

As she sat beside him in the Wolsey on the way to Bude, Daisy's fingers played with the fine folds of the red coat she had made for herself – warm against the wind, slim at the waist with a huge skirt. She hated telling even the smallest white lie and she did sometimes meet her friend, Val, but for the last two Sundays, she had wandered out to the beach on her own. If there was a chance she might bump into Jack, she didn't want anyone else tagging along. As it happened, he hadn't turned up, but that didn't stop her wanting to see him or getting swept away by crazy dreams about what she would say to him (and he to her) if she did.

'You look topping,' Dan Jewell's face wrinkled into a smile. 'Who's the lucky fellow?'

Daisy thought, for one moment, that he had been reading her thoughts. But that was because she had a guilty conscience.

'He'd better behave himself . . .'

'Dad!'

Dan just grinned. Daisy waited until he had steered the Wolsey around a slow-running bend before launching a diversionary exercise by telling him about what was happening up at Lizzah.

'You should have seen Mr Garland when he was brushing the moths out of the tapestries. Dust in his hair and his eyes and up his nose. He says they were made in Flanders.'

'In Flanders fields the poppies grow,' said Dan.

'Mother's poem.' They had printed it in the *Cornish and Devon* when the Great War ended and Dora Jewell had cut it out and put it in a frame in memory of Uncle Will.

'Every year,' Dan said, 'she put a jug of poppies by it for his birthday.'

'And sometimes the brooch he sent her. Or the hymn book with his name in it.' Daisy said, 'I remember him singing me to sleep.'

'He was fond of a tune. And fond of nut-milk chocolate. It never lasted long if Will was about.' If you find a young man half as good, Dan thought, you'll do all right.

As soon as Father had dropped her off, Daisy strolled along the Wharf to the lock gates. There was no sign of Jack on the dunes or the beach. Her spirits began to plummet. She had almost convinced herself that he would be here, but it was a flight of fancy.

Browned off, Daisy wandered across the beach below the lifeguard station. The breakwater loomed ahead of her. Enormous waves were crashing against Barrel Rock. She picked her way over wet shingle, her eyes on her feet. Then looking up, her heart flipped. Jack was coming across the beach towards her.

He saw her and smiled. Daisy smiled back but after that her eyes went down and she couldn't look at him. The sky was brimming with light, the stones slipping under her feet.

'Careful,' Jack said, grabbing her as she slithered into a rock pool. Even after the bust-up with Lil, he had told himself he mustn't be tempted into seeing Daisy again. She was too young, too innocent. But here he was, breaking his own rules and, to be honest, he couldn't make himself regret it.

He said, 'Now your shoe's wet.' Her shoulder felt warm through her sleeve.

'It doesn't matter.' Daisy let the wind – a huge, seaside draught – whip at her hair. 'It'll dry.' She took the shoe off and shook it out.

'So where are you off to?'

'Not sure. I was just wandering. Is Mrs Jago having tea with the canon?'

'No. She's laid up with her arthritis. I just fancied a walk.'

'Me too.'

Daisy threw him a sideways smile. She felt she was in an American movie. The sea pinks and the gorse on the clifftop and the wider blue of the bay were all in glorious technicolor. The gulls wheeling past and that boat bobbing away on the water deserved a swelling sound track. She felt happy and scared at the same time.

'Haven't seen you for a while,' he said.

Daisy put her shoe back on. It felt squelchy. She wasn't quite sure what to do next, so, glancing shyly at him, she began to walk on. Jack hesitated, then turned and walked with her. He wanted very badly to light a cigarette, but he wouldn't have been able to stop his hand shaking, so he chucked the idea. They chatted, inconsequentially, about things that didn't matter. Both of them had a sense of being enormously alive. Neither of them could have told you afterwards what had been said.

'Tide's on the turn,' Jack said when they reached the top of the breakwater.

'Help!' The wind was tearing at Daisy's voluminous skirts and threatening to blow her away.

'More sheltered under the rocks. Come on.' He grabbed her hand and ran her, laughing, down to the sand on the far side. They stopped at last and Daisy collapsed, gasping, on to the nearest rock. Her cheeks glowed and her hair was all over the place. She didn't bother trying to put it straight. Not a bit of vanity in her, Jack thought, his heart doing that terrible melting thing.

He said, 'How are they treating you up at Lizzah?'

'Very well. Your mother runs the kitchen like clockwork.'

'That's Mother. Bossy as hell.'

'I didn't mean . . . What I meant was, she's . . . very organized.'

'And you're very tactful.'

Daisy had turned pink. 'No, really. I like her. She makes me laugh.'

Jack said, 'She likes you. She says you're a hard little worker.'

'It's easy to work hard when you like what you're doing. I'd rather be sewing than working on the farm.'

'And she says you're always turned out nice. Which is true. Did you make that? Your coat?'

'Yes,' Daisy said. She laughed. 'Out of some old curtains and lining material. I was sick of square shoulders and lovely shades of army brown.'

'Clever girl.'

'Not really.'

'You could make yourself a fortune if you set up in business.'

'Maybe I will. One day.' She smiled up at him. He gazed at her. Sweet Jesus!

'What's wrong?'

'Nothing,' he said in his normal voice, and then, with sudden unsteadiness, 'It's just that you're the most beautiful girl I've ever seen . . .' Just looking at her made him want to weep.

Daisy stared down at her shoe. A wedge of wet sand was stuck to it like a toe-cap.

After a moment, he said, 'I don't say this kind of thing all the time. I'm not like that. And I can't let myself go on feeling like this, because I'm married. But every time I set eyes on you, it's like the sun coming out from behind a cloud.'

'And you can't see anything for the dazzle,' Daisy said, with a steadiness that belied her inner confusion.

From a distance, Mabel saw Jack Trewarden wave goodbye to Daisy. Mabel lived a bare three miles from the beach, but only once a year, on the anniversary of Stephen's death, did she ever go near it, so that she could take their favourite walk up over Compass Point and along the footpath to Widemouth.

A steely woman, Mabel did not often give way to emotion. A level plain, that was what she longed for these days. But on this one afternoon in the year, she allowed herself to wallow. Oh, she never told Edie. She could always find some trite excuse for disappearing on her bicycle for an hour or two. Edie, simple soul that she was, always swallowed it. She had probably forgotten that Stephen ever existed except in her sister's snapshot album where, gaitered and kit-bagged, he stood to attention with his rifle by the wicket gate at Apple Cottage, that huge grin of his belying the military stiffness of his back.

Mabel always brought the same little things with her on her annual pilgrimage to the cliffs: her opal and diamond engagement ring, which for the rest of the year resided in the little blue sugar bag full of sixpences in the dresser drawer, and the tin biscuit box that held every card Stephen had ever sent her. She read them sitting on the hollow in the cliffs where he had proposed to her thirty-one years ago. She could see it in her mind's eye, like a little act in a play. Two figures in a summer landscape, quite separate from her workaday life. Stupid, no doubt. And self-indulgent. But she could not live without those memories of quivering beauty.

Deep feeling was a difficult thing, on the whole, to deal with. She found it easier, for the rest of the year, to push it all away. In this she was like Myles. He never showed what he felt to anyone – especially Virginia.

Virginia . . . Mabel was still smarting from their confrontation. She had told Myles about it; he hadn't said much, merely mumbled an apology

and said he wouldn't involve her in his private affairs again. That had upset
Mabel even more. Dammit, she liked him to confide in her! He was the
only man who was ever likely to, at this advanced stage of her life.

She stood on Compass Point gazing down at the beach. Jack Trewarden
was still there in his open-necked shirt and dark trousers. And his eyes
were still fixed on the point where Daisy had vanished into the distance.

Of course, it might just have been a chance meeting, but Mabel didn't
like the way the boy stood there mooning long after Daisy had disappeared
over the breakwater. She was fond of Jack and she wouldn't have blamed
him in the least for leaving that trollop of a wife of his. But to have Daisy
involved . . .

That was a very different matter.

Jack had finally moved. He was drifting back across the beach with his
hands in his pockets, looking for all the world like a lovesick Romeo.
Mabel stood on the clifftop, a stoutish figure in a green coat and hat. She
felt a rush of worry for the boy, mixed with irritability.

'Something is going on there,' she thought.

Oh, my word.

Nipper was in the snug talking to his dog, but he stopped when Jack
walked in. Nipper was wearing a purple suit and ginger shoes and his old
army haversack stood on the floor beside him. The Acland was the black
market headquarters in the village. You could pull a gallon of petrol behind
the bar, they said, and a nice fat little pheasant, wrapped up in somebody's overcoat, would walk past you most nights of the week.

Jack said, 'All right, boy?'

'Fair to middling.'

'And Cis?'

'Not too bad.'

'When's it due?'

'December.'

A long pause. Nipper was either totally clam-like or the life and soul
of the party. Tonight he was on the silent side, all shut up in himself. Even
the dog didn't seem right. It sat, chin on paws, looking at Jack with a
glum expression.

'What is it? A pint?' Jack said. He needed one badly. At the end of a
perfect afternoon, he couldn't bring himself to go home and his mouth
felt dry and salt-washed.

'Shan't say no.'

In the bar next door, Den Pooley was kicking his heel against the skirting board as he coaxed a tune out of his squeeze-box. Jack put up a hand to attract Pru's attention. 'How's business?' he asked. 'Mother reckons you've been taking a few risks.'

'You don't know what risk is.' A laugh came from Nipper's chest, a bronchial spasm. He said, 'Know what the Japs did if they caught you stealing food?'

'No.'

'Well, I wouldn't tell 'ee, boy.' Nipper drew hard on his cigarette.

'Just don't get caught. That's all I'm saying.'

Nipper's eyes went on moving round the room. 'No chance,' he said. 'The usual, Jack?'

'Two pints, please, Pru.' He watched her pull them. 'Busy tonight.'

'Tell me about it!'

People got their news from The Acland, which opened at six. But it wasn't just locals. 'Plenty of visitors about,' Jack said.

'You're right there, Jack. I've had a bellyfull of 'em. Looking for accommodation, but never satisfied with what you can offer. Making out they're used to more sophisticated entertainment.'

'Good for business, though?'

'I suppose so, but I'd rather a few more of 'em was gents like Mr Garland.'

'He's a good bloke.'

Nipper gave Pru one of his fleeting grins. 'Our Jack's mixing with all sorts. Turning into a proper nob.'

'Nothing wrong with that,' Pru said. 'The world may be going to pot, but we don't need to go with it.' She propped her bulk on the bar edge and asked if they'd heard about the ex-officer and his wife who'd taken Baker's Cottage. 'Back from Greece, so I heard, and brought his submachine gun with him. Comes in most nights of the week. Wears Saville Row suits and drinks like a fish. I *heard* that he sprayed the side of his last place with bullets, but the court set him free because he's a war hero.'

'Plenty of that sort about,' Nipper said to the little dog. 'Stick a medal on, drink a pint or two, talk a good war.'

Pru asked Nipper how the dog had got on at the vet's and started on about the gas shortage in London and how Clar Piper, the resident village conchie was having a hard time of it. Not that people said much to his face. They just froze him out.

Nipper sat fiddling with his pearl tiepin. Pru pulled them another pint. Jack sipped his and breathed in the very particular Acland smell of dusty

plush and cold mutton and let her ramble on. The memory of that hour with Daisy made him feel he had been given a meal when he was starving.
Or water in the desert.

October. Crisp morning sun, berried afternoons with a faint, musty, burnt-bracken smell in the air. The grass out in the park had that long, glistening, autumn look. Then squally gales began to roll in from the west and vicious little winds funnelled through the elm walk. The major decided to take himself off on army business for a day or two.

Trewarden drove him to the station. In the Bentley, they went through their normal chaps-talking-but-not-saying-much routine. They had got it down to a fine art. The major would choose the subject and Trewarden would set about teasing some life into it. They had already covered the second crop of roses that was coming into bloom, last month's serious gas strike in London, and the blots that those damned new-fangled biros made when you tried to write with them. Trewarden didn't know what they would invent next, except that there probably wouldn't be any need of it. He asked the major how long he would be away and Myles said three or four days, long enough to get him away from the womenfolk for a while.

The weather remained wild and wet while he was in Aldershot; the sea blowing so rough, you could hear the roar of it miles inland. The day Myles caught the train back, the trees were tossing and the carriage was now and again buffeted by the wind.

When he was crossing the bridge to change trains at Okehampton, Mabel Petherick suddenly appeared from nowhere with a laden shopping bag on her arm.

She said, 'Why, Myles! Fancy meeting you here!'

'At the tail end of the afternoon.' He took her bag from her with evident pleasure.

'You've been off soldiering. How are you?' Mabel asked.

'Oh, you know, roaring along.'

'We've got half an hour's wait. I was just going to have a cuppa.'

They found a table by the fire in the station buffet. Mabel asked how he was getting along with the Trust. Myles told her they were haggling at present over who was to meet the kitchen garden expenses. 'Apparently, they'll reap the produce, so I propose to charge them for the use of my tractor, my gang-mower and his man at the rate of twenty pounds a year. I also want to know what will happen if the government decides to take over the Trust's activities. There are rumours, you know . . .'

'You look very dapper in your uniform,' Mabel said, more to calm him down than anything else.

'Like the smell of it. Never thought I'd say that. Had dinner last night with a fellow I chummed up with in Germany. Can't tell you what a relief it was to get away from the problems at home. Damned lawyer chappies coming down on you like a ton of bricks. I had to agree to a ten thousand pound capital endowment, you know. Or securities to yield four hundred and fifty pounds per annum.'

'How's your mother?' Mabel asked.

'Much as usual. Acting like the empress of all the Russias.'

'And Virginia?'

He fiddled with his tie, his sock suspenders, his hair, his belt. 'Still mad at me. There's about as much give in her as a starched linen sheet. I told her she needn't have had a go at you, but that just seemed to make matters worse.'

Mabel wasn't surprised. She attempted to find a happier topic. 'But Daphne's blooming? I bumped into her in the village. When's the wedding to be?'

'Heard mention of June. Feel bad that I can't settle anything on her. Had a word with young Noel about it. He said there's no need, but it makes you feel embarrassed. Damned nice chap. She's done well for herself there. Shan't worry about her once she's up at Trebartha.'

Mabel poured a second cup of tea. She sat gazing at the pressed glass cake stands, the pile of newspapers, the notice pinned to the wall advertising a Women's Institute lecture. 'Christmas will be here before we know where we are. Will you be holding the staff party?'

'Could do without it with everything else on our plate, but we'll have to make the effort.'

'Want me to organize the nativity play?'

'If you would, but we'd best play safe. Not a word until I've broached the subject with Ginny.'

She cleared her throat and arranged her coat buttons. 'Before that, of course, there's the new plaque for the war memorial.'

His face was as still as if it had been cut out of stone.

'It will be an ordeal,' she said gently. 'But you helped me get through when Stephen's name went on it and I shall be there for you when Kit's name is added. She had already seen the plaque with **CAPT. CHRISTOPHER JAGO** at the top, followed by the names of the privates and gunners from the village.

Myles said, 'Case of gritting your teeth and getting on with it.'

'I'm afraid so.'

'Like old what's-his-name – the Roman emperor.'

'Seneca?' Mabel suggested. 'The philosopher?'

'That's the chappie.'

'Well, at least you've got your girls.'

'There's that, I suppose.' His face brightened. 'Daph's a brick. And she'll be just around the corner.' He took his glasses off and put them in his breast pocket. 'She's got her heart set on a memorial window, you know.'

'Daphne?'

'No. Ginny.' His voice was abrupt, staccato even. 'I said, if it makes you feel better. The architect chappie has found a stained glass studio that suits her. Nothing Burne-Jonesy. No sentiment. Can't get too much sense out of her, but I gather it's to be a skyscape with a yellow kite.'

Mabel said, 'Well, that's . . . interesting.'

He was looking at his watch. 'What time does the train leave?'

'Fifteen minutes.'

'I told Trewarden to be at the station at five. He's having another child, by the way. At least, his wife is.'

'Good God! Is it his?' Shouldn't have said that, Mabel thought, but it was her first, involuntary reaction. 'It's just that his marriage is on thin ice,' she added. 'Lil Trewarden's a trollop of the first order.'

'A baby might improve things.'

'I shouldn't think so for one minute.'

'Funny old business, marriage,' Myles was saying. 'Did you ever see a perfectly happy one?'

'Edie and Fred were happy enough. But neither of them was sharp enough to spot the other's faults.' She said, 'My parents were happy.' Then, 'No, my father could be an awkward old cuss. But they stuck it out.'

'Perhaps that's what it boils down to, in the end.'

'Good thing I never got to the altar then.'

'You don't mean that, Mabs.' He said, 'Tell you what would be nice. Getting to the stage where you could keep each other company.'

Like you and me? Mabel thought. She wouldn't look at him. She began to gather her shopping together. 'We'd better make for that train,' she said.

Approaching Bude, on that darkish afternoon, they stared out on mile upon mile of hedge-divided hills. It was a landscape that was filled with memories for them both. Watching the dark woods and the thrashing of wet branches outside the carriage window, Myles felt an aching nostalgia for his childhood. Passing this spot as a ten-year-old, coming home at the end of term, he'd had a sense of the Big House, shabby and beautiful, waiting in the distance to greet him.

Not the same now, he thought.

All lost. They were smartening Lizzah up, but destroying its essential nature. A house had to evolve. It could never be a 'made' place.

The train whistled and pulled into the station. The engine ground to a halt and sat wheezing steam. Mabel stepped on to the platform and breathed in the dark, smoky smell, which ought to have been disgusting, but was, instead, faintly comforting. Young Jack was waiting for them by the luggage trolley. He took the major's bag and, at a signal from Myles, her own.

'We'll drop you off. Can't have you catching the bus.'

Mabel followed them to the Bentley that was parked in the station yard. 'How are you, Jack?' she asked.

'Bearing up, Miss Petherick, thank you.'

'I hear congratulations are in order?'

His face told her a great deal. He wasn't happy about the baby. Not one bit. 'At least,' she said, 'you'll be around to enjoy this one.' She was about to ask if Lil was keeping well, when her attention was distracted by a man in a black overcoat who was about to board the Trewenna bus.

'Isn't that the Polish fellow? Romily's young man? No, it can't be. He's on his own. My eyes must be deceiving me.'

Twenty

PEN'S DIARY

29 October

On Friday we were sent home from school. Ursie Hogan was rushed to hospital, she has infantile paralysis. They scrubbed the dorms down with carbolic disinfectant and we had to change our clothes and gargle before catching the train home. We might not go back until January (here's hoping). Matron said to send for the doctor immediately if you get a stiff neck.

30 October

At breakfast, I was sure I had a pain in my neck, but all Daph said was, never mind, rub it with something. Granny said *she* was in pain all the time. I do not think they will care if I finish up in an iron lung. This morning everything was as still as can be in the fog. Daddy and I walked up to The Barton to tell Mr Jewell the Trust will take on his dairy herd and the farm and I sat in the inglenook with all the irons and the bundles of twigs for lighting the fire. Daisy is always nice to me, unlike some at home that I could name. She took me up to see the new dress she's making for the Christmas dance. It's green pan-velvet (not sure what the pan bit means) with a collar that stands right up and is lined with rose pink.

31 October

Tilley thinks that if there's one thing that will stand by you through thick and thin, come rain or shine, it's a bit of dripping. You can fry rabbit's joints in it or make gravy or slap it on a bit of toast for your tea. Uhhhgh! She has a nasty rash on her arm from all the cleaning fluids.

Daph made me go with her to visit the Plymouth family. There was a chip and a bean on the rug in their sitting room. I do not think much of babies, they try to climb on your lap. I came home absolutely stinking of wet nappy.

1 November

Daddy has been turfed out of the library because a bald old bibliophile (I just learned that word from Mr Garland) has come to sort through the books. Mr Garland says there has to be 'a drastic cull'. Granny said the army had got there ahead of him, several of the most valuable volumes (along with one or two pictures she was fond of) having disappeared while 'our boys' were in residence. Granny says reading makes you think too much anyway and is best avoided.

2 November
We had a visit from cousin Arthur. The awful Julia was with him and she said she couldn't understand why the law refused to protect Arthur's interests. She said it was breaking his heart. Mummy said perhaps Arthur should speak for himself for a change. Mummy said, he wasn't a ventriloquist's dummy, was he? Julia said there was no need to be offensive, people did have feelings. Mummy said tommy-rot, you didn't even have the good grace to send a condolence letter when my son died. Julia went a bit red and said it must have gone astray in the post, letters did, you know, and Mummy said, and I'm a Dutchman and if you aren't jolly well out of here in two minutes, I'll knock your head off.

3 November
Mr Garland found Granny's Venetian glasses. They were in a wardrobe in one of the attics. She said I could almost kiss you. Mr Garland said that would make his day and I thought for one weird moment that she might. But then she said, yes, well, I only say one nice thing a year, so you'd better make the most of it.

4 November
Woke to rain rattling against the window. Went to church. Mr Garland came with us. He is going back to London tomorrow and I said I didn't want him to. He looked at me with what they call in books a kindly twinkle and said I'll miss you too. I have decided that the thing I like best about him is his floppy hair.

5 November
Mummy had a letter from school to say that Ursie Hogan died in the isolation hospital. I went up to the green landing and sat on the stair with my rabbit Buster for a while. I did not cry much, but enough to make my nose run. I only talked to Ursie once, she was a bit sappy-looking, which of course one shouldn't say when she is, well, dead.

Mummy came up to see if I was all right. She said she has a bad back from humping piles of books. She looked at me through her glasses for a moment, then stood staring out of the window at the garden, I don't know why, because you couldn't see anything, it was all grey and blurry. She said, this is all rather alarming for you but you must try not to worry. She handed me her handkerchief to wipe my eyes and when I asked her if she wanted it back, she said, no, thank you. She said we would go and buy some more kilts and perhaps a Burberry to replace the ones I had to leave at school, that would cheer me up. Or find a dancing class so that I could talk to other children. I said does that mean I can have a velvet dress and go to the Christmas dance in the village but she said no it jolly well does not.

6 November

Not having anything else to do, I had a nose through the little drawer in Daph's bureau, the one from which the ivory knob is missing. I found half a packet of birthday candles, a Girl Guide badge, a small silver key (to fit what?), six odd buttons, a fountain-pen filler, a concert programme for the Wigmore Hall with a cinema ticket inside and a ticket for the V&A.

Then I opened the bigger drawer and found a pair of french knickers with pink roses on the gusset.

Well!

I was still sitting there aghast when Daph walked in. She accused me of snooping. I said, you haven't got any secrets, have you, and she went bright red and said, don't you be so cheeky. I said, then don't you be so snippy and she said anybody would be snippy having you around. I told her, we did not ask Mr Rude to tea and walked out, quite dignified, I thought, under the circumstances.

7 November

I went out for a long ride on my bicycle before Daph could find me. I saw Daisy up by Ham Wood. Trewarden had stopped the car to give her a lift. I waved hard and Daisy waved back, but she looked a bit flustered. He is not supposed to give people lifts.

8 November

The rector came to see Granny. I was expected to brush my hair and have tea with them. When Tilley brought in the tea tray, Granny told her off because her collar button was undone. Tilley said that was because the cat had got at the remains of the pie and she had had to chase it out of the door. The rector said, what a delicious-looking plum cake, had she made it? Tilley said, yes, sir, she had, but it had sunk in the middle. I wanted to ask the rector if he thought Ursie was in heaven, but it didn't seem the right kind of thing to say when you had a mouthful of cake and bits of plum sticking to your teeth. The rector asked Granny to give a donation to the Fund for Poor Children. Granny said it was all very well, but the poor must expect to stay poor if they insisted on having a quiverful of children. In the end, she put something in his box, but she told him not to ask too often because everyone knew that the working classes were naturally indolent, these untrained dailies, for example, had no idea how to clean silver and were no substitute for proper, residential servants.

9 November

Mrs Trewarden thinks that dogs can have depression as well as human beings. She said you can see it in their eyes. I know what she means because Punch sometimes looks at you as if he is sighing deep inside. Today I decided I would much rather be called Berenice, then perhaps people would listen to me and take me seriously. Oh, and they could call me Berry for short, which has altogether more character than Penelope or plain old Pen. Having the right name is just as important as wearing the right clothes. Mr Garland turned up (hurrah) with a new housekeeper called Mrs Harmsworth. He says she will pull together his frightfully good staff team. He kept that under his hat, Mrs Trewarden said, what a vinegary looking old crow, she needn't think she can boss me around, how about you, Bess?

10 November

I had a letter from Jen, she says she is bored stiff. She sent me a drawing of herself all hunched up with a scowling face.

I put the picture on my bedroom wall with a couple of thumbtacks. Bos came after lunch to see Daph, but she had gone off to a Girl Guides meeting. For a moment he looked lost. I was sticking old postcards into an album and he asked if I'd like some from Cairo. I said if he could spare them. So he said if I came back to Trebartha, he would look them out. I ran off and found my coat while he had a word with Pa. His dog, Susy, licked the back of my neck all the way up to Trebartha. We went round by the coast road. The sea was calm for a change and such a pale, cold grey, you would almost think it frozen. We were just turning in through the gates when we came across a hedgehog snuffling around at the bottom of the hedge. Bos said, he's a nice little fellow, so we stopped the car and watched him nosing around for worms and beetles and caterpillars and earwigs. Bos likes hedgehogs. He says they are useful, modest little chaps, it's rotten that so many of them come to a sticky end.

Why, Penelope, Mrs Boswell said, how nice to see you. She said, and where is dear Daphne? I said at one of her meetings and she looked at me as if I'd broken one of her china figures. She said, I do so admire her energy, but I think it will have to be channelled elsewhere once she is married. She said there were so many Things to be seen to. That made me ask, what kind of things? She said, well, there is a Household to run. I said, Daph gets all strung up if stuck indoors, she is much happier mucking around outside in her work clothes. Strung up? she said. Well, difficult, I said. She must get it from Granny. Once she's made her mind up about something, she can really dig her toes in.

The postcards are fantastic. There is one boring one of the infantry base depot but the others have men in nightshirts leading camels and women in black with babies and fruit sellers and the Sphinx being battered by a sandstorm and pictures of what Bos called colonial relics. Mrs B looks like a colonial relic and she is mean, too. She confiscated the tissue paper the postcards were wrapped in because it might be useful.

11 November

Remembrance Day. A crisp blue-sky morning cold enough to see your breath. After church everyone walked down to see Pa unveil the new plaque on the war memorial. Pa and Miss Petherick led the council procession and the rector billowed along ahead of the choir. I wish Daph would not sing so loud, she sails way above all the others. It is not that she does not have a good voice, just that I would rather she did not stick out. The square was a squash of British Legion, relatives of the Departed and the Home Guard Association. Mrs Hicks brought a chair out of the shop for Granny to sit on. She sat in the front row, very erect, feet together, hands in her lap, as if paying a call. Mummy said she hates symbolic occasions, she did not cry, just stood twisting her three rings around and staring at nothing. Miss Petherick handed the poppy wreath to Pa. I was very proud of him. He looked most distinguished in his army greatcoat, though Granny did not think so, she told him in the car that he needed a good haircut.

Over the ten names on the new plaque, it says:

Pray for the souls
of the gallant dead

whose names are written here.
Though their bodies
lie in earth
they gave their
lives for King and Country

There should have been eleven names inscribed, but somehow John Hambly got left off. Miss Petherick is furious. She said people would think it her fault because she was the one who went round knocking on doors and noting down who should be commemorated. She knew John's name had been on the list she sent to the engraver, but the rector read his name out with extra emphasis as if to make up for it. Captain Christopher Jago is at the top of the plaque. Mummy asked me last night what I remembered about Kit. Not much, I said, I was only five when he went away. Mummy looked fed up, so I thought harder and said I remembered him coming home on leave and we all picnicked on the beach and sat in the wind so long that my legs got mottled. Mummy said did I still have the ebony elephant he brought me, I said, yes, but I didn't tell her I broke its trunk.

We sang 'O God Our Help' and then all the men took their hats off and we stood under the churchyard trees listening to the two minutes' silence, which went on so long that when the bugle broke it, you felt surprised.

Trewarden's wife was the only person not wearing black, she wore a pink swagger coat. Granny said this was a disgrace and an insult to the Fallen and she would tell her so when she got a chance, which she did just as everyone was coming away. Trewarden's wife was most indignant, she said her dark coat did not fit on account of her bulge and if Granny thought she had the spare cash to buy a black coat which would only be worn for six months, then she had another think coming. Granny said she might have borrowed one for the occasion. Trewarden's wife said she should mind her own bloody business, at which point Trewarden dragged her away, he said it was neither the time nor the place. Tell *her* that, his wife said, bossy old cow, they don't own the place any more. Trewarden said, no, but they paid his salary and if she wanted to be without a roof over her head with a baby coming, then she was going the right way about it.

Granny made a big fuss of getting herself up with her stick and thanked Mrs Hicks for the chair, she said it was most thoughtful, which was more than you could say for some in the village. Think nothing of it, m'm, Mrs Hicks said, we'm all going through the same hell. Mrs Hicks' son, Billy, went down with his ship in Scapa Flow. She put a bunch of chrysanthemums from her garden next to all the poppies.

The rector shook Pa's hand and said, most moving, most moving. And then, to cheer things up, I suppose, he said, I almost joined you and Mabel in the station buffet at Okehampton the other day. We could have had an extraordinary meeting of the Church Finance Committee. I think this was intended to be humorous, but Mummy was not in the mood for jokes. She gave Pa a look and said she would wait for him in the car.

12 November
Mummy is walking around the house with a contemptuous look on her face, and Pa says he is in the doghouse. Daph said she would take me to the flicks to get us out of it.

13 November
The film was very soppy, I can't imagine why Daph liked it, but we had baked beans in a nice little café afterwards. The best bit about going to the pictures is the thick, patterned carpet and walking past all the photos of the film stars on the way in.

14 November
A letter came for Daph from London, but she won't say who it's from. It was lying on the brass tray in the hall. From the way she snatched it up, I think it is something secret to do with her wedding.
  The rector walked up to see Mr Garland. Something is up, but I could not catch what. The rector, who is usually very kind and Christian, sounded very cross. It is something to do with Romily, but Mr Garland shut the breakfast room door before I could hear much.
  I do not have to go back to school until January. Two more girls have got infantile paralysis; one of them is Rosamund Sheridan, she died last week. Ros once got out of doing cross country by putting the thermometer near the gas fire while matron's back was turned. She hated games because she ran knock-kneed, but I really liked her. It is odd, but it seems to be all dead people this month. I am so scared. Suppose I catch it and they have to bury me next to Kit?

15 November
I woke up with a temperature. I am sweaty and hot all over.

Twenty-One

'Christmas was much nicer in the days of lamps and candles,' Evalina said. It was twelve noon. There was a light scattering of snow. Leaning towards the window, she saw Mr Garland cross the terrace. She wondered where he was going and why he was carrying a grey stuffed elephant.

'There was no electricity until 1913, you know. The doctor was worried about my chest. It's as tight as a drum.'

'Mine was, m'm.'

Tilley handed her a tray with a bowl of chicken broth, a silver spoon and a linen napkin. Evalina was recovering from a bout of flu. Penelope had gone down with it first and it was now making its way through the household.

'He fears this thick cough might turn to bronchitis. I shouldn't be at all surprised. My feet are like icicles.'

'The broth will warm you up, m'm.'

'I doubt it. That fire looks reluctant. Give it a good rattle. And turn the wireless on. One pays ten shillings a year for the thing, one may as well use it. Oh, and before you go, throw a shawl over that mirror. I caught myself in close-up this morning and I have no wish to repeat the exercise, thank you very much.'

Her mother's clock ticked away on the Oriental side table. Eva let out a sigh. She grew bored, sitting up here in her room all day. It gave her the hump. But her legs were still so wobbly that a glass of brandy at teatime was the only thing that put the stuffing back into them. Can't do handstands any more, she thought, can't dance, not like in the sunshine days before 1914. Not that it matters, since there's no one to impress any more. All I can do, she thought, is sit and sew. She stitched to keep herself sane, to fill her empty life, to keep her arthritic fingers exercised while she could.

You are old, Father William, the young man said,

And your hair is uncommonly white . . .

The lines, popping suddenly and unaccountably into her head, reminded her of the schoolroom at Stowe House, where she had lived as a child. There had been an oak table with a red leather top on which she and her sisters had done their lessons. And of the fire escape, a thick canvas chute attached at the top to an iron frame hinged to the window sill. When required for use, it was tipped up and the tube fell outside on the ground where the hammock-like end could be held out to catch you coming down. Every few months they would have an exercise with menservants and gardeners assembled below to hold the hammock. You got in, pressed outwards with your bottom and knees and whizzed down it. Mother would go first, wrapping her skirts around her ankles and descending with great poise. Then the children. Then the nursery maid. Wouldn't it be convenient, Eva thought, if, on one of these painful and interminable days, you could simply jump into a chute for the next world?

Punch had been sick over Mrs Harmsworth, Tilley was saying. 'Mrs Trewarden says that dog's more intelligent than she gave him credit for.'

Eva motioned to her to turn up the volume on the wireless. A BBC voice said, '*A latticework of laurel leaves at Christmas-time will have a wonderful effect. Strips of calico, half an inch wide, must be covered with laurel leaves, each sewn on separately. This task will furnish a few pleasant evenings' work to the younger members of the family.*'

'They obviously haven't met Penelope,' Eva said. 'Try the Light Programme. Find some music.'

Tilley found a lunchtime concert. 'I'm not in the mood for violins,' Eva said. 'Switch it off.'

Tilley made a face behind her back.

'And you can take the bread away, I don't want it.'

There was a tap on the door. Tilley opened it. Daisy was standing in the passage clutching a linen basket stuffed with blue and white crewel work. Eva said, 'Who is it? Daisy? Come in, girl. Don't hover. What have you brought me this time? Ah, the William and Mary hangings. Put the basket where I can reach it.'

Daisy was wearing a print dress with a soft, gathered bosom.

'How neat you look,' Eva said. 'Every inch the seamstress. I've a mind to send you over to the cottage to show Lily Trewarden how to dress.'

She almost regretted having said it. Daisy had flushed scarlet. She was obviously not used to compliments. At least not compliments from an old termagant like me, Eva thought. She changed the subject.

'I've finished the bell-pull. You can take it back down to the drawing room. Did you make your frock yourself?'

'Yes, Mrs Jago.'

'I've a dress-length of black silk somewhere. I'll have you make it up for me. You never know when you might need it for a funeral.'

* * *

'I can't say I'm mad about posh people,' Peg Trewarden said, 'but I like their stuff.'

The rest of the staterooms were still bare on that Christmassy day, but the hall was now all grand and romantic with scrubbed, shining flag-stones, a sofa in the window recess, a Turkey carpet (covered in bundles of holly) and a Charles II armchair on each side of the fireplace. And the windows were so clean that the landscape outside seemed to jump in through the glass.

'Very swish,' Peg said. It was a dry, cold afternoon. The men were hauling the tree through the big window in the drawing-room and on into the hall. 'Stop there!' she told Jack, as he guided it past the blue Chinese vase in the alcove. 'Right. No, not right. Left. Left! Which way is left, Jack? Keep going. No! Mind the window—'

'What *is* all the noise about?' Mrs Harmsworth, a thin woman with sharp eyes, appeared from nowhere.

Peg ignored her. 'Now – turn it!' Jack heaved. The tree swayed. There was a crash as one of the chandelier crystals smashed on to the floor.

The housekeeper said, 'Now look what you've done!'

'Accidents *will* happen.'

'I'll direct operations from now on,' Mrs Harmsworth told her.

'Have you noticed,' Peg said, 'how some people only turn up when the job is done?' She took herself off upstairs. After a couple of wrong turns she found Mrs Jago on top of a stepladder by the linen cupboard. 'Here. Take this,' she said, hauling something from the top shelf.

The box of Christmas decorations was fastened with a straggle of tinsel. Three more boxes came down after it, each with its own cloud of dust. 'Good gracious!' Peg said. She whipped a duster from her overall pocket and gave the boxes a going over. 'Christmas makes a lot of work, but I suppose it's worth it.'

'You think so?' Mrs Jago asked.

Peg hooked up two of the boxes. 'I'll take them down, shall I?'

Mrs Jago's hair was bound up in a green scarf. With a desperate shove, she realigned the heavy pile of linen. 'If you like. I don't much care.'

Christmas is the worst time, Peg thought, when you've lost somebody. The toffs are no different to anybody else in that respect. 'I'll put them by the tree then.'

'Fine,' said Mrs Jago after a moment.

'Then I'll come back for the others.' Peg edged herself carefully past the stepladder. She started towards the stairs. As an afterthought, she added, 'I'm afraid Jack broke one of the chandelier crystals.'

'Yes?'

'He caught it with the top of the tree.'

Mrs Jago wedged a pair of sheets into the remaining space. Then she said, 'Oh, God, what is any of this for? I do not want Christmas, I see no point in Christmas, so why the hell are we damned well bothering?'

On her way home, Peg called at Apple Tree. Edie's daughter, Annie was visiting. A nice girl, if a touch on the soft side. The green plush cloth was on the table. Edie was putting apples on to stew with honey to save the sugar. Mabel was struggling with the jumble sale accounts. 'I shouldn't worry if it doesn't tally,' Annie was saying. 'Who's going to care about the odd pence?'

'I care. That's who,' said Mabel, ungrammatically for once.

'Well, the thing is, Auntie, no one else would do the job.'

'Make yourself useful and get the cups out,' Mabel said. 'Sit down, Peg. You look worn out.'

'And no wonder,' Peg said. 'It was murder up there today.'

'At the manor? What's up?'

'Christmas is up,' Peg said, 'that's what. The new housekeeper's throwing her weight around and they're doing the bran tub for the Christmas party so we were treading bran everywhere, and then Miss bloody Penelope, pardon my French, decided to make silver paper flowers and stars for the tree and we ended up scraping cheese off the carpet.'

'Cheese?' Mabel didn't follow.

'She pinched the silver paper from the processed cheese packets. And then the blessed architect turned up and he's staying the night, which meant I had to make an extra pie as the other one wouldn't stretch to him. I turned out a pair of green rep curtains you might use for your toymakers' club. They're in a bag by the grandfather clock.'

Mabel ran the club in the school hall on Wednesday evenings from September until Christmas.

'I caught Mr Garland this morning. Sold him one of the elephants you made from Stan Pierce's old flannel trousers. He's a soft touch. Mr Garland, I mean.'

Mabel said, 'I can imagine.' Then, 'Edie!'

'Sorry, dear.' Edie stopped whistling to herself.

Mabel said, 'How's Cis?'

'Due next week, thank God. She can scarcely walk. But it's Nipper I'm worried about. Cis says she's not sure he wants it.'

'The baby?' Mabel said, 'Those boys have been through a lot. Samuel especially. Give him time.'

'I suppose you're right.' Peg brightened. 'At any rate, Jack's happier than I've seen him for ages.'

Mabel's gaze went back down to the account book. Her face said nothing, but she sat tapping her pencil.

'Maybe having another child will settle Lil down.'

'Neither you nor I believe that, Margaret.'

That was true enough. I haven't forgotten, Peg thought, the Yank who used to ride the little trollop home on his handlebars while Jack was off fighting for his country. I called her all the names under the sun, but she took not a blind bit of notice.

'Agnes says there are eight women in the parish newly pregnant and three christenings coming up.' Edie fetched a plate from the dresser and filled it with ginger nuts. 'And five pairs of banns have been published and two more are to be delivered to the clerk next Saturday.'

'The rector will have his work cut out,' Peg said.

'Also, there are three weddings coming up—'

'The kettle's boiling,' Mabel said pointedly.

Edie picked up the teapot. 'Agnes has lost her big tabby. Did I ever tell you about the tabby cat we had when we were children? He was called Boxer and he used to trot across the road to the schoolroom and sit under Mrs Bertram's chair when she took her Bible class. And one day he didn't turn up and she came across and said, "Where's your cat, Mrs Medland? He didn't come to my Bible class." He suffered from asthma, you know. The poor thing used to get it from licking his fur. Mother used to dose him with syrup of blackthorn.'

Mabel asked if they were going to get their tea today or tomorrow.

Tom said he had come to check the bulge in the butler's bedroom ceiling, which had probably been caused by snow melting through the chimney seam. He said he had called in on his way back from Cotehele, and Daph said, 'Wouldn't it have been easier to call a local builder? It's not that big a problem, is it?'

He didn't answer the question, just pulled off his muffler and asked if she could find him a torch and a bucket and handbrush and take him up there. The worst of it was that when he said the word bedroom, she coloured up.

'What, now?' she said.

'If you wouldn't mind. I'll wait here, shall I?'

Daph said, 'I'll . . . see what I can find.'

She went down to the kitchen, where Mrs Trewarden was tying up Christmas puddings, and Tilley located a torch on the shelf in the back pantry. She came back out with it in her hand. 'I didn't put dried elderberries in the puddings this year,' she confided, 'because between you and me and the gatepost, they was blinking horrible. Will you be carol singing with the choir, miss?'

'On Christmas Eve,' Daph said. 'Seven o'clock.' She had a tempting thought. She would stay down here with Tilley until Tom got tired of waiting and then Charlie would deal with the lump in the ceiling. But Mrs Harmsworth, she of the thin lips and the sour smile, came marching in, so there was nothing for it but to make her way back upstairs.

'Good,' Tom said. He took the bucket and left her with the torch. 'Lead on, Macduff.'

It was eerie up on the second floor. The passage wound gloomily past a number of spare bedrooms, at times lit by cold light from a window and at others almost pitch black. The torch wasn't really much use. 'I think it's at the end here,' Daph told him.

'Right or left?'

'Right,' she said.

'Are there light switches?'

'Yes, but I can't remember where. Haven't been up here in an age.'

As she waved the torch, her hand brushed his arm. She pushed open a door and found a light switch. 'That's better,' she said. The bulge in the ceiling was to the left of the fireplace.

'Good,' Tom said, 'there's a trapdoor.' He fetched the stepladder from outside the linen cupboard at the far end of the passage and banged the trapdoor open. 'Charlie was right. There's snow on the rafters. Pass the bucket, could you?'

He disappeared into the roof. Daph heard knocking and sweeping and a muffled clinking. When he lowered the bucket, it was full of snow. 'That's most of it,' he said. 'What's left won't hurt. Charlie will have to get his local chap to check the lead around the chimney.'

He planted the bucket out in the passage and brushed his hands dry on his jacket.

'Will the ceiling have to come down?' Daph asked.

'Shouldn't think so. They'll just knock out that bit of plaster. Actually,' he said, fishing into his inside pocket, 'what I really came for was to give you this.'

The package was scroll-shaped and wrapped in red tissue. 'A Christmas present?' She was horrified. 'But I didn't get you one.'

'Doesn't matter.'

'Oh, but it does.' She felt mortified.

He said, 'You can give me one after Christmas.'

'I might not see you after Christmas.'

'Yes. You will.'

He stood gazing down at her as if he never wanted to look away. 'Don't open it until Christmas morning,' he said.

'I won't.' But that sounded so brisk that she was embarrassed and finished up stammering like a complete idiot. 'It's . . . it's very— Much too kind. You really shouldn't have.'

'So how long are you home for?' Daph asked Romy, as the spotlight on the revolving, multi-faceted glass ball cast splinters of light on the dancers.

'Not sure. Probably until the new year.'

'Can you shove those prizes into the box? And after that, we'll put the sandwiches on the plates. Or will they dry up before we get to the interval?' She consulted the list Edie Medland had given her. 'I wish Mabel hadn't gone down with the flu. I'm hopeless at catering. So does your Pa know why you moved flats?'

'Good God, no. And don't you dare tell.'

'But don't you think—?'

'No. I don't! Here's Bos.'

'Yes. He offered to help with the raffle.'

'He really is stuck on you. Rather sweet really.'

Daph stood by the long refreshment table in her black lace with the imitation carnation, watching Bos duck his head to avoid getting caught up in a paper streamer. 'He's bought me something in a huge box for Christmas. He says I'll like it, but his mother won't. I've been wondering how I'll get on with her. He says we'll be company for each other.'

'There's company and company,' Romy said. 'I thought she was moving into one of their cottages.'

'I hope so, but I haven't had the courage to bring the subject up.'

By now Bos was dropping a kiss on her cheek. 'Happy Christmas! What a spread. You must have been working like a Trojan.'

Whenever he smiled at her like that, a kind of anxiety filled her, as if her crush on Tom might have been found out. 'Romy helped,' she said.

'Well done. How are you, Romily? I hear you're working in another book shop.'

'I wouldn't exactly call it work,' said Romy. 'I flick a duster around. Look up when the bell pings. Knock off for lunch dead on one.'

'Whizzo!' The three-piece band (piano, drums, saxophone) changed tempo. 'You two should have a dance,' Romy said, 'while you can. Might not get a chance later.'

Daph shook her head. 'There's far too much to do.'

'I can manage,' Romy said. 'Go on. Have a canter. Don't look so embarrassed. It's Christmas.'

'Yes,' said Bos, surprisingly. 'It's a slow number. I think we might manage that.' He took her hand. They moved together in strict tempo, Daph fiercely concentrating, trying to anticipate the steps he was going to take before he took them. Slow-slow-quick, quick – slow. Double reverse, turn at the corner. Oh, help, she'd trodden on his toe.

Bos said, 'Sorry. My fault.' His hand was resting on the small of her back. 'I must say, you look rather fetching tonight.'

Daph said, 'I look a sight.'

Bos replied, 'Not at all,' gallant as ever, and she made a determined effort to smile up at him and look as if she was enjoying herself, but it was no good, she would rather have been out in her old clothes, taking the dog for a run.

'Mother wondered if you would come over for lunch on Christmas Day. Make a change from just the two of us. Would your people mind?'

'I'll ask,' Daph said vaguely.

'Good. Romily looks well.'

'Does she?' Looks can be misleading, Daph thought. Romy might act fearless, but there was a watchfulness about her that hadn't been there before.

They swung left and almost bumped into Trewarden, who was dancing with Daisy Jewell. Trewarden whisked Daisy (in pale green velvet) away from them.

'What's happened to the Pole?' Bos asked.

'Don't ask. He's stale news.'

'Good riddance, from what I hear. There's Charlie Garland. Has he turned into your lodger?'

Actually, Daph thought, Charlie *was* beginning to feel like one of the family. A sort of replacement brother, only under the circumstances, you could scarcely say so. He was making a beeline for Romy; pushing his way through the dancers like a man sleepwalking.

'You won't mind if I ask,' Bos was saying, 'but I'm not quite sure what she's wearing.'

'Romy?'

'Yes. Is it a frock or a boiler suit?'

Charlie was saying something to her. Romy's hair (tied up with a scrap of ribbon to match her white silk whatever-it-was) shone in the spotlight. 'Frock. Maybe.'

Another turn. Trewarden and Daisy had stopped by the doorway. Daisy was laughing and out of breath. She looked very pretty and very sweet. It was as well that Lil Trewarden was nowhere in the offing.

Bos said, 'Is there something going on? Between Romily and your lodger?'

'Possibly,' Daph said, gazing over his shoulder at the banner that said: **GRAND CHRISTMAS DANCE.**

'He seems a good sort.'

'Yes.'

The music was coming to an end. Bos squeezed her hand. 'I enjoyed that.'

'Yes,' Daph said. *There ought to be more to Christmas than this.*

'We should do it more often.'

'Perhaps.'

'All work and no play . . .'

'We'll see.'

I am going to have to settle for this calm, prosaic form of love, she thought. It's more sensible. And much less likely to burn itself out. But her mind would keep taking itself back to Tom. She remembered standing with him in the V&A before she caught the train home. They had whizzed round, dashing from one glass case to the next, finishing up in the print room in front of a geisha with bone carvings in her hair. *Pictures of the Floating World,* Tom had read. And they had burst out laughing. There had been such a sense of . . . delight.

Why can't you make me feel like that? she wanted to ask Bos. But that was unfair, when he was always so good to her.

In the East End, during the Blitz, there had been one fear-filled night when a bomb had destroyed the house opposite. After the blast, her room had moved a foot out of place, hesitated for a terrifying second, then it had fallen back into place.

Things would drop back into place between her and Bos.

They had to.

Every morning when she woke up, Romy wrapped herself in her dressing-gown and stood gazing shallowly out of the window at the berries on the holly and the white mist behind the winter trees. Christmas was following much the same course as it always had at the rectory; shepherds watching, angels singing, red crêpe streamers draped around the fireplace. Her brothers had turned up, one by one – Peter first, cheerfully unannounced, then Philip, all muffled up, with a new girlfriend called Angela – but she couldn't savour any of it. She loved Christmas, but this year she felt shut off, glassed in behind a wall of horrible little anxieties that inserted themselves between her and the world outside. Oh, she put on her usual breezy act, keeping up the appearance of everything being as normal, but all she really felt was deathly tired. And bruised. Not bruises that an inspecting doctor could find, more the kind that ached inwardly.

Now and again Charlie could make her laugh. He saved up funny stories expressly for that purpose. How he had found the major sitting at his desk writing letters with a hot water bottle in either pocket. How old Mrs Jago had told him, in that choppy, old-fashioned voice of hers, that the best thing one could say about doctors was that they were not all rogues, like lawyers. Yes, Charlie was a dear. And soft about her. She knew that. But he wasn't really her sort and she found herself shying away from the quiet intensity of his feelings for her. At the moment, violent forces of any kind made her feel apprehensive. Not that trying to deter him made a blind bit of difference – Charlie was a tiny bit dim that way. On Friday he had driven her down to the Ceylon Café, wedged her into a corner table, and told her that she was looking thin and he was going to sit there while she consumed a good, square lunch. (She had managed thick soup and minced chicken hash, but no pudding.) Then yesterday he had walked in on them while they were decorating the church. She had been helping Daph and Edie Medland trail ivy around the pew ends in a shove-it-on-and-hope-it-will-stick sort of way, while Virginia Jago put together the chancel arrangement of holly and yew and Christmas roses.

Daph was the first to spot Charlie. 'Come to help?' she called out. 'We could do with an extra pair of hands.'

'Just passing through. Sorry.' He said he had spent fifteen minutes thawing the film of ice on the car windscreen with a warm sponge. To Romy he said, 'I called at the rectory. Your mother said you were dressing the church in its Christmas best.'

'I got detailed. What time are you off?'

'Right now. I just wanted to wish you a Happy Christmas.'

'You too.' She grabbed another stem of ivy. She split the stem in half, hung it on the high, square pew. No good. It dropped off. He picked it up for her.

He said, 'Only another twenty-five to do.'

Romy gave him a look.

He gazed back at her with sudden seriousness. 'What I really came for is to ask if you'll be OK?'

'Of course. Why shouldn't I be?' She looked at him, at his windswept flop of hair, at the knapsack on his back and the three cumbersome files he was carrying. She said, 'Life's a bit dull here, but that suits me at the moment. I'm making myself useful. Playing the parson's daughter.'

Charlie said, 'Good. So . . . how long are your brothers staying?'

'Until the new year.'

'I'm glad.' He didn't say why. 'Well – take care.'

Romy wanted to say, I'm not made of glass, you know. I don't like being treated like a complete weakling, but just as she was about to say so, Edie came trotting up.

'Romily, dear, I can't stay any longer. Mabel's still poorly and as prickly as a porcupine. That's what happens when you cough all night. She broke Mother's best teapot this morning . . .'

Charlie, backing off, mouthed a silent, 'Happy Christmas!'

'. . . not that we ever used it. Well, only when we've got company. I got the blame, of course. *And* for the custard pudding turning runny.'

In the chancel, Mrs Jago stepped back to check the symmetry of her arrangement. Edie lowered her voice to a whisper. 'Mabel can't abide her, but you can't help feeling for the bereaved at Christmas. I lost a son, you know. He was only a year old. I pour myself a sherry every year on what would have been his birthday. Cis Trewarden had her baby. A dear little boy. Did you know? I'm so glad you've found yourself another young man, dear.'

Romy said, 'He's not my—'

'I shouldn't say it, but the other one wasn't quite the ticket. Mabel had no use for him. She thought he was looking for a goose that could lay him golden eggs. That night she saw him getting on the bus—'

'The bus?'

'Three weeks ago. Or was it four? She said he had a face like . . . well, you wouldn't want to meet him in the dark.'

Romy said, 'Which bus?' Her knees had gone.

Edie adjusted her gold spectacles. 'From the station, dear. Up to the village.'

'Are you sure?'

'Pretty sure. Agnes saw him get off. He stopped outside her house to light a cigarette, then headed for the rectory. We couldn't work out why, because you were up in London.'

* * *

The rector was sticking candles on top of an old biscuit tin. He turned as Romy opened the vestry door. You look tired, she thought. Mother could help more, but she won't put herself out. Pigeons were scrambling in the roof.

'Did I hear Charlie's voice?' he asked.

'Yes. He popped in to say goodbye.'

'How are things coming along at the manor?'

'He says the house is settling down nicely.' She came in and shut the door behind her. 'Can I ask you something?'

'Fire away.' He set the biscuit tin aside.

'Did Jan come to see you?'

It was cold in the vestry. White, translucent diamond panes framed the rector's head. At last he said, 'I wouldn't have told you, but . . . yes, he did.'

'Why wouldn't you have told me?'

His dark eyes met hers. 'I suppose I needed time to think.'

'About what?' But she thought she knew the answer to that. 'Did he bring you my letters?'

He said nothing. Romy's heart sank. 'Did you read them?'

'One or two. Just enough to . . . get the gist of it.'

Romy felt shabby and dirty and ashamed, like some tart trying to talk her way past St Peter. 'Daddy, I'm sorry,' she said. 'I care very much about what you think. If I could turn the clock back, I would have done a lot of things differently. But I can't and I didn't and I know what you must think of me.'

'Do you?'

'I've let you down.'

'Look, Romily—'

'He's such a—'

'Darling, listen—'

'Towards the end, it . . . he was awful.' There was some kind of obstruction, now, at the back of her throat.

'I know,' the rector said. 'Charlie told me.'

'Charlie?'

'He was worried about you. He thought I should know what was going on.'

She stood staring at him.

'I wanted to come up to London, but he persuaded me not to. He said you wouldn't want it. That you were quite safe and he would keep me in the picture.'

Romy thought, he didn't choose to keep *me* in the picture. She said, 'Does Mummy know?'

'Best not. Don't you think?'

Romy looked at her father, at his quiet, humorous eyes, his greying temples, his old-fashioned dog-collar. The rector's expression had not changed. He said, 'I'm not such an old fogey as you might think.'

She thought, I should have known that. But she was still mad as hell at Charlie.

Christmas Day came with its familiar festive smell. The weather was sharp, the bells pealed, the best china adorned the table. They had a huge fire, for once, in the dining-room, and a bountiful dinner of turkey and brown potatoes and sprouts, all from Farmer Jewell. Pen had made Tilley a kettle holder and Mother a case with needles and cotton and buttons in. Pa had a shoe polisher. 'Very good. Well done!' he said. Evalina wore her diamond earrings and grey velvet gown and, over one too many glasses of wine, told of a young poet from Oxford who had once proposed marriage to her, though the spirit of romance hadn't lasted long. 'He was a little too fond of a tipple,' she said, helping herself to the port.

The major proposed a toast. 'Absent friends,' he said gruffly, as the candlelight flickered in the mirror and in the windows. And for a moment, no one knew what to say. Daph fiddled with her linen napkin. Virginia, in plum-coloured taffeta, stared hard at the portrait Pen had done of her. It was squinny-eyed, but there was, actually, some faint resemblance.

After dinner, the major walked the dog and Daph slipped up to her room to open Tom's package. She slipped off the ribbon, then the red tissue.

It was a sheet of music. Jerome Kern. 'The Song is You'.

I hear music when I look at you
A beautiful theme of every dream I ever knew . . .

The parchment was smooth under her fingers as she read on.

Why can't I let you know the song my heart would sing?
The music is sweet and the words are true . . .

At the top of the title page, he had written:
What more can I say? With love. Christmas 1946

So after six wobbly months, Daphne sat on her bed with a shawl wrapped round her shoulders and a wildly blissful smile on her face.

Twenty-Two

Charlie woke at ten minutes to eight to find that it was still pitch dark. There were ice ferns over the bedroom window. Icicles a foot long hanging from the water spout.

When Tilley brought up an enamel jug of hot water, she told him that the lane to the village was impassable and Dan Jewell hadn't got through with the milk. 'But I can do you a nice soft-boiled egg, sir.'

'No time, Tilley. Just black tea and toast.'

'Proper job. I'll peg on, then.'

By the time he had washed, breakfasted and made his way down to the drawing room, it was beginning to be light. Heard and Sons were already measuring the dado panelling. The sections ripped off by the army needed to be replaced, the carved cornices restored and the large pair of oak doors into the dining room rehung. And then there was the rotten wainscoting in the library . . .

He was already crossing things off the list of jobs that could realistically be done by early June.

'Don't you worry, sir,' said a voice behind him. 'Us'll get there.'

Charlie turned, wondering if his thoughts were that transparent. Heard Senior had taken off his cap and was smoothing his sparse grey hairs, as befitting the head of the family of carpenters who had worked at the hall for at least a century. He carried around with him a wonderful tawny aroma of wood shavings and old pencils and cedarwood.

'I hope so,' said Charlie. 'This weather won't help.'

'''Tis a likker,' Heard agreed.

'I'm surprised you got here.'

'Dug our way over Top Wood. Well, the boys did.'

Charlie wanted him to look at the rickety mitred rails on the first floor landing. The wood smell moved with them into the hall and up the stairs. Heard bent to examine the rails quickly, expertly, knowledgeably. You didn't have to tell him anything; he knew exactly what was needed.

'That'll be no problem, sir.'

Charlie asked if there was anything he couldn't deal with.

Heard laughed and said not much these days. He went off back down the grand staircase looking entirely at ease, more like a poor relation of the Jagos than a tradesman. Well, he'd been in and out of the place for seventy years or more. It was not just those who owned the stones and mortar, Charlie reflected, who had a relationship with the house. All those unseen village hands that had tended the place for generations, they held shares in it too.

As he stood staring out of the crinkled glass of the window, a name and a date carved on the chimney stack caught his eye. Hicks 1540. Another maker and mender, another shareholder leaving his mark on the house and proud of it.

Charlie went down to telephone Romily. On the first day of the new year, Pearl Matheson had slipped on ice and broken her ankle and Romy had agreed to stay at home for a month to help her father out. To be honest, she hadn't much seemed to mind delaying her return to London, her new job at the book shop being only temporary. She had said to him, 'I can't seem to be able to gel.' And it was true that she seemed full of restless energy, which was good because she brought herself up to Lizzah to help out when she had had enough of Pearl's grousing. But she wasn't easy. Had she forgiven him for what she called blabbing to the rector when she had asked him not to? Charlie wasn't sure. Did she like him? He had no idea. As he picked up the receiver, he reminded himself to act imperturbable and stick to light banter.

'Trewenna one four two.'

'Romily, this is Charlie. Cold enough for you?'

'Bloody freezing! Fifteen degrees of frost last night. I'm wearing three layers of everything.'

'How's the invalid?'

'Don't ask. I've just taken up the post. She says the village boys are making far too much noise waging snow fights in the street, no one has any idea how much pain she's in, and arthritis will probably set in and cripple her in every limb. Except your tongue, I almost said. She is driving me up the wall! She won't read, she won't knit, and if I don't answer the bell, she thumps on the floor with the poker. To get out of earshot, I salted and shovelled a path from the front door to the gates. Daddy sneaked off to take some soup to a sick parishioner. Very convenient, I thought. He took the nine o'clock communion in an empty church.'

'Not surprising. Are you coming this afternoon?'

'How, for God's sake?'

'Got any skis in the attic?'

'Actually, that's a thought. What do you need help with?'

'The guide book needs typing up. Biddy was going to do it, but she's stuck in London.'

'I should warn you, I'm not terribly accurate.'

'Neither is Biddy.'

'And I'm not very fast.'

Charlie said nothing.

'Oh, very funny,' she said. 'Is Biddy fast?'

'Depends if Mrs Hackett has her eagle eye on her or not. Mrs Hackett runs the office. When she cracks the whip, we all jump.'

'I wasn't talking about her typing. You must tell me about her.'

'Nothing to tell. Old Fossett and Miss Waterhouse work in one room; Biddy and I share the bigger room with the filing cabinets.'

'And are you still sharing a bed?'

He certainly wasn't going to answer that one. He pretended that the major had just walked in and said he would, hopefully, see her later.

The major sat in the library in his greatcoat reading about the remaining Nazi leaders in concentration camps (large hotels inside barbed wire with the dirty blackguards sitting in basket chairs on the terrace), about blocked roads and railways, food shortages, coal shortages, trees collapsing and farmers digging horses out of drifts. Outside, blue smoke from the chimneys twirled straight in the freezing air. Charlie had said that fires must be kept going in the staterooms all through winter no matter what the cost. Well, some good came out of everything, Myles supposed. Virginia's voice, discussing paint samples, came now and again, disconcertingly, through the gap in the door. Only part of his mind registered the fact, for the rest of it was wondering whether he should have bought the load of wood Samuel Trewarden had tried to sell him that morning. Cheap enough, he thought. The thing is, you can't be sure where it came from. My own trees, probably. I won't say he's a pilferer. More a flash-Alf. Then quickly, he softened his uncharitable criticism. The poor fellow's been through hell, he told himself. I've seen some sights myself. Dachau. Never told anybody. Best not. Wish I hadn't asked about his dog. What a blunder, but how was one to know it was on its last legs?

A cloud of smoke rose from the major's pipe. He got up and took himself over to the sideboard. There was a glassy tinkle and a clink as a stopper went back into a decanter, then Virginia's voice said, 'That won't help.'

'Cold hands,' the major said, vexed at being caught out.

'That's the lamest excuse I ever heard. Come and polish silver with me. That'll get your circulation going.'

'I'm not a batman.' He said irritably, 'Couldn't we get out of here for a day or two?'

'While all this is going on?'

'Why not? When did we last have a holiday?'

She did a mental calculation. 'Eight years.'

'Well, then?'

'Just buzz off? Are you mad?'

'No.' Actually, it was the sanest thing he'd thought of in a long while. She said, 'The whole country's snowbound.'

'It'll clear by next week.'

'And where would we go in the middle of winter?'

'Where would you like to go? The south of France? New York? Australia?'

'You are joking?'

'Yes.' A pause. Then he said, 'How about a few days in London? Posh hotel? What do you think?'

'We can't afford it.'

'Perhaps we can't afford not to.'

She knew what he was getting at. 'But . . . January in London?' she said.

'You could shop. We could do a gallery or two. You used to like that in the old days.'

She remembered staying at the Clarendon the year after they were married: fur coat and hat for the journey; hot chocolate every morning in Bond Street. Boozy lunches and the luxurious bed with gold hangings. That was where Kit had been conceived.

Kit. Her gaze strayed over the Persian carpet, the lovely, battered old desk, the cardboard snowman Pen had made Myles from an old Vim container.

What on earth would we talk about? she wondered.

Myles said, 'So what do you think?'

'It's not possible,' she said flatly. 'Too much to do, what with the opening in June and the wedding two weeks later.'

The pattern of the planning lunches had set itself in place some months ago, more by accident than design when Charlie, grabbing a quick bite in the Summerleaze Hotel in Bude, had bumped into Virginia, who had promptly come across to sit herself at his table. She had wanted to ask about the repairs to the cottages. Over salad and very tough steaks, followed by Monmouth Pudding, they had sorted out the village repairs, the tree felling, the staircase ceiling and what they thought Mr Churchill ought to say at the University of Zurich. Now the lunch meetings were a regular thing. Sometimes the major joined them, with sheets and sheets of notes in his tiny, meticulous handwriting, but on the whole, they got on better without him. Charlie prided himself on being able to handle the most awkward clients, and there were days when the major seemed almost approachable, but he had a habit of drifting off. 'Myles,' his wife would say, 'don't disappear on us.'

However, today it was just Charlie and Virginia, sharing cold grouse and rowan and apple sauce at a small round table in the little parlour under the back stairs. First they had discussed the decorators' estimates. Charlie favoured Pompeian red for the dining room, which Virginia had felt would look much too gloomy, but Charlie said not with glasses and silver catching the light on the dining table, you have to trust me on this, I know what I'm talking about. Virginia said didn't he think it would look like a Venetian bordello and Charlie looked amused and said not for one moment.

Then Virginia said, 'What I want to know is, how are we to show the public around? Because my husband would run a mile. And quite frankly, I haven't got the patience.'

Charlie said, 'The British Legion will be happy to provide guides. They have chaps on their books who are crocked up and in need of part-time work.'

Virginia laid down her knife and fork. She sat gazing at him from across the table, which had been drawn as far away from the window as possible. Every stir of the curtains brought an icy chill.

'And where will all these paying customers come from? We're in the middle of nowhere and petrol's rationed.'

'They'll walk from the station. It's only three miles.'

'You've got more faith than I have.'

The fire was crumbling. Charlie got up and threw on another log. 'Don't you like looking around other people's houses? Everything's been so bleak. Looking at lovely old things will cheer people up.'

'Make them hate our guts, more like.'

'I know what's wrong with you,' Charlie said.

'What's that?'

'Cold feet.'

When she laughed, her whole face lit up. You should do it more often, Charlie thought. It makes you look quite different.

'Kit made silly jokes,' she told him. 'I miss that.'

'Of course you do.'

'Jokes never work when Myles tells them,' said Virginia. 'He does his damnedest to get them right, but they always sound rehearsed.'

Charlie grinned.

'When he proposed to me, I think he must have been practising for days. "Will you make this place your home?" he said. Offering the house as if the man on his own wouldn't be good enough. I was so touched, but if I'd had my head screwed on, I would have said, "I'll take you, but not the house."'

'You don't mean that?'

'Yes. I do.' She poured herself another glass of wine. 'We'd have been far happier. Lizzah has drained the life out of our marriage. Oh, it was fun at first, finding myself mistress of a country house. We had parties, people were always dropping in and out. You'll never believe this, but when he was twenty-something, Myles was almost sociable.'

Charlie waited, wondering if she wasn't more than slightly tiddly. He looked out of the heavily curtained window into the blizzard. The swirlings were hypnotizing; framed in flakes, there was a reflection of the whole room.

'But then the gilt began to wear off the gingerbread. What money there was disappeared on the upkeep of the house. Myles began to worry himself sick.'

'Well, soon,' Charlie said, 'he won't have anything to worry about.'

'He'll invent something. Did it ever strike you that the country is in the same state as these old houses? In a complete mess. Delapidated. Bankrupt.'

'Attlee will haul it up by its bootstraps,' Charlie said.

'I hope so. It's a pity you can't do the same for a marriage.'

'Attlee is to nationalize coalmines, transport, electricity and aviation,' Evalina was saying at that moment to Daphne down in the kitchen. 'I don't know what the world is coming to! India and Burma clamouring for independence. Palestine in conflict. And that young man has stripped the place. I miss all the little tables. And the ornaments.'

'How can you miss them,' Daph asked, 'when most of them have been squirrelled away in your new quarters. Don't think we haven't noticed.'

'I don't know what you're talking about.'

'I'm talking about the way you sent Trewarden to pinch the Dutch chest with the brass handles from the stuff Charlie has in storage.'

'Pinch? It's my chest! I keep my hats in it.'

'You *used* to keep your hats in it. It'll have to go back. It belongs to the Trust.'

'Oh, to hell with the Trust!' Evalina said.

'You'll also have to return the dolls' house.'

'I will not! You children used to play with it. Kit loved the boy in the sailor suit. And the bewhiskered policeman.'

Daph said, 'I know. But Charlie needs it for—'

'Charlie! Charlie! Charlie! Has the man charmed you? He's got us shut away in desolate prison cells at the back of the house—'

'Prison cell? You have the nicest little rooms. You've never been so cosy.'

'All I can see through the window is a gravelled triangle.' Since Christmas, Evalina's suffering tendencies had come back with a vengeance.

'When you were at the front of the house, you complained about the noise.'

'Also, I hate gas fires.'

Daph looked at her with raised eyebrows.

'And there isn't a bookshelf.'

'You don't read.'

'I didn't say I wanted to read. I just like to look at a line of books. There's a hurricane coming under that door. Tell the Harmsworth woman to get it stuffed up. I don't like her. She's not top drawer.'

'Servants are rarely top drawer, Granny.'

'But they should be of sound character. Like Trewarden's mother. She talks too much, but she's capable and she makes me laugh.'

Give that woman a medal, Daph thought.

Outside, the wind was rising. Fat, white flakes, like goose feathers, were sticking to the windows. Daph watched the room take on a peculiar light. This week, she thought, has seemed like a month.

Tom had telephoned her on the first day of the new year. 'Did you have a good Christmas?' His voice, full of warmth, had made her instep tingle.

'Yes. Yes, we did. And you?'

'Mother has a nasty cold. But apart from that . . .'

A dead silence. Then Daph said, 'Thank you for the present.'

'Did you like it?'

Another silence. 'Yes, I did. So much.'

'Good.'

'I feel bad I didn't get you anything,' Daph had added.

'Doesn't matter,' said Tom. 'Have you got snow? We had to dig ourselves out. I kept thinking about you. Is that allowed? Probably not, but I don't care. I have to see you. Please don't tell me I can't.'

Daph listened to her grandmother going on about Churchill and Stalin. It's funny, she thought, how some people sound better on the telephone than others: Tom so close that you could almost feel him breathing; Bos like an officer in khaki, jolly, but clipped.

But he would never, ever cheat on you, whispered the sensible, if sanctimonious, half of her brain. You should be ashamed of yourself, wanting to be with Tom. All right, she thought, but the thing is, a relationship is bound to feel crumbly if a man hasn't tried to make love to you before you walk down the aisle with him. How are you supposed to know you'll enjoy sleeping with someone if he always acts like the perfect gentleman?

Tom would pounce. If I let him.

Is that good or bad? She stared down at the ring on her third finger. The solitaire glinted back at her. Bad, of course.

Dear God, let me not feel like this. Let Tom be sent away to work on another old wreck of a place miles and miles away, so that I can forget about him and it can all go back to what it was before.

She had never felt like this about anyone. Stirred up. Exhilarated. But how could she know if such feelings would last? How could she take the risk of stepping out into a sheer drop, a thousand miles down? Bos might seem old and sedate, as dull as ditchwater, but he was safe and had a heart as big as a bathtub. He'd given her an electric bed warmer for Christmas. Quite hideous, and not at all romantic, but a godsend at the moment, when the bedroom chill ate into your bones.

She gazed out at the fast-falling snow that was blurring every outline and thought how solid Bos was, how much he cared about her. She told herself sternly, this thing with Tom must stop. It did not strike her that it might not, in the end, be as simple as all that.

The world these days, it seemed to Mabel, was one of empty cupboards and thick utility socks. She sat sipping her cup of cocoa and listening to Father's clock ticking off the hours. She had drawn the curtains against the wind and stoked up the kitchen fire. At least there was wood, thanks to Samuel – real wood, not just parings or faggots. The back door was hung with curtains against the cold. Her feet were on the brass fireguard and for knee warmth there was Mother's fat old cushion with the mock Jacobean linen cover. Every now and again she chafed the chilblains on her finger.

Where are the fruits of victory? she wondered. The new Utopia? Unaccountably delayed, it seemed. Edie didn't seem to mind the country being in such a mess. She made light of the big freeze ('Don't the trees look pretty?'), the electricity cuts ('It's like old times, don't you think, dear?'), the scraggy meat, no soap and no potatoes. But Edie's was a saintly nature. It occurred to Mabel, as she flicked through the parish magazine, that her sister took after Granny Lane, who had once brought the parlour ceiling down by hammering on it to frighten the mice away before they got caught in the nasty traps. Which reminds me, Mabel thought, *I* must set some. Fieldmice, in from the cold, had been eating the corners of Father's books.

She finished her cocoa and laid the table for the morning. After that, she straightened the meat plate that she had hung on the newly distempered wall and decided that Edie should have been home a long time ago. She had gone to Agnes's sewing evening, which was no more than an excuse to catch up on the latest scandal. What if she had come a cropper on the ice and broken something? Mabel felt vexed at having to worry about her.

She went to the door and looked out. The gooseberry bushes were muffled blue shapes, ice crystals frosted the wall. She stayed there until she heard Edie walk crunchingly up the path.

Mabel said, 'What time do you call this?'

'It's hard walking,' Edie said, by way of explanation.

'Then you shouldn't have gone.'

'I enjoyed it.' Edie stamped her boots on the doormat, sending clumps of slush over the immaculately polished linoleum. 'Aggie's getting an electric washing machine. She says we must keep up with the times.'

'Throwing good money after bad.'

'And Cis's baby is to be called Frederick John. He's a nice little chap. Feeds well. And that Plymouth family have moved in two more. But that's not the real news.'

'I don't listen to gossip.'

'You'll want to hear about this. It's all over the village. It seems that Jack Trewarden has been carrying on with Daisy. Dan came across them in the barn together. He threatened Jack with a hay rake.'

For once in her life, Mabel felt flurried and stupid. Oh, eff! she thought.

Twenty-Three

'*Lord, I hear of showers of bless-ing, Thou art scattering full and free,*' sang Tilley as she sat cleaning a handsome but tarnished old jug that Mr Garland had asked her to have a go at. Tilley loved to polish. Copper especially. It kept her warm and left her mind free so that her thoughts could go wandering.

Showers, the thir-sty land re-freshing;
Let some drop-pings fall on me,
E-ven me, E-ven me?
Let some drop-pings fall on me.

Sankey and Moody propped her up when cowboys singing lonesome songs about tumbleweed didn't suit the circumstances. Tilley was worried about Daisy. And about the Trewardens, for that matter. Jack hadn't been in for his mid-morning splits and jam and he'd missed lunch. Had the major fired him? Whispers were going round that Dan Jewell had been up to the hall and kicked up a proper to-do.

Quite right too, Bess supposed.

Not that she disliked Jack. Not many chaps would go out of their way to help you fill the lamps with evil-smelling paraffin. Some of the village girls liked him because he looked like Humphrey Bogart, but the lamps won every time for Bess. It was just that Daisy was a dear and too good to have married men taking advantage of her and folks quacking on about her behind her back.

The beautiful gates will unfold,
The home of the blood-washed I'll see—

It struck Bess as ominous that Daisy hadn't been to work all week either. Mr Garland, saying they couldn't possibly let things get even more behind, had sent work up to the farm for her.

The city of saints I'll behold!
For oh, there's a welcome for me.

Bess was about to embark on the second verse when the outside door opened and Peg Trewarden came in, stamping snow off her boots.

'The magic of winter!' she said. 'Stop that caterwauling, Bess, and put the kettle on. I can't feel me feet.'

Bess disappeared into the dark cave of the scullery and reappeared minutes later with the filled kettle. She heaved it on to the top of the stove where it began to hiss.

'Now, I know exactly what you're dying to ask. Yes, Jack's been a proper young lerrup and I could cheerfully strangle him, but that's all I've got to say about it, even to you.'

'I wouldn't have dreamed of asking,' fibbed Tilley.

'I like Bess,' Peg said. 'Her's a good maid, but her passes stuff on to her mother and Flo Tilley would tittle-tattle to the world and his wife.'

Mabel said, 'I wish I'd said something when I saw them that day on the dunes.'

'*I* wish you had.'

'Does Lil know?'

'What do you think?'

Mabel thought that Agnes would run to the lodge faster than forked lightning.

'And?'

'Her's cussing him up hill and down dale. Threatened to walk out and take the children with her.'

'And will she?'

Peg gave a dry laugh. 'That little tramp? She knows which side her bread's buttered. You can't gallivant with kiddies to look after.'

'It didn't stop her during the war. Do we know how Daisy is? Has anyone been up to the farm?'

'Jack tried, but Dan wouldn't let him through the door.'

'Would you like me to go?' Mabel asked. She was thinking hard. She had been planning on getting her oatmeal costume cut down and remade. Dan couldn't stop her asking Daisy's advice on that.

'I don't want Miss Petherick interfering.' Jack said, 'I'll deal with it myself.'

'Like you've been dealing with it up till now?' Peg said, 'I could kill you, Jack, I really could. You haven't been home five minutes and you land yourself in this pickle.'

'*You* try living with Lil!'

'You made your bed, my son, and you must lie on it. Thank God Dan didn't take the shotgun to you, that's all I can say.'

If it had been anyone else he was talking to, Jack would have said that, in his opinion, God was a bit of a shit. But he didn't reply. He didn't need reminding that he had made a mess of his life and Daisy's too.

Peg melted some dripping in the frying pan and, when it was smoking hot, jammed in some cold cooked potato. She said, 'You look as though you slept in your clothes. And you stink of drink.'

'All I had was a pint.' He was morose and combustible. More fed up than he had ever been in his life. He needed to see Daisy badly, but how, with her father keeping her virtually under lock and key? 'You've got the wrong chap, sonny,' the normally mild-mannered Dan had said, 'if you think you can play fast and loose with my daughter. I'll dig your grave sooner.' The memory of Daisy in floods of tears caught at him. He dug his hands in his pockets and thought that for two pins he would drive up to The Barton and force his way in. Only Daisy wouldn't want him to and he'd do anything sooner than make things worse for her. If only he could speak to her. Explain that she was all the world to him.

'You can have a bite to eat,' Peg said, 'then you'd better be getting home.'

'It's not a home. She wouldn't know how to make one.'

'Feeling sorry for yourself won't help.' Then she added more kindly, 'You've got to pull yourself together, boy. Oh, I can't say I blame you for wanting something more than Lil. But Daisy's a decent little girl. You should have known better than to make her a laughing stock.'

'I would never do anything to hurt Daisy.'

'But you have. And you're a grown man and you should have known better. How's she going to show her face in the village?'

Jack looked desperately at the frying pan.

'I wasn't playing around. I love her.'

'Love? You're as maize as a brush.'

'She smooths me out. Makes my life worth living.' With a sudden, rough movement, Jack got up. The oil lamp gave a hiss. 'I won't give her up,' he said.

'Then you're a bigger fool than I took you for.'

Peg flipped the potato over and seasoned it with a dash of salt. It was no good trying to tell your children anything. They never listened.

'I thought he'd be home by now. Where is he?'

'God knows. You'll never guess what he brought home yesterday. A squeeze box and a mouth organ.' Cis said, 'He swapped them for a large cock pheasant.'

'One of these days, he'll get a hand on his shoulder.' Jack took the chair by the range. The kitchen smelled of wood smoke and boiled ham.

'That's what I said, but you may as well talk to that wall.' Cis sank, with the baby, who was wailing, into the armchair opposite. 'I've put his supper in the oven.'

'So how are you?' Jack asked.

'Oh, you know. How's Lil?'

'Giving me hell. I suppose the news has got round?'

'I did hear something.' Cis kept her eyes on the woodash in the grate. 'Mother just gave me a rollicking.'

'Oh, dear.'

She looked uncomfortable, so he took pity on her and changed the subject. 'How's the dog?'

'Not eating. Poor thing.'

Jack, who liked Cis, though she was a bit p dingy for his taste, stretched his legs to the blaze and listened with halı an ear while she told him that the baby slept all day and wailed all night, and Nip got a bit impatient. Some days he was lovely, but at other times she couldn't do a thing right.

'Give it time,' Jack told her.

She sat bouncing the baby on her floral lap. 'Dr Murdoch says he'll be his old self in a month or two.'

Jack couldn't think of any way to tell her this, but the fact was that the old Nipper had gone for good. He had been through too much. They all had. They were all in the same bloody boat.

'I can't believe he brought her over on the tractor,' Romy said to Daph.

'She had cabin fever,' Bos had said as he ushered his mother into the house. 'We've been snowed in for weeks, so I thought I'd bring her over to see what you've done to the old place. The Massey Ferguson was the only thing that would get through.'

'I've got frostbite,' Bos's mother said. 'Goodness gracious, you've painted the hall yellow.'

'It's called honeycomb,' Daph told her. 'It's the original colour. Charlie found it underneath layers of old paint. We're in a bit of a state, I'm afraid. Clearing up after the decorators. The paint may still be wet, so I wouldn't touch anything. How are you, Mrs Boswell?'

'Not brilliant, Daphne. But you can't expect to be when you get to my age. I suppose your Mr Garland has been to lots of lectures and such, but I think, dear, you might ask for a second opinion on the yellow. After all, you'll have to live with it for a very long time. That is, Myles and Virginia will have to live with it. You will very soon be in pastures new.'

Over Mrs Boswell's port-coloured felt hat was a neatly tied headscarf.

Both now came off. She fluffed out her thinning hair. 'I hear that wedding preparations are forging ahead? Noel tells me you are to have orange blossom for the church.'

'From the garden. Yes.'

'And your mother's wedding veil. Oh, dear, I suppose that's letting out secrets.'

Daph glanced at Bos. Sometimes, she thought, I wish you would tell her to shut up.

'Veils can be tricky to handle if they're at all bulky. Mine stretched halfway up the aisle and the pageboys trod on it.'

Bos said, 'I'll just dig out my grey suit.' A look of anxiety crossed his face. 'I'll get togged up in tails if you want me to. But you wanted a quiet affair.'

'Absolutely.'

'No one's said what the bridesmaids are wearing.' Romy said, 'Honestly, Daph, it's a bit late to be asking.'

'I know. Sorry. It's all this.' She waved a vague hand. 'There hasn't been a minute.'

'Bridesmaids are a waste of money,' Romy said. 'I shall get Daisy to make me some old rag. That business with Trewarden was a bit of a turn-up.'

'It'll be a nine-day wonder,' Daph said.

'A lot of marriages have come to grief of late.' Bos held his hands out to the fire. 'Ours won't. I'm more than ready to face the big day. The only thing that's worrying me is the speech.'

In the drawing room, Mrs Boswell was shaking the snow from her headgear and peering at the fireplace wall. 'Now would you call that orange? I suppose I'd better ask, or I might get it wrong again.'

'I'd call it pumpkin,' Romy told her.

Mrs Boswell eased off one boot and stood wriggling her toes back to life. 'I wouldn't have it in my dining room. Not that we're likely to be redecorating. There's the cottage to be done up first. I'm afraid I shall be with you for some time, Daphne, dear. There's no way we can get builders in until the severe weather has passed. But you'll put up with a tiresome old mother-in-law, I'm sure. I started *my* married life with my mother-in-law. It wasn't easy. She had a habit of walking into our bedroom in the middle of the night. It had been hers as a child, you see, and she tended to sleepwalk. Your father used to get quite tetchy with her. Well, he got tetchy with me, but I took no notice.'

She started pestering Daph about her trousseau coupons. She said that lace was coupon free; you could get any amount of it if you wanted. But then again, it was nasty, scratchy stuff. Personally she wouldn't wear it next to her skin. You would get rashes and such.

'There's one thing,' Romy said on their way up to Daph's room. 'You'll never be lonely. Not with Mrs B. around for a chat.'

Daph skirted a great froth of stripped-off wallpaper and a tall stepladder 'She means well. I'm sure I shall grow fond of her.'

'You think?' Romy was laughing.

'I don't see why not.'

'Daph – this is me.'

'All right.' Daph said, 'The thing I find hardest is that she's so dependent on him. She's so glad to have him safely home. It's touching, but she sticks to him like glue. I can't see how one would have a life of one's own.'

'You won't,' Romy was blunt about it. But then she said, 'I was wrong about Bos. He's actually rather sweet. Charlie's sweet, too. Only I'd never tell him.'

'I see.'

'No, you don't.'

'I hope you're not playing games with him.' When there was no reply, she said, 'Do you ever hear from Jan?'

'He telephones now and then.'

Daph was astounded. 'I thought it was all over.'

'It is.'

'I'm sorry, I don't understand.'

'He telephones, but doesn't say anything. Sometimes in the middle of the night. There's just this threatening silence. Then he puts the thing down on you.'

Daph said, 'Are you sure it's him? It could be a fault in the system.'

'In his system.' Romy's voice was hard.

'Have you told the police?'

'Daddy had a word with PC Eliot. All he said was take no notice and sooner or later it would stop.'

'What are you two whispering about?' Pen had come creeping up behind them.

'Mind your own business.' Romy said, 'Shouldn't you be at school?'

'Can't get there.'

'You'll be absolutely ignorant.'

'I don't mind.'

'No, I don't suppose you do.'

'Want a game of Ping-Pong?' Pen asked.

'No, we don't. We're far too busy.'

'You don't look busy.' Pen wore a thick red jersey, a tweed kilt and two pairs of knee-length socks over patterned lisle stockings. 'Charlie's looking for you. They're putting some of the furniture back. *He* puts a table or chair in place, then Mother decides she doesn't like it. He says it would eat up less time if he had an adjudicator. By the way, Mrs Boswell's got orange paint on her coat. Tilley's scrubbing at it with white spirit. And they're staying for lunch. I don't think Mummy's very pleased. She looked as if she'd like to spit on the carpet.'

'I think,' Daph said, 'you might have put that more politely.'

'Why?' Pen was walking in circles around them, stopping every now and again to study them with interest. 'I wish you would cheer up. You're growing frown lines. I expect it's what they call the ravages of time.'

Down in the hall, the gong sounded.

'You look a bit like Granny on a bad morning.'

'Oh, shove off!' Daph told her.

After lunch, Romy went off to adjudicate for Charlie, while Bos and Daph looked over the travel brochures he had picked up with their honeymoon in mind.

'We'll have two whole weeks. How does that sound?' His face beamed with good humour. 'We'll find a good hotel. Scotland, I thought. Or Wales. The cricket season will have started. And we might manage a game of tennis or two.'

'Sounds good,' Daph said.

'This hotel looks excellent. The Seabank. It's on The Mumbles. Two En Tout Cas tennis courts. Dinner dances every Saturday with resident band. Beautifully appointed bedrooms, all with hot and cold water, bedside lights and sprung interior beds throughout.'

'Bedside lights?' Daph's voice said.

'We might ask for breakfast in bed.' He put his arm around her and gave her a little shake. Then he removed it again.

'Imagine . . .' Daph smiled.

But that was when the panic started.

Next day, Charlie extricated himself from the snowball fight he had got into with young Penelope and went in to call the rectory. 'Any more phone calls?' he asked Romy.

'No.'

'Good. Do you want me to sort him out when I get back to town?'

'No. He'd murder you.'

'I did boxing at school.'

'That was years ago.'

'Not that many,' Charlie protested. 'So are you coming over? The tack room needs scrubbing out.'

'You really know how to give a girl a good time. Why the tack room?'

'Because it's going to turn into the tea room.' While she went on about a lump of snow dropping on her head when she had nipped out for a crafty smoke, he stood there imagining a sofa, the two of them on it and all sorts of things ensuing.

His shining blonde . . . Shapely legs in indigo flannel trousers. He liked arty girls. It was like when you walked into a house and they tried to tell you why you should fall for it, but they didn't actually need to. You knew already. He thought about trying to explain all this to her, but she would think him quite mad . . .

'You still there?' Romy demanded.

'Of course.'

'But drifting off?'

'No.'

'You know what surprises me?'

'What?'

'That you're so good at your job. Half the time, you don't know what day it is. But you get things done.'

'I hope so,' Charlie said. 'In five short months, by some miracle, we have to be up and running.'

Daph pushed open her bedroom window. The curtains quivered stiffly as they filled with freezing air. It was a starry night and the park was visible all the way down to the lodge. The cold lawns, the frosted yew hedge, the snow-mounded terrace . . .

So very beautiful, she thought.

Luminous.

Schubert lifted quietly into the ceiling. It was Saturday night. She wanted to be doing something, going somewhere, feeling something . . . not living life inside her head. It was only a mood and it would pass, but as a rush of air blew into her face, she took a deep breath and allowed herself to say out loud what she was thinking. *I feel awkward with Bos, whereas I didn't before. And it's getting worse. I can't marry him. But I can't tell him either.*

I can't deal a blow like that, she thought, to such a considerate man.

I may have done the wrong thing. I may have been hasty in agreeing to marry him. But dumping him at this stage is a hellish way to treat someone you've been fond of for the biggest part of your life. You have to get on with it, she told herself.

What if I can't? What if this feeling lingers that getting married should be like opening your presents on Christmas morning.

For heaven's sake, grow up! Marriage isn't like that. Look at Ma and Pa.

But it should be. The landscape lay bathed in silver. She remembered a wedding she had played for in the next village. The clear look of love in the eyes of the bride. And her very young husband. Not a fashionable wedding, but . . .

Radiant. It was the only word.

If it was Tom I was walking down the aisle with . . .

Oh, stop it!

Lil Trewarden's baby was born two weeks late, in a flurry of snow, on the last Saturday in January. A little girl, six pounds and four ounces. Trewarden didn't come in that day. At nine thirty the following morning, Daphne washed and dressed and pulled on a red jumper and corduroy trousers. Before leaving the room, she stopped and gazed at her reflection in the mirror for a couple of seconds. She slipped quietly down the back stairs, paused to listen at the bottom, then went to the telephone. She took a piece of paper out of her pocket with a number written on it. She dialled, then, touching the wood of the table, waited. When Tom's voice answered, she said, all on the jump, 'It's me.'

Twenty-Four

Tom Fermoy's sister, Fiona Shaw, was thirty and she had three noisy children who, periodically, drove her bonkers. So now and again, she left them in the capable hands of the nanny and came up to town to straighten her head out.

On this particular visit, she had had several interesting but mostly useless chats with her brother about the state of his love life. He was rather a good actor, and quite expert at good-humouredly staving off her questions, but she knew him well enough to sense that something was going on. She could hear all the things he wasn't saying. Also, he had been trying to get her out of the house at least two hours before they needed to head for the station.

But the telephone call, straight after breakfast, had let the cat out of the bag. It turned out that he was expecting some girl called Daphne Jago. He'd promised to be in when she arrived and now he couldn't because there was some sort of emergency at the office.

'Could you hold the fort for an hour?' he asked.

Fi didn't say so, but she couldn't have been more delighted. And so on a bitter morning with a wind that made your eyes sting out in the slushy, shabby streets, she opened the door to a girl with a mass of glorious auburn hair and a cinnamon-coloured coat that matched her freckles. A girl of a different sort, Fi decided. Quirky.

'You must be Daphne,' she said. 'I'm Tommy's sister. Fi Shaw.'

'Um. Hello.' The girl looked flustered.

'I'm afraid he had to dash off. Some flap at the office . . . but he'll be back by eleven.'

'I'll come back.'

'Nonsense! He said he'd kill me if I didn't hang on to you.'

Daphne said, looking panicky and trying to back off, 'I don't want to inconvenience you.'

'You won't. Honestly.' Fi pulled her in and shut the door. 'You look frozen. Tea? Coffee?'

'Um. If it's no trouble.'

'It's no trouble.' Fi, who was enjoying herself, eyed her visitor. 'Have you known Tommy long?'

'Just a few months.' The girl unbuttoned her coat, then buttoned it up again. 'Since June.'

Interesting. In the pause that followed, Fi remembered what Tommy had said: Don't ask too many questions, don't frighten her off and don't, under any circumstances, ask about her ring.

Ah, yes. The flawless, simply enormous diamond solitaire on the girl's wedding finger. 'I'll put the kettle on,' she said, transferring her gaze to the plum-coloured scarf wrapped round the girl's neck.

In the kitchen, she put on the kettle and set out two cups. 'China or Indian?' she called through the door.

'Indian. Please.'

'Damn. He's eaten all the biscuits. And I was going to pinch some for the train.'

'Train?'

'For Oxford,' Fi called out. 'I'm catching the twelve-thirty.'

'You're the sister who's a doctor,' Daphne said.

'He told you?'

'Just in passing.'

Fi warmed the pot, made the tea and carried it in on the tray. 'I worked at the local hospital all through the war. Now I help out at my husband's practice.' Then, ignoring her brother's instructions, she said, 'So . . . do you live in town? Were you here during the Blitz? Or did they post you somewhere?'

'I live in Cornwall, but during the war I was a children's officer in Whitechapel.'

'Really?'

What she ought to have said next was something bland and innocuous like, 'Isn't this weather foul? Isn't life strange without bombs coming down? Isn't it dreadful about the floods?' But what she said was, 'Tommy was very cagey about you. And he spent almost an hour this morning trying on shirts and rejecting them.'

'Really?' Daphne said. She had turned bright red.

'He's normally a complete scruff.'

'I quite like scruffs.'

'Me too.' Fi put down her cup. 'One thing I *did* get out of him was that you're musical.'

'I . . . play the organ in church.'

A *churchy* girl wearing another man's ring! It got more intriguing by the minute. The sky outside – lemon yellow – suddenly transformed the blue-green half light in the park.

'Would it be ill-mannered,' Fi said, 'to ask what the situation is between you and Tommy?'

'I . . . We're just friends. Good friends.'

And I'm a Dutch uncle, Fi thought.

A draught rushed in as the door opened. 'I'm back,' Tom said. He stood looking at them for a moment. 'Everything all right?' he asked.

Half an hour later, they were on their way to Paddington. Fi's carpetbag sat on the back seat of the car next to Daph. From the front, there came a trickle of chat and laughter. They're awfully fond of each other, Daph thought. She didn't contribute much to the conversation. She was doing her best to fight off a suffocating panic.

All at once, she saw that she should never have come. It didn't feel right. It was too uncomfortable. Well, when they got to the station, she would make some excuse and do a bunk. Back to safety. I don't know him at all. *Tommy.* I don't know myself either. The face she had just caught a glimpse of in the driving mirror (blank, expressionless, all made-up) was one she scarcely recognized.

Tom said, 'We're almost there.'

Almost where? She couldn't bear to look at the back of his head. I'll break it off with both of them, she thought. I'll turn into a spinster aunt and knit socks for the rest of my life.

Like Mabel.

'You're very quiet,' he said.

'I'm fine.' She couldn't get beyond the repetition of those two words.

Yes, I'll make a dash for it. Thank God she hadn't chosen to stay with Marina. Duke's Hotel (crummy, mediocre, but anonymous) had been one of her better ideas.

A jeep cut across them and disappeared down a side street. Fi said she would never drive in London. Daph said, 'You get used to it,' and wondered where she could grab a cab.

Tom parked the car by a bombed-out church. He glanced at his watch. 'We've left it a bit late.'

'I'll get my skates on.' Fi reached back and grabbed her bag. 'Bye, darling. See you at Easter.' To Daph, she said, 'I hope we meet again sometime.'

There were some children playing tag in the road. Fi legged it straight through them. The rear door was still open. Daph eased her way towards it. 'Don't you dare,' said Tom. That was at twenty-eight minutes past twelve. By one fifteen, they were being shown into a very classy café called The Buttery.

'I'd like a table for two,' Tom told the waiter. 'And two gin and limes.
Right away, if you could.'

Everything in the café seemed extraordinarily vivid. The lobster-coloured
lampshades, the blue menus, the daffodils blazing in the cut-glass vase in
the window. It felt like a stage set to act out some odd kind of scene that
Daph didn't have a script for.

'I'm glad you telephoned,' Tom said. 'I was on the point of coming
down.'

He wore a rough linen shirt and, over it, his jacket was bluish grey.
In his top pocket were stuck three pencils and a rolled-up piece of
tracing paper. He took his gin from the waiter and sat with it in his
hand, looking at her for so long that she began to wonder if she had a
smut on her face.

She said, 'It's like a lunatic asylum. Lizzah. I had to get away.' She felt
suddenly manic, as if caught in a sugar rush. 'I like your sister. I should
have asked how her husband is. You told me he was invalided out. But it
threw me, I suppose, to find her there instead of you.'

'John's quite well now.'

'Is he? Good.'

'They're blissfully happy. *I'd* like a marriage as happy as theirs.'

She took a swig of gin and felt it burning down inside her. 'This is a
nice place. Have you been here before? It's very warm. Most places these
days are absolutely freezing.'

He didn't say anything and she thought she was safe. Then, 'Will *you*
be happy, when *you're* married?' he asked.

One, two, three seconds passed. Daph swallowed hard and said, 'I . . .
hope so.'

'Shouldn't you know so?'

She said, 'I don't see how you can be absolutely sure.'

She sat hanging on to her glass like grim death. His gaze was very
direct and very strong. It was fearfully hard to look away. He said, 'I'd be
sure. If I was walking down the aisle with you, I wouldn't have a doubt
in the world.' His hand came out to touch her face. She thought her bones
would melt.

'You must know by now. I seem to have a thing about you. Will you
forgive me for that?'

She went on twisting the ring on her finger.

'I came alive the day I met you.'

'You were alive before,' she said.

'Not like this.'

'We scarcely know each other.'

'I know you inside out,' he said.

'Yes,' she said, 'I'm afraid you do,' and a rush of happiness poured through her. She felt clear and free and sharply defined. If I'm still groping around not knowing where I'm heading, she thought, at least he has made me aware of who I am. If Tom thinks well of me, loves me even, perhaps I'll do. 'Look,' she said. 'I'll admit to being in a blue funk about the wedding. That's because Bos . . . well, he doesn't expect thrills. At least, I don't think he does. But he's a dear,' Daph persisted, seeing Tom's eyebrow lift. 'He really cares about me. And I sort of love him. That's why it would be very hard to hurt him.'

'Better to hurt him now than for the rest of his life.' Tom lifted her fingers to his lips and kissed them.

She let out a shaky breath. 'What I mean is, you know and I know that I shouldn't be here.'

'I'm glad you are. Say you love me.'

The waiter, out there in that other world, gave a little cough. He proceeded to open menus and explain about *carrots a l'anglaise*. He then put pencil to paper, brought wine, and unrolled napkins with a cherishing if knowing smile on his face. At last, he sprinted off to the kitchen so that romance could flow again.

'Say you love me.'

Daph said, 'You know I do.' Then, 'What in the world are we going to do?'

'Run off to Paris?'

'Be sensible.'

'I mean it. We could catch the boat train. I know a perfect little hotel.'

If only, Daph thought, if only.

At teatime, they went to see an improbable film about white slave traders who injected the heroine with needles and carted her off to South America. 'How about Rio de Janeiro?' Tom said in her ear.

'Too far. Too hot.'

'All right. Brighton.'

'Too cold.'

'Cheaper, though.'

'I didn't know you were a cheapskate.'

'Most architects don't have a bean. Didn't you know that?'

'Don't Charlie's lot pay you?' she whispered.

'Very small cheques a month or two after they're due.' His arm dropped around Daph's shoulder.

The heroine was dying to a crescendo of violins. 'About time,' he said. Daph let out a giggle and in the middle of it, he kissed her.

They ate doughnuts and strawberry tarts in the Lyons Corner House. He bought her a bunch of violets that smelled like wet hedgerows. They drove back to Camden Town and parked the car in the street outside his house. By this time, the skies had cleared; stars were scattered in tiny bursts above the trees. The evening was slipping by more quickly than she wanted it to.

While Tom made coffee, Daph dropped into one of the cream-coloured armchairs by the fireplace. She felt comfortable and dreamy. The room was filled with a hotchpotch of nice old things. There was a tea table, a wonky bookcase, a Bechstein piano, framed watercolours of Florence and Siena, and the gramophone, of course, with a library of records. He had put on a Harry James.

Tom came back in with a laden tray. He found her reading the invitation cards on the chimney piece.

'You're very popular,' she said. 'Who's Lady Julia O'Donnell?'

'Just a girl I know.'

'Pretty?'

'Chic. And a little bit saucy. Why?'

'Just wondering.'

'I thought about having a fling with her, but I couldn't be bothered.' Is this a fling? Daph wondered. Even if it is, I don't think I care.

'Have you had many? Flings, I mean?'

'One or two, when I was on leave. Three night stands and, "I'll love you forever, darling," but you knew they wouldn't.'

A pause. Daph's fingers fiddled with her pearls, a lock of hair, her skirt seam.

'There was a girl I thought I was keen on in France, but she was half Jewish and got hauled off one night, so I never got the chance to find out if I was really in love with her.'

'I'm sorry.'

'Feel sorry for her, not me.'

'I am. I do.'

'I know.' He said, 'And you?'

'Flings? Just one. He was married, but didn't think to tell me,' Daph said, wondering if cheating on one's fiancé was worse than sleeping with another woman's husband. She said, 'I'll pour the coffee.'

'I don't really want it,' he said. 'All I want is you.' He cupped her face in his hands and kissed her mouth so lightly that it made her knees wobble.

'You've got me in such a state,' she said. 'I can't think straight.'

'Me neither.' He kissed her again. Then he took her hand and led her out into the hall. Daph felt like a sleepwalker. They climbed the uncarpeted staircase – wine-dark walls, lined with sketches and theatre programmes and brass rubbings and dimly framed photographs – to the first floor landing where a couple of cabin trunks stood piled with books and a rolled-up rug. Tom led her past these to his bedroom, which, over a couple of years, had metamorphosed into a studio-cum-den. He opened the door. Daph was forced to smile.

'What's so funny?'

'This room. It's so like you.'

'Messy?'

'Messy and arty, yet utterly traditional.' She felt her spirits lift. There was this sense of feeling entirely at home. 'What an enormous bed!' *Oh, God, I shouldn't have said that.*

'I inherited it.'

'Really?'

'Really.' It was his turn to smile. 'You've gone pink.'

What an idiot! You always end up putting your big, fat foot in it.

He didn't touch her. He just said, 'It's very comfortable. Want to try it?'

There was a hammering in her veins. 'I didn't mean—'

'I know you didn't. Darling Daph . . .' He was no longer laughing. 'I want you, I want you, I want you.'

Towards dawn, just before they slept, Tom said, 'I could drink that coffee now.'

'It'll be stone cold.' They lay in the huge oak bed. The house stood quiet around them. Daph's lips had a tingling aftertaste, like strong fizz. The rest of her was melting into space. 'I'll make some more,' she said.

'No, don't.' His arm came out to stop her.

'Sure?'

'Quite sure. You might try to run off again.'

'Not until Friday.'

'That's only three days. You can't go back to Cornwall.'

'I have to. Pa needs me.'

'I need you,' he said, kissing her and sliding his hand down to the little hollow at the base of her spine.

Can I knock this bit of my heart out? Tom asked himself, *if she goes ahead
and marries him?* He had always been the hopeful type, looking for the
next good thing to come round the corner, but it suddenly struck him
that happy endings were only for children.

Halfway through the morning, Daph telephoned Bos to tell him her shopping wasn't going so well and she needed to stay on for a day or two.
('Well, wrap up warm,' he said. 'Mother says there's influenza in town.')
She fetched her things from the hotel, hung them in Tom's wardrobe and
was startled to find how normal this felt. The trouble with happiness, she
thought, is that it makes you selfish, indifferent.

She took her ring off and hid it away in the locked compartment in
the side of her hold-all. She was not at all proud of this, in fact, she was
sorely aware that her principles were slipping. I'll do penance, she thought,
like the Catholics. I'll wear sackcloth and ashes. Whatever it takes. But I
won't . . . can't . . . spoil these few precious days by feeling guilty when
I don't seem to have the strength left to stop myself.

Tom telephoned his office to say, hamming up a wheezy cough, that
he had gone down with influenza. Then they did everything they could
possibly cram into the next three days. They went to concerts and galleries
and book shops. They went dancing, they sat in parks and threw crumbs
at the sparrows. Tom bought her a Japanese kimono and she sat around
in it in the evenings while they explored his record collection. The nights
were something else; they travelled not to Paris or to Rio de Janeiro, but
to a whole new continent.

If there's a spark, as Tom said, light the fire.

And then it was Friday and he was taking her to the station. The wind
(a raw north-easterly) carried tension with it. Daph sat on the tube
watching faces and wondering where they were all going and who they
were going to meet. When the carriage emptied, Tom kissed her. 'I'll miss
you,' he said abruptly. 'Can't you stay?'

'I can't. Kit's window's being dedicated on Sunday.' There was this
feeling of dislocation, of no longer being in control. At Marylebone, she
started rabbiting on about getting stuck there once, in a wartime blackout.
'They couldn't . . . or wouldn't . . . open the doors. You couldn't see a
hand in front of your face. It got hotter and hotter—'

'Daffy, shut up for a minute.' A woman got in. Blue coat and hat that
almost matched. Tom said, 'Are you going to give him back his ring?'

'Let's not talk about it,' she said. 'Not here.'

'We have to talk about it. You have to tell him. We'll go together. Face up to it.' He was very pale, but he meant it.

'No. I'll tell him.'

'Cross your heart?'

'Cross my heart.'

Paddington, in the early morning, seemed startlingly real. The trains whistling and shrieking and shunting, the dark smoke puffs, the wheezing steam. They sat in the buffet drinking coffee out of thick, chipped cups. Outside, a man who had lost his luggage ticket was having an argument with the porter.

Whatever's going to happen will happen, Daph told herself. But it didn't help.

'I'll come down,' Tom said desperately. 'I'll tell Charlie the south front wants checking.'

The train came all too soon. On the station platform, he held her. 'Take care of yourself,' he said. She watched him walking away in that loose way of his.

She found a seat, the city fell away. People got on and off, the voices changed. By the time they got to Exeter, London was not just a couple of hundred miles away, but a world apart.

They crossed the Tamar. At Shebbear, she put the ring back on her finger.

Twenty-Five

Hesther Baring was disconcerted, even a little shocked by Kit's window. The jumbled up yellow segments, according to Virginia, were meant to be a kite. The flash of green was a tent. Unless I'm missing something, Hesther thought, modern art, well it doesn't make much sense. And then there was Virginia's choice of music. Who in their right mind, Hesther wondered, as she sat in the family pew next to Evalina and surreptitiously fished in her bag for a peppermint (which turned out to be slightly fluffy), would choose 'When I Was Young and Twenty' and 'Over the Rainbow' for a dedication service? The rector's wife – fidgeting, tut-tutting – had definitely taken umbrage.

But young Mr Garland, sitting in a side pew, had tapped an appreciative foot. That was because Daphne had the most wonderful voice; expressive but unshowy, a rich mezzo soprano. Hesther thought, I enjoyed it too. Should one say that on such a sad occasion?

Outside, February slipped into March. Sun gleamed on dry hedges. The church seemed to shake in the wind.

She remembered how one of the guests at Myles's wedding had lost her hat in a sharp gust. She had had to run after it. They all wore cloches in those days. Hers had been powder blue and she had looked hideous in it. Virginia had looked wonderful in a plain veil with a circlet. A flapper, Eva had said when Myles brought her home. She won't last the course. But she had.

Well, so far, Hesther told herself. But really one might wish her to be a kinder soul. She fastened her gaze on the strange bits of coloured glass and thought, I hope Myles is going to be all right. She was fond of her nephew. He had been such a very determined little boy; solemn as a judge, sensible but never boring.

Mabel Petherick, taking Daphne's place on the organ for once, struck up the last hymn. Evalina, leaning over to stare at Hesther's hands, said in a stage whisper, 'What kind of gloves are those?'

'Driving gloves,' Hesther said through the first bars of 'Morning Has Broken'.

'Well, really, Hesther! You might have worn something more fitting!'

* * *

Soon they were spilling out into the church porch. Gin, wearing a grey lace coat and her keep-your-distance manner, stood talking to Bishop Paul.

'Unusual window,' he said. 'Most . . . imaginative.'

'Kit would have liked it,' she said. And the cheerful music, she thought. And that psalm he always liked. The one about trampling on the young lion and the dragon.

I wouldn't trample a dragon, Mummy, would you?

Behind her, Myles was talking to Boscawen Senior, who was stout and pompous. A browbeater, if only you let him. There was a mound of snow still up on the top field and stunted trees, blown sideways by the westerly wind.

'I was glad to see the brass had been cleaned,' Evalina was telling the rector. Aunt Hesther was attempting to move her on.

The new heir, told Hugh Matheson the service had been top-hole. Evalina said it would have been better with decent hymns.

The rest of the congregation began spilling out. A blast of cold air flattened the long grass around the headstones. *I'm glad there's a wind,* Gin told Kit. *Perfect kite weather.* She had been talking to him in her head all morning.

Charlie Garland advanced towards her. He said, '*I'd* like to be remembered with a window like that.'

She could think of no answer that wouldn't put a lump in her throat, so she asked if he was comfortable staying at The Acland.

'Very comfortable.' He said he was looking forward to Pru Hockin's pork chops with her special pork and apple stuffing. 'Better than the Great Western three and sixpenny lunch.'

How nice he was, trying, with his light touch, to lift her morning out of the dumps.

'I've got Biddy with me,' he said. 'You remember Biddy? The van will be here good and early in the morning with the extra bits from the museums and elsewhere.'

'We're running short of soap,' she told him. 'For the cleaning. Can't get it for love nor money.'

'Don't worry. We'll beg, borrow or steal some. I'll see you tomorrow.'

Myles joined her. 'Think I might walk back,' he said. 'Across the fields.'

'Are you up to it? You look tired.'

And older, she told Kit. *His eyes look . . . cheerless.*

There were voices all around her in the crowd. Mabel Petherick saying, 'Daniel's not here. He never misses.' Evalina putting her oar in with,

'My father-in-law let parishioners know of his displeasure if they were irregular with their attendance.' Hesther shushing her up. 'What we need is lunch. Come along, Eva.'

But the one voice she couldn't hear – for the first time in almost two years – was Kit's.

Myles said, 'I'd like to walk.'

'Well, if that's what you want.'

'It is . . .' He was silent for a moment, then he added, 'Things like this somehow make it worse. I almost wish you hadn't done it.'

He didn't even stop to speak, thought Mabel. He always speaks after church. She plodded on up the lane to The Barton. And he didn't kneel to join in the responses. Something's wrong. I'd ask Virginia, but she won't even have noticed. All those flowers she bought and arranged must have cost a fortune. Where do you get lilies, dozens of them, for heaven's sake, in March? And we don't usually have incense except at Christmas.

Mabel didn't much care for smells and bells.

Up by Ham Wood, the trees were about to burst into bud. It was the moment before spring. A painful time, Mabel thought, if you've lost anybody. She forced herself on – hearing her stomach rumble – over the brow of the hill and suddenly the Barton fields were spread in front of her. If you stopped to listen, you heard nothing but the wind whistling. Then a curlew.

She glanced at her watch. Twelve thirty. Not a decent calling time, but for once it wouldn't have to matter. She eased up as she approached the farmhouse. She was in a sweat. Not half as spry as you used to be, she told herself. The place seemed deserted, but then she saw Daniel hoeing the border by the dovecot.

'Gardening on a Sunday, Daniel? Your mother would turn in her grave.'

Nothing was done at Apple Tree on the Sabbath. Mabel and Edie went to church, then sat in the parlour or went for a walk. Mabel had consented at the beginning of the war that it was permissible to listen to the radio. Or read. But no newspapers, no knitting and no sewing. It was a day away from the world and its sins.

'The weeds don't know the days of the week,' said Dan without his usual smile.

'I can't stay. Edie's got the roast on. You look as if you could do with a sit-down. I wondered if Daisy could do something with my old suit,' she said, pulling a brown paper parcel out of her bag. 'I'm fond of it,' Mabel went on, lying for England, 'but I tore the hem a couple of years ago when I tripped over the bucket of sand on the landing. I thought Daisy might put it right. My word, there's a wind. We missed you this morning. Was it your sciatica? If so, you shouldn't be hoeing. I really am in a rush. Shall I go on in?'

She was careful to keep on walking with a sort of careless flurry, so that there would be no time for him to stop her.

In the farm kitchen, there was a rich smell of roasting meat, but no sign of Daisy. Mabel slipped through into the hall. She could hear movements upstairs, so she went on up.

Daisy was in the room over the porch that she had turned into her sewing room. Mabel was glad of that. There would be less chance of Daniel walking in on them. She walked quickly in and shut the door behind her.

'No, don't get up,' she said to the girl, who looked startled. 'If your father comes up, we're talking about my oatmeal suit.'

Mabel sat down on the chair by the window. Her face softened when she saw how pale and almost plain Daisy looked. 'Now I know you're worried about what people will say. And I can't approve of what's been going on, but I blame Jack rather than you—'

'Don't. Don't blame Jack.'

'He's old enough to know better, my dear.'

'It wasn't his fault. I . . . I could have stopped, but I didn't want to.'

Daisy's face was so frighteningly eager that Mabel sat shaking her head. 'You're so young, child. This will fade.'

'But I don't want it to.'

'And where in the world do you think it will end? He's married, Daisy.'

'To someone who doesn't deserve him.' Daisy's cheeks were stained with pink.

'Granted. And in an ideal world, Lil Trewarden would vanish in a puff of green smoke when true love came tootling along. But we have to live with the realities. They are married, for better or for worse, and there are two young children to consider.'

'Yes, but one of them might not be his.'

Mabel smoothed the hem of her tweed skirt. She could see the dovecot and farm buildings through the side window. 'Look,' she said, 'it is quite possible that the second child isn't his. Lil . . . well, between you and me and the gatepost, she's a contriving little slut. And Jack's a favourite of mine and I'm very fond of him. But men will sometimes make up little fictions when they . . . When—' Mabel stopped, unable to find the right words. Why, oh, why, she thought, isn't your mother alive to deal with this? I'm too big and too clumsy and too old for this kind of caper.

'He doesn't tell lies,' said Daisy, with that guileless look of hers.

'He might not *think* the child is his, but he can't be sure.'

'He can. He is.' Excuse me,' Daisy said, her face suddenly changing. 'I . . . don't feel well.'

She rushed from the room. When she came back, minutes later, she was as white as a sheet. Mabel looked sharply at the girl. A thought had just occurred to her. A terrible suspicion.

'My dear girl,' she said, without beating around the bush. 'You're not . . . pregnant?'

Daisy sat down hard on the little sofa. She looked terrified. She looked as if all the stuffing had gone out of her legs.

'My dear soul!' she said. 'You are.'

Daisy burst into tears. 'Don't tell Father. Please.'

'He'll have to know.'

'But not yet, Miss Petherick. Please. It'll kill him.'

There had never been a problem about spreading hot news around the parish. Idle curiosity would send the latest scraps of gossip from Agnes Bolitho's tea ceremonies spinning around the village from post office to bakery to the grocery-store-cum-apothecary's-corner at the bottom of Forge Lane. Charlie wished he could employ a system one tenth as efficient to broadcast the date and time of the Lizzah Grand Opening (June first. Eleven a.m.) to the wider world, but instead, all he could do was place the usual advertisements in all the usual periodicals and call the press in.

News conferences, he thought, as the hacks began to roll up on Tuesday afternoon, were like slippery pigs that sometimes managed to get away from you at the point when you thought you had them cornered. This one was turning out to be no exception. He had arranged an introductory talk followed by questions and tea in the stag room followed by a tour and a brief photo call with the major and his family. But half the reporters had turned up late because of the still-iced-up roads and the floods upcountry, the major was nowhere to be seen, and Daphne had seemingly taken offence and walked out when he mentioned the wedding that was to take place two weeks after the opening.

Also the Dowager Duchess, whom he had hoped to keep well out of the way, was bending the ear of the *Country Life* correspondent, berating her about the state of newspapers in general and telling her in ringing tones, 'Did you know that we are to have someone else's furniture? I said to Mr Garland, we may have been nationalized, but we are not a charity! My doctor tells me my blood pressure is rising. Is it any wonder, one might ask?'

Finding one of Mrs Trewarden's little cinnamon cakes and taking a comforting bite, Charlie was accosted by Penelope.

'Your friend says you used to take her to the pictures.'

'My friend?'

'Biddy. The one in the orange cardy. Are you keen on her?'

Charlie stood imagining a solitary room, a sofa, a malt whisky and total silence. He said, 'I quite liked her for a while.'

'But now she gets on your nerves?'

'I didn't say that.'

'Daph gets on my nerves,' Penelope said. 'She's unbelievably bad-tempered at the moment. Bos won't half have a shock when he finds out her true nature.'

In the dining room, Mabel Petherick stopped to say, 'Those chairs look good.'

'Genoa velvet,' Charlie said. 'Cost over three hundred pounds to re-cover, but it was worth every penny.'

'Remind me never to sit on them,' Mabel said. She went off to find Peg Trewarden.

Later, in the drawing room, escaping from the *Western Morning News* man, who was attempting to chat her up, Romy said, 'It seems to be going well.'

'You think so?' Charlie asked.

'Well, not bad. How was Pru's pork?'

'Delicious. How was lunch with Bishop Paul?'

'Endless. I had to keep nipping out for a cigarette.' She was looking elegantly grown-up for once. He liked her pale green suit and high-heeled shoes. 'Will you tell me if you see Daph? I'm worried about her.'

'She's probably with the prospective bridegroom.'

'No. He's talking to the photographer. What I want to know is, what's going on between Daph and Tom? Are they having an affair?'

Charlie stood there looking amazed at the idea, which he was.

'She didn't stay with Marina. In London.'

'No?'

'No. I tried to ring her there. You're not going to tell me, are you? You men stick together like glue.'

'Look – how would I know? I haven't seen Tom for weeks.'

'But you'd be on his side if he'd seduced Daph. Of course you would.'
'Seduced?'

'Well, Daph wouldn't have the faintest idea how to start anything.' She was glaring at him.

Charlie kept quiet, feeling that whatever he attempted to say would be held against him. What have I done? he asked himself. Why is she being so hopelessly irrational? Why, for that matter, did you feel that, with Romy, it was always one step forwards and two back?

She let out a long sigh. 'You're being so patient and I'm being a complete bitch. There's a reason for that. He's plaguing me again. Jan. He sent Mother a photograph of us necking at a party. She opened it at the breakfast table. One minute, she was sitting there straightening a fork and the next she was having a fit of the vapours. It was pretty explicit, you see. He sent me a note in the same post. *'Don't think I won't get you.'* She said, 'Oh, Charlie – I'm so scared.'

Peg said, 'Does Dan know?'

'Not yet.' Mabel saw Myles walk past the kitchen window. She thought, babies popping up all over the place. It wasn't like this in my day. Well, it was, but you hushed it up more. She helped herself to a split from the plate on the table.

'He'll have to.'

'Of course he will.'

Bess came rushing in with a tottering pile of cups. 'I've had enough of they newspaper chaps,' she said, breaking into the conversation. 'They use dictionary words you can't understand.'

She riddled the range furiously, then tore off out again. Peg said, 'I thought when the boys came home, we'd have some peace and quiet. That's a laugh.'

Mabel said that peace was always a temporary affair. Then she brushed the crumbs from her beige dress and stockings and went to look for Myles.

Myles had had a wretched afternoon. Making a dash for the woods, he had bumped into a photographer – a real upstart, cocky as a robin – who had had the cheek to ask if Myles was the gamekeeper and if so, could he snap him with the dog and the gun? All his life, Lizzah – the house, the gardens, the park – had been the one place the world didn't intrude on. Now that he had lost the sense of comfort it had always given him, Myles felt a paralysis of loss, a heaviness that would not lift.

He had sent the chap off with a flea in his ear, but his mind was now obsessed with the future and its miseries.

Back in his den, he couldn't even read a book. No one, he thought, should have strangers tramping over his home. It's an impertinence, an intrusion on one's very soul. The copper beech outside the window seemed ominously dark. He knocked out his pipe, filled it and lit it, then knocked it out again. 'Not worth carrying on,' he said, 'if this is what it's come to.'

'Talking to yourself?' Mabel's voice said. 'That won't help.'

Myles turned to find her standing in the doorway.

'You ran away,' she said. 'That's not like you.'

'Felt blank. Took a constitutional.'

'You went off in a grump,' Mabel said with some severity.

'Got the blue glooms.' His expressive, slightly intimidating eyebrows frowned at her.

'The window service upset you. I can understand that. And today was never going to be easy. But you know and I know that running away is not an option.'

Does she think I'm one of her pupils? Myles wondered, feeling the sharpness in her gaze. Her beige straw hat was stuck with a fearsome silver pin. 'As a matter of fact,' he said, 'I thought about shooting myself.'

Mabel was so outraged by this that she almost laughed. 'Oh, tosh!' she said. 'I've no patience with melodrama.'

Myles threw a longing glance at the grog tray. 'I miss the boy,' he said suddenly, without meaning to.

'Of course you do,' Mabel said gruffly. 'And I feel for you.'

'And I can't bear the idea of strangers intruding into my private space.'

Mabel said, 'Neither would I, I suppose, if truth were told. But there comes a time when you have to grit your teeth and get on with it. People do, you know.'

Punch was nosing for nothing in the crocuses out on the terrace. 'Dash it, Mabs – how can I, when nothing will ever be the same again?'

'Things have changed,' Mabel said, 'for a lot of people in this village. Men have died, families are struggling. Good God, the whole country is fumbling its way through a crisis.'

He said nothing. Try to sound kinder, she told herself, sweeten the pill, but somehow the rest came out with the same no-nonsense fierceness. 'I don't like saying this, but it's time somebody did. There have been gassings and concentration camps. Bombings and burnings. Half the world's

population is hungry and the other half displaced. Now, no one is asking
you to house them here, in your very pleasant mansion with its six
thousand acres, but it's a rum thing if you can't throw open your doors
occasionally to let a few of them – a very few – take a peep at your
drawing room.'

Had she gone too far? Yes, she had. His back had stiffened. There was
something stubborn and unchanging about his expression. Mabel didn't
know what to do next, so she gave his arm a quick pat. He stood wood-
enly, not responding. 'Virginia was looking for you,' she said.

'Right.'

Chill blue shadows filtered into the mauve beech leaves. A car
scrunched on the gravel outside and at the other end of the house, a
telephone bell rang.

Mabel had a terrible feeling she had just ended a precious friendship.

When Peg told him, Jack looked absolutely wretched. She wanted to hold
him and hit him at the same time. 'You silly young fool,' she said. 'I
thought you had more sense.'

Jack said, 'I'll pay for her to go away and have it.'

'And what's she going to do with the child when she comes back?
Hide it in a suitcase? Can you imagine what the village is going to say
when it gets out? Which it will, before long.'

Jack said, 'Oh, God, Mother, don't make me feel any more guilty.'

'I'm not concerned about your feelings. You're a grown man. But that
little girl – you've ruined her life.'

'I know.' He was almost in tears. 'What do you want me to do?'

Peg hadn't the faintest idea. There was a silence and then she went
on, 'Oh, well, I suppose there'll be a few more pupils for Mabel's
school. All Trewardens. They'll want a new classroom at this rate.' She
thought of something else. 'I wouldn't want to be in your shoes when
Lil finds out.'

'Damn Lil,' he said. 'She's the cause of it all.'

He had a point, but that didn't mean she was letting him off the hook.
'You didn't have anything to do with it, then? Immaculate conception,
was it? You're married, Jack. And Daisy's a sweet child who deserves
better.'

'For God's sake,' he said, 'stop rubbing it in.'

'I'm sorry, son.' And she was, but regret solved few problems. She
reached into her pocket for her cigarettes. All through the war, there had
been this daily thread of anxiety. Would her boys come back in one piece?

Would they come back at all? What she hadn't anticipated was that the worry would go on and on.

That evening, Gin and Myles had supper on their own. Daph, looking, for some reason, grimly determined, had gone up to Trebartha. Penelope, thankfully, was back at school. Myles did not say much. There was a slight vagueness about him. If only, Gin thought, there was a window in his head, through which I might glimpse his thoughts and feelings.

She had said her piece about his disappearing act that afternoon, but there had been no reaction. It was as if there was a glass bell, shutting him off from her. She lined up the handle of her coffee cup with the gilded flower on the saucer. 'Charlie thought we might put the Georgian outfits on display,' she said. 'What do you think?'

'As you wish.'

'The house is really beginning to look very nice.'

He answered with a kind of grunt.

Gin reached for the coffee pot, fighting off a sense of unease. 'I opened the last of the trunks from the attic,' she continued, 'And guess what I found? My diamond clip.'

He didn't know what she was talking about.

'You bought it for me. On honeymoon.'

She sat there, remembering the utter romance of it. A winter tour in the Med with the Ellerman Line. Five whole weeks . . . Gibraltar, Genoa, Leghorn, Naples . . . On the steamship, he had secured a deck cabin with three berths and she had packed three trunks with her hundred guinea trousseau. For those few magical weeks, he had almost worn his heart upon his sleeve. That was before it all started to go wrong.

There was a silence. Then Myles said, 'In Ancona. The night it rained.'

She took the clip from her lapel and sat gazing at it. Her emotions seemed to be balanced rather unsafely between now and then. She said, 'It must have been put away with the jacket. Listen, I've changed my mind. We should get away. It's better than sitting here going quietly potty. We should go now. Before the deluge. But not London. How about Bath? That rather good hotel in The Crescent . . . if it's still there?'

He'll refuse, she thought. He looks absolutely dreadful. Black under the eyes. Not a glimmer of his usual awkward courtesy.

What he said was, 'For how long?'

'I don't know. Three . . . four days?'

'Better book it, then,' he said.

She did, the very next morning, before he could change his mind.

Dan Jewell, burly but no longer jolly, refused to look Peg in the eye. He said stiffly that he wasn't a pauper and wouldn't take a penny from her blasted son. Mabel told him that Jack was a good boy at heart. He was dependable, desperate to support both Daisy and the child. Daisy, her hair falling around her frightened face, said it was all her fault and she wished they would stop quarrelling. Mabel wanted to hug her, but that would never do when she had this reputation for wearing barbed wire next to her skin. So she told Dan they would all look after Daisy, for Dora's sake.

The sun shone brilliantly on Dan's hunting prints, the cushions in the window seat, the white blinds with a deep crocheted edge. Lambs gambolled in the field outside. 'I'm just thankful my Dora's not here,' he said, 'to feel the shame.'

Peg picked up her bag and walked out. At home, she ripped around the whole cottage, giving the place a good cleaning.

Charlie drove Biddy back to London in the little car. Biddy slept most of the way, but when they reached the outskirts, she woke up and, giving her arms a long stretch, suddenly said, 'I just remembered – some chap with a foreign accent keeps calling the office. Polish, maybe? He wanted to know if you're in town or down at Lizzah.'

Twenty-Six

'Had you realized,' said Mrs Boswell in the sitting room at Trebartha, 'that you will have an odd number of bridesmaids? Will that be a problem, do you think?'

'No one will be looking at the bridesmaids,' Bos said with a fond smile in Daph's direction.

'When your Uncle Fern got married, the bridesmaids were dressed in his racing colours. Blue and white. Of course, that wouldn't always be feasible. Orange and black, for example, would be far from attractive.'

'Oh, I don't know. Romily might take to it.'

'I don't doubt it for one moment. She was late for church yesterday, did I tell you? She waltzed down the aisle in the middle of 'O Day of Rest and Gladness' wearing the most outlandish hat.'

'She made it from an old dressing-gown. She liked the colour,' Daph said. Why, oh why, she wondered, won't she leave us alone so that I can say my piece? Twice, during the last fortnight, she had attempted to break off her engagement, but on both occasions she had flunked it. Oh, she had rehearsed a hundred times what she was going to say to Bos. '*Look — I haven't been fair to you. I've been seeing someone else,*' or, '*I've come to realize that being fond of you isn't enough.*' But deciding on the most suitable sentiments was not the same thing as actually spitting them out.

'Well, I hope she won't look so outlandish as a bridesmaid,' Mrs Boswell said. 'And I hope you'll have a word with your father, Daphne, dear, about the pace of the bridal procession. He mustn't walk too fast. My own father led me up the aisle as if we were fox hunting. I got to the chancel all of a gasp with the bridesmaids panting behind me.'

Mrs Boswell took herself off to change for tea at last. Daph glanced nervously at Bos, whose solid figure was leaning against the mantelpiece.

'You look worried,' said Bos. 'Don't let Mother fuss you.'

Daph took a good, long breath. 'There's something we have to talk about.' Her heart was being rearranged with great jerky tugs. This is beastly, she thought. Absolutely beastly.

'If it's about the fol-de-rols,' he said, 'the bridesmaids and such—'

'It isn't. I don't care a toss about the bridesmaids.'

'I knew you wouldn't. Much too sensible.' He hesitated, looking slightly embarrassed. 'Look – I think I know what you're going to say. I told the major a while ago, it doesn't matter if he hasn't the wherewithal for a marriage settlement. He keeps apologizing, but there's honestly no need.'

'He gets het up,' Daph said.

'He'll be fine once things settle at Lizzah. How's your Mr Garland getting on?'

'He's in a state, too. The guide books have been delayed because of mistakes in the proofs. Also, we've got rats in the drawing-room. Charlie says they've been disturbed by the underpinning of the foundations.' She realized that they were straying from the subject. 'What I wanted to say is—' But just as she was cranking up, so to speak, for one more go, she was interrupted by Doris, the maid, who came in to mend the fire.

And then Mrs Boswell was back, telling Doris it was time the lamps were lit. Daph fled, not wishing to be invited to stay for tea. As she skimmed the dogcart around the grass-grown bends in the lanes, she cursed herself for not coming to the point with Bos at once. She wished she were more ruthless and didn't worry so much about people's reactions. And she would have liked to see or hear from Tom. He hadn't been in touch since putting her on the train three weeks ago. Was she worried? Yes, a little, because this kind of thing had happened to her before. You let a man . . . well . . . get somewhere with you and he didn't bother to come back. Surely Tom wasn't like that?

When she walked into the house, all hell was breaking loose. Doors were slamming, Trewarden was banging a broom around and Tilley was standing on a chair in the passage uttering dreadful shrieks.

'Rats?' she asked Charlie, who was standing by the window with an anguished look on his face and some shards of broken china in his hand.

'Two great monsters.'

Daph didn't hang around. She went to the back hall and telephoned Tom. The thing went on ringing for ages. Then, just as she had given up, a girl's voice said, 'Sloane three five four.'

'Um . . . I must have the wrong number.'

'Do you want to speak to Tom? He's not here, but I could take a message.'

She sounded beautiful. One of those sure, confident girls who never, ever, felt inadequate.

Daph hesitated. 'No . . . that's all right.'

'You could leave your name.'

'Daphne. Daphne Jago,' she said. She put the phone down and stood for a moment looking distraite and tense. It was good, she supposed, that someone had answered.

Absurd to worry that the someone had been female.

The telephone rang several times that evening. At first, she raced to answer it. But after two or three days, she stopped hoping it would be for her. Tom didn't ring back.

Pen wrote:

> Tilley insisted I should call on her mother to inspect the renovations to her cottage. She likes her bedroom the best because she no longer has to keep a bucket in there to catch drips when it rains. She used to fall over it. I resisted the temptation to make a joke about kicking the bucket. We are to have a wedding hop, but they can't agree on the date. Bos came over this afternoon to introduce his best man. He also brought chocolates. Chocolates! I took the lumpy one with the squiggle on the top. The best man sat in the basket chair that creaks every time you move. He is training to be a clergyman. The dressmaker has been here all morning, crawling round, pinning the hem of Daph's wedding dress. My bridesmaid's frock sticks out in all the wrong places. I said I wish Daisy could make it, her dresses always look elegant. Daph told me off later for being rude to the dressmaker. I said it was the pot calling the kettle, as she has been in a foul mood all week.
>
> I wonder how Daisy got pregnant? I did ask, but no one will tell me.
>
> I asked Mother if I could go to Bath with them. I wish I'd kept my mouth shut, because Granny went into this long story about arriving in Bath on a blacked-out train during the first war. When Romy came, I asked if *her* bridesmaid's dress stuck out. She said not to worry, she would fix it for me. I said the other bridesmaid (Bos's niece) is a little horror. Romy said she wouldn't fix her frock, we would let her look a fright.
>
> I heard Bos tell Daph they would make it comfy up at Trebartha and that it would be good to have her put her mark on it. I was behind the sofa reading a book. I didn't mean to eavesdrop, but if I had come out, I would have startled them. He then said he would like a child – children – to play bears with. Daph said that would be nice, but not just yet. I think he had his arm around her. Then he said, Why don't we take a run down the coast. Daph said Romy

and Pen can come too. I don't think it was quite what he intended.
We saw Trewarden's brother on the beach at Tregoze. He was pulling
his little dog on a trolley. Romy said he was collecting driftwood
to sell at extortionate prices. Bos said people these days make a
living as best they can, which I thought very kind of him.

Charlie says we can't put the stuffed birds back into the bathroom. The damp temperature will do for them and their eyes will
pop out. He has ordered posts and ropes to stop people touching
things. Daph looked at me and said guess who will be first to trip
over them. There was no need for that. Romy said she was ratty
because of wedding nerves. I think she is turning into a sour, bitter
woman. After tea, she sat playing the same tune on the piano over
and over again. 'That's nice,' Bos said. She stopped at once.

Daph rattled back the curtain rings and stood gazing out at the daffodils
that were flooding the park. When all that yellow made her eyes hurt,
she found a pen and paper and wrote list after list. Every time she stopped
because she had run out of steam, her hands fell into her lap. Words like
fool and *gullible* kept popping into her mind. 'Why did I believe a word
he said?' she asked. 'Did I really think he was in love with me?' In the
house around her, another scuttly day was beginning. She heard the
builders' lorry roar up the drive. 'Why didn't I stop and ask myself what
he was after? Because,' she said fiercely, 'just once in my life I wanted to
float in a rose-tinted dream.'

Well. She squared her shoulders and blinked hard. *Real life is a sensible
navy blue and the sooner you get used to the idea the better.*

The wonder is, she thought miserably, that he ever wanted to get me
into bed in the first place. Hockin's lorry forked left, braked and stopped
by the orangery. So . . . what was the procedure after a crash landing?
You extricated yourself from the wreckage, shook yourself down and
when you next took off, you made sure it was in a machine that was solid
and safe and reassuring.

Which meant Bos. Briefly, she closed her eyes. She would never be in
love with him, but she forced herself to sit there and tot up his good
qualities, like when you saved all the odd bits of string in wartime and
tied them together. He was considerate, he made sweet, appreciative
comments, he took an intelligent interest in what was going on at Lizzah
and he was never, ever, beastly about his tiresome mother, which made
him a saint at least. He was sometimes funny. He took her back to her
childhood where everything was safe. And the fact that he was devoted

to her was, it had to be admitted, some sort of balm to the raw mess
that was her heart.

And that other thing? The thing called sex?

She tore the top page off her notebook, folded it over and over and
dropped it on the bed along with the other bits of paper. She said, 'We'll
have to deal with that when we get there'

Every Wednesday evening, Edie Medland caught the five o'clock bus into
Bude and spent the evening with her daughter. Sometimes she stayed
the night and helped Annie scrub out her larder or trace out designs for
a blouse front. On this particular Wednesday – a soft, wet evening in
the middle of March – Edie went off with her overnight bag. As soon
as she heard the bus leave, Mabel sped upstairs and tidied herself up.
She made herself a sandwich, lit the fire in the front room and sat knitting until her visitors were due to arrive.

She had spent an agitated week wondering what could be done for
Jack and young Daisy. Dan Jewell had been adamant that Jack would never
see his daughter again. But Mabel the arranger, gruff but loving, keeping
a formidable weather eye on every child in the village, had convinced
herself that the young people needed an opportunity to talk things over.
Jack is not a rotter, she thought, impaling the ball of wool on her knitting needle and lighting the little spirit kettle. How does Dan think this
baby that's coming along will manage without a father? How will Daisy
cope, for that matter, shut away up at the farm with no one to talk to?

She picked up the knitted tea cosy. If we can turn ourselves into a
team to try and keep Lizzah up and running, she thought, then we can
pull together to sort out this little lot. Gumption. That was all you needed.
And a spot of covert organization behind the scenes.

She heard the knocker rap as she poured the water into the pot. She
did not take the lamp to the hallway, but opened the door to Jack in
semi-darkness. He said, 'This is very good of you, Miss Petherick.'

'Very stupid, more like,' Mabel said with her usual brusqueness. 'I'll
give you half an hour together. Then you can take yourself off and Daisy
can stay for supper.'

'Fair enough,' Jack said.

'Daniel will be picking her up at ten o'clock, so there's no point in
your hanging around.'

'Yes, Miss Petherick.'

She suddenly saw him as a seven-year-old at the annual concert her
pupils used to put on for their parents. A modest occasion, but terrifying

for the children. She had coaxed him into doing a solo performance. He had grown paler and paler while waiting to sing 'The Minstrel Boy'.

'I worship the ground she walks on,' he said now.

'I dare say, but I'm not sure how that's going to help. How's Samuel?'

'I'm going fishing with him tomorrow. I'll ask.'

'Do that.'

On the stroke of eight, Daniel Jewell dropped Daisy outside the house. If he ever finds out, Mabel thought, I'll be for it. But she didn't care. Daisy wore a scarf over her head and she shrank from meeting Mabel's gaze. 'In the front room, dear,' Mabel said, as if to an upset child. 'There's some tea, if you feel like it.'

Well aware of what curiosity could do to cats, Mabel shut the door on them, found her old hat that hung on the back of the kitchen door and fetched some logs in. After that, she went up to her bedroom and sat talking to the standard lamp with the beaded fringe as if it was her friend.

'I'm all of a sputter,' she said. 'That poor child. Plunging into the reality of life through the trapdoor of young love.'

She sat listening to the wind in the chimney and the murmur of voices in the room below. There was a gripping feeling in her stomach. Someone had once told her that the war was over, but she couldn't honestly say she believed it.

Jack sat next to his brother on the riverbank. Every now and then, with a sigh, the wind would run through the willows. They had fished together since they were boys. Nip liked catching fish – his basket was almost full – and Jack liked having the space to think. He remembered how a tearful Daisy had clung to him in Miss Petherick's front room. In another life, he thought, I might have had sweetheart days with her.

The dog lay flopped out with his nose on his paws. Nip had just dosed it with something from a medicine bottle. Time it was put down, Jack thought. He had tried to say so, but all Nip would say was that you got attached to them. I'm attached to you, Jack thought, but I can't get through to you like in the old days. Then again, I can't tell *you* about Daisy's shock and distress.

'They won't make me give our child away. I won't do it, Jack.'

The day was cloudy, with a little mild sunshine. Nip said, 'So what dost think of Lady Muck's window?'

Jack dragged his mind back from the night before. 'Window?'

'In church. I told the rector, my dead mates didn't get memorial windows.'

'Nor mine,' Jack said.

'I thought about putting a brick through it,' Nip said. 'But it made more sense to sell the brick.'

'What I want,' Lil's mother said, 'is one of they posh new council houses with a bathroom and indoors lavvy. But you have to know somebody. Slip 'em a pound or two. That new lot from Plymouth have got one. They should look after the locals before the foreigners, that's what Aggie says.'

Jack looked daggers at her. 'Aggie Bolitho says too damned much. One of these days she'll be found dead in an alley.'

'Is that a threat?'

'No. A prognostication.'

'Those who keep their noses clean,' Florrie said, 'won't get themselves talked about. Naming no names, of course.'

Jack wanted to beat the old witch to a pulp. She was sitting in his favourite chair, lighting a cigarette that illuminated her hard face. He said, 'Isn't it time you were getting off home?'

'Didn't Lil tell you? I'm stopping for tea. I'll try and eat with the right knife and fork. Mustn't let the side down, now that you're hobnobbing with the gentry. How many millions have they spent this week, doing the old place up?'

'It's in your interest,' Jack said, 'for the Trust scheme to work.'

'And how d'you make that out? I shan't get the entrance fees when they open the doors.'

'If the Jagos go down, so will the village. And hobnobbing with the gentry, as you put it, keeps a roof over your daughter's head.'

'I keep myself, thank you very much,' Lil shouted from the kitchen.

'You spend everything you earn on glad rags. I don't see you buying food for the table or clothes for the boy.'

'His name's Cliffy! How many times do I have to tell you?' Lil came banging through the door, wearing a scarlet jumper and a skirt that was halfway up her thighs.

'What *do* you look like?' Jack asked.

'I'm not the wholesome type.'

'Don't I know it.'

'And neither is Daisy Jewell, by the sound of it. Getting knocked up by all and sundry—'

'Shut your damned mouth,' Jack said. At which point, the baby started to bawl.

'Why should I?' Lil demanded. 'What do you think it's like for me. And for Cliffy?'

'Cliffy?'

'Yes. Cliffy.' Lil marched into the kitchen. She came back steering the boy in front of her. 'Tell him,' she said.

The boy hung his head.

'Go on. Tell him what they're saying.'

'No.'

'In the playground. Tell him what they call you.'

'No.' The boy had blushed scarlet.

'Tupper Trewarden. That's what they call him. He didn't know what it meant. I had to explain.' A look of crafty satisfaction was written all over her face. She had the edge over him at last.

Jack said, 'I'm sorry, son. Tell me who said it. I'll sort him out.'

The boy turned on him. 'It's all of them. You can't fight all of them. I hate you!' he shouted. 'I really hate you. I wish you'd never come back.'

He ran off upstairs sobbing. Lil gave Jack her painted smile. 'There,' she said. 'Now look what you've done.'

Charlie suggested a tea party to get everyone together. The new staff, the Trust people, the family. 'We could lay a table in the hall,' he said. 'Or in the garden, if it's warm enough. I find it helps everyone to pull together.'

His words were met with a stiff silence.

'Have villagers to tea?' Evalina said, aghast.

'We do it at Christmas,' Daphne told her.

'That's different. That's . . .' A long pause. 'Them and us.'

'Well, now we shall all be one big happy family.' Daph sounded a little savage. She stomped off in her turban and her dungarees to weed the flowerbeds.

Evalina said, 'She's got the wedding jingles. I shall be glad when Myles and Virginia are back. Not that they care one bit about my feelings. They'll be sorry when I'm on my deathbed.'

'Perhaps two weeks on Friday . . .' said Charlie abstractedly, his mind still on the tea party. His mind was leaping around all over the place worrying about possible bottlenecks, up and down the great staircase; about the whereabouts of the Stuart casket that had gone missing at the V&A's workshop; about how he was going to find three more gardeners and two more guides; also how he would ever find the time to train the ones he had already engaged. Mabel Petherick was a natural – if a touch officious when the wind was in the wrong direction. Flight Lieutenant

Taylor, on the other hand, had a tendency to invent what he couldn't remember about the history of the house. As for the other chappy . . . Meredith . . . well, a warning note had been sounded when Charlie had caught a hint of whisky on his breath.

Life was easier, he thought, when there were only experts to deal with.

The old lady was still boring away at him about estate workers and evacuees. His head hurt and he wished he had another pair of hands. Also another brain would help. He went to make a call to the office, but there was a fault on the line. The telephone system was as unpredictable as the weather. So far today, there had been open-necked shirt sunshine, face-whipping gales and hammering rain.

The front lobby was empty except for Peg Trewarden. She took one look at his face and said, 'You look rattled, Mr Garland. Why don't you shove off for an hour or two? I won't tell on you.'

'Shoving off won't get the work done,' Charlie said.

'Well, if they can bugger off to Bath, pardon my French, I don't see why you shouldn't get yourself a breath of fresh air.'

Maybe she was right. Maybe Romy would like a spin out.

Peg was still looking at him through the small wire spectacles that she wore when she was working. 'Go on,' she said. 'Admit it. You're tempted.'

'You'll get me into trouble,' Charlie said.

'I might have done when I was younger, given half a chance.' Peg made for the green baize door with the tray she was carrying, calling over her shoulder as she elbowed it open, 'Do what you're told for once and scarper. If anyone should ask, I'll say you had an urgent letter to post.'

He heard a conspiratorial chuckle as she disappeared through the door. But Charlie didn't smile back.

He stood there as if he had been struck by lightning.

Oh, God, he thought. Tom's letter.

I left it on my desk in London. He'll kill me.

Twenty-Seven

In Bath, Gin felt almost alive again. If shabby. Everyone seemed to be immensely smart. A woman in Orange Grove had sported an enormous rose, set in foliage, perched over one eye with the aid of a kirbi-grip. The hotel in Pulteney Street was warm and welcoming. She took a hot bath, with eau-de-cologne, up to her neck, slipped on a pair of stockings, fine and silky like cobwebs, and her favourite velvet dinner frock and they ate braised beef and salad and coffee mousse in the Georgian dining room.

'Not bad,' Myles said. 'Not bad at all. Good to be out of Tilley's clutches.'

'Good to be warm for once.'

They were actually enjoying themselves. Gin had three glasses of wine and found herself talking too fast and too much about how wonderful it was, for once, not even to think what was happening back at Lizzah. And next morning, when the waiter lifted the lid of the silver dome to reveal not a pre-war breakfast of bacon and eggs but two miserable mushrooms each on two tiny rounds of toast the size of a penny, she even had a fit of the giggles.

'Haven't seen you laugh like that in years,' Myles said.

She wiped her eyes. 'It was the anti-climax.'

They made short work of the mushrooms and sat for ages drinking coffee and watching the passers-by outside in the spring sunshine. They explored the Royal Crescent and the Circus and lunched in a restaurant below the Abbey Yard. Gin felt that their relationship just might be springing back to life. But then something niggled up and spoiled it again.

Afterwards, she blamed the well-corseted widow who took the table next to theirs and made sheep's eyes at Myles all through dinner. 'You don't mind if I introduce myself?' she asked with the confidence of one who was going to do it anyway. 'Gloria Kelley. You do so remind me of my dear late husband. We used to come here together. It was Bill's favourite place.'

'Really?' Myles replied.

'One always meets the right kind of people. My son warned me against coming back, but I'm glad I did. Do you have children?'

Myles cleared his throat. 'Two daughters.'

'What age?'

'Twelve and twenty-two.'

'You don't look old enough,' she said roguishly. 'I expect they're the apples of their father's eye.'

Myles managed to give a vague nod.

'I never had the pleasure of daughters. But I'm immensely close to my son. He's a dear boy. I honestly don't know how I'd manage without him.'

She threw him another fatuous smile. For a moment there was silence. Then Gin, sitting there like a spare part, drained her glass and said, 'Oh, for heaven's sake—'

The woman stared at her.

'How many sons,' Gin heard herself asking, 'have been killed in this war?'

The Merry Widow turned her gaze back to Myles as if to ask for his protection.

'Far too many.' Gin's voice crisped up. 'But I haven't noticed too many mothers chucking themselves on funeral pyres. They soldier on. There's no alternative, as you would find out if anything happened to your son.'

Myles said, 'Steady on, old girl.'

'Well,' Gin muttered. 'She deserved it.'

'I don't see how. She wasn't to know.'

Men! Gin thought. They're so gullible.

She pushed her chair back and said she was going for a breath of air. She marched upstairs and changed into her day things. Crossing the bridge into town minutes later, she thought, I shouldn't have attacked her like that, but what the hell?

She ended up walking into a cinema and crying all the way through some unmemorable film. She came out with her face in a mess and her heart numbed.

'You were a long time,' Myles said when she went upstairs to find him. She put a bright smile on her face. 'I walked too far. Got myself lost.'

'Right.' For one second, Gin thought he was going to add, 'I was worried about you.' Instead of which he said that he was tired and thought, if she didn't mind, he would turn in.

She fixed her eyes on the lamp outside the window and felt a stab of loneliness.

'I'm so sorry,' Charlie told Daph. 'Tom called at the office to ask me to give it to you. I dropped it on my desk to deal with later. Should have

put it in my briefcase, of course, but we had the audit people in and old
Fossett sent me off to a Historic Buildings Committee meeting. And afterwards I had lunch with Biddy—'

Daph said, 'What has that got to do with it?'

'Well, we consumed rather a lot of wine.'

'So Tom's letter is still on your desk in London?'

'I'm afraid so.'

'It's been there for three whole weeks?'

'Yes.' A shade crossed his face. 'I can see you're cross.'

'Well, what do you expect? You know the trouble with you?'

'I'm an idiot.'

'You're an idiot.'

'I'm so terribly sorry.'

'Saying sorry,' she said, 'at this point is about as much use as . . . as . . .'

'Bombing a graveyard?'

She refused to be charmed. 'Do you know what was in the letter?'

'Not exactly, but his mother was taken ill. He had to rush off to
see her.'

'How ill?'

'Um . . . not sure.'

Her eyebrows went up. 'You mean you didn't even try to find out?'

'Sounds bad, doesn't it?'

'Very bad.'

'He'll kill me. Tom, I mean.'

Daph said, 'That's if I don't kill you first.'

Romily said, 'So why is he sending Daph letters?'

'I told you. His mother was taken ill.'

'Yes, but why should that be anything to Daph?'

'Well . . . you know . . . they're friends and all that.'

Romy said, 'Oh, Charlie, you are dense.' He's like Rufus, she thought.
Rufus was a pony she had had as a child. Unassuming, well-mannered . . .
but you had to kick him like mad to get anything into him.

'Why not ask Daphne?' he suggested.

'I did. She said it was something to do with the roof joists.'

'There you are, then.'

Romy propped her elbows on the table and her chin on her clasped
hands. Charlie was saying something about ordering china for the café
and getting some old railings back from the scrapyard – things he understood. Then he showed her a sixteenth-century line drawing of the house

that had turned up in a Christmas number of *Punch*. Romy thought the dun-coloured sketch quite dreary, but looking at Charlie, in the spring sunshine that suddenly filled the room, made her suddenly feel all lazy and loose. I like you, she thought. I like you a lot. In fact, it might even be somewhat deeper. Why don't I want you to know that? Because I'm not sure where the feeling has come from. Or if it will last.

'He won't be there,' Daph thought as she dialled Tom's number. 'Just as well,' she told herself as it rang on and on. 'I shouldn't be doing this.'

Two more rings. Then, 'Tom Fermoy.'

'Um – Tom, this is Daphne.'

'Daph! I just this minute got back.'

Just hearing his voice made her so happy, she wanted to cry. 'I didn't even know you were away. Charlie forgot to give me your letter.'

He let out a hissing sigh. 'Idiot!' Then, 'You must have thought it odd. My sudden silence.'

'Yes.'

'Daffy? You didn't think—'

Daffy. Appalling to be so taken apart by one silly little word. 'Perhaps. Sort of.'

He said, 'You're an idiot, too. I missed you so much.'

She drew a line on the dusty table with her finger. 'I did call you. Some girl answered.'

'Must have been Vanessa. She lives next door. Keeps an eye on the place while I'm away. I want to see you. When can you get away?'

She scribbled the line out and rubbed her finger on her skirt.

'Daph?'

'Yes . . . Um . . . how's your mother? Was she very ill?'

'Pneumonia. She almost copped it, but she's recovering well.'

'That's wonderful. The recovering bit.' Her voice unsteady, she said, 'Charlie's planning a tea party. He says it'll mix us all up and we'll get used to working together—'

Tom said, 'You haven't told him.'

Daph started twisting her hair.

'Sorry?'

'You haven't broken it off.'

'I . . . tried.'

'And?'

A long silence. Daph thought of the wedding dress spread out like frothy cream on the window seat in her bedroom. Of the invitations that had gone out, the huge salad bowls Tilley had just washed in the back scullery.

'I . . . He's looking forward to it so much.'

Tom's voice, intelligent and downright, said, 'I don't care.'

'Well, I care—'

'Not enough to spend the rest of your life with a man you don't love.'

'I do . . . sort of love him.'

'You're fond of him. I respect that, but not enough to sit back and watch you marry him. I'm coming down.'

'No. You mustn't.'

'I'm coming down,' he said. 'I'll tell him if you won't.'

Evalina sat watching the rooks out in the trees. 'They won't settle,' she said. 'There's something wrong with them.'

Peg Trewarden set the tea tray on the table next to the fire.

'My father-in-law would have taken a gun to them. He kept it on the mantelpiece next to the clock. Always took it with him on long, dark journeys. That boy of yours—'

'Which one?' Peg asked.

'The one who married the trollop. Has he always been a problem to you?'

'Not at all,' Peg lied.

'I wanted him dismissed, you know, for getting that sweet child into trouble.'

'So I heard.'

'But Myles said his personal life was none of our business.'

Hooray for the major, Peg thought.

'Put a match to the fire,' Evalina said. Then, 'The rector wants Daisy to have the child adopted.'

'No grandchild of mine will ever go to strangers.'

'Well, I think you're very foolish.'

'And I think,' Peg said, 'that you should mind your own business.'

'What happens on this estate is my business.'

'Not any longer, dear,' Peg told her.

Dear? Evalina gave her a black look. 'I could have you dismissed for being lippy.'

Peg said, 'I rather think Mr Garland might have something to say about that.'

Evalina attempted to wrest the conversation back into her court. 'Your fingers are stained,' she said stiffly. 'What have you been doing?'

'Cleaning silver.'

'Well, rub them with lemon before you serve tea again.'

And where the frick, thought Peg, would I find a blinking lemon?

Daisy was by the bus door, waiting to get out. She hung on to the strap by the driver's blind and stared down at the corrugated surface of the floor. The bouncing of the springless seats had brought on the nausea. Also, she no longer met people in the eye because of the way they looked at her. Even if they smiled and made some pleasant remark about the weather or asked how she was, she had found they were just as likely to be talking about you behind your back.

But at this particular moment, she was not thinking about her fellow passengers. She stood remembering what Jack had said to her at Miss Petherick's. '*You're shaking. Don't cry. I'll look after you. And our child. I promise . . .*'

The bus ground to a halt. The driver said, 'Everybody out. That's your lot,' but all Daisy heard was Jack saying, '*I love you. You know that. We'll be together just as soon as I can sort things out.*' She let go of the strap. In front of her, a girl with a baby heaved herself to her feet. The baby smiled at Daisy, but she turned her face away, staring through the steamy window at the Buttercup Café, the good, solid-looking Labour Exchange, the blue sky full of billowing clouds. She swallowed hard, hoped very much that she wasn't going to be sick. Miss Petherick said the sickness would pass, but it hadn't yet.

She followed the other passengers on to the pavement and Pru Hockin said, 'How are you, Daisy?' and, 'Still a bit on the chilly side.' Daisy, smiling rather wanly, said, 'Yes, isn't it?' before escaping across the road to the chemist's shop.

She bought some lint and a bottle of linament for Father's back. While the assistant was closing the cash drawer and Daisy was putting her purse back into her basket, the shop bell tinkled. She was about to turn for the door when someone grabbed her arm from behind.

'Why, if it isn't little Miss Goody Goody. I don't think!'

Lil Trewarden had appeared from nowhere and was giving her a spiteful once-over. 'Not feeling too good?' she asked with false concern.

Daisy's stomach contracted. 'I'm fine,' she said.

'You don't look fine. You look a bit green about the gills. Jack will go off you, if you start looking seedy.'

'I . . . don't want an argument,' Daisy said quickly.

'You don't want an argument?' Lil dropped her cigarette on the floor and stepped on it. 'I bet you don't! But I've got a few bones to pick, so we're going to have one whether you like it or not. How long have you had your beady little eye on him?'

'Let me pass, please.'

'I'll let you pass when I feel like it. How long has it been going on, you sneaky little whore?'

'Now look here—' the assistant said.

'You keep out of this,' Lil snapped. 'So go on. Tell me. How long have you been giving him one?'

'I say—' said the assistant.

Lil picked up a bottle of liquid paraffin and swung it at him.

'It . . . wasn't like that,' Daisy said. The assistant had ducked. Shattered glass, in a gooey mess, was sliding down the wall.

'No?'

'No.'

Lil laughed outright. 'You'll be telling me next that you were the only one he was carrying on with.'

'Don't—' Daisy said.

'Don't what? Give you a good solid dose of the truth?'

'It's not the truth.' Daisy's face was suddenly white. 'He loves me.'

'Yeah, and I'm the Queen of Sheba.'

'You're a lousy wife,' Daisy fired back, 'and he deserves better.'

'Why, you little—'

First Lil grabbed her wrist. Then she gave Daisy a stinging slap across her cheek. When she stumbled backwards, the assistant reached out as if to help, but slithered on the runny mess and disappeared under the counter.

Lil grabbed a handful of Daisy's hair. 'Well, I hope you enjoyed yourself, because I'll make damned sure you and your little bastard pay for it.'

Daisy felt the strength leave her legs. But a flare of colour touched her cheeks. 'I'm not afraid of you,' she said.

'No? Well, you will be when I've finished with you.'

Lil yanked hard on Daisy's hair then lost her grip as someone hoisted her aloft and dumped her against the door. 'That's enough,' Pru's voice said.

Daisy slumped on to the floor.

Pru dragged a bentwood chair over and lifted her on to it. 'It's all right,' she said. 'Sit there. Take a deep breath. We'll call Nurse Gotch when we get home.'

'That's right. Take her side.' Lil came lurching back across the shop floor.

But Pru's mighty bulk stood in her way. 'Leave Daisy alone or I'll flatten you,' she said, '*And* I'll call the police. Now scat! Do you hear?'

There was a tense, sparring moment. Then Lil fell back on her usual cocky pertness. 'I shan't set foot in The Acland again.'

'As if we'd have you.'

As Lil flounced out, Pru thought: Good riddance to bad rubbish. But she was frowning slightly. Lil wouldn't let it rest there. You could be sure of that.

On the day of the tea party, they opened the long windows and laid tables on three sides of the terrace. It was April, after all. Leaves were rustling and buds opening. Charlie spent the morning delving into this and that and Tilley (her face all screwed up with worry) went hopping around behind him with stiff tablecloths and vases and tea cups, with tea knives and cake forks and sugar bowls. Tilley couldn't see, at first glance, how this all-muck-in-together thing – what Mr Garland called 'the bigger family of the village community' – would work.

She told him with some gusto, 'The old lady won't have it, for one thing. Do or die, that's her motto. And then there's Annie Ridgeman as you've appointed to run the tea room. Mother heard her carrying on something chronic at the WI last week about how madam talks down to her. I mean, you set they three down to sip tea together and there'll be ructions. As Wes says, you can't strain carthorses into collars alongside your thoroughbreds.'

But in spite of – or perhaps because of – her reservations, Tilley had wangled an invitation for her mother, who was going to sit in the butler's cubby-hole at the bottom of the stairs and take coats and such. If there was going to be a bust up, Mother said, she wasn't going to miss it. The cloakroom, as it was now termed, was a perfect place for keeping an eye on comings and goings. When she went in there to rootle for extra chairs at one fifteen, Bess heard the major making one of his quick exits.

He don't hang around at the table, she thought. He's had a taste of her tongue again.

He was tapping the clock with his stick to settle the minute hand. She took a quick peep, just in time to catch him propping something – a white envelope – behind the spill jar. Secretive, like.

She could have taken a look after he'd gone, but she didn't like to. And besides, time was lerruping along.

* * *

Cliffy heard their voices before he even got inside the gate. Mother was screaming. Dad shouting, 'Clear off, if you like. But the kids stay here.'

Cliffy took the stem of wood sorrel out of his mouth. The bitter, lemony taste stuck to his tongue and his throat contracted. *What shall I talk to him about if I have to live with him on my own?*

'And who's going to look after them? Your bloody girlfriend?'

'She'd make a better job of it than you would.'

Cliffy's round, worried eyes stared down at his boots.

'So you want to move me out and her in? We'll see about that. I'm going up there. To the farm.'

'You bloody won't.'

'You can't stop me.'

At least, the boy thought, they won't notice how late I am. On his way home from school, he'd dawdled around chucking pebbles through the newly restored manor gates.

'I'll stop you.'

'You and who else? Charlie Chaplin?'

There was a spider's web in the grass next to Cliffy's boot. Not all spiders spin webs, Miss Petherick had told them, but when he had asked why not, she had told him to open his book and draw the garden spider on page six.

'If you so much as ever go near Daisy again—'

'The same might apply to you,' Mother snapped.

There was a scrape and a thud as if a chair had gone flying. Then a sudden bark from the other direction. Uncle Nip was coming through the gate with his dog draped around the loose shoulders of his demob suit. Like a hairy scarf, Cliffy thought.

Uncle Nip said, 'All right, boy?'

The screaming and shouting was getting worse. Uncle Nip's face was bare and blank. He said, 'Afraid to go in?'

'A bit.'

'Can't say I blame 'ee.'

The garden was quiet for a minute, then Dad came slamming out through the door. When he saw them, he stopped dead.

'What's up?' Uncle Nip asked.

'Nothing. Everything.'

Cliffy wondered if the storm had passed.

Dad said, 'Not working today?'

'No.' Uncle Nip shifted his haversack to the other shoulder. 'I wanted a word.'

'Bad time, Nip.' Dad said they could talk down at the pub later. After Uncle Nip had gone (the dog, with its gluey eyes, gazing balefully back at them), Mother came flying out to clip Cliff across the ear and ask where the hell had he been.

He ran up to his room. A gust of April wind slammed the door behind him. The rooks went on swearing and grumbling over the elms. 'Your mother's a bit crabby,' Dad said when he came to fetch him down for his supper. 'Doesn't mean anything.'

Bos hovered on the terrace, thinking he ought to volunteer for something, but not knowing what exactly. All round him, clumps of people were drinking tea with thin sandwiches and scones and sponge cake. Half a dozen women, recruited from the village, were helping serve. He admired the stiff folds of the tablecloths, the newly trimmed box hedges and the clean, bright green of the park, which was looking better that he'd ever seen it. Whenever there was a lull in the conversation, Charlie's voice floated effortlessly into the void. 'But sometimes,' he was saying now to a group of women with homely villagers' legs, 'ignorance can be a great asset. When you're faced with a problem, you just have a go.'

'They'll put things in their pockets.' That was Granny Jago's voice, extraordinarily piercing. She sat, grim-lipped, in a basket chair by the large south-facing windows. Daph went across, unsuccessfully, to hush her up. 'They'll make a jolly fat living out of us, mark my words.'

'Drink your tea,' Daph said, 'before it gets cold.'

'It's already cold. Do you realize, they're holding this . . . this shindig on what would have been your grandfather's ninetieth birthday? He would have been heartbroken. I'm heartbroken.'

Bos wanted to grab Daph's hand and walk her down to the woods or the fallow field with the lambs and gorse linnets. She was wearing a green frock adorned with an artificial rose. Every time he caught a glimpse of her, it was as if he had been knocked off his feet. Couldn't somehow get that over to her. He would, though, one of these days.

Miss Petherick was sporting a crunched black hat. She was looking daggers at Agnes Bolitho, who was big and bosomy and always first at the food trough. One of Aggie's little clique of women had been making sheep's eyes at Trewarden, who had arrived late and was being told off for it by his mother.

'We need more chairs, Jack. The rector had to fetch his own. And Charlie says to see if you can find the major. He was due to make a speech ages ago. Oh, and get that Plymouth woman to send her kids packing. Tell her it's not a Sunday school treat.'

It's like sitting stranded on a rock, Bos thought, with the tide swirling all round you. Backwards and forwards they flowed. Charlie had got himself washed up with Pearl Matheson, who was informing him that in her opinion tea should have been served in the new tea rooms. 'It would have been less draughty for those of us with a delicate disposition.'

'Not quite finished, I'm afraid,' said Charlie, smiling apologetically.

'Of course, the ideal option would have been the big marquee. The one we put up for the summer fête.'

'And who does she think would have time to erect it?' asked Virginia, who had come up behind Bos.

'Anything I can do?' he asked.

'Strangle Pearl? Or Mother. I don't care which you do first.' Virginia stood rubbing her temple with her fingertips. 'Do you have the faintest idea why we're putting ourselves through this?'

'Mustering the troops? Getting them on your side?' He finished his tea and put the cup down. 'Where's the major?'

Virginia sighed crossly. 'God knows. He said he wasn't any good at this sort of thing. Best left to the ladies.'

'But he has to be here.'

'Tell him that. If you can find him.'

'He's probably potting pheasants. I heard a couple of shots a while back. Want me to be the search party?'

'Would you?'

'Of course.'

'You're an angel.'

'I've been called some things . . .'

He cut across the lawn and along by the yew hedge. Beyond the orangery, he saw Tom Fermoy getting out of his car. He had an overnight bag.

'If I were you,' Bos said, 'I'd turn round and go straight back again.'

Tom seemed startled to see him.

'Unless, of course, you're a masochist, in which case, ask Granny Jago if she's enjoying the occasion.'

Children's voices mingled with a sharper sound. That of a woman screaming. Bos glanced around.

A second scream, wilder this time.

Lil Trewarden was tearing up the drive with the baby in a pram. She looked wild-eyed and beside herself. Bos thought, Oh, God, there's going to be a scene.

Lil was waving a frenzied arm. Trewarden, who had just come out of the house, stood like a man transfixed. Lil skidded the pram to a halt and made for him, still screaming. That was when Miss Petherick took charge. Moving surprisingly nimbly, she headed Lil off, taking hold of her by the shoulders.

Lil said something, but it couldn't have been very coherent, because Miss Petherick was shaking her and telling her to calm down. Lil struggled to get to Jack, swinging round as Miss Petherick hung on to her. Then she said something else and Miss Petherick's hand went to her mouth.

By this time, Virginia had run down from the upper terrace. Miss Petherick said a word or two and –

Good God! Virginia, too, was running, oblivious to the startled faces watching as she headed for the wood.

House, masts of trees, hedge thorn blossoms mingled into one terrifying blur. Behind her, there were shouts and the sound of running feet. Finally, Gin stopped. There he was, stretched out in the clearing. She put a hand to her mouth, but when she took one more step, the worst, for her at least, was past. The man lying among the wild daffodils with a shotgun to his head wasn't Myles.

It was Samuel Trewarden.

Twenty-Eight

Daphne brought her mother back to the house. Virginia was distraught, sobbing and hardly able to catch her breath. In shock, Daph thought, which was where her wartime training kicked in. Down in the kitchen, Tilley was ambling around filling up milk jugs and cutting slab cake. 'Hot, sweet tea, Bess,' she said. 'Quickly. And a blanket.'

Mother was saying, over and over, 'I thought it was Myles. I thought it was Myles.'

Daph wrapped her in Tilley's woollen shawl. Held her to stop her shaking. 'No. It wasn't Daddy. Really. He's fine.'

'Are you sure? Where is he? Is his gun in the case?'

'I don't know. Why?'

'Could you go and find out? Could you find him? Please?'

'Of course. Have your tea. I'll be right back.'

'Find Doctor Owens,' she told Mabel Petherick when she got back upstairs. 'Ask him to go down to the clearing. And telephone the local constable.'

In the drawing-room, she told Bos to clear them all out. 'Tell them the party's over. Then find Nurse Gotch and take her to Peg Trewarden. Just do it. I'll talk to you later.'

Out on the terrace, she removed teacups, gave Pru Hockin a litter basket, then went to see if Pa was in the den. He wasn't. Why was Ma so worried about him? And about the gun? Daph had never seen her in such a state. Surely she doesn't think he shot Samuel?

'Daphne!' Granny was there behind her, fumbling with her wrap and looking harassed. 'What is all the rumpus about? No one will tell me. And what's wrong with your mother? I need to sit down, but my hip won't let me. Fetch Tilley. My legs are going . . .'

'It's all right, Granny. There has been an accident. Nothing for you to worry about. Here – take my arm.'

'One minute, the place is chock-full and the next they're running for cover. What kind of accident? Stop. Stop! I've seized up.'

Daph passed the old lady over to Edie Medland, who had come fidgeting after her, and went to look in Pa's gun cupboard, only to find it locked and the key missing from the pigeonhole in his desk. The clock on the filing cabinet seemed to tick ominously. Standing there, gazing out of the window at the slabbed courtyard and the newly laid drains, she had a sense that they were approaching some sort of zero hour.

Mother a weeping mess? How could she have just fallen apart like that? I didn't think I loved her, but it's horrid, seeing her so . . . collapsed. A new thought came to her. Might Pa have had something to do with Samuel's death? Was it possible? Though for the life of her, she couldn't imagine him shooting the dog too.

Was that particularly dim? To think someone would kill a man, but not a dog?

Daph couldn't decide. Her legs had lost their stuffing. She didn't know what to think about anything any more.

PC Eliot was in the library, taking statements in shorthand. Pen sat next door picking at a tune from *Madam Butterfly* on the piano. It's like an opera here at the moment, she thought, hitting F sharp instead of F. I didn't know Mother could cry like that. I wonder if they'll cart her off to the psychiatric hospital. I hope, Pen thought, she's going to stop soon. Grown-ups aren't supposed to sound like that.

F mixed very oddly with B. She banged the chord again. Harder.

The door flew open and Daph's voice said, 'Could you stop that row?'

'I'm only—'

'Well, don't!'

The door slammed shut. Pen slammed the bad chord one more time, just to get back at her.

Daph had given up her search for the key by the time Charlie stuck his head around the door. 'Sorry. I was looking for the major.'

'He's not here.'

'I can see that. Are you all right?'

'Yes. No. I'm looking for Pa's gun.'

'Isn't that it? In the corner behind the plant stand?'

'Oh, yes. Yes, it is. Oh, thank God.' She sat down hard in the chair by the window.

'Why did you want it?'

'I don't. I was just worried—' Then she came right out with it and said, 'Mother thinks Pa might have shot Samuel.'

'Samuel shot his dog,' Charlie told her, 'and then himself. His sister-in-law saw it.' Then, 'Why would she think the major shot him?'

'I don't know. I don't know. Dear God, what will Peg do?'

She shut her eyes and leant her head back against the chair. When she opened them again, Tom was standing behind Charlie in the doorway.

'There you are,' he said. 'I've been looking for you.'

She gazed and gazed at him, but all she could say was, 'Not now, Tom. Not now.'

It was all too much. She felt dazed and abstracted and overpowered by the events of the last hour. If he had said one word more to her, she would have gone all hysterical.

The major strode doggedly back down the lane from Bursy Moor. Somewhere above his head, he heard the call of a cuckoo, that cunning bird that lays its small egg in the nests of wagtails and meadow pipits and white-throats . . . the dupes, you might say, of the bird world. Jolly good lesson in survival, he thought, one could learn from it – though he was hard pressed to pursue the analogy any further.

A skylark, its little wings working in top gear, dropped a cascade of notes into the sky. Proud-pied April, the major thought. The best month. At least, it ought to be.

It was five o'clock. As he dropped down into Mill Lane, a dog barked, but apart from that, the village was quiet. The children all indoors. Even the distant murmur of the sea seemed muted. Surely they couldn't all still be up at Lizzah? He quickened his step. I'll be in trouble when I get back, he told himself. Jumping ship. Ducking out and leaving the women-folk to run the show. Jolly bad form. When he thought about it, he felt a pang of guilt.

He said, 'I'll make it up to them. Must buck up. Must make more of an effort. God knows how, but—'

'Myles!'

He stared. Mabel was half-running towards him.

'Yes?'

She was short of breath. She called, 'Thank God I found you!'

'What's up?'

She told him. In those first, disbelieving moments, his world shifted once more. 'Better get home,' he said.

'Yes. You had. Your wife needs you. She's falling apart.'

'Virginia?'

'Yes, Virginia.'

The major's face registered alarm at the thought. Mabel's showed very little.

*   *   *

Romy manoeuvred the last of the chairs into the coach house and went back to the terrace to find Charlie. She had taken off her woollen jacket and tied her hair back with its soft belt.

Charlie was sitting on a trestle table in his shirtsleeves. He was in a world of his own, gazing down across the lawns and the park as if making an inventory of the golden and green thyme, the early plum trees, the young cyclamen growing at the base of the lime tree, the purple flowers of the ground ivy and the church tower, which seemed to hang in a line of haze in the very distance.

'Penny for them,' Romy said, heaving herself up beside him.

'Pretty bloody,' he said, 'to be dead on such a day.' Then he added, 'It's way too early, but I could sink a large whisky.'

They sat in silence for a while. Without looking at her, he said, abruptly, 'I thought I was a goner in '43. Got caught in crossfire. Spent the whole summer in hospital.'

'You never told me that.'

'You never asked.'

'Too wrapped up in my own worries. Sorry.'

'No need.' He turned his head to look at her. 'Do you believe in the afterlife? I suppose you have to, being the parson's daughter.'

'I don't have to.'

'Of course you don't. Stupid of me. Your father would let you make up your own mind.'

'Yes.'

'I like him a lot. He's what a chaplain should be. Gentle, shining light and all that.'

'He likes you too.' She stared down at her hands that were laced in her lap. 'I don't know about the afterlife. I want to believe. Sometimes I almost get there.'

'I hope there is. For *his* sake.'

'Nipper's?'

'Yes.' His face had closed itself right up. After a silence, he said, 'There was this Welsh fellow Biddy picked up at a party in London. Lewis. He helped out at the office for a few weeks and, well, he gave a good impression of being bright . . . self-sufficient. Smiling face and all that. Then, one night, he went clean off his head. Jumped in front of a tube train. Biddy went to the funeral, where she heard that his regiment was the first to liberate Belsen.'

'We're all strangers to each other,' Romy said.

'There are strangers inside us, too. The people we used to be, before the war hit us.'

Romy touched his hand for a moment, then slid off the table. 'Come on. We'll walk down to the rectory. Get that drink.' Something caught her eye, down among the elms. 'Here's the major,' she said.

'About time,' Charlie told her.

Daphne explained to her father how distressed Virginia was. 'She's been crying for hours. Dr Owens thinks the shock of finding Samuel like that triggered something off. She's been holding things in, he says, ever since Kit died and now that she has started to cry, she can't stop. She thought it was you lying in the woods, covered in blood.'

'Good Lord!'

'Then when she knew it wasn't, she somehow convinced herself that you might have shot Samuel.'

'Why the devil would she think that?'

'I have no idea. He's given her a sedative. Says it will make her sleep, but it doesn't seem to be working. She'll calm down now you're here. I'll have Tilley bring some tea up.'

Myles found Virginia curled up in a heap under an eiderdown. Her eyelids were swollen and red, her hair an untidy mess; she looked as unlike her usual elegant self as it was possible to imagine. He perched himself awkwardly on the edge of the bed.

'Ginny? It's me. Come along. Come along,' was all he could think to say. 'What's this all about? Eh?'

She grabbed his hand and clung on to it. 'Thank God you're back! I couldn't think where you were.'

'I told you I'd gone out for the day. Left a note behind the clock.'

'I kept thinking, *It's my fault. I drove him to it.*'

'Drove me to what?'

'I thought you might have taken your gun. And you were worked up about Charlie's tea party—'

'Look – I might have felt like shooting myself, but I wouldn't have had the nerve. And I certainly wouldn't have shot the dog.'

'The dog? Oh, Myles . . .' She was laughing and crying almost in the same breath. And then crying again. She cried until she was exhausted, like a child.

Myles sat holding her, because he didn't know what else he could do. And after all, he told himself, it was better out than in. But then he began to be alarmed that this violent fit of weeping would be in some way harmful, so he reached for the glass of brandy he had brought up with him. (Damn tea, he had thought, this is not one of your everyday crises.)

'Here. Have a drop of this. It'll buck you up.' He forced her to take a sip or two, then set the glass down on the bedside table. 'There. That's better. All right now?'

'No. Haven't been right in ages. I shan't ever be right again.'

'Yes, you will. We will.' He bent to drop a kiss on top of her head. She still had a tight grip on his hand.

'I don't know why I'm crying. I didn't even know him. Peg's boy. The spiv. I suppose it's because he's yet another victim of that . . . barbarian. What the poor people of this country have had to endure in the last seven years!' She mopped her eyes on a corner of the starched sheet. Myles stroked her fingers.

'All these lost sons,' she said. 'I can't bear it.'

'I know. I know.'

'You just have to endure. But it's so hard.' Another fat tear was rolling down her cheek.

'It'll get better—'

'Don't say time will heal, because it doesn't.'

'We'll be all right,' Myles said gruffly. 'We'll get there. Now it's time you stopped crying. Kit wouldn't want to see you like this.'

Gin turned her head so that it was buried in his shoulder. 'I wish I could see him just one more time.'

'Me too, old girl. Me too.'

'It's so unfair, Myles. I loved him so much.'

'Of course you did.'

'You'll never know how much I wanted you here when the telegram came. Dealing with Kit's funeral on my own was dreadful.'

'You think I didn't feel pain about that?'

'Of course you did. Sorry. I'm being stupid. And selfish.'

'My darling girl—'

She passed a hand across her eyes. 'It hurt so much, following our son's coffin into church without you. But I'll tell you one thing . . . whatever hell we've been through . . . however much we miss Kit, it can't be quite as bad as what Peg's going through. For a son to die at his own hand . . . Always to have that coming back into your mind—'

'Dreadful. Dreadful.' Myles wondered what he could say that would divert her from this train of thought. 'It's cold in here. I'll get Tilley to light the fire.'

'It isn't Sunday.'

'It isn't Sunday, but I think we're in need of it.' He patted her hand.

'The children always had fires when they were ill. Remember when—'
He stopped.

'When Kit had you set up his train by the fire and a hot coal jumped into one of the wagons? Is that what you were going to say? He had the measles. He was absolutely pickled with spots. The only thing that kept him happy was the train going round and round.'

A muscle tweaked in the major's cheek.

'Darling. I'm sorry. I shouldn't have reminded you—'

'It's all right. Actually . . . it's a relief to talk.'

It was late afternoon. The light was fading, but outside the windows, sparrows were twittering. We're as battered, Myles thought, as this house was when I came home to it, but great chunks of it have been restored and I daresay we shall manage to haul ourselves up by our bootstraps.

Gin must have been reading his thoughts, because she said, 'I thought if I got the house back together, I'd somehow get him back. Kit. Stupid of me.'

'Not stupid at all.' In a way, he thought, it had worked. Being forced to make drastic changes on the home front had come as a walloping shock; but in doing so, he . . . they . . . had been made to face deeper issues that they might otherwise never have found the courage to tackle.

He was acutely conscious, all at once, of Kit's boyhood self here in the room with them. Of the past existing side by side with the present . . . not behind it.

And though there was no way he could, even now, find the words to express the sense of comfort that it gave him, he squeezed his wife's hand and said he would get Tilley up with the fire makings.

The whole village attended Nipper Trewarden's funeral. His brother, Jack, who had kept vigil in church the night before, with four candles by the flower-covered coffin and just the altar lit, walked Cis and his mother into church behind the rector. Peg wore her black dress with the padded shoulders. Cis scrubbed at her eyes now and again with the turkey towelling bib that was tucked under the baby's chin.

I am the resurrection and the life, saith the Lord. He that believeth in me, though he were dead, yet shall he live . . .

Jack, a raw look on his face, held his mother's arm as if to prop her up. Cliffy, shoved into a jacket that was too small for him and with his hair vigorously pruned, now and again shot a look at him. Lil Trewarden looked unnaturally subdued, her lips pale for once instead of tomato-coloured.

'I was taking a shortcut through the woods,' she had said, walking round and round Cis's kitchen, 'on my way to The Barton. And I saw him in the clearing. He shot the dog and then—'

Cis sat clutching the note Nip had left on top of the bread tin on the scullery shelf.

'If I'd been two minutes earlier, I might have stopped him.' Lil turned to look at her sister-in-law. Cis seemed bewildered more than anything. 'Jack says it's his fault. If he hadn't turned him away—'

'It was that camp,' Cis burst out. 'He wouldn't talk about it. Except that one night he said the devil's a real person. You meet him everywhere.'

Poor Cis. A single shocked whisper passed from pew to pew. What could have tipped the boy over? Oh, he'd been moody of late. He'd told Pru on Friday night that there was living death and dead death – whatever that meant. Also, he'd been upset about the dog, who was past praying for, but the village had vehemently agreed that dogs are ten a penny.

They did not know what to make of a man who could feel more for an ailing mongrel than his wife and child. None of them spoke, in the house of the Lord, of the stash of cash Nip had left in the tin box with Cis's name on it in the upstairs back bedroom.

'Let us pray . . .'

Miss Petherick and her sister creaked to their knees. Charlie, squeezed into the pew behind, was startled to catch Mabel wiping her eyes. We've come full circle, he thought, with a keen memory of a bride's smile shining out and the groom, huddled inside his suit, throwing her a quick, intense grin. Too intense. Most servicemen on their return had slotted themselves back into some pigeonhole or other, but when you thought about it, Nipper had deliberately kept himself displaced.

Mabel, intoning the Lord's Prayer, felt indescribably old. You spend your life quietly and determinedly doing the best for your pupils, she thought. You teach them spelling and mathematics and grammar and music. You talk to them about books and nature and good manners and history. You ask after them, you keep a weather eye on them and do your damnedest to turn them into useful members of society. And then they go and blow their brains out. *Samuel, dear Samuel.* Her only comfort, this morning, was the sight of Myles's stiff, military back three rows in front. It was good of him to have sent a note telling Peg that he would lay on refreshments in the church hall after the service. Hall and village drawing together, as always, in times of trouble. The rector, in his starched surplice, was heading for the pulpit. Peg looked deathly pale. She doesn't see any of us, Mabel told herself. What on earth could he find to say that would be of the least bit of comfort?

The rector told a hushed congregation that the church had been adorned with flowers from the woods that Samuel had always loved and with rosemary for remembrance. He said that Samuel, like many thousands of other young men, had been plucked by a mad wind from an obscure country parish and dropped halfway across the world into conditions that the rest of us would find unimaginable. He spoke of a dear son and brother who had come home damaged but defiant; proud and close, yet deeply resourceful. He said that dying for one's country took many shapes and forms and that we should be poor Christians indeed if we judged Samuel for being unable to bear the burden of pain that had driven him to such a drastic action. 'I hope,' he said in conclusion, 'that you will all remember Samuel's soul in your prayers. I hope you will help Cicely treasure her memories of her husband and that you will help nurture the child that is her hope for the future.'

The organ swelled around them. Outside, some of the oaks behind the rectory were showing green. *Forasmuch as it hath pleased Almighty God of his great mercy to take unto himself the soul of our dear brother here departed* . . .

The coffin was lowered into the grave. Peg threw a bunch of jonquils in after it. The heavy tolling of the bell and the soft, aromatic smoke of wood fires hung over the churchyard. Jack eased Cis and his mother back down the church path. Charlie almost expected to see the little dog running after them.

'Wonderful sermon,' he said to Romy. She looked subdued (for her) in a grey coat and blue hat.

She shoved her handkerchief back in her pocket.

'I couldn't even think,' Charlie confessed, 'what to put on the card with the flowers.'

Whichever way you looked, people were grim-faced.

'I can't bear to think about it,' she said. 'Have you got your car? Would it be too horribly selfish to cheer ourselves up by going for a drive?'

Peg Trewarden was tackling a pile of ironing in her back kitchen. It was the kind of violent and repetitive activity you could thump away at when you didn't know what the hell else to do with your pain and grief.

Jack had brought her home from the funeral when she couldn't take any more of people's well-intentioned sympathy. He had told her to rest, that he would be back within the hour, but lying on the bed made her feel worse (was that possible?), so she had exchanged her black funeral

coat for her flowered pinafore and had fetched out the ironing table, a
basin of cold water and a piece of soft rag to remove specks or creases,
and had already thumped her way through three double sheets.

When the front knocker rapped, she closed her eyes and ignored it.
Whoever it was would give up and go away. Peg dumped the cooling iron
back on the stove top, picked up the hot one and swung it over the collar
and cuffs of Jack's shirt.

The knocking went on.

She listened to the low roaring sound the range made when it was
burning well. Then she put down the iron and went to the front door
and opened it.

Evalina Jago was standing in the porch. She looked like the old queen
in her long coat with its fur collar and her crêpe cape and her pearls and
her gloves. She said, 'Your son said you had had enough. He tried to put
me off, but I told him I wouldn't stay long.'

'I *have* had enough,' Peg heard herself say. 'But as you're here, you'd
better come in.'

The old lady hobbled, with her stick, into the dim hallway. 'I shall have
to sit down,' she said. 'My hips are the very devil.'

Peg pulled her pinny off (not that it mattered; not that she cared) and
led her visitor into the front room, where Mrs Jago lowered herself
gingerly on to the rayon-damask couch and sat smoothing her skirts down
with crippled fingers. It was five past four in the afternoon and Peg had
a sick feeling in the pit of her stomach.

The old lady peered for a moment through her quizzing glass at the
chintz cushion covers and the upright piano and the nineteenth-century
seascape (over the mantelpiece) of a little ship being tossed about on a
dark green sea. She telescoped the glass up and put it away in her bag.
Then she said, 'I am so very sorry, my dear. I'm an old woman, with very
little purpose in life. I would willingly have gone in his place.'

Peg turned away to the window. She rubbed a hand over her eyes.

'If I can do anything . . . Doctor's bills. Funeral expenses——'

'Thank you, but Cicely . . . Samuel left funds for that.' Peg sounded
stiff, stony, precise.

'I was telling Trewarden that the day your son shot— The day he
died . . . happened to be my husband's birthday. That has no real bearing.
None at all. I'm making things worse. Clumsy of me.' Her voice trailed
away. She looked down at her hands, then said, 'You must feel such pain.'

Like having slivers of glass inside you.

'He couldn't have meant it. It was some terrible accident.'

'He meant it,' Peg said. She had more control now. The nausea was passing. 'He left a letter.'

'My dear—'

'He'd changed. You wouldn't have known if you'd had dealings with him. But when he was at home, he went inside himself.'

It was cold in the front room. Peg walked over to the door and turned on a switch. In the grate, a three-barred fire came on. It glowed well, but not much heat came out.

Evalina Jago sat very upright. At last, she said, 'There are widows in almost every English village. Young women whose lives have been blown apart. And you feel for them. Of course you do. But if you ask me, it's the mothers who suffer most. A widow, for the most part, will meet someone else . . . marry again. There is no way in the world that a son can be replaced.'

Peg stood by the window in her plain black frock. She didn't . . . couldn't . . . speak. Her heart was so full, she wouldn't have known where to start.

'It's eighteen long months since Kit died, but neither Myles nor Virginia can bring themselves to mention his name. You try to think what you can offer in the way of comfort, but what is there to say? That they have other children? It's no consolation. That every cloud has a silver lining? Too many of them don't. And of course, it doesn't help that my daughter-in-law is far from the most approachable girl you ever met. I can't talk to her about anything.' A short pause, then, 'Shall I tell you what I would do, if I had my way? I would put women in charge of the world. They would think twice before sending all these young men off to face God knows what.'

Peg could hear the sound of the sea three miles away. Better that, she thought, than the sound of silence. She turned from the window. 'I should have offered you tea.'

'Most kind, but there's no need. Your piano is just like the one we had in the schoolroom at Stowe when I was a child. We were taught by German frauleins . . . one of them had a black moustache. They made us hammer away at our scales for hours. Are you eating? I told Trewarden, you must eat. Keep your strength up. He's taking it badly. Only to be expected, of course.'

'Jack blames himself,' Peg said.

'Whatever for?'

'Nip went to see him just before it . . . happened and Jack was too . . . busy to talk to him.'

'You must tell him we can none of us be responsible for other people's actions.'

'Yes . . . well. Jack's sensitive. Though much good it ever did him.'

'What you must make him see is that, try as we might, we can't bring back yesterday. All we can do is attempt to put it right for the next generation.' She grasped hold of the sofa arm and got up. 'And the only advice I can give you, my dear, is that you have to be a sticker. But you are. I can tell. I shall be glad to see you back at Lizzah just as soon as you feel up to it. Until then, you must rest and—' She was hunting through her bag for something. 'Here. I brought you this. It was the only thing that helped when I lost my Alex.'

A half bottle of Remy Martin was pushed into Peg's hand. 'Just a tot . . .' the old lady confided, 'when things get on top of you. It will do you a power of good.'

For the third time since his return to London, Tom tried to telephone Daphne. This time Virginia answered. It was seven o'clock in the evening and he could hear some kind of hammering going on in the background.

'I'm afraid,' Virginia said, 'that you've just missed her. She's just gone up to Trebartha. Would you care to leave a message?'

'No,' Tom said. 'It doesn't matter.'

Up to Trebartha, he thought. What, after all, is there to say?

Twenty-Nine

In the weeks after Samuel's funeral, village tongues continued to wag. Agnes Bolitho knew for a fact that Nipper had left Cis more than two thousand pounds in gold sovereigns; Flo Ricketts said the autopsy had revealed fearsome scars over every inch of his back; Annie at the post office said fancy old Mrs Jago and Peg Trewarden getting tipsy on pink gin together while the rest of the mourners had to make do with tea in the village hall – and the barmaid at The Acland had heard that the old dragon had been to Boscawen and Boscawen to make provision for Cis's cheal in her will.

To Mabel, who visited Peg and Cis every day with a few leeks left over from the winter or a pot of honey or a jar of Edie's prize-winning pickle, the tittle-tattle was both predictable and depressing. If I had my way, she thought, I would hang gossips from those new-fangled lampposts that have gone up in Church Street and Agnes Bolitho would be the first to swing and I would happily volunteer to pull the ladder away from underneath her.

Pru Hockin had had enough of them as well. Pru had knocked on Agnes's door one morning to warn her that if she and her cronies didn't stop picking young Daisy to pieces, their husbands would be banned for life from the bar parlour. Daisy had looked as pale as a plucked goose at the funeral, thought Mabel. It had been brave of her to come to pay her respects.

Jack had reported back to work the day after the burial. The major had told him to go home, but Jack had said if the major didn't mind, he would rather be doing something. But he was looking almost as bad as his mother. Mabel had said as much when he called at Apple Tree to deliver a note from Myles, inviting her to a planning meeting for the grand opening.

'You're going to be ill,' she told him, 'unless you look after yourself.'

'I'm all right,' Jack said. 'Thanks for keeping an eye on Mother.'

'It's no more than anyone else would do.' Mabel pulled off the wool hair net she wore in the house. 'You look worn out.'

'Can't sleep,' Jack said.

'Then you shouldn't be driving.'

'I'm all right,' he repeated, staring without seeing anything at the garden wall and the path that was edged with beach pebbles and the forget-me-nots that were beginning to come.

'I'm serious, young man.'

He stared at her, too, as if unable to comprehend her words.

It was at that point that Edie came suddenly trotting out from behind the coal-and-potato shed. 'Oh, my!' she said, when she saw Jack. After which, she got into a proper stew about how to continue. 'How are you, dear? I didn't expect . . . Mabel didn't say . . . And Cicely and that poor little cheal? You must excuse my gardening apron. I've been digging. I've been looking for . . .'

'Finish just one sentence, Edie, and we might get somewhere.' Mabel said, 'What she's trying to say is that she's been searching for a hoard of groceries that we buried in '39, in case of emergencies.'

'In case the Hun should make a nuisance of themselves,' Edie said. 'Three pots of blackberry jam, some tins of baked beans and two of sardines—' She looked at Jack, her eyes filling, then she said, 'Dear Samuel . . . He always kept a few things for us. If I could have got to Berlin, I'd have smashed that Hitler!'

'The boy needs tea,' Mabel said. 'Hot and sweet.'

'I can't stay,' he said, when Edie had taken herself indoors.

'Nonsense! Have you seen Daisy?'

'No. She took some flowers in to Mother.'

'Yes. She would.' A pause, then she said, 'The rector went up to sound her out about having baby adopted.'

'And?'

'Dan agreed with him, but Daisy refused. Point blank.'

Jack's head went down. A lorry passed in the lane outside. The breeze from the sea touched their faces. 'How is it,' he asked, 'that I finish up hurting the people I love most in the world? If I'd left Daisy alone, she would have met some decent young chap and they would have walked out for a decent space . . . then all in good time, the banns would have been called and she would have walked down the aisle in white and nothing bad would ever have happened to her.'

'Bad things happen to us all, Jack.'

'Not to Daisy, they wouldn't have. And then there's Nipper. He came for help that afternoon and I turned him away,' Jack said, and his voice began to shake. 'I'm the one he turned to if he had things on his mind. Ever since he was a little tacker. You know Nip. He wouldn't hurt a fly and yet he finished up— What the hell could I have been thinking of, letting her work me up to the point where——?' He covered his eyes with a shaking hand. 'He needed me, Miss Petherick. And I turned him away. I killed him——'

'I have no time for such nonsense.' Mabel, when nonplussed, tended to become brisk. 'These prison camps have a legacy. And you're a BF, Jack Trewarden, if you think Samuel's death was your fault. Now come along in and have a cuppa. But get yourself together first or we'll have Edie blubbing and then where should we be?'

Mabel hurried into the planning meeting just as Mr Garland was saying that, with regard to publicity, advertisements had been placed in the national papers and periodicals and that a BBC film unit would be visiting Lizzah in a month's time with a view to giving it further coverage.

She dropped into the vacant chair between the rector and Daphne. The room was extremely sunny. Really, she thought, this part of the house was a good deal cosier than in what they had thought of as the good old days. The dust all gone, the crystals on the chandelier positively sparkling and the long table, the wooden floor and panelling polished with oil, so that there was a pervading scent of cedar trees.

Quite honestly, Mr Garland had proved himself a perfect trump.

He went on to announce that the Trust chairman would be coming down from London to receive the deeds of the place from the major, in what would be an official ceremony on the terrace steps on the afternoon before the opening. Mabel tucked one lisle-clad ankle over the other and waited for Myles to explode, but he merely asked that the proceedings should be kept as brief as possible and sat tapping his pencil with apparent unconcern.

Well!

Mabel cocked a glance in Virginia's direction. She was gazing at her husband with a doting expression in her eyes. Then – you could have knocked Mabel down with a feather – she put out a hand and touched his face.

Mabel looked flabbergasted.

'I've arranged for young British Legion attendants to man the gates on opening day,' Mr Garland said, turning a page in his notes. 'They will continue to be on call, as a back-up to our home-grown guides.'

Roland Kerslake, who was to act as the Trust's local agent, asked if the Legion people had been vetted by Charlie personally. Not that you wanted to doubt their integrity. Or honesty. And he was sure they would be splendid chaps. It was just that with strangers coming into the picture, one felt . . . well . . . obliged to ask. Mr Garland said he had found the Legion pretty dependable, on the whole, and he would now call on Mrs Jago to tell them more about the security arrangements and the geography of the guided tour.

In the adjoining chair, Daphne drew a bar of crotchets on her notepad.

She's miles away, Mabel thought, watching Daphne add a scribbled sketch of what appeared to be a Japanese kimono.

Virginia began by saying that their only real concern was that the layout of the rooms might cause delays and overcrowding. 'If anyone turns up, that is. But Charlie assures me that they will, in droves,' she said playfully, 'in which case, we shall have to rely on his excellent judgement and prepare ourselves accordingly.'

This, Mabel thought, I do not believe. Jokes? Skittish little glances in Mr Garland's direction? Also Virginia seemed to be all jazzed up in a bright spring outfit – a floral frock and a slim little blue cardigan. Mabel wanted to tell her n'er to cast a clout until May was out. Virginia waffled on for a bit about dogs and children and roped off areas and the guide training sessions that Charlie (Charlie, indeed!) would be holding on Tuesday and Thursday evenings until the opening

'So how are these droves to get here from the station?' Romily asked when Virginia had sat down again.

'There are buses,' Charlie told her. 'And I imagine the local taxis will pick up extra business.'

Romily fished a peppermint from the brown paper bag on the table in front of her. 'What happens if coach parties turn up?'

'Special coach parties will be restricted to one mid-week day. We wouldn't want to find ourselves overwhelmed.'

'You're hopeful,' Romily said.

'Oh, I'm an optimistic kind of a chap.' He smiled at her. She popped the mint into her mouth and smiled back. What it is to be young, Mabel thought with a sudden twist in her stomach.

Noel Boswell asked how many days the house would be open.

'Tuesday to Thursday all through the year,' Virginia told him, 'and the grounds every Saturday and Sunday.'

A babble of anticipatory talk broke out. Bess Tilley came into the room with teacups on a tray. The sun made an auburn flame of Daphne's hair. Myles smiled at Virginia and said something that was meant for her ears only. Mabel took in only the last of these. She sat, straight and stiff in

her chair, looking as if something very cold and hard had entered
into her soul.

Virginia said, 'You remember that trunkload of silk bellpulls we found in
one of the attics? The ones with the ivory rings identifying the servants
that were to be summoned? Well, Charlie had them cleaned. They look
wonderful. He's planning to hang them in the basement corridor leading
out to the tearooms. By the way, I forgot,' she told Daph, 'the architect
telephoned while you were up at Trebartha last week. He wouldn't leave
a message. Said it wasn't important.'

It couldn't have been, because one week passed, then two, then three, but
there was no telephone call, no letter, nothing. The reason that Daph did
not call him back (to apologize for snapping his head off, to ask about his
mother, to – oh – just hear the sound of his voice) was that, the more time
that went by without hearing from him, the more panicky she felt about
striking off on to yet another wrong path. She felt as if she had come to a
signpost on whose right arm was written TO TREBARTHA. MARRIAGE.
    And the left one? It was a complete blank.

The wedding hop was to be held up at Trebartha. Bos told Daph that she
had quite enough on her plate with opening day so close and he was
perfectly capable of organising a jolly old knees-up.
    'Are you sure?' Daph said.
    'Quite sure. All we need is the gramophone and a spot of champagne
and a few fireworks to round the evening off.'
    The events of the last week or two had taken their toll on her. She
didn't seem to be grasping much of what he said. He rather thought she
might be still in a state of shock. So he had decided to take custody of
the entire show – catering, guest list, invitations – as if it were a military operation.
    By the night itself, he was hoping that Daph had taken stock and had
put things into context, so to speak. She had come up to the house after
lunch and had spent the afternoon helping Doris lay the buffet table with
the best china and cutlery and set up cribbage tables for the older guests.
He said, 'It all looks splendid.'
    Daphne picked up a tangerine jelly and placed it further down the
table. 'Does it?'
    'I'm afraid I had to ask the Greville aunts. Hopefully, the music will
drown them out.'

Daph took a pile of plates from Janet and set them down on the table. 'Is that the time? I must nip up and dress.'

She got into her green silk and was downstairs again, sneaking a large sherry from the decanter when the first guests – the Greville aunts – arrived, both of them worked into a state of dignified disgust about the state of the roads these days. Aunt Gussie (small and sniffy) remembered when there wasn't a single pothole. Aunt Win (more of a porker) declared that she had been shaken into a blancmange. She stood breathing heavily and casting her eye over the room. 'This place has got smaller,' she told Daph.

'Er – has it?' Daph said, like an idiot.

'Of course, Freda never had the means to do a. hing with it. Instead of letting her in for a spot of cash, Arnold put everything in trust for Noel. Which means that you'll be all right, as long as he allows you to get at it.'

'Um – let me take your coat,' Daph said.

'Thank you, but I'll keep it on until the place warms up.'

Daph passed them on to Bos who put on his hearty voice and said how well they looked and promptly handed them (like ticking time bombs) on to his mother. Daph poured herself another sherry and went on meeting and greeting, outwardly in control, but feeling . . . unconnected. People would keep clapping her on the shoulder and asking silly questions. 'How does it feel to be getting married in a couple of weeks?' 'How will you like living at Trebartha?' 'How do you think you're going to manage a husband?' When she said she had no idea, they laughed and said it would be no end of fun finding out and there was nothing like jumping in at the deep end and it wouldn't seem so bad once she had done the first ten years.

'You look surprisingly calm,' Romy said, when she walked in with Charlie in tow.

'Do I?' Daph thought again, then said, 'Dutch courage.' She poured champagne for them and a large one for herself while she was at it. The music had started. People were edging on to the dance floor. As she passed through the hall, her father, pottering about as if hoping to escape at any minute, caught her by the arm. 'Everything all right?'

'Fine,' she said, automatically.

'Your mother's had a spat with Freda.'

Well, at least, Daph thought, something is normal.

'She asked if Freda bought her porcelain by the ton. Thought I'd keep out of the way until the dust clears.'

Daph smiled and dropped a kiss on his cheek.

'Always getting herself into scraps. Just as well. It keeps her afloat.' He laughed awkwardly, then said, 'I couldn't manage without her, you know.'

Daph found her eyes filling. She touched his arm and went to tell Janet to heat the soup. Someone put on 'Zip-A-Dee-Do-Dah'. The drawing-room looked enormous with all the furniture cleared out of it. Bos was standing on the edge of the dance floor, deep in conversation with the rector. She drained her glass and joined them. Bos stood looking at her, a fond expression in his eyes. 'I was about to come looking for you,' he said. 'It's going swimmingly, don't you think?'

Daph simply nodded, because her head seemed to be going swimmingly as well. Romy's frock, in the middle of the dance floor, was a blob of pink and those shimmering, odd-shaped spots of blue (like moonlight) had just turned themselves back into a string of paper lanterns.

'Your glass is empty,' Bos said. 'Can't have that.'

He handed her a refill. She hung around while the rector told them about a book he was reading about the Canadian prairies. But slipped away when the rector got on to the subject of chipmunks and wandered, feeling odd and lost, down to the little parlour with the bowls of potpourri at the back of the house.

She sat knocking back her champagne until Freda's symmetrically placed line of sofa cushions began to annoy her. She picked them up, one by one, and flumped them back down again, any-old-how. One of them landed on the floor. Picking it up, she hugged it to her, closing her eyes until the room began to spin, at which point she opened them again. Every now and then, as if a door had opened, a bar or two of music wafted by. After a long spell, the waftings consisted of voices, not foxtrots.

They were moving into the dining room for supper.

'Don't let me eat too much pastry.' That was Freda.

'My sister-in-law has just come down with a hernia.' Pearl the doom-monger.

And then, Doris's voice, saying, 'Napkins? You'll have to ask Miss Daphne, m'm.'

Time to go back to the fray. She was heading (weaving? possibly) for the dining room when her mother caught up with her. 'Bos is looking for you. He wants to propose a toast. I'm afraid I've managed to upset your future mother-in-law. Were I ever to find myself locked up with her, murder would be done. Oh, God. I forgot. You *will* be shut up with her.'

'For my sins,' Daph said, and added, 'I'm slurring.'

'Just the tiniest bit. How much have you had?'

'I've had . . .' She couldn't remember. 'Rather a lot. Doesn't matter. It's my party.'

Mother actually seemed concerned. 'Darling, are you all right?'

'Not sure. Good of you to ask, I suppose.'

Oh, Lord, it had come out sarcastic.

A pause. Then, 'You're angry at me,' her mother said. 'Well, you've a right. You look very nice tonight. Did I tell you?'

It took Daph a minute to get over that one.

Then her mother said, all in a rush, 'Do you think we could have a talk some time? I've got rather a lot to explain.'

'I'll . . . think about it.' Daph zigzagged carefully into the large, old-fashioned dining room. She pushed her way through the crowd and Bos said, 'Here she is,' and gave her a full glass and raised his own and said, 'A toast! To my bride-to-be.' He cleared his throat, then added, 'I got collared by a girl with red hair who ordered me around when she was ten years old and who, with a bit of luck, will continue to do so throughout a long and happy marriage. To Daphne.'

'To Daphne,' everyone said.

She smiled a wildly contrived smile back at them.

'Speech! Speech!' called Romy from the far side of the room. Freda turned her head to glare at her, but Romy took no notice. 'Speech from the bride!'

Charlie was gazing down at her with his crinkly grin. He was dressed in a dark evening jacket and soft cord trousers and he was plainly batty about her. Daph felt a pang. She downed more bubbly and said, 'Thank you all for coming. I didn't feel very much like a party, to tell the truth. You all know what happened down at Lizzah last week. It has been an odd sort of a time. A sad time.'

Scanning the crowd, her gaze wandered from Doris, who was waiting to serve out the supper, to Miss Petherick, who looked more old and cross than usual.

'You suddenly realize . . . You want to say . . . Sorry . . . I'm bit fuddled. You want to shut the door and hide behind it. Like when Kit died—' There was an uneasy silence between this sentence and the next. 'But as Granny is fond of saying, life is not all chocolate eclairs.'

She was actually beginning to feel quite eloquent. 'She can't be here tonight, by the way. Not feeling good. Says her dancing days are over.

But here's—' She raised her glass and her voice. 'Here's to her indom – indomin—' She thought some more and had another go at it. 'Indominability!'

Amazed to have got it safely out, she added, 'To Grannies everywhere!'

'Grannies everywhere!' Bos's hand was around her waist. He was steering her, gently, back towards him, but she hadn't finished.

'And to my brother, Kit.'

'Kit.' Glasses were raised again.

'Who would have wanted us to have a good time. The thing is,' she said, all at once more chatty than she had ever been in her life, 'that when it comes down to it, we're all in the same boat – losing our moorings – washed around by the night in the wind – the wind in the night—'

They were all staring at her, especially Pa from the back of the crowd. She was overtaken, suddenly, by a rush of affection. It was as if her whole body had a lump in its throat. 'But we keep puttering along. Trying to repot ourselves. Earth, roots dangling everywhere. Mixed metaphor. That's no good—'

The space around her had little wobbles in it. 'Actually,' she said, 'I don't feel well—'

For his height and bulk, Bos moved surprisingly quickly. He managed to catch her just before she passed out.

When she woke up, her stomach felt like a curdled junket. Somehow, she found, they had moved her out of Trebartha and got her into her own bed back at Lizzah. The curtains were being rattled back and an unbearable amount of sun and light was flooding in. 'Tilley has brought you some tea and toast,' Mother's voice said. 'Can you sit up?'

'No tea,' Daph whispered, 'and no breakfast.'

'You must eat. Bos thinks that was what caused the problem. You'd had nothing to eat all day.'

'Wasn't hungry.'

'And I suppose you didn't sleep for thinking about it all the night before?'

'Something like that,' Daph said.

'Then it was no wonder you got plastered.'

'Whizzed as a newt. Was I too awful?'

'Quite funny, actually. And I liked what you said about Kit.'

She hadn't mentioned him by name for months. Well done, Daph wanted to say, but she didn't know how to open up about things like that with Mother. We're intimate strangers, she thought. We have a lot to learn about each other. But she didn't know how to say that either.

Tilley bashed the tray down and said, 'There you are, miss. The tea's a bit wishy-washy, but I dare say that's all to the good.'

'Thank you, Bess. Sit up,' Virginia told Daph, as Tilley hopped off out. 'Have some toast.' She waited while Daph eased herself up against the pillows and then she said, in quite a different tone, 'Talking of Kit – this is probably not the best time, but I wanted to say that since his death, I've been . . . well, a bit rocky. And I've taken it out on you and Daddy. And that wasn't at all fair.'

Hang on, that was an apology. Daph tried to work out whether she preferred the sarky, combative Mother that she was used to or the new, astonishingly soppy version.

'You must sometimes have wanted to push me in front of a bus,' Virginia said.

Daph couldn't argue with that. The room was a quiet space. After a moment, she said, 'I sometimes wanted to yell that you wouldn't ever get Kit back, but *we're* here. Me and Pen,' she added ungrammatically.

They sat watching one another. There was an image fixed firmly in Virginia's mind, filed away somewhere between Kit's death and his funeral. It was of an exhausted Daphne holding her sister tightly, while Pen howled her eyes out.

'I've neglected you both,' Gin said. 'And I'm sorry for it.' Her tone crisped up. 'But, believe me, I intend to make it up to you.'

She took Daph's hand in both of her own. 'You are going to have the best wedding,' she said, 'that we can possibly lay on—'

Daph's headache went through the roof.

'I don't want any fuss,' she said.

'Oh, darling,' Virginia said. 'A happy occasion will do us all a power of good.'

Bos came over in the afternoon. Daph had decided to attempt a spot of weeding, because she needed the air, but her brain was feeling as soft and fat as a slug.

'Feeling better?' he asked.

She put the trowel down. He held out his hand and pulled her to her feet. Daph said, 'I'm so sorry. I made a complete fool of myself.'

'Doesn't matter one bit.'

'But it does. Your mother . . . All those people—'

He took hold of her shoulders and kissed her fondly. It startled Daph, and he seemed to find the kiss a little surprising himself. 'You had a wobbly. A fit of nerves. Most brides do.'

He was being far too kind about it – which made her feel even more guilty. She had spent the morning lying on her bed with her eyes closed, trying not to think about Tom. Every time a memory of the hasty joy of that week in London threatened to enter her head, she batted it out again. But from time to time that morning, her own words echoed through her head. '*Not now, Tom,*' rapped out so fiercely that she had probably frightened the life out of him. Words that had neither been thought about nor weighed up. Her inner, instinctive self had sent him away. And examining this fact, she came to the reluctant conclusion that it was all to the good.

I'd rather have a steady conscience, she told herself, than live a head-over-heels, hell-for-leather life that is bound for a bumpy ending.

All that happened is that I went off the rails for a bit and slept with a man I barely know. It happened because all of us here at Lizzah have been through hell and back. There's no sense in beating yourself up about it. Calm down, clear your head, focus on leading a calm and sensible life.

'I don't deserve you,' she told Bos.

He laughed. 'That's what Aunt Gus said.'

'Oh, dear.' The sun came out. Daph covered her eyes with her hand and said, 'Much too bright.'

'What you need is strong, black coffee.' He reached for her hand. 'Isn't the air fine? I like a change of season. It was what you missed in those hot countries.'

Isn't it a blessing, Daph thought, that not all of us are tormented souls?

'She told me she always felt second best.'

'Middle child,' Myles said.

'No. It isn't that. I've always bitched at her. I can't think why, because she was such a dear little girl.'

'Polar opposites. You and Daph.'

'Not entirely. I was thinking, yesterday, *I* was quite the tomboy once upon a time. I played wicket and climbed trees all summer with my brothers. There may be more of me in her than I thought.'

They stood, Myles and Virginia, by the window in silence. The park shimmered in the early summer haze. Behind them, Kit's Japanese screen and the Moroccan rug glowed in a patch of sunshine.

Gin said, 'It was Kit who caused the problems.'

Myles nodded. 'Losing him got to us all.'

'What I meant,' Gin said, 'was that he was my favourite. Daphne reacted to that. She had to try and elbow her way into my heart.'

There was a pause. The room was flooded with unaccustomed light and air. That was because the door and both windows were open.

Letting me out, Ma? It's about time. I'm fed up with you wandering around like an unhappy ghost. Gorgeous day. You should have brought along a brass band. And a bottle of bubbly . . .

Gin said, 'I shall try to perk her up. *I* got into a flap before *our* wedding.'

'Can't say I noticed,' Myles said.

'Yes . . . well . . . you're a man.' Gin pushed her wedding ring round and round on her finger. She said, 'Your mother walked me round the house the afternoon before the wedding. She told me I was lucky to have you. She didn't think you were in safe hands. Or the house. I used to think of her as the old witch. Now, of course, I can see that it must have been hard for her to have to share you with some chit of a girl she didn't particularly like.'

'Not many girls,' Myles said, 'would have stood up to her.'

'That's because my temper is as foul as hers. In fact, I may have turned into a witch myself.'

Myles said, 'I thought I'd won the jackpot when you agreed to marry me.'

'You wouldn't have said that last year when I brought Charlie down.'

She turned from the window. On the round, gate-legged table stood a silver frame, with a snapshot Kit had taken of them all on the beach. Daphne, aged twelve, and Pen, just a toddler.

'I'm going to take some of these bits and pieces downstairs,' she said. 'It's time. Do you know, I was thinking, in the night, about this whole process. Losing Kit. The taking apart of your gingerbread mansion.'

'Gingerbread mansion?'

'That's how I thought of Lizzah when I was proposed to by a young man with enormous worldly advantages.'

He looked at her with a wry grin.

'I decided last night that wrestling the house back together and getting to grips with life without Kit . . . well, it's as though the two processes have sort of turned into one. The clearing out, the laying bare, the opening up—'

Myles said, 'If you say so, old girl. Bit deep for me.'

An old-fashioned silence hung over the room. She reached for the framed photograph and Kit's little knife box and his scrapbook and walked to the door with them.

'We'll leave everything open. Let the air in.'

Good idea, Ma. No more weepiness. The years are whooshing by. Time to get on with your life . . .

''Er passed out,' Bess told Wes. 'Went down like a ton of bricks.'

'Get on!'

'It's God's truth.' She had been bursting to tell him all week. 'They all thought as 'er'd gone dotty with joy. But it turned out – you won't believe this – her was plastered!' She giggled, but he only looked abstracted.

Wes mostly appreciated a story with a bit of go to it, but for once, it was going over the top of his head. 'Talking about weddings –' he said. 'Well . . . um—'

'You're all of a sweat,' she said. They were at the halfway point down Lovers' Lane.

'Talking about weddings,' he ploughed on, 'I knocked into the boss by the barn the other night. Wes Colwill, he said, how long have you been courting Bess? Eleven years, I said, come Michaelmas.'

In eleven years, she had never heard him put three sentences together. Not all in one go. Not without a squeeze or two to help them along.

'Well, then he let out . . . the boss, I mean . . . that Jack Hambly's rheumatism has got the better of him and he's off down to Camelford to live with his sister.'

'Jack Hambly's rheumatism?' Bess said. 'What's that got to do with anything?'

Wes grew even shinier. 'If you'll hang on a minute . . . Where was I?'

'Jack's rheumatism.'

'That's right. Jack's off to live with his sister. Down to Camelford. So there's a cottage going. If we wants it. The boss says 'tis time we tied the knot.'

'Well, you can tell the boss to mind his own blessed business,' Bess said sharply. 'How can I get married, when I've got them to see to.'

'If you'm talking about the major . . . I've got nothing against him . . . he's a lovely chap . . . but I've gone from agricultural labourer to horseman and I'm earning a steady living and us can't go on walking out till the cows come home.'

Bess was shocked. Steam off and get married? Just like that? She couldn't think what had got into him.

'I can see I've caught 'ee on the hop,' he said. 'But the cottage won't be empty till Christmas, so there'll be time for you to get your puff back and arrange things, like.'

Bess was three-quarters dazed at the best of times, but Wes's sudden flight of rhetoric had sent her into a knickers-in-a-twist silence. She said, 'I can't think about it what with that opening loomin'.'

'Dreckly will do,' he said and patted her on the arm and pointed out an aircraft wandering up the coast.

Thirty

Two weeks after her son's funeral, Peg Trewarden hung her mourning frock back in the wardrobe and forced herself to go back to work. Sitting at home crying your eyes out, she told Jack, wasn't going to bring Nip back. Walking across the fields to the hall every day, on the other hand, and scrubbing and cleaning and polishing as if her life depended on it when she got there, drew at least some of the heavy grief out of her.

Evalina Jago, noticing that every floor gleamed, every object in what she now called 'Mr Garland's domain' glittered and shone, called Peg a wonder-worker, which, coming from Evalina, was praise indeed. But then she went on to spoil things by adding, 'It's a pity the Trust won't pay to give our private rooms the same treatment. *Our* cleaning woman only comes for half a day.'

Virginia said it was being so cheerful as kept Evalina going. Myles said they would all go light-headed if Ma reinvented herself as a ray of sunshine. It was the last morning of May, a fine one that promised heat. In just a few hours, he was to hand over the deeds to one of the Trust bigwigs. The place had an up-tempo air: the light very bright and shimmery, bunting on the terrace, Charlie Garland zipping around the place as if shot out from a pressure cooker.

And Myles, filled all of a sudden with a rare burst of optimism, thought, I've dealt with it as best as I know how. The world won't come to an end if we let a few people in. At least I've got her back. Ginny. The return, miraculously, of conscious affection more than compensated.

'This is a time of winding up and new beginnings,' Charlie said, 'both nationally and here at Lizzah.'

He spoke crisply, because he wanted to get this most delicate stage of the proceedings over and done with. The little octagonal table from the breakfast room had been set on the terrace by the front steps, with chairs behind it for the major, his wife and mother and old Fosdyke. The rest of the hand-picked guests stood in a half circle under the fluttering bunting. Daphne, in a silvery tweed jacket, and Noel Boswell, with Penelope wedged between them. The heir and his sharp-boned wife.

The rector and a handful of churchwardens. Also Mabel Petherick and Edie Medland, who wore summer coats of English cloud grey; Mabel's topped off with a gold filagree brooch and Edie's with a buttonhole picked that morning from the garden at Apple Orchard.

'Lizzah is simply the tops,' Charlie went on. 'I am sure it will be a huge success. There has been an awful lot of interest. I had a letter this morning from a furniture designer who wants to feature the house in a series of BBC broadcasts.'

A whisper of excitement passed around the gathering. The photographer for the *Western Morning News* ducked to get a shot of the major.

'But that is for the future. It now gives me great pleasure to instigate the formal part of the proceedings. Let me introduce the chairman of The National Trust, Mr H.G. E. Fosdyke, who will receive the deeds of the house from Major Jago.'

Old Fosdyke was, unfortunately, as long-winded as ever. Always pleased with the sound of his own parroty voice, he waffled on and on about the problems the Trust had had during the war. He went on to pontificate about Charles II chimneypieces and staff reorganizations and Georgian Group meetings. After twenty minutes or so, he somehow got on to the subject of Labour MP's being, on average, three inches shorter than their Tory counterparts. Then, just as his audience was growing squirmy, he peered hard at the major from behind gold-rimmed spectacles and said, as if drawing his ramblings together and casting off the stitches, 'We have done all we can, by advertising, to entice visitors to this remote property. I hope we succeed. But we shall see. We shall see.'

Charlie grabbed the slim file that contained the deeds and slipped them to the major, who let a pause fall before rising to make his own speech. He praised the staff, old and new, who had worked so hard to get the project to this point. He praised Charlie's tact and humour, without which the process would have been much more thorny. 'I don't mind telling you that when my wife brought this young man down here, I had him down as some flash cad who was attempting a fishy try-on. But I was wrong. The Trust's Mr Garland has had the interests of this old place very much at heart. We couldn't have gone on as we were. Couldn't have stayed in a 1930's time warp. When there is no option, even an old boffer like me has to learn to adapt.'

A wood pigeon called in the elms. The major gazed down at the file in his hand.

'All over the world, there has been a seismic shift. New systems are being born from the ruins of the old. Knowing that Lizzah will go out of our family after four hundred years gives me great pain. But seeing it as it looks today – well, what else could you ask for? My wife,' he said, 'the other day, called it a gingerbread mansion. I was thinking about that. About the hall being a source of sustenance not only for my family, but for the village as a whole. For centuries, my tenants have relied on the Big House for a living. It works the other way as well, of course. We have always been dependent on the village for help. So perhaps it is time for us to think of Lizzah as a joint responsibility. And as spiritual and aesthetic nourishment for the thousands of visitors – we hope – who will come to enjoy its gardens and contents.'

A scattering of applause ran round the ring of guests.

'We have had enough sad and bad days. I now have . . . I won't say enormous pleasure . . . but a sense of certainty that in transferring the care of the house to the safekeeping of The National Trust, I am doing the best thing for my family, my tenants and future generations of both.' The major handed the deeds to old Fosdyke.

'He has natural good manners,' Edie whispered to her sister. 'Born in him, not made. I hope they didn't hear my stomach rumbling. It was all that talk about nourishment.'

The first of June, 1947. An opal sky. Larks resting in the short grass of the park. Take the track between the sea and the moor and, when the early morning mist clears away, there, standing in a wave of dog roses and rosebay willowherb is an old house whose walls are wreathed with climbers. A house that has been there almost as long as those trees of ancient magic – the oak and ash and thorn – on the shouldering hill behind it or the distant, heathery ridges of Rowtor and Brown Willy. It is summer; now and then, the sound of church bells comes floating across the fields. In between-times, there is only a whispering stillness. 'Make the most of it,' Evalina tells herself, 'before the hordes descend.' And it is already beginning, as a large, green van delivering supplies for the tearoom rattles through the granite gateposts. New world indeed! She wouldn't give tuppence for it. 'I shall keep every one of my things locked in my room.'

The plan was to put everyone – staff, guides, and the famous Shakespearian actor who was to act as master of ceremonies at the opening – through their paces at an early morning rehearsal. But by the appointed time, half the guides hadn't turned up, the makeshift staff from the village (a motley crew of obliging but giggly village girls) were all but uncontrollable and Charlie's famous air of imperturbability was beginning to crack.

'If you would just listen for one moment—' But his mannered, hesitant drawl cut no dash.

Mabel Petherick, a more commanding presence, took over. 'Annie Gilbert – Dora Pett – what did I always say to you about empty vessels?'

'Sorry, Miss Petherick.' Dora, a shrill girl with more mouth than sense, said, 'Us was laughing at—'

'*We* were laughing. I do not care for people who cannot speak the king's English.'

'We was laughing . . .' Dora said, 'because the lavatories in the old brewhouse baint . . . aren't . . . finished. Annie reckons they might all have to go in the bushes.'

'Yes, well, you always were a silly pair.' Mabel's expression was as tough as her mannish shoes.

This is going to be a fun day, Romy thought.

She tried to catch Charlie's eye, but he was showing Sebastian O'Flynn (Was it obligatory to have a name like that to be a theatrical Titan?) where to stand to direct the proceedings.

Jack Trewarden, fixing a broad ribbon across the front door, was fed up with the sound of the actor's strikingly plummy voice. He wished he knew if Daisy would turn up for the opening. Mrs Jago had sent her a special invitation, but he couldn't decide whether he wanted her to brave the prying eyes or not.

Dora and Annie were tittering again. They found the actor's imperious brow and lobster eyes a hoot. In a voice of intense irritation, Mabel said, 'Neither of you. Has the sense. Of a goose-chick.'

The bunting went on flapping in the breeze. Roses were in bud. The house had an air of almost flawless perfection. Which was more than you could say for Charlie's preparations.

Daphne, in the grip of a major fit of the heeby-jeebies, seemed to be able to see all the things that were going wrong at the same time: Biddy wrestling with a tennis court marker to produce a wriggly white line around the Red Cross enclosure; Trewarden chasing the sheep that had got into the garden through a gap in the fence; his mother scattering a tray of freshbaked sausage rolls over the cobbled yard when she spotted a rat.

Scraps of frenzied conversation floated through the summer air.

'No, we haven't the funds to put a guide in every room. You'll have to keep moving around and keep your eyes peeled. Romily will be by the ticket desk, acting as trouble-shooter . . .'

'The bloody thing ran straight across in front of me! They've been all over the place since the stable walls was knocked into.'

'My dear . . . I don't know what the heck I'm supposed to be doing.'

'Has anyone seen the programmes? I left them on the ticket table . . .'

'That actor chappie's a bit . . . well . . . thespish . . .'

Daph realized that this last had come from Bos and forced herself to pay him some attention. 'That's why Charlie hired him. To take centre stage. Make himself audible.'

'Charlie could do that.' He changed his mind. 'Well, perhaps not.'

As if on cue, Charlie joined them. 'Hear about the rat?' he asked.

'Should add a certain *je-ne-sais-quoi* to the cream teas.' Daph took a sip of coffee. 'Anything I can do?' she asked him.

'Not at the moment. Unless you want to help Tom organize chairs for the silver band.'

'Tom?' she said.

'He turned up half an hour ago. Said he wanted to make himself useful.'

'Oh. Right,' she said.

The day was suddenly so much warmer and brighter. It was as if, until now, the garden had been painted with a limited set of colours. And now she was being treated to the whole spectrum. Daph's heart did a flip of pure delight. And then steadied itself. Well, almost.

At first, they came in a trickle through the sun-washed lanes. By two thirty, the trickle had turned into a steady flow. The chap on the gate kept up a cheerful, rambling conversation as he took money and dispensed tickets and sent cars down to the field behind the park.

After the first hundred visitors, Charlie cracked open a bottle of fizz, saying that it was the custom to take a little celebratory breather. Women pushing babies in sunsuits were clogging up the lawns, the silver band was playing a medley of wartime melodies and the queue to get into the house wound all the way round to the orangery. The major thought it extraordinary. Virginia, in grey, ruffled silk, said she had told him all along. Evalina said it was jam for all and leisure for all and who on earth did they think was going to pay?

Daphne, stationed at the top of the wide oak staircase, was simply happy to see how people gathered around the little water-colour portrait of a very young Kit that Charlie had hung next to the tallboy. Most people admired the background of wild waves and the thunderclouds gathering in the distance behind Kit's head. He was sitting in a niche in the rocks down on the beach, hanging tightly on to a Yorkshire terrier whose name

Daph couldn't quite remember. (Scrap? Jack?) The brushwork had caught Kit's springy smile and the fresh, clear air (could air be caught?) blowing in his face.

She remembered, as a child, rushing into the sea with him. Laughing and splashing and screaming as the surf crashed over them. I wish I could go back, she thought, to when life was intimate and unguarded and filled with unselfconscious delight.

I must not, she told herself with sudden fierceness, wish for magic carpets. They don't exist. And if they did, I'd fall off on the way to some fabulous paradise.

Mabel Petherick, down in the library, was talking with missionary zeal about the Prayerbook Rebellion. 'In 1549, Sir Bevil Jago saved the rector of this parish from being strung up on the tower of his own church for sticking to the old Latin mass instead of using the new English prayer book.'

Another voice said, 'I wondered where you were hiding—'

While Daph was deep in thought, Tom had come up the stairs. He stood watching her, with his hands in the pockets of his snuff-coloured suit. The first thing she thought was, *He looks so right here.*

Daph said, 'I'm not hiding.'

'No? You didn't come to help with the chairs.'

'Bos said there was no need.'

'Right,' he replied, deadpan.

Quickly she looked away, before it got out of hand.

Mabel said, 'The inhabitants of this parish would have spoken Cornish, not English. That's why the prayer book on the table is defaced.'

'So how are you?' Tom asked. 'Last time we spoke, you were in shock.'

'I'm . . . very well,' Daph said awkwardly.

'Good.' He turned. He faced her. 'I've had time to think, these last few weeks. I decided that when I saw you again, there would be no small talk. Just big talk.'

'Look – Tom—'

'You're not in love with him and you never will be.'

'You can't say that—'

'Yes. I can.'

Daph said, 'You've only known me two minutes.'

'Some new things you know better than the old. I thought,' Tom said quietly, 'I could push you into breaking your engagement. Then I realized . . . the only person that can make the break is you.'

A woman in brown came pushing past them. Guide in hand, eyes darting all over the place, she looked like a frantic pheasant.

'We only have one chance at life, Daph. Getting things right sometimes involves a leap of faith. There's no point in being scared. That's all
I have to say.'

Daph, when he had gone, smiled at the pheasant woman without
seeing her.

Daisy thought, it's five thousand years since I was last here. I shouldn't
have let them talk me into it. She saw herself among the crowd, with
everybody nudging and whispering, and knew that she stuck out like a
sore thumb. Not that she was showing – yet – or looking green or feeling
nauseous. It was just that, walking into the dining room with Father, she
felt like the most stared-at object in the whole mansion. Father was
uncomfortable, too, but nothing on earth would make him show it. ('We'll
get through this together,' he had said when she had offered to go away
and have the baby. 'I lost your mother. I'm damned if I'll lose you.') He
might have looked stern, but his stance was fiercely dignified and his hand
on her arm both gentle and protective.

'Well, I reckon you made a good job of those curtains,' he said.

Daisy did, too, though she refrained from saying so. Together they
stood admiring the original deep fringe with its heavy silk knots and
valance and the view of the garden through the long windows and the
painted ceiling so high that you could imagine sparrows flying around up
there. It was the first time Daniel had been in this part of the house. His
normal territory was the rent office out by the kitchen garden.

Daisy spotted Cis Trewarden pushing a pram along the lower terrace.
Cliffy was with her and it looked as if he was on baby duty too, only he
wasn't such a dab hand with the second pram, which had got stuck on
the rim of the step and wouldn't go any further. Daisy watched him nervously, wondering where Lil was. 'Come away,' Dan said gruffly.

They joined the trail of visitors shuffling their way around the library.
Daisy gazed at the gilded and leather-bound volumes trapped behind
diamond-paned glass and wondered if any of them had ever been read.
Father said he'd rather have a copy of *Farmer's Weekly* any day, so they cut
back across to the drawing-room, where Miss Petherick was shooing a
group of people towards the fireplace. 'Daisy! Daniel!' she said.

'Mabel.' Daniel spoke stiffly. He hadn't yet forgotten their last
encounter.

'I'm glad you came. How are you both?'

'Not so bad.'

'Come and join my little tour.'

'Actually,' he said stiffly, 'Daisy wants to inspect the bed hangings she worked on.'

'You made a good job of them,' Mabel said.

'I made a mess of everything else,' Daisy told her.

'I can't think,' Virginia said, 'that it would be anything to do with us.'

The person on the other end of the telephone seemed to argue otherwise. Tilley, rushing past with her collar awry, thought the missus looked hot and bothered.

But all she said, in that posh voice of hers, was, 'I'll tell Trewarden. He'll keep an eye out. It was kind of you to telephone.' She put the receiver down and sat there in the back hall for a minute, pondering.

What I wouldn't give, Tilley thought, to kick *my* shoes off and take the weight off my pins and have time to think. But that was for people who had got a few bob. If you were scat, thinking was a blooming luxury.

'We are the owners,' Evalina said haughtily, 'on behalf of the nation. My father-in-law once painted that view of the broad walk.'

'Imagine!' The paying customer, a fifty-something provincial widow, was quite awed by the old lady, never before having spoken to a member of the aristocracy, let alone one who was sporting a hat like a stately galleon.

'He also did a large oil painting of his favourite dogs.' Evalina was up to speed now, having trapped the latest member of her captive audience in a sunny corner of the terrace between the garden seat and the fig tree. 'It now hangs in the yellow bedroom above my mother-in-law's trousseau trunk – a huge black affair lined with linen and with her initials painted on its lid.'

On this bright and beautiful day, leaves rustled, blackbirds called in the chestnut candles and, behind the symmetrical coach houses, a kite swooped. The harpist Charlie had hired from a London symphony orchestra threw her arms out from the elbow and plucked music from the air around her. It's going well, Charlie told Romily, who bought him a rock cake and asked if he thought Tom was capable of seething lust. How on earth would I know? Charlie said, thinking, Ask me what I'm capable of, why don't you? Over her shoulder, he could see Bos being indescribably polite to the rector's wife. And a momentary parting of the crowd revealed Daph, who appeared to be gazing, blankly, down over the park.

Romily waved her hand in front of his face. 'Hello? Am I boring you?'

'Far from it.' When he smiled at her, she said, 'Are you all right?'

'Right as a trivet.'

'Only you looked sad.'

'Coming to the end of a project,' he said. 'You get attached to places.' And people. He was about to say this, about to ask, tentatively, if they could meet when he was back in London, when there was a flurry on the far side of the crowd. The dog seemed to be barking its way along the terrace. And a man was shouting.

Charlie went to see what was going on.

Three other people had made their way down the steps to investigate: the major, the rector and Jack Trewarden. The shouting was coming from the pretty little rose bed on the lower terrace. Some maniac, shoulders back, arms raised, was whacking the bushes with a cudgel-like stick that looked as if it had been pulled from a hedge bottom. A couple of them had been decapitated. The rector looked aghast; but it wasn't the roses he was staring at. It was . . .

Krawczynski.

I should have expected it, Charlie thought. All those adverts in the London papers about the opening. He knew I'd be here. And Romy . . . Where is Romy? I must stop him before he gets to her.

The Pole sliced another bush with his stick.

The major was suddenly energized. 'Stop that! Stop it at once!'

Krawczynski, drunk and swaying, yelled, 'You English and your houses! You old-fashioned, bloody English toffs!' Suddenly and unexpectedly, the stick went flying in the direction of Pearl Matheson and her ladies' brigade; he made a rush for the open doors at the top of the steps.

Meredith, who was at the ticket table, tried to stop him. Krawczynski shoved him so hard that his head cracked against the door. Glass shattered.

Charlie and Trewarden went in after him.

'Where is she? Where's that stupid whore?' Krawczynski was slewed and slurring. He picked up a marble bust and launched it at the fireplace. There was a nasty smashing sound. Next one of the porcelain jars hit the chandelier crystals, with the sound of alarm bell tinklings.

'Stop it! For God's sake, Jan—'

He turned and saw Romy. Stood looking at her for a moment. Then he flung his jacket off and went for her. Trewarden made a lunge for him, but was knocked back against the staircase.

The Pole had Romy boxed into the corner by the fireplace. 'You . . . bitch. You don't bother me. You think you got away. I'll give you something you won't forget in a long time—'

He hit her across the face.

Charlie saw red. Right, he thought, launching himself at the bastard. What he forgot was, there was a difference between being swipe-happy and knowing how to win a fight. A moment later, he found himself on the floor with what felt like a broken jaw.

Krawczynski went for Romy again. Then three things happened at once. Daphne, appearing as if from nowhere, launched herself at him with a shooting stick. Trewarden came back with a rugby tackle. And the dog – Punch – leapt at his throat. In the mêlée, Daphne was flung sideways, ending up in a heap in the fireplace.

'Christ almighty – Daph—' It wasn't Bos who tore to her side, but Tom. 'Are you all right?'

'Hit my head.' A trickle of blood was running down her forehead.

'He could have killed you.'

Shaking as he held her, Daph said, 'Oh, well . . . he didn't.'

With a muffled laugh, Tom pulled her into his arms. 'God, I love you.'

And Daphne, clutching him hard, said, 'I love you too.'

Behind them, a yard away, Bos's face wore a frozen expression of incredulity.

Pru Hockin said, 'He was drunk when he got to the pub and he knocked away a lot more during the lunch hour. That canary-brained barmaid let out that Miss Romily would be up at the hall and sold him a bottle of whisky while she was at it. I telephoned Mrs Jago, but she thought I was fussing.'

'And it was all going so well,' Edie Medland remarked.

'Wes has got him in the lock-up, while Jimmy Eliot finishes his cream tea,' Pru said. 'Here comes Mr Garland with his black eye. Did the Red Cross put a steak on it?'

'Arnica,' Charlie said. It was hard to get more than a few syllables out of a swollen jaw.

The silver band was playing again. 'Here,' Pru said, 'what was Miss Daphne doing going off with that architect?'

'It's off,' Charlie told her.

'What's off?'

'The wedding.'

'Bless my soul,' Edie said. 'What else can happen?'

Mabel, meanwhile, was drinking tea with the major in his private quarters. He had insisted on calling her in. He had felt, of late, that she was being short with him and he couldn't think why. 'Have I done something to upset you?' he asked.

'Why would I be upset?' Mabel wouldn't look at him.

He mumbled something about a decline in energy and going inside himself and not being on his best behaviour.

Looking round at the old rugs and the furniture and the things that had always belonged, Mabel felt that it was pointless to try and explain. 'We've all been jumpy.'

'I suppose so. But I've eased up.'

'Good. It's about time.'

'I just wanted you to know . . .' He looked at her intently. 'Look – I don't often say things like this, but I wanted to say . . . well, I value it. What you've done today. Your friendship. Happy times past. All that.'

Her heart soared like a lark, but all she said was, 'Now don't go all sloppy on me.'

'Sorry.' A long pause. Then, 'Extraordinary day,' he said. 'All those people. Fisticuffs. Daph calling the engagement off. I didn't know what to say to Bos. Can't think what to make of it.'

'Oh, for heaven's sake,' Mabel said. 'Let her choose the one she loves.'

The door opened behind them. Virginia walked in. 'Miss Petherick!' she said cheerfully. 'Mabel. How have you survived the day?'

'I'm well enough, thank you very much.'

'Good. Is that tea? I expect it's stewed. I'll have Tilley make a fresh pot.'

'That would be nice,' Mabel said, surprising herself.

Virginia rang the bell. 'Charlie said there'll be colourful reports in all tomorrow's papers. It'll be brilliant for business. He looks dreadful. Romily's taken him off to the rectory.'

'And how is Romily?'

'A little shaken. But the young take things in their stride.' Virginia said, 'Pearl doesn't know whether to be mortified or theatrical.'

Mabel almost smiled. Which must prove, she supposed, that if this kept up, they could learn to pull together.

'It's a pity about the roses,' Virginia went on.

'Oh, well,' Myles said. 'They were German roses.'

Intoxicating scents of hawthorn and elderflower drifted through the windows. Gazing down at her hands, Mabel gave herself a little lecture. Did you really expect a butterfly to emerge from this middle-aged chrysalis? You'll get used to it. Having to share him. If you cannot have what you want, try to want what you have.

Jack thought, Why the hell isn't she here? I'm starving. The baby will be starving. It's not right to leave them with Cis all this time. That bloody salon! It's got to stop. He stood in the empty cottage, brooding and stewing. She's no more use than a wet weekend in Whitstone. I suppose I shall have to go down and fetch them. He went into the kitchen to put the kettle on. The window was open and the curtain flapped in the breeze. There was a dirty nappy festering on the draining board and a pile of dishes in fetid water in the sink. It was as he reached for a cup that he saw the note propped against the teapot.

Dear Jack,

I've got to get out of this dump. You don't ring my bell any more and I don't ring yours. I'm only twenty-eight and I'm damned if I'm going to spend the rest of my life being bored. I'm going to open a beauty salon in London with this chap I know. I don't imagine you'll be too mad at me, except for the kids, and Peg will look after them. They'll be better off with you. As you're always saying, I'm not much cop in that department. I'll come and see them some time. I wish you better luck next time. I don't suppose you'll have to look far.

Lil

PS I'm sorry about Nip. He was a good sort and didn't deserve it.

Thirty-One

Mabel Petherick said, 'So – Daphne – you're back.'

'Just for a day or two.'

It was August. Hot, midsummery breezes shifted the leaves above their heads. In a cotton tea dress and sloppy old sandals, Daph felt cool and easy. She twisted her fingers into Tom's and said, 'I don't know if you've met my . . . Mr Fermoy.'

'Not yet. But we can put that right.' Mabel held out her hand. 'How do you do?'

'I'm very well, thank you,' Tom said.

'Good.' She took him in for a moment, then addressed herself to Daphne again. 'And what are you doing with yourself in London?'

'I'm working for a charity fund in aid of East End children.'

'I'm pleased to hear it. You remember the parable of the talents? If you have a brain, you should use it.'

Daph was amazed and not a little relieved. She had expected the cold shoulder for running out on Bos. She still felt sharp regret for the pain she had caused him, but she was no longer floundering around in the everlasting guilt. As she had said when she had given back his ring, going ahead with the wedding would have been totally unfair to him. 'The last thing I want is to hurt you. I've made it worse by leaving it until this point, but I'm not in love with you and I can't pretend any more. If Tom hadn't come on the scene, it might have been fine. But he did. And it isn't. I'm so desperately sorry, but the day he walked into my life, every-thing changed.'

At first Bos had said nothing.

It was the look in his eyes that was killing. A look of raw disconnection.

Then, with immense dignity, he had said, 'Well if that's what it takes to make you happy . . .' Which had reduced her to tears.

'If you hate me,' Daphne had said, 'I'll understand.'

'These things happen, dearest Daph. I could never hate you.' Then, in an attempt to get them both through it, he had added, 'Perhaps I'll wait for Pen.'

Beyond the shade of the elms, the garden blazed. The place was alive with visitors. 'I must go,' Miss Petherick said. 'I'm on duty in ten minutes.'

You've spent your whole life on duty, Daph thought with a sudden spurt of affection. As she was debating with herself whether to say so or not, Tom said, 'Here's Charlie.'

Miss Petherick said, 'Good heavens alive, I didn't expect to see you again!'

'Surprise visit,' Charlie said. 'Spot check. Daphne and Tom very kindly offered me a lift down.'

'And what's the verdict?' Mabel asked. 'Have we passed muster?'

'You most certainly have.' Charlie waved a hand towards the incomparable view of the granite mansion set among fields and grass and air. 'I mean, you only have to look. Arcady or what?'

'That is not a sentence, young man!'

Charlie didn't seem to have heard. 'One more stupendous old place saved from the rumbling landslide,' he said happily. 'Open any room and history will tumble out.'

All that youthful enthusiasm, Mabel thought. She allowed herself to soften for a moment, let a wistful nostalgia engulf her. Let them be transported while they can, she thought; Daphne and her new man, Jack and Daisy (well, once the divorce has gone through), this young missionary who has hitched our lives to his optimistic dreams.

All she said was, 'I'd better push on. Do my stint.'

She gave them a nod and marched on up to the house. At the terrace steps, she allowed herself a glance back. They were still there, under the elms, but they had been joined by the Matheson girl, who had come skidding up on her bicycle and was flinging herself at young Garland.

Really! Miss Petherick thought.

Then, before she could help it, *Arcady or what?*